PRAISE FOR
VISITATION STREET

"Fans of Richard Price will immediately recognize his New York here, with its barely concealed ethnic tensions played out on a landscape of grit sprinkled with flecks of beauty. . . . *Visitation Street* is an impressive entry into the field . . . of female suspense novelists—among them, Tana French, Laura Lippman, and Kate Atkinson—who are arguably writing more serious genre fiction than their male counterparts." —*New York Times*

"Masterful . . . a novel that pulls you deeper and deeper along in its powerful current. . . . While Pochoda brilliantly depicts the grime and submerged violence of Red Hook, she also soars above it, showing us the powerful aspirations of characters who hope and dream despite every reason not to. Like Lehane, Pochoda is an author with a profound understanding of human resilience, our indefatigable determination to seek light through the darkness. Her characters don't want to be rich, but to find their better selves, move beyond their limited circumstances. In Pochoda's telling, these aspirations are heroic." —*Boston Globe*

"A good story . . . an urban drama with shocking secrets at its heart. . . . *Visitation Street* contains elements of both mystery and ghost story. But thanks to Pochoda's lucid style and her gift for psychological exploration, the novel transcends genre to become a poignant chronicle of loss, isolation, and the human need to wrest meaning from the senseless workings of chance." —*Dallas Morning News*

"*Visitation Street* is urban opera writ large. Gritty and magical, filled with mystery, poetry and pain, Ivy Pochoda's voice recalls Richard Price, Junot Díaz, and even Alice Sebold, yet it's indelibly her own." —Dennis Lehane

"*Visitation Street* explores a community's response to tragedy with crystalline prose, a dose of the uncanny, and an unblinking eye for both human frailty and resilience. Marvelous."

—Deborah Harkness,
bestselling author of *A Discovery of Witches*

"Ivy Pochoda makes the saltiness of Brooklyn's Red Hook come to life so vividly that every time I looked up from the pages of this intoxicating novel, I was surprised not to be there. Reading *Visitation Street,* imbued as it is with mystery and danger, I am utterly convinced that Pochoda is herself a medium, capable of communicating across boundaries real and imagined, across noisy courtyards and over rough waves. She is simply too good at hearing voices—and sharing them—for that not to be the case."

—Emma Straub, author of *Laura Lamont's Life in Pictures*

"*Visitation Street* immersed me completely in the neighborhood of Red Hook, and brought its inhabitants to life in beautiful, haunting prose. Ivy Pochoda brings forth the full palette of human emotions in this gripping urban drama, a story that hurts you on one page and gives you hope on the next. A marvelous novel."

—Michael Koryta, award-winning
author of *So Cold the River*

"Pochoda's premise is inspired, the novel that unfolds even more so. Rich characters, surprising shifts of plot and mood. I loved it."

—Lionel Shriver, award-winning author of
We Need to Talk About Kevin

"Rich with characters and mood. . . . Red Hook itself feels like a character-hard-worn, isolated from the rest of New York, left behind and forgotten. A terrific story in the vein of Dennis Lehane's fiction."

—Kirkus Reviews (starred review)

"Exquisitely written, Pochoda's poignant second novel examines how residents of Brooklyn's Red Hook neighborhood deal with grief, urban development, loss, and teenage angst. . . . Pochoda couples a raw-edged, lyrical look at characters' innermost fears with an evocative view of Red Hook."

—Publishers Weekly (starred review)

"Riveting . . . will keep readers enthralled until the final page. The prose is so lyrical and detailed that readers will easily imagine themselves in Red Hook. A great read for those who enjoy urban mysteries and thrillers with a literary flair."

—Library Journal (starred review)

"Pochoda doesn't need the conventions of genre fiction to tell a compelling story. . . . With deep insight and a merciless eye, the author has created a cast of richly imagined characters who, in turn, bring the fading community of Red Hook to vivid life. This is the kind of novel the reader closes reluctantly, wishing it were possible to follow the characters into the future and make sure everything turns out well for them."

—Washington Independent Review of Books

"There are certainly mystery elements in this deeply nuanced, well-crafted tale that has the disappearance of a teenage girl at its core. However, it is more of a character-driven work, somewhat reminiscent of Lawrence Block's Small Town in its kaleidoscopic snapshot of a Brooklyn neighborhood and its residents."

—Bookreporter.com

VISITATION STREET

VISITATION

STREET

IVY POCHODA

Dennis Lehane Books

ecco
An Imprint of HarperCollinsPublishers

VISITATION STREET. Copyright © 2013 by Ivy Pochoda. All rights reserved. Printed in the United States of America. No part of this book may be used or reproduced in any manner whatsoever without written permission except in the case of brief quotations embodied in critical articles and reviews. For information address HarperCollins Publishers, 10 East 53rd Street, New York, NY 10022.

HarperCollins books may be purchased for educational, business, or sales promotional use. For information please e-mail the Special Markets Department at SPsales@harpercollins.com.

A hardcover edition of this book was published in 2013 by Ecco, an imprint of HarperCollins Publishers.

FIRST ECCO PAPERBACK EDITION PUBLISHED 2014.

Designed by Mary Austin Speaker

Library of Congress Cataloging-in-Publication Data has been applied for.

ISBN 978-0-06-224990-6

14 15 16 17 18   OV/RRD   10 9 8 7 6 5 4 3 2 1

For Justin Ames Nowell

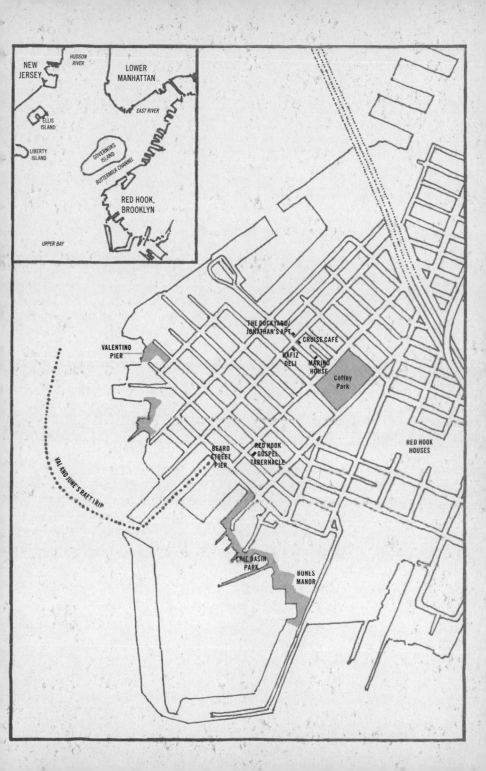

VISITATION STREET

CHAPTER ONE

Summer is everybody else's party. It belongs to the recently arrived hipsters in their beat-up sneakers and paint-splattered jeans spilling out of the bar down the block. It belongs to Puerto Rican families with foil trays of meat, sending charcoal smoke signals into the air, even to the old men in front of the VFW, sitting out, watching the neighborhood pass them by.

Val and June lie on Val's bed on the second floor of her parents' house on Visitation. The girls are waiting for the night to take shape, watching the facing row of neat three-story brick houses.

Although June has the phone numbers of twenty boys in her cell, ten she'd willingly kiss and ten she swears are dying to kiss her, the girls are alone. June's been scrolling through her phonebook looking for someone she's missed, her polished nail clicking against the screen. If she keeps this up, the battery will be dead by midnight, which is what Val's hoping for.

The girls spent another day working at Visitation of the Blessed Virgin Mary day care, watching the summer escape while they tended a bunch of babies. They missed the community pool and the open fire hydrants. They missed sitting on the stoop in their bikinis. They missed the shift from afternoon to evening, the gradual migration from hanging out to going out. Still, they made a little cash for when they are old enough to spend it on something interesting. But at fifteen, all the interesting stuff seems beyond their grasp.

This is one of the nice streets in Red Hook, tree lined and residential, on the predominantly white waterside of the neighborhood. Cut off by the expressway from the stately brownstone-lined streets of Carroll Gardens, Red Hook is a mile-long spit stranded at the southern point of Brooklyn where the East River opens into the bay. In the middle of the neighborhood sits Coffey Park, which splits the "back" with its decaying waterfront from the fortress of housing projects and low-cost supermarkets at the "front."

All around the girls the night is heating up. The stoops are filling, some with newcomers dressed in secondhand clothes, others with grizzled men sucking air through their teeth as if this might cool things down. It's a hot night in a calendar of hot weeks. The community pool has been packed, its surrounding concrete a mosaic of bright towels. The local firehouses, the Red Hook Raiders and the Happy Hookers, have been clocking overtime, circling the neighborhood to shut off illegally opened hydrants, telling kids to go cool off elsewhere. People have been doing their best to stay out of each other's way. By this point in the summer everyone's developed a beat-the-heat routine—a soaked do-rag tied around a scalp, a tiny fan held inches from a nose, a cold beer cracked before lunch.

In the backyard, Val's sister, Rita, and her crowd have taken over the aboveground pool, still celebrating their high school graduation two months on. The paved yard is littered with cans of Coors Light and rolling bottles of high-proof lemonade. Val and June stood at the edge of the party for a while. But the talk turned to things they weren't supposed to know about. Eventually, Rita sent them indoors.

"That boy in the lawn chair?" June said, as the girls climbed the stairs. "He grabbed my ass. He totally grabbed it." She's glowing beneath her outrage.

"Your butt fell into his hand is all," Val said.

June's curves are everywhere these days, especially where they don't belong, bursting through the buttons of her school uniform or falling out of her too-short shorts. The girls, once a matched set, now seem to be fashioned from different material. Val, whose pale skin repels the sun, is made of reeds and twigs—like the sad saplings planted in the park that shoot up but never seem to leaf out. June, blessed with an olive complexion even in winter, is formed from something soft and pliant, clay, maybe, or cookie dough.

Somewhere, Val suspects, there may be boys who admire her bamboo limbs but out in Red Hook everyone goes for June's generous shape, her elastic breasts and rear that she seems to resculpt every night, giving the neighborhood something fresh to look at. Even her wavy brown hair appears mischievous in the way it curls and bounces. Val's hair, an unremarkable straw color, strikes her as lacking in enthusiasm.

Val knows that time is short for kids' stuff. When school starts, they'll be expected to turn up at parties, looking on-point, made up and polished. But sometimes Val can't restrain her silliness. After being cooped up in that day care, she wants to be naughty. Not that in-your-face naughtiness of scoring a bottle of something sweet and alcoholic or sneaking a cigarette. What she's after is a prankish secret the girls can share someday when they are on some guy's couch tipsy or even high.

The window is open wide. June's positioned herself near it and hops to her feet each time she hears footsteps. She stretches out her arms, grasping either side of the window frame.

"I'm gonna get my groove on tonight," she says loud enough for anyone passing to hear. "I'm gonna turn it up." She rotates her hips and thrusts her chest forward. Her shorts strain at the seams. Val worries that if June arches her back another inch, the whole package is going to burst. "I'm going to show them how it's done," she says.

Something about June's posture reminds Val of a bag of microwave popcorn. She falls back on her bed, her laughter pouring out into the street.

"Baby," June says. "You laugh like a baby." She leaves the window, flops down on the bed, but keeps her distance from Val. She checks her nails and pulls out her phone. "Let's do something."

"We could camp out on the roof," Val says.

June does not look up.

"Or watch a movie."

"You want the world thinking we're babies forever."

"There's nothing wrong with movies."

June stands up. "I'm getting us a drink."

Five minutes later June returns with a half-empty bottle of alcoholic lemonade. "Did you pick up someone's empty?" Val says.

"I drank half on my way up."

"We could take the raft out," Val says. "It's something."

June finishes the drink. "You have some stupid ideas."

"Your only idea was stealing a half-empty bottle from my sister."

"Just get the goddamned raft," June says. She tilts her head upward, tosses her hair, exhales an invisible cigarette.

"Don't be such a bitch," Val says.

The rubber raft was a gift from a crew of older guys who'd

taunted and teased them, and finally made a play for the girls at the pool last weekend. What they wanted with a hot pink rubber raft Val and June didn't know but they took their prize. Tonight, hot and stir-crazy, Val decides what the raft is for. Take a float in the bay, cool off, see what's what from the water.

The girls hit the street, the raft bumping awkwardly against their legs as they walk. "It's your raft. You carry it," June says, dropping her end.

Late summer smells hang in the air—ripe sewers, cookouts, and the scent of stagnant water that lingers in Red Hook no matter the season. The night echoes with other people's noise, laughter falling from windows and the call-and-response of competing boom boxes. The girls approach Coffey Park at the edge of the Red Hook housing project. June's walking a few steps ahead, putting a couple of feet between her and Val and the raft. Val lets her go on, not quite sure about the sway of June's hips and the way she's shaking her hair like a show pony. At one end of the park is the old luggage factory, now converted into lofts, at the other, the first of the project high-rises, and in between a battleground of basketball and barbecues.

The park benches are filled, many of them turned into soundstages for newbie rappers whose rhymes are muffled now and then by the bass of passing cars. Girls in fluorescent clothes, wrapped tight like gifts, are clustered around the benches, bumping and dipping to the beats. June and Val envy their doorknocker earrings, their careless voices, the grip of their halter tops, and the cling of their short shorts. The way they hang out late and loud.

Sometimes on Sundays, when the service at Visitation of the Blessed Virgin Mary has ended, June and Val slip away from their parents. Fearless in the daylight, they cross Coffey Park and pass through the heart of the projects, until they arrive at the Red Hook

Gospel Tabernacle—a small storefront church on a side street where they're not certain they're welcome. In spring and summer, the doors are propped open and they can see into the small, fluorescent-lit room, with linoleum tiles and folding chairs. The girls know some of the singers from their old elementary school, before Val and June were sent across the expressway to Catholic school.

It's nighttime now and the girls aren't bold enough to enter Coffey Park. They walk along its periphery. Val watches as June rolls the waistband of her shorts so they ride higher.

"You can wear anything. A paper bag would look hot on you," June told Val the other day. "Me, I've got all this to worry about," she added, cupping her breasts. "You know, my burdens."

June's body doesn't seem to be burdening her too much at the moment. She dawdles in front of each bench, untangling her hair from her silver hoop earrings, adjusting her bikini top beneath her shirt. Val hovers a few steps back, half in, half out of a streetlamp's yellow glow, her lanky shadow stretching out in front of her.

There's a girl in one of the groups June knows from their early years in public school. She's sitting on the back of a bench not far from the park's entrance. Back then, Monique would hang with them in the Marinos' basement, helping make broken furniture into castles, spacecrafts, and ships. The three of them dressed up in Rita's clothes, clomping around the basement in her heels and smearing her makeup on their faces. Once in a while they went to June's place, for her grandmother's homemade orange Popsicles or to spit cherry pits from the second-story window. They never went to Monique's apartment in the projects.

"Hey, Monique," June calls. "Monique."

"Someone out for you, Mo," one of the guys says. He's rocking a sweaty forty in his palms. He wipes his hand on his baggy basketball shorts. Monique checks June and Val. "You asking your friends to join us?" the guy says, nudging the bottle toward Monique.

"Nah," she says, turning away.

June stays put, but Val moves on, bumping her with the raft.

"Watch it," June says.

The guy holds out the bottle. "Thirsty?"

June hesitates, shifts her weight from one foot to another. Val knows she's trying to catch Monique's eye to see if this is cool. But Monique's still looking away, laughing with a group of older girls.

"Thirsty?" the guy repeats, swigging from the bottle and holding it out once more. He licks his lips then shows Val and June his teeth, two of them capped in gold with diamond chips. The gems catch the light, giving him a jack-o'-lantern smile. He shakes his head. "Yeah. Didn't think so." He drops the empty in the grass.

"You didn't save me some?" Monique says, swatting his leg.

"Didn't know you wanted it." He and Monique stare at Val and June.

"Let's go," Val says.

"What's your hurry?" June says.

Val grabs June's wrist. She knows Monique and her crew are about to explode with laughter. She pulls June away from the park.

"You saw how he was looking at us?" June says.

Val links her arm through June's. "Totally."

As they move along they try on the streetwise rhythms of Monique and her crew. Trying out words they'd be afraid to use at home or school. Calling each other "ho." Feeling the nervous release of each curse. Waiting for repercussions that don't come. Because they are alone on the streets now. They're skirting the edges of the projects and approaching the water along dark, cobblestone streets with only the burned-out streetlights and abandoned warehouses for company.

The moon is riding high and full. The last lights of the projects are at the girls' backs. The summer noises and chatter from the park have faded so they talk louder now, raising their voices against the silence. They wave their arms, gesture large, beating back the shadows that stretch from abandoned doorways and broken windows. They know the rumors, but they try to ignore them—the stray dogs, rabid and feral, that breed in the abandoned sugar refinery, the haunted junkies, the homeless, the insane.

A couple of blocks from the water there's an abandoned lot strewn with trash and knee-high weeds. In the middle of this lot a dilapidated fishing boat is moored in the rubble. The weeds rustle as the girls pass. They pick up the pace. There's a whistle from somewhere near the boat. The girls turn and see Cree James, a kid from the projects who used to hang with Rita before Val's parents put an end to their friendship. He's good-looking—round face and wide eyes, high cheekbones. He keeps his head shaved in the hot months.

Cree is sitting on the boat's prow, legs dangling toward the dirty ground.

"Where you girls off to?"

"Somewhere," June says.

"How come you're all alone?" Val asks.

"I got things to do."

"Doesn't look like it," the girls say in unison.

"What you two know about it?"

"We know stuff," Val says.

"Like what?"

"More than you think," June says.

"Yeah?" Cree drums his feet on the hull.

"Yeah," June says, wrapping her fingers through the chain-link fence that blocks the lot from the street. "So why don't you come find out?"

Val digs a finger into her side.

"Big words for a fourteen-year-old," Cree says.

"Fifteen."

"Big words all the same."

"So, you won't be kicking it with us?" June says.

Cree shakes his head. "I got somewhere to be."

"Shame. We know where the party is," Val says. Normally Val

would be nervous flirting, even in jest, with an eighteen-year-old. But out here on unfamiliar territory, she feels bold.

"Sure you do," Cree says.

"We got it going on," June says.

The girls begin to walk away. June's voice has lost its saucy edge. Val feels her relax, as she falls into step with their adventure.

"We know where it's at," Val says.

"We know how it's done."

"We know how to do it."

Cree watches the girls disappear up the dark street, carrying that pink raft between them. They used to hang with his cousin Monique when they were little, back when he and Rita were tight, before her parents taught her that kids from the Houses were off-limits to waterside girls. He'd never expect Val and June to turn up in this part of Red Hook, especially so late. He usually has this corner to himself at night. Even people from the projects keep away from these streets after dark. And no one takes much notice of a boat moored in the weeds, just another sliver of old Red Hook lore, the vanished world of dockworkers and longshoremen.

But this decaying fishing boat never belonged to any of the guys who cluster in the VFW or in the last waterfront bar. It belonged to Cree's father, Marcus, who bought it from a salvage yard in Jersey. The boat was beached after Marcus, a corrections officer, caught a bullet meant for no one in particular—collateral damage in the now dormant drug wars. Cree guesses the boat is his now.

Cree's mom, Gloria, believes that Marcus's spirit lingers at the spot in the courtyards where he fell. Gloria's often out there with a thermos of iced tea. But Cree knows better. No ghost, especially not his father's, would bother haunting a bench. But a captain always returns to his ship. One day Cree hopes to get the boat back in the channel and take Marcus farther out on the water than he'd ever been in his lifetime.

On certain nights Cree tricks himself into seeing his father's shadow moving through the weeds and climbing aboard. He imagines him sliding into the tiny cabin and taking the wheel. Then Cree pretends that he and Marcus are crossing the Upper Bay to New Jersey where they'd once visited another desolate cobblestone waterfront. There was the same smell of silt and water and the same sound of wind slapping empty buildings. But there were no projects near the Jersey waterfront, and no one over there gave Cree and Marcus a glance that told them they didn't belong.

On that trip back to Red Hook, Cree had found himself staring across the Upper Bay trying to pick out his project from the distant mass of Brooklyn gray. Odd, how only a short ride away turned his hometown unrecognizable. Like it had nothing to do with him.

Cree can't focus enough to summon Marcus. Maybe the girls scared him off. Cree vaults off the prow and lands in the dust and grass. He picks up a bucket and fishing rod from beside the boat and hits the street, his footfalls replacing the echoes left behind by Val and June.

His pace is slow. His shoulders slump as if gravity is too much. He reaches the end of Columbia Street and catches a whiff of the water, a brew of fuel and fish. He heads out on the pier that juts into Erie Basin at an obtuse angle. He skirts the impounded cars in the police lot and walks until the pier starts to double back on itself. He sits and dangles his legs over the water, looking past the docked tugboats at the abandoned shipyard and the remains of the sugar refinery that burned before he was born.

This is the place that gives Cree the end of the world feeling he likes, the sense that he can go no farther and still never be found. The clang of buoys, the rustle of the water, the absence of voices and streetlights, and that hunk of moon melting all over the place are as close to the country as Cree can imagine. From here he can look back at his neighborhood, and not see it at all.

When he was younger and his father took him out in the bay, Cree often dreamed of the places the water might lead him. But recently he finds it difficult to envision the world beyond the twin Ms of the Verrazano and the single hump of the Bayonne—the two bridges that hem in his horizon.

He casts his line into the water. Out here is where he has witnessed the secret underside of Red Hook. He's seen a flaming car pushed into the water and what he would swear was a severed arm floating by, shriveled and blue like a sea creature. He's seen people catching fish and cooking them in a rusted trash can. He's seen women turning tricks in the back of a rowboat, two Asian men in wet suits snorkeling with spears in their hands. He's seen all sorts of makeshift crafts hammered together out of driftwood and debris.

Cree drags his line through the water, leading it away from a web of seaweed and trash that's bobbing near the pier. He always tosses back his catch. But the fish are taking the night off and the water looks dirty and sluggish. Grimy foam coats the rocks at Cree's feet. Even the tugs sound unhappy, their engines choking on the water, never settling.

But where there should have been only the noise of the water and some clatter from the tugs he hears voices. He reels in his line, imagining that somewhere nearby Val and June are teasing him. He stands up, spins once, like he's looking for the turnaround jump shot. And then the voices vanish, leaving him gaping at the dark, wondering if he heard anything at all.

The girls choose the water between the Beard Street Pier and the rotting factory where a two-masted sailboat is taking its time sinking into the murky basin. Never mind that the water is dirty and that they aren't the best swimmers. And never mind that they are going to have to paddle through that grimy water with their hands. They figure they'll float around this pier and past the next two, then get out on the little beach next to Valentino Pier. Couldn't take more than half an hour.

It's crazy dark down by the water. Their footsteps are loud and hard, bouncing off the warehouses. Only a ten-minute walk from home, yet they'd never been to the waterfront at night. Never been to this stretch of the waterfront period. Until they got in sight of the water, they pretended their parents' warnings were a lot of nonsense. But now there seems to be something hiding in each shadow, scattering the litter and rubble. It doesn't seem possible that they have this place to themselves. There must be someone lurking behind the cracked windshield of a rusted-out station wagon, someone watching them from the ruins of the sugar refinery.

The waterfront creaks and resettles—the decaying groan of old wood is a ghostly moan, the rhythmic bang of a boat against the pier is the approaching of footsteps.

Something clatters down the refinery's dilapidated chute and plunges into the water. The girls grasp hands and start singing, chanting, making a lot of noise, trying to outdo whatever fell down that chute, attempting to subdue the darkness. But the brick warehouse and the basin throw the song back, distorting their voices so they sound unfamiliar to themselves.

June points at the sugar refinery. "Heard it's haunted. Probably someone over there right now, watching us."

Val glances at the skeleton of the refinery.

"Ghosts better not mess with us," June says.

"You want to go back?" Val says. There's movement in the refinery. She's sure of it. Something—someone—rattling in the large metal dome.

"Nah," June says, turning her back to the building. But Val can't take her eyes off it. She watches the chute, checking to see if it sways.

The girls turn up the volume, chanting louder.

They tiptoe onto the green-fuzzed rocks and lower the raft into the water. June stands back. "You first."

Val shakes her head.

"Your raft. Your idea."

Val squats down, trying to avoid touching the rocks, and falls back on the raft. It buckles under her weight and she's swamped by the oily water. "Nasty."

June closes her eyes and scrunches her face, then sits down behind Val. The raft submerges, soaking the girls up to their chests. "Damn that's cold." June shakes as if she can escape the wet and nearly knocks the girls into the drink. Then the raft adjusts to their weight, pops back up. And they float.

The water is chilly and slick. The girls paddle hard and erratically with their hands, pushing away the junk that keeps approaching the raft and trying not to look at the gloomy area underneath the crumbling sugar refinery. The raft swings close to the half-sunk sailboat and the girls kick frantically, not wanting to tempt whatever went down with it. The water smells rank.

There's something pulling from below that makes the raft spin.

"What is that?" Val asks. She feels the raft buckle in the middle. She stops paddling and lets the pink rubber flatten out beneath them.

"It's like a waterslide," June says through clenched teeth.

"Yeah, just like Coney Island," Val says. She checks the shoreline that is quickly sliding away behind them.

They clutch the raft with rigid hands. They are unwilling to let go, unable to pull themselves out of the swirling current.

"Don't rip it with your nails," Val says. They're out deep now, too far from the questionable comfort of the shore. "We've got to paddle."

They let go and slap the water with their hands. Finally, they get out past the pier and let their arms rest. They float into the basin where the water has a regular beat. The moon's shining like it's out of its mind. The raft is handed from one wave to the next. To their left Staten Island is glittering, its houses lighting up its hills with an LCD display of red, green, and white. Tankers, like shining islands, sit in the bay, heavy and motionless. Straight across, the cranes in the port of New Jersey look like some kind of Jurassic fantasyland.

A tugboat passes in front of them. The girls scream and bend forward and try to balance, so they're not swamped in its wake. Small waves break over their legs and waists.

Floating is wilder than Val expected. The silhouettes of the city and Jersey rising on all sides, the water stretching out dark and vast. But it's the silence—only now and then disturbed by the call of a foghorn, the crash of a wave tangling with the pylons, the rhythmic beat of a boat somewhere out there—that grabs her.

They float by the wreck of a tugboat. The moon is trapped in one of the sunken windows, its reflection struggling through the dark water. The girls grasp the edge of the raft and see the blank eyes of the portholes staring back at them. There's a new swell in the water, a deep insistent tug. If Val could forget the bay's depths, she would be willing to follow this current wherever it leads her.

"We could keep going forever," Val says, looking over her shoulder at June. June is no longer clutching the raft. She's trailing her hands in the water, small ripples receding from her fingertips.

As the raft rounds another pier, the Manhattan skyline bursts into view towering over the black hump of Governors Island. The buildings claw the sky as if they are desperate to get out. The girls are pulled forward by the fresh current of Buttermilk Channel. But it seems to them that the city is drawing them in.

"That's where we belong," June says. She raises her arms and snaps her fingers. "No more wasting time."

"Stop it," Val says. She's not looking at the city; she's watching its reflection stretching out into the water in front of them. "Stop."

.   .   .

Cree stashes his bucket and line and begins to pick his way along the waterfront. He passes underneath the chute of the refinery where sucrose refuse was dumped into the basin. He rounds the Beard Street Pier, balancing on the jagged rocks at its short edge along the water. From the far side of the pier he can see the pink raft bobbing in the middle of the bay.

The girls' voices carry, their laughter electrifying the lonely water. They're taking over the gloomy basin with their dinky raft, exploring the currents and depths shut off to Cree since his father's death. He wonders how far they dare to float.

The raft rounds another pier and bobs out of view.

Cree scrambles. He wants to keep the girls in sight. Somewhere out in the bay a foghorn cuts the silence, its low groan rolling across the water like a shudder.

There's a rocky outcrop between the next two piers. A large warehouse blocks Cree's view. He stumbles, gashing his knee on a cement pylon. Stagnant water is pooled between the rocks. Cree cups his hand over his wound, trying to avoid the water's grimy foam.

He's on the next pier now and can hear the girls again. Their words are indistinct. He catches sight of the raft bobbing in the water heading toward Manhattan. Cree turns and runs toward Valentino Pier, now a promenade for old fishermen and young couples. This late he expects to have it to himself.

He can hear the girls as the raft approaches. He crosses the small park that leads to the pier and hurries to the end of the concrete walkway. The raft is crossing in front of him—the girls, two dark silhouettes against the distant Jersey docks.

And then they are gone.

CHAPTER TWO

If asked, Jonathan Sprouse might describe his life as a landslide, a series of descents. His best year came at the age of twelve, when he was chosen for the lead in a Broadway musical—a glittery mashup of Grimms fairy tales. The show was a flop, one of those spectacular Great White Way disasters that get front-page coverage for the duration of their blink-and-you've-missed-it runs—when the whole city fixates on the spectacle of a show that closes before it opens.

In the year after this almost success, Jonathan went from potential Broadway star to unremarkable chorus member. Later he was demoted from Juilliard to a public high school for performing arts, from Carnegie Hall to fly-by-night practice spaces. After college he moved from the Upper East Side to the Lower East Side, then from Brooklyn Heights to Red Hook—a neighborhood below sea level and sinking.

As a child, he never imagined that he wouldn't succeed. His father, Donald Sprouse, had enough money to collect houses in all the best sea and ski locations and to scoop up Jonathan's mother, a respected Broadway star. Eden Farrow couldn't open a show like Bernadette Peters or Patti LuPone, but no one complained when she stepped into their shoes at the end of their runs.

The Sprouse family fortune and Eden's moderate fame were enough to guarantee Jonathan attention from conservatories and invitations to important auditions. He had the best vocal coaches and music instructors. He turned up at auditions dressed in a sailor shirt and matching cap that his mother had hand-tailored on Lexington Avenue.

As a teenager, he was known less for his talent than for his parents' frequent absences and their spacious apartment. The Sprouse-Farrows had a well-stocked bar and fridge and their doorman's hand was easily greased with a C-note. Liquor for Jonathan's underage set was delivered through the service entrance. Jonathan was one of those New York kids everyone knows. In with the Upper West elite, the Village kids, even the Harlem hoods from a couple blocks north whom Jonathan invited to the Sprouse penthouse to mix things up.

Although his short-lived Broadway career fizzled, Jonathan continued to audition in his early twenties—classical, jazz, off Broadway. He was an understudy who never got called up. He didn't make it through conservatory. The auditions stopped. Eden's agent dropped him. He sat in with a couple of bands, sang and played keyboard. He joined a quartet that got written up in the New Yorker. But then Eden died, or because Eden died, the quartet let him go. Jonathan fled from the spotlight that had briefly threatened to illuminate him.

After Eden's death, Jonathan dropped her last name and reverted to Sprouse. He taught at Carnegie Hall where he'd once had lessons. He taught at a private high school in lower Manhattan. He taught spoiled kids in their homes. He taught jazz band at a public school where there weren't enough instruments to go around.

Ever since he moved to Red Hook, Jonathan has been teaching music appreciation at St. Bernardette's, a Catholic girls' school just outside the neighborhood. He also has a steady gig Friday nights at a gay piano bar in the city where he hammers out show tunes accompanied by a drag queen who gets all the tips. From time to time he writes advertising jingles for cut-rate brands. He tells himself he's a commercial success.

Old acquaintances from as far back as high school, conservatory, and Broadway sometimes come to Jonathan's apartment. They know that out here dealers stay up late, and Jonathan has their numbers. They hang around his place, waiting for delivery and pretending it's Jonathan they've come to see.

His studio apartment is upstairs from the Dockyard bar, which keeps unwholesome hours. He has a choice of listening to its noise filtered through the loose floorboards or coming downstairs and experiencing it firsthand.

Although Jonathan only meant to stop into the Dockyard for a couple of drinks, he's slipped from a prime spot in the middle of the bar to a shadowy corner, from top-shelf whiskey to swill. He's gone from laughing along with the regulars to being laughed at. Lil, the bartender, urges him to shut up. She's suggested that he go home even though it's only one A.M.

Jonathan can't remember when the evening got away from him. Maybe he insulted Lil's honky-tonk music. She's a little too old to be working here. She has a toxic red dye job and faded tattoos that look like bruises. Her gray eyes tighten as the night drags on. By last call they look like the heads of two screws.

Sex with Lil was unremarkable, the kind of late-night mistake Jonathan can't bring himself to give up. Something about the whole mess reminded him of the racetrack—the clop of Lil's cowboy boots, the slap of his hand on her ample flank, her exhausted whinnying when the thing was over.

The Dockyard's walls are covered with buoys and life preservers, grainy photos of steamers and tugboats. There's coiled rope and collapsed lobster traps, as well as flies and lines, bait and tackle. The mounted trout and bass are missing eyes and shedding scales. The place is supposedly filled with nostalgia for the humming waterfront of yesteryear. But it's really a shipwreck. Lit by strands of green Christmas lights, the bar looks as if it's sunk into the grimy basin a couple of streets away. The busted ship's clock helps the patrons ignore the time and keep on drinking.

Nicknames are big here. It took Jonathan a couple of weeks to sort out the crowd. There's Guitar Mike and Biker Mike. There's Whiskey Bill and Pirate Bill, Old Steve and New Steve. None of the women have nicknames.

Everyone calls Jonathan "Maestro," although he suspects none of them believe he actually writes music. One day he plans to take them by surprise. His head is crammed with riffs composed from neighborhood noise. These are usually suggested by something simple—the howl of the hinges on the door to the Dockyard, the lonely twang of the telephone wires on Van Brunt Street, the uneven, metallic rattle of a bicycle with loose fenders riding over cobblestones.

Days pass in Red Hook like musical compositions. Sometimes they are fugues, sometimes sonatas. The wildest days, when a storm blows in from the Atlantic and water surges down Van Brunt, are certainly symphonies. But Jonathan doesn't try to explain any of this to the patrons of the bar.

Lil's playing hard to get, fiddling with her CDs and ignoring Jonathan's signal.

"I thought you were keeping quiet tonight, Maestro," she says, not pouring him another. "At least I was hoping."

"Too hot to head upstairs," he says. "I thought I'd stick around and pay you to keep me entertained."

Lil wears a shot glass on a chain around her neck. It bumps against her breasts as she works. Instead of tipping her, patrons can buy her a shot. It's the best way to get on her good side.

Jonathan grabs the glass. "Let me buy you one."

Lil's shirt is wet from wiping down the bar and rinsing glasses. She shakes free. "No thanks, mister."

"My money's no good?"

"Leave your money on the bar."

He pisses Lil off a lot these days, especially when he's trying to be charming. "I thought no one around here turned away a free drink. Booze keeps you keeping us happy."

"You talk too much, Jonathan."

He drops a twenty next to his glass just to show her.

The bar is full even in this heat wave. There are a few leftover locals—salty types and retired detectives. But mostly it's a new crowd—artists, chefs, and odd craftsmen. Men in baseball caps for losing teams. Women in clogs or cowboy boots. Lots of women tonight. It's the dead of summer, and they still wear cowboy boots. It makes Jonathan feel old watching them and he's not even thirty.

Earlier, Jonathan tried talking to a few of these women. But now they're keeping their distance. He's not sure what went wrong. Maybe they were offended when he bought them a round of drinks and said that women only drink whiskey to impress men. Now they make a point of not looking his way. He's spent a year watching, noticing their short, choppy haircuts and new tattoos. He's watched them drink more, sleep less, and try on the tough postures of the old waterfront.

The women grow grungier and sexier the later it gets. Soon they bear no resemblance to the morning commuters who will tuck themselves into bus shelters along Van Brunt on Monday, polished and brushed and reasonably presentable to the world outside Red Hook. Nighttime abrades them, tangles their hair and chips their nails. Colors their speech. At night, the hundreds of nights they've passed the same way begin to show, revealed in their hollowed cheeks and rapid speech. Jonathan wonders how long it takes for their costumes to become their clothes, their tattoos their birthmarks. When will they let the outside world slip away and forget to retrieve it?

The new drink hits his stomach fast, a sign that he's had enough. He takes a walk around the bar to sober up. There are two drunks in the booth in the back. One has been passed out since happy hour. The regulars are taking turns decorating his face and clothes with Magic Marker. Someone is opening his shirt and drawing a pair of claw marks above his nipples.

"Got a song for us, Maestro?" a woman asks. She turns away before he can reply.

He drops to one knee and takes her hand. She tries to wriggle free, but he's got her tight. The song that comes into his head is Irving Berlin's "Let's Face the Music and Dance." The crowd is laughing at him, but Jonathan doesn't care. He sings loud, louder than the rockabilly pouring out of the speakers. He flings his free arm back and knocks a woman in the stomach. Lil wraps a calloused hand around Jonathan's wrist. Her strong grip feels good. "Out," she says.

Lil sees him to his door, only a few feet from the Dockyard's entrance, and makes sure he goes inside. Jonathan lingers in the doorway, listening to her cowboy boots beat time on the pavement—*Too Hot. Too Late.*

Upstairs, he opens the window, letting out the stale cigarette air and letting in more heat along with the night sounds. The storyboards for a new commercial are scattered on the floor—black-and-white drawings of dancing soda cans waiting for a tune.

He lights a cigarette and props his elbow on the sill, exhaling into the thick air. A few days ago at the piano bar in the West Village, he'd had an idea for this jingle. The blunt way his drag queen partner Dawn Perignon outlined her lips in cola-colored pencil then filled them in with cherry gloss inspired the first bars. He scribbled some notes on a napkin and shoved it into his pocket.

Since Jonathan only wears black jeans, locating the pair from that night is difficult. He turns out the pockets of his entire wardrobe. He finds matchbooks, phone numbers of women he doesn't want to call. He finds a few crumpled napkins from Cock 'n Bulls, but they only have doodles on them.

He lies on the couch staring at the storyboards. The only thing they bring to mind is merry-go-round music from a state fair.

He picks up his phone and calls Dawn, hoping her voice will suggest whatever it was her two-toned lips inspired.

She picks up after the third ring, house music blaring in the background.

"Hello?"

It always catches Jonathan by surprise that offstage Dawn talks like any other guy from Jersey. She has a deep voice, filled with guttural sounds and heavy consonants that are at odds with her lilting onstage inflection.

"Hello? You going to say something or what?" Dawn barks before switching to her stage voice. "Jonathan, baby? Cat got your tongue?"

"Forget it, Dawn. I had a question. It's not important."

"Don't tell me this is a booty call after all these years. You lonely tonight?"

"Screw you."

"With pleasure."

Jonathan hangs up. He's always wondered if Dawn is a little sweet on him.

He looks across the street to the Lebanese-owned bodega. If it

were open, he'd head over. Instead Jonathan extinguishes his cigarette and flicks it into the street. He takes two Tylenol PM and
chases them with whiskey. Then he puts on a recording of calypso
music in case the tropical rhythms inspire the dancing cans.

Jonathan usually wakes up when the bar quiets down. After the
noise drains slowly into the street, he knows Lil is in there alone.
She lowers the music and he can hear her footsteps as she clears
glasses and wipes the counters.

Lil sings after closing, a lonely performance for the half-empty
bottles and overflowing ashtrays. She's got a decent voice with a
rusty country twang. Jonathan imagines that she sits on the bar
with her feet on a stool, serenading the yellowed nautical charts
and photos of old sea captains.

She finishes her song and heads outside. She pulls down the
grate. The padlock falls into place with a bang.

Jonathan sticks his head out the window. "Hey, Lil."

"You still up?" She's holding a bottle of whiskey.

"You want to share that with me? I need a little inspiration."

Lil holds the bottle by the neck and waves it like a pendulum.
"Well, I'm not sharing my inspiration with you."

Jonathan watches her walk away. It's 5:15. This is the hour
when the four businesses—two bodegas, a luncheonette, and the
Dockyard—on the four corners of Van Brunt and Visitation per-
form their daily concert of opening or closing, the grind and
bang of recoiling metal welcoming another day.

The Greek is already struggling with his iron shutters. He has
roused the little wino who sleeps in the luncheonette's doorway.
The wino's shadowing him. One of the gates is stuck—the right
side won't budge higher than three feet. The Greek is tugging on
it. The wino's shuffling around, trying to help. He breaks a dead
branch off a tree and offers it to the Greek.

Jonathan has never eaten at the Greek's. The place caters to retired dockworkers, tollbooth clerks from the graveyard shift at the tunnel, and early arrivals for the methadone clinic.

The wino's voice catches Jonathan's ear. It's dissonant, all flats and sharps with no clear words. He looks eager, ready to invent odd jobs so the Greek will pay him to go away. The Greek gives his shutters a final shake before going inside to heat up the grill, make coffee, display yesterday's meatloaf.

Jonathan drops his blinds, but angles them just enough so that when daylight comes, it will descend on the diagonal.

It's too late for sleep. The first morning bus is rattling over the bumpy street, hitting each pothole and fissure made by the new sewage pipes.

When he was eight, Jonathan spent the summer in London with Eden who was appearing in a West End revival. They rented an apartment next to a Hasidic Jew. In the evenings, after Eden had left for the theater, the Hasid would come out onto his balcony and sing as the sun set. Although Jonathan could not understand the song, there was something in his voice that sent him to sleep. For a summer Jonathan could not sleep without this song.

There is no one to sing him to sleep now. There is only the metallic grind of the morning. He peeks through the blinds. In the half-light, the wino is sweeping a single square of pavement. He's got it blocked off with sawhorses scavenged from a ruptured manhole up Visitation. If he keeps this up, he'll get the boot and be drunk by nine. Behind him the Greek has found a crowbar and is trying to wrench the grate up. It sounds like he's milling steel.

To escape the commotion, Jonathan walks down to the water. Although it's steaming out, this is not a bad hour to be awake in Red Hook—too late to encounter the all-night revelers, too early for what's left of the local industry. The sun is beginning to rise behind him, fighting through the projects at the back of the neighborhood, promising a full-on Brooklyn bake.

The few streetlights on the side streets go out with a buzz. These blocks are quiet. The chop shops and warehouses are not open yet. The guard dogs protecting empty lots still sleep.

Jonathan turns down a cobblestone street that leads to the water—one of two decent residential blocks in Red Hook, a street filled with single-family homes in various stages of disrepair. From here he can already smell the water, its stagnant summer scent of diesel and salt.

The dark is lifting and Jonathan can make out Valentino Pier ahead stretching into the water like a long, horizontal ladder. He used to come down to the pier at sunset, but the skyline was an insult, its glittering lights a sad reminder. In the evenings, the pier itself became a trial. A place for couples. A scenic spot where the women who don't speak to Jonathan at the Dockyard show off the neighborhood to their Manhattan friends. So he started coming down in the mornings instead. He usually has the tugboats and seabirds for company.

He crosses the small park and heads onto the pier, passing a kid dressed in a low-rent imitation of the local dealers—nondescript baggy clothes that camouflage his frame. He juke-steps as Jonathan approaches, changes direction, and darts off toward the abandoned warehouses to the left of the pier.

There's a fog over the river hiding the skyline. It's claimed both the Verrazano and Bayonne bridges, stolen Staten Island, and obscured most of the Jersey waterfront.

A ferry crawls into view, creeping across the flat water like a caterpillar. The buoys are calling to each other, a long low horn followed by a quick high response as if the second buoy is mocking the first.

There's a little beach to the right of the pier, a collection of trash, sand, shale, and foam. It's strewn with chunks of wood too splintered and waterlogged for driftwood. The logs move in and out with the modest waves. Some tangle with the pylons below the pier. They get trapped and beat against the metal supports, their rhythm welcoming the arriving day. Jonathan leans over to watch them.

A girl is lying underneath the pier, faceup, beached on the jagged shale. Jonathan grips the pier and closes his eyes. The night was too late, the morning too soon. His insomnia has conjured worse imaginings. When he looks again, she is still there. Despite the suffocating air, Jonathan feels chilled.

He climbs down to the dirty sand and is ankle deep in cold water. A film of oil coats his calves. The girl's clothes are torn and muddy. She's barefoot. There are small cuts on her hands and feet. Her face is unscathed. Her fingers and lips are shriveled. Even in the dismal light under the pier, Jonathan can make out the watery pallor of her skin. Her hair is spread over the rocks. It's hard to tell whether it's brown or blond since it's matted and tangled with debris.

Jonathan knows that he should squat down next to her. But perhaps it would be simpler to rush off, phone for help, or even let her be someone else's discovery. Then he kneels at her side and listens for her breath. She too smells of seagulls.

Jonathan presses an ear to her lips. They are cold and dry. At first, there is no sound. He is about to pull away, when her breath echoes in his ear. It's short and sharp, as if catching on a pebble. Jonathan recoils, then presses his ear to listen again.

He knows that if he screams for help, the tugboats will pass in silence and the empty warehouses will turn a blind eye.

Jonathan rolls the girl's head to one side and a foamy stream slides from her mouth. He wipes mud from her cheeks. It's Valerie Marino, one of the few students from Red Hook who attends St. Bernardette's.

He lifts her carefully. Her limbs are long. She is dead weight.

He presses his body into hers, trying to warm her. Her heart beats against his own chest—a faint staccato patter. He cradles her head over his shoulder and feels her clammy skin against his collarbone. It has been months since he has held anyone so close.

He makes his way up the beach, trying not to stumble over the sharp and slippery rocks. Her body is cold. Her wet clothes stick to his skin. Holding her does nothing to ward off the suffocating day.

CHAPTER THREE

Fadi's late. But few will notice. On one hand he can count the people in the neighborhood who know his name. *Hey. Hey thanks. Coffee light. Coffee. The regular. The* Post. *The usual.* How do you order "the usual" from someone and not know his name?

The F train stopped on the elevated bridge just before Smith and Ninth. Fadi was stuck for twenty minutes in an un-air-conditioned subway car watching the sun's slow climb over the Red Hook Houses. The temperature had barely dropped all night, simmering in the low nineties. The radio says it'll crack a hundred today, menacing the power grid and threatening the neighborhood with a brownout that'll kill Fadi's dairy and ice.

Van Brunt is waking up slowly. The Puerto Rican place is still shuttered. But the Greek across from Fadi on Visitation is battling with his roll gate, hammering it with a crowbar. The string of Christmas lights that spans Van Brunt between the streetlight in front of Fadi's store and the one in front of the Puerto Ricans' sags in the heavy air. The colored bulbs hang lazy and limp, the lights hibernating until winter.

The papers are waiting outside his bodega. Both tabloids have front-page photos on cooling off. The *News* has snapped an elderly woman in the Bronx pouring a twelve-ounce bottle of water on her head. The *Post* shows a teenager jumping into the bay right off one of the piers in Red Hook.

The kid is in midflight, arms above his head, right leg extended straight, the left bent back behind. Below his feet is the inky bay. A ferry is passing beneath his legs. His arms cradle the crown and torch of the Statue of Liberty. Three of his friends are hanging from the railing, waiting to jump, heads upturned, admiring the flying boy. It looks like a perfect leap, high and clear of the railing, far beyond the pylons, into the heart of the water.

Fadi wipes his brow, unlocks the padlock, and lets the iron gate roll back revealing the cigarette ads that cover the shop's windows and keep daylight from bleaching his stock. He shoulders the bundled newspapers and pushes his way into the bodega.

This bodega was the idea of Fadi's father, Hafiz. While his brothers opened bakeries and restaurants on the Lebanese strip of Atlantic Avenue, Hafiz wanted something besides counters lined with sambousek, awamat, and baklawa. He believed that what Americans want is a drink that's orange because of the dye not the fruit. They want ham and turkey breasts pressed into neat cylindrical versions of hams and turkeys.

Hafiz's Red Hook bodega is only a twenty-five-minute walk from Atlantic Avenue, but Fadi figures his father might as well have set up shop in Staten Island for how often his uncles visit.

Even Hafiz has given up on the neighborhood. He now spends

his retirement on a camp chair, watching Atlantic Avenue roll by. He'll be awake soon, drawn into one of his brothers' shops by strong Lebanese coffee and a favorite honey and pistachio pastry while Fadi's out here with knock-off Maxwell House and powdered Donettes.

But Fadi still believes things are going to turn around out here, especially with the first cruise ships set to dock at the terminal at the end of Visitation in two months. Last night he gave his black-and-white linoleum an extra once-over with some premium cleaner from the shelves. His bodega shines a little brighter than the others in the neighborhood. His Puerto Rican competitors across Van Brunt have pared things down—generic beer, cigarettes, soda, chips, and only the *Post*. Fadi's got a range of beers, from sickly sweet forties of malt liquor to microbrews with ironic names. He's even got a kosher brand called He'Brew. He caters to everyone. But it's getting harder to keep up with the trends. The hipsters now brown-bag Colt 45 down by the pier while old-timers from the projects cart cases of Pilsner Urquell to their barbecues.

He stacks the newspapers in their racks and brews two pots of coffee. He turns on talk radio, props the front door open with a cinder block, then peeks inside the cooler. The ham's beginning to sweat nitrates in its plastic sheath. Fadi turns the thermostat to "cold" and checks the store to see what else might be suffering.

English muffins. Sliced bread. He stacks these in the cooler with the meat and cheese. By now much of Fadi's inventory has found its way into this cooler, leaving portions of the shelves empty until fall. He settles behind the counter with a mug of black coffee and a Danish pastry ribboned with white icing. Most of the icing still clings to its plastic wrapping. Even made at maximum strength the coffee doesn't come close to Lebanese brew. Twenty ounces of watery caffeine whose dregs don't tell his fortune. His chair wobbles. He should replace it. Or maybe he should lose weight. Stop eating the junk he sells. Living on the local diet of fried chicken from the bulletproof Chinese window and greasy garlic knots from the third-rate pizza joint has helped Fadi fill out.

Fadi wears XXXL white T-shirts like the local dealers and their hangers-on. With his dark complexion and gold chain, he could easily slip into their ranks. Sometimes from the close interior of his shop he envies their lazy days, their portable business, their flexible hours. But the maniacal chatter from the bar opposite and the sallow ghosts riding the bus to the methadone clinic up the block set him straight and make him sad.

When he's honest with himself, Fadi has to admit that, despite his improvements, he doesn't do much better than the Puerto Ricans in their dingy store that smells of ammonia and kitty litter. Ambiance doesn't exactly matter when you're buying liter bottles of Coke or cigarettes.

Yet Fadi hopes that his bodega is a place for neighborhood news. A year ago, he hung a bulletin board near the door so that customers can learn about council meetings, hairstylists, dog walkers, babysitters, yoga classes, carpet cleaners, handymen, Reiki sessions, and Tarot readings. He's a local authority on available apartments—someone people go to when they've been kicked out or need a change. This summer he began leaving a couple of folding chairs in the shade of his metal awning, enticing people to linger awhile, and let him treat them to a soda or beer in a paper bag.

They don't know he reads the three major newspapers thoroughly—that he's an expert on metropolitan news and local crime patterns through daily study of police blotters. No one would guess that the guy in the bodega can name all the members of the city council, the five borough presidents, or that he votes in every election right down to the ones for his local school board.

Fadi knows he's never going to get rich selling Tylenol PM to night owls from the bar across the street, but he believes in Red Hook. He's taped a collection of local news stories to the plexiglass cabinets on the counter. He wants his customers to know that they are an important part of the city and that his bodega is their center. In the four years since the shop opened, he has papered the counter with stories about a local war hero, a retired detective turned real estate developer, a neighborhood kid who made it to the NBA, another who landed a record deal.

In his years clipping local news from the major papers, Red Hook never earned the front page until today. A flying boy. A heat wave poster child. A jump that captures the city. Fadi tears off the front page and tapes it in the place of honor, just to the right of the register.

A while back, Fadi started a weekly community newsletter that he presses into his customers' hands along with their change. Although he asks for submissions, he rarely gets any. Most of Fadi's items are drawn from incidents he's witnessed—a drunk driver plowing his van into the doorway of the Dockyard, trapping the drinkers inside for hours, or an alligator discovered in a basement apartment on Visitation.

This summer he's written several articles about the changes he hopes the cruise ships will bring to Red Hook. He tried to interview his Puerto Rican rivals as well as Christos, the Greek owner of the recently renamed Cruise Café across Visitation. But they mistook his interest in their businesses for snooping, so Fadi mainly reports his own opinions.

He peers into the cooler. The ham is still sweating. He lifts the cylinder of meat and begins to wrestle it from its sheath. It plops onto the counter, the slick of greasy water making it do a one eighty. He grabs the ham before it can slide to the floor. He cups it to his chest, cradling it as the salty juices soak his shirt. He's still holding the ham tight when the door opens.

It takes a moment for Fadi to recognize Jonathan, who lives above the bar. His dark brown hair is matted, and mud is streaked across one of his cheeks. He's carrying a girl. He's got her head carefully balanced on his shoulder. Her arms and legs dangle like they have nothing to do with her body. There is a smell of brine and garbage.

Jonathan's arms are trembling under the girl's weight. Blue veins emerge on his biceps. His breath is quick and heavy.

"I found her," Jonathan says.

"Set her down." Fadi points to the floor.

Jonathan doesn't move from the doorway. "She's cold."

"Set her down."

Jonathan adjusts the girl in his arms, holding her tighter. Fadi rushes to him. "Jonathan, you need to put her down."

They join arms, cradle the girl, then squat and lower her to the shiny linoleum.

"She was under the pier," Jonathan says. He sits beside her, leans against the ice cream freezer, and takes the girl's hand and rubs it between his palms. "She looked broken. Like driftwood."

The girl is barefoot. Her nails are blue. Jonathan's are ringed with mud.

Fadi reaches for the phone and dials 911. He recognizes the girl. Val, the younger of the two Marino kids. Two days ago she and her friend June had tried to buy cigarettes from him. He'd asked for their IDs, then handed them each a menthol from the pack he keeps for his cousin.

Fadi heads into the mop closet for a clean T-shirt. He lays it over the girl's narrow body where it looks as big as a beach towel.

"She going to be okay," Jonathan says, still rubbing Val's palm. "She's going to be okay." He glances at Fadi. His gaze is uncertain. His eyes are submerged in dark circles.

Fadi looks at the girl, the faint rise of her chest underneath the shirt. Her lips are colorless. "I don't know," he says.

Fadi remembers when Jonathan moved in above the bar. The place had been empty for months. The Dockyard was too loud for most people. But it didn't seem to bother the musician. Fadi's overheard people from the bar calling Jonathan "Maestro," but he doesn't dare use the nickname himself.

Fadi used to see patrons from the bar go in and out of Jonathan's. But it seems he's been spending time alone these days. Fadi likes Jonathan's manners. The intelligent way he talks to Fadi. He appreciates the musician's dark trousers and dress shirts—even if they're wrinkled and frayed. Jonathan's always talking about different composers or humming music he challenges Fadi to identify. Fadi never can, but he plays along.

Nearly every day Jonathan tells Fadi about a piece of music that's perfectly suited to the moment. Last week he said, "It's an afternoon for Gershwin. Mostly sunny, a little bit snappy, but with a hint of rain." And two evenings ago he asked, "Did you see the sunset? Only Philip Glass would write a sunset like that."

Fadi has no idea what Jonathan means. But he enjoys listening. He settles back in his wobbly stool and lets the musician ramble. Jonathan gestures theatrically as he talks, conducting an orchestra hidden somewhere in the bodega or serenading some offstage lover. He usually turns the counter into an invisible keyboard, hammering a few chords or running through scales between the penny tray and the lighters. Then he thanks Fadi for his time and leaves. Fadi hands him a free newspaper on his way out.

Fadi imagines that if there were no counter between them he might be able to talk freely with Jonathan, tell him about his own Brooklyn neighborhood ten subway stops away where he tries to mistake the sound of traffic for the ocean.

He glances at Jonathan now, slumped on the floor. The musician's dark hair is matted and pressed down like a wiry skullcap.

Both men look up as a bus pulls up in front of the Greek's. They listen to its geriatric noises as it rumbles off.

"I know her," Fadi says. "She's from up the street." He checks the store clock, counting backward to when he dialed 911.

"She's going to be okay," Jonathan says. "I got to her in time. So she's going to be okay." His words sound like a prayer, Fadi thinks. An incantation.

Jonathan rubs Val's hands.

Fadi checks the coffee and pours a cup for Jonathan.

The neighborhood falls silent. The bus stop is empty. No trucks rumble past. Fadi goes outside. The street is empty.

Inside the bodega the only sound is the whir of the clock. Fadi empties the coffee filters and refills them. He considers telling the musician to leave the girl's hand alone.

"I don't know why I looked under the pier. I could have walked away. What if I had walked away? What would have happened?"

Soon they hear the slow wail of a siren rolling down Van Brunt. Two ambulances arrive. Paramedics push Jonathan aside. The crackle of their walkie-talkies drowns out Fadi's radio.

They bring in a stretcher and transfer Val. Clutching his coffee, Jonathan follows Val to the ambulance and tries to step inside. One of the paramedics leads him back into the store.

Three cop cars arrive. Their dark uniforms drag in more heat.

"I should go to the hospital," Jonathan says. "She shouldn't go alone."

"You should stay here," one of the cops says.

Fadi takes his place behind the counter as the officers question him. He crosses his arms and lets them rest on his belly. He turns his weak fan to high and offers the policemen coffee.

"I know the girl," Fadi says. "Val Marino. She lives up the street."

They go outside so he can show them the Marino house. Fadi points out the three-story brick around the corner from his shop. He watches the officers knock on the door.

Fadi sees Val's sister emerge. She's wearing a boy's T-shirt and boxer shorts. She puts a hand on her hip. Then her posture changes, as if a string holding her upright was cut. She doubles over. An officer puts an arm around her. Carrying her shoes in one hand, she follows the policemen up the block and gets into a squad car.

Fadi returns to the store. The sirens have brought people to their windows. The curious begin to arrive at the bodega. They pace the two aisles trying to collect the latest news. At the least, they're hoping for a free coffee.

Two plainclothes detectives appear—one middle aged and one fresh on the job. "The sister says she had a friend with her," the older detective tells Jonathan. "You see both girls or just the one?" He flashes his badge: Coover.

"Just one."

"You sure?" Coover massages his jaw. There's a flush of razor burn on his florid neck. His tie is crumpled.

"Was it a rough night? Maybe you missed something down there," Coover's partner asks. He's holding his badge out for Fadi to read. The leather case is new, and the badge shines; the detective's name is Hughes.

"She was alone under the pier. I almost didn't see her at all." Jonathan's fingers are restless. They are playing scales on his pants.

"June," Fadi tells the detectives. "She and Val are always together. June lives with her grandmother. The grandmother likes cream and three sugars. I don't know where they live. They go to the church around the corner. They pass by on Sundays."

Two police officers take Jonathan outside and place him on one of the folding chairs. Fadi slides a pack of Jonathan's brand of cigarettes into the musician's hand.

Soon reporters will arrive, Fadi thinks. Tomorrow there will be a picture of his store in the newspaper. He heads inside and wipes down the counter, removing the sweaty palm prints. He takes a coffee cake from the shelves and cuts it into slices and passes it around to the officers outside. He glances back at the store, hoping no one is stealing.

A crowd has gathered on the corners of Van Brunt and Visitation, facing off like the points of a compass. The story develops slowly. Several policemen and the two detectives remain in the bodega. Their walkie-talkies crackle and beep. Fadi keeps them supplied with bottled water and soda.

"They're good girls, June and Val," Fadi says, handing Hughes a cup of ice.

"Know 'em well?" Hughes removes his suit jacket and rolls up his sleeves. His clothes are new, pressed and creased. Fadi glimpses a military tattoo inside his forearm.

"They're in the store a lot."

"You see them outside the store?" The younger detective smells of cologne. His hair is beginning to sweat pomade.

"On the block sometimes."

Hughes exhales and shifts his weight, releasing a creak of gun belt leather. "That's it?"

"They're nice girls," Fadi says, refilling the penny tray.

The detective withdraws a notepad in a leather case from his belt. He flips it open. "And the guy who found her. He's nice too?"

"Yes," Fadi says.

"You know *him* well?"

"He comes in every day. We talk."

"About?"

"Music."

Hughes does not write this down. "You two like the same kind of music?"

"I like talk radio."

"You see him outside of the store?" Beads of sweat are collecting at the detective's temples.

"At the bar."

"So you drink together." He uncaps the pen.

Fadi has often been tempted to offer Jonathan a beer. He imagines the two of them standing under the awning, their bottles concealed in brown bags. "No. From here I see him going in and out of the bar."

"You don't drink there yourself." Hughes closes his notebook, leaving the page blank. "You'd guess he drinks a lot?"

"They all seem to drink a lot."

"You live nearby?"

"Avenue N." It's miles away, but Fadi knows his neighbors as well as anyone in Red Hook.

With Val's sister's help, the police locate June's grandmother, who confirms her granddaughter's absence. Officers are dispatched to canvass the neighborhood. They take a photo of June with them.

Fadi asks to make a copy of the picture on his dilapidated copier. The photo is from June's yearbook. She's looking over her right shoulder at the camera. Her hair is pulled into a tight ponytail. She has undone the top three buttons of her blouse. Underneath the photo Fadi writes "Have You Seen This Girl?" and lists the phone numbers of the bodega and the local precinct. Everyone who comes into the store will leave with one of these flyers. By tomorrow he'll have printed up a special edition of his newsletter with a tip line and information on missing children and grief counselors.

He watches pairs of officers file up Visitation. The canvass moves between the waterfront and the projects. Police rescue boats are dispatched. The detectives ask Jonathan to accompany them to the precinct for routine questioning. The musician's shoulders droop as he gets into the back of their unmarked car.

After Jonathan leaves, the locals are more forward. They want to know if Val looked beaten or abused. They insist that Jonathan looked drunk. They all seem to know why he was down at the pier before sunrise.

"He wasn't arrested," Fadi tells his customers.

The customers like their version better.

"Better concentrate on the missing girl not the musician." But the locals are more interested in Jonathan.

News ripples through the neighborhood. Fadi learns that the girls haven't been seen since last night around eleven.

Customers keep coming into the bodega to buy things they

don't need. Fadi is selective about the information he gives out. He keeps things to himself. He refuses to talk about Jonathan.

"You can read the official account in the paper tomorrow," he tells his customers. He wonders if he should double up on the next day's tabloids. He keeps an eye on his phone, hoping the *Times* will call.

During a lull in the action, he calls his office supply distributor and orders extra ink and toner for the copier. His newsletter will no longer be something people discard at the bus stop, but an essential community resource. He keeps his ears open for anything newsworthy, something that will grab his readers.

Christos has been loitering on the sidewalk in front of his café all day. Something's still wrong with his grate. The place looks closed. From across the street, he waves to the officers, trying to siphon some of Fadi's business. But no one trusts a dark restaurant. All the business is Fadi's today.

He runs out of ice. He runs out of pastries. He's low on rolls.

A black teenager turns up. She's wearing a tight pink crop-top, short denim shorts, and fluorescent basketball sneakers. She buys a pack of watermelon gum. She unwraps the gum, pops a piece in her mouth. She points at the flyer. "Saw her last night," she says. The gum is like a stone she needs to work around. "She tried to kick it with my crew over in Coffey Park. She and her friend. They had some kinda raft with 'em. She was acting crazy. Then she took off." The girl stops chewing and purses her lips to one side. "Can I ask you something? You think I shoulda stopped her?" Fadi grabs a pen and turns over one of the flyers.

"Never mind," the girl says, blowing a bubble.

"What's your name?"

"Monique."

"Monique what?"

"Monique isn't enough?"

"You should stick around in case someone wants to talk to you."

Monique laughs and says, "Where you think I'm gonna go?"

June Giatto, last seen in Coffey Park by a young woman named Monique and her friends, Fadi writes. *According to Monique, June seemed agitated.* It's a scoop. His first.

People arrive with candles, flowers, and photographs of June taped to poster board. Fadi worries that it will appear as if a crime was committed in his store, but he allows the shrine to build. He hands out cookies. The owners of the bodega across the street eye him. They've put out lawn chairs and are blasting Latin pop music.

Late afternoon, Fadi begins scanning the radio stations for news of Red Hook. But all the airwaves care about is the heat—grid overloads, possible brownouts, water shortages. In the Ravenswood Houses in Queens, an elderly couple died from heatstroke. A kid in Harlem died when an electric fan fell into his bath. Babies die in cars. There is concern about animals in the Central Park Zoo. Fadi spins the dial and finds a station playing Christmas music.

As the light softens, the crowd thins. Fadi's not handing out free beer. There's no reason to hang around. A few women transport the shrine down to the waterfront. Fadi's left alone in his store with only the occasional customers for company.

The streets are empty. The neighborhood settles down, exhausted from the day. The bar fills. Half the patrons stand outside smoking. Their laughter carries across Van Brunt.

Fadi keeps an eye on Jonathan's window, hoping to see a light go on.

He orders takeout from the bulletproof Chinese. Fadi expects the delivery boy to say something about the disappearance, but he just holds out his hand for the money and slides off.

Just before closing, a boy comes in. A tall, lanky kid from the Houses Fadi's never seen before. He circles the aisles. He's wearing enormous red basketball shorts and a matching jersey. He grabs an iced tea out of the cooler. The stuff's so sweet just thinking about it makes Fadi's teeth hurt.

He puts the drink on the counter. "Gimme the rest of the *Post*s," he says, pointing at the papers.

There are over thirty copies left. With all the commotion today, the papers were ignored. The kid slings these onto the counter and Fadi counts them.

"How come you're interested in yesterday's news?"

The kid looks up. When he smiles, his lips go jagged. He points at the flying boy on the cover. "That's me, man." Then he grabs the papers and swaggers out.

CHAPTER FOUR

Val keeps her eyes closed, her body curled sideways. She stays tucked into herself, feigning sleep, feigning absence. *Three, two, one,* and it will all be over. *Five, four, three, two, one.* The detectives, the doctors, her sister, Rita—everyone will be gone. *Ten, nine, eight, seven, six, five, four, three, two, one.* June will turn up; she will be installed in the hospital bed next to Val's. They will talk long after the nurses switch off the lights in the ward. They will camp out as if they are still kids.

Val's lungs feel scraped and sore. Her eyes are dry. A dull throbbing that seems to originate at the base of her skull rises into her head and crowds her brain like a tight helmet. She is on the tenth floor of Long Island College Hospital in a room that overlooks the river. The walls are beige. The tiles are the color of Listerine. Her pillow and mattress feel like crumpled newspaper. She keeps her eyes closed. She doesn't want to see anyone or anything.

She tells the detectives that she doesn't remember what happened after she fell into the river. She doesn't know where June is. *Five, four, three, two, one.* Val counts backward with her eyes closed as one of the detectives keeps questioning her. The buzzing of the detective's cell phone will be the news that June has been found. The information whispered from his partner will be the clue that will bring June home.

You don't remember anything? Anyone?

Val shakes her head, eyes closed.

Nothing? Nothing at all? It sounds like an accusation.

Val flinches and curls tighter.

Nothing? Nothing? You're sure, nothing? What knocked you off the raft? You don't know? You're sure you don't know?

"I don't know," Val says, her face buried in the crinkly pillow.

And you wound up on shore and June just disappeared? Was she swept away? Did you see her? You didn't see what happened? Nothing? Nothing at all? Nothing?

"Nothing."

Your friend is missing, Valerie. You're the last person who saw her. You can't help us? You can't help at all?

Val shakes her head. The pillow cracks and rustles. She squeezes her eyes tight, so tight that she needs to hold her breath. If she can hold her breath for a minute, the detectives will leave her alone. If she can hold her breath for two minutes, she will rewind back to the raft and June will not slip away.

You can't help? Do you know something? Something you're not telling us?

Her stomach turns and plummets. She reaches out to grab June's hand, but all she catches is the frayed edge of her brown polyester blanket.

Eventually the detectives leave. Her panic subsides to a simmer. *Five, four, three, two, one.* Val counts backward, willing herself to sleep. When she wakes, this will be over.

Her parents arrive from a weekend at the beach cut short, bringing with them the artificial coconut smell Val associates with her uncle's place on Long Island. Val sits up in bed so she can focus on the view—the million-dollar lookout over South Brooklyn down to Red Hook with its grids of town houses, white and brown and brick. The view reveals a hidden rooftop world—kiddie pools, putting greens, barbecue grills, lawn furniture, beach towels, laundry lines, pigeon coops. A tar beach paradise.

Between the roofs, Val can see the dips that hint at vest pocket parks and community gardens—squares of green and shade. The sunken expressway is clogged with cars, bolts of sunlight bouncing off their chrome and paint. She watches the piers and warehouses, the waterfront world demystified in the daylight. Beyond these lie the tip of Manhattan, the Statue of Liberty, the industrial port of New Jersey, the suggestion of Staten Island. But most of all there is the water—the river and the bay where she last saw June.

From up here, the water is a startling cornflower blue that darkens as it reaches the piers and waterfront. It's crosscut with white wakes from tugs and ferries. A stripe of sunlight runs down the middle of the bay, so bright it swallows the boats as they cross it, momentarily hiding them from view.

If the red tug with the "M" on its smokestack crosses the stripe of sunlight before the orange ferry, they will find June this afternoon.

Val's mother wears a beach cover-up over her jeans and jelly sandals. Jo's a short, round woman and her shapeless terry-cloth top makes her look like a ball of toweling. Her skin is shiny with aloe and suntan lotion. She places a plastic figurine of the Virgin next to the bed.

"You pray for that angel, Val," she says. "You pray for Juney every minute. Even when you're sleeping, you pray for her." She taps the Virgin with a peachy nail. "You talk to her. You tell her to bring Juney back. You tell her."

"Sure, Mama."

"At the church I'm gonna light candles. One from each of us." Jo shakes her head. "And we'll have a potluck at VFW. You better pray for June to be back before then. I don't know what I'm gonna say when I see her grandmother."

"You want to tell me what happened out there?" Paulie Marino says. He's a broad man with a tight brush cut. He keeps his forearms crossed over his stomach. A tattoo showing his firehouse shield sneaks out from the sleeve of his T-shirt.

"You're out on the raft? You banged in the head? And none of these doctors or police can tell me if it's an accident or an attack."

"I don't know," Val says.

"What don't you know? Tell me this scheme wasn't your idea," Paulie says.

"I had the raft," Val says.

"And what? Then what? June wanted to go out on the water?"

Although Val had done her best to ignore it, June had grown tired of the adventure. Val had been able to feel her mounting irritation, her restless need to be elsewhere with others. "I guess," she says, turning away from the window, blocking out the view of the bay and basin.

"You know the kinds of sicknesses you get from that water?" Paulie says. "Not even the homeless wash themselves down there." He takes a lock of her hair and combs it out with his fingers. "Jesus," he says. "What if it'd been you?"

"No," Jo says. "Don't say that, Paulie. Don't you say that."

Jo has her telephone pressed to her ear, keeping tabs on Red Hook. She cups her hand over the phone and says, "They're building a shrine to June. They're sweeping the projects."

Paulie stands by the window, scowling first at the distant shapes of the Red Hook Houses, then focusing his wrath on the river.

"No one lies underneath one of the piers unmolested. I know Red Hook. You were out cold for hours," he says. "Anything could of happened. There's no reason for you to be down there. No reason for my kid to be creeping around at night. And those drunks from the Dockyard. Who knows what they're capable of."

"We weren't creeping. We were floating."

"Floating? You just thought you'd float around the waterfront."

"Leave her alone, Paulie," Jo says.

"I just want to understand, that's all. Kid's in a hospital bed and I have no answers."

It's useless to tell her parents about the sunken tugboat. Something glimmering in the wheelhouse. Something else hiding behind the portholes. The skyline reflected in the river, an unreal, melting city. The strange pulse of the water, the river's heartbeat.

"And then what?" Paulie says. "June decides to swim away from you?"

Val's breath catches in her throat. She senses her stomach preparing to go into free fall.

"She doesn't remember," Rita says. "God."

"You're the one who was supposed to be watching her," Paulie says to Rita.

"She's fifteen," Rita says.

"And?" Paulie says. "I don't seem to remember you being an angel at fifteen. We left you in charge. Which means, you watch her."

"I can't help what she does when she goes out."

"Who said she is allowed to go out?"

Rita goes to the small mirror outside the bathroom and wipes last night's makeup from the corners of her eyes.

"They're done with the Houses," Jo says. "They're taking out police boats." She turns to Val. "You better be praying for June every second you're not talking. You better pray for her in your sleep."

"I am," Val says.

Val groans and rolls over. Jo mistakes her daughter's anxiety for pain. She summons the nurse who shines a flashlight in Val's eyes and instructs her to sit up. The nurse holds a finger in front of Val's nose. She moves the finger back and forth, front and back. She asks Val to say her name, her age, what year it is, what year she was born. Val glances at her mother, sitting forward on her chair, mouthing the answers to the nurse's questions, worried that Val is going to fail this test. The nurse reprimands Val for taking her eyes off her finger. She makes notes on a clipboard and leaves.

Val's concentration is broken. Although her parents beg her to, she won't try to piece together the hours after she fell from the raft. Instead she tries to recall all that happened before. To turn it around, examine it from all sides, shake it up like a kaleidoscope then let it fall back into place.

But all she can think of is June falling into the water. Each time she sinks into her memory, lowering herself back onto the raft with June behind her, sliding into the slick water at the edge of the first pier, she sees June slipping away.

Throughout the afternoon Jo's questioning gaze lingers on Val's face. "Anything, sweetie?" she says.

"Anything what?" Val says.

"Anything else you want to tell us about Juney?"

"Jesus, Mama."

Visiting hours end and the Marinos leave. A nurse disconnects Val's IV. The hospital grows quiet as the sun begins to fall behind the skyline, throwing the buildings into silhouette, making the sky burn four shades of orange and pink. The river goes from blue to black. Only a hemline of sun remains behind Manhattan skyscrapers.

Now the hospital is whirr and whisper. The nurses creep along the halls, poking their heads in from room to room, adjusting machines, checking IVs. Val tries to imagine that she is in June's bed and that June is next to her. She pretends they are sleeping head to toe—a habit June's grandmother believed would prevent spreading colds.

She tries listening for the familiar sounds of June's bedroom— the hiss of Mrs. Giatto's humidifier, the whine of the neighborhood's gate, the rumble of the school buses pulling into their parking lot across the street. The girls were forbidden to play in this lot. This hadn't stopped them. After they'd heard a rumor about a boy who was left overnight in a school bus and died, they sneaked into the lot, trying the doors of all the buses, attempting to see if there were any forgotten children. Back in bed the girls tried to spook each other by tapping on June's window, pretending to be the school bus ghost. They'd compete to see who could catch the other off guard, at the cusp of sleep. Who could make the other scream.

During the night, the nurses shine flashlights in Val's eyes so often that she gives up on sleep. She wanders the halls. The hospital is a freestanding building and her ward takes up the tenth floor. It's laid out like a donut—the nurses' station and the elevators in the middle, the patients' rooms on the outer edge. At least the views belong to the sick.

Except for an elderly man with drooping shoulders doing laps with his drip pole, Val is the only patient in the halls. From one end of the floor she looks deeper into landlocked Brooklyn to the fortresses of projects looming over middle-class neighborhoods. From another side, she stares out at the affluent brownstones of the Heights and the outline of the Brooklyn Bridge poised at the neighborhood's back. Val calls June from a waiting room that overlooks Manhattan's skyscrapers, the water below alive with their reflections.

The phone goes straight to voice mail. An automated voice tells Val that June's mailbox is full. She crosses her fingers, holds her breath, counts backward from ten. She calls again and again, listening to June's message, which she knows by heart, trying to believe that June will "get right back" to her.

Val dials Rita.

"Because of you I'm stuck at home tonight," her sister says. "They say I'm responsible for you. Like I can keep track of every one of your crappy ideas."

"What about June—"

"Nothing," Rita says.

Val hangs up. The buzz of the fluorescent bulbs in the waiting room makes her head hurt. She fingers the bump on the back of her skull, tracing her stitches through the bandage. She closes her eyes. She counts to ten. Then she calls June until she exhausts her phone's battery.

She presses her head against the window. From behind the heavy glass she watches New York stream and flicker—taxis shooting up the river-side drive, the blank-faced office buildings still lit up at night. She turns one of the handles on the window but it's painted shut. She pulls the handle trying to shake the window loose. She barely rattles the glass. She turns and presses a shoulder against the pane but nothing happens.

Val wanders through the hospital, passing the incubated glow of the maternity wards and the locked double doors of the psych unit. She takes the elevator to the ground floor and finds herself amid the chaos of the emergency room where patients clutch and groan and sleep until someone notices.

She lingers by the desk, watching relatives and friends demand care, demand to see doctors, demand to talk to the person in charge and the person in charge of that person.

She heads into the lobby where there's a Taco Bell and an Au Bon Pain, and beyond these a revolving door that leads to the street. No one is watching her. No one would notice if she slipped out. It would be simple to leave and start looking for June.

When she takes a step toward the exit, the door revolves, bringing in a hot gust of Brooklyn night. It spins again. And then three paramedics burst through the wheelchair entrance, pushing a gurney carrying a female figure into the hospital. They shove Val aside.

One of the paramedics heads to the admitting desk while the other two go to work on the figure on the gurney. All Val can make out are matted reddish-brown curls and a face smeared with blood. A thin sheet poorly disguises the ample curves of the body beneath it.

"I know her," Val says, pushing her way toward the gurney. A nurse takes Val by the arm and pulls her out of range.

"June," Val screams.

The paramedics make room for a doctor and two nurses. All of them are yelling at once, speaking in code. They wheel the gurney out of the waiting room and into a hallway.

The doctor grabs a set of paddles from the paramedic and presses them onto the patient's chest. Her body heaves and flops. He jolts her again.

They are doing something to her throat, cutting, inserting a tube. They are pounding on her as if she is incapable of feeling.

No one notices Val. "June," she says. "June!"

All the girls' minor transgressions and small truancies fly into Val's head, their childhood misdemeanors and thoughtless disobediences. Val runs the numbers on these, desperately calculating if a cigarette, a stolen magazine could have brought June here.

In eighth grade the girls skipped school for the first time. They took the back stairs. They shed their uniforms, revealing tank tops and shorts. They planned on taking the subway into the city, but they lost their nerve. Instead, they walked deeper into Brooklyn than they ever had been before.

They crossed from Red Hook into Sunset Park, stomping through the wilds of its industrial waterfront. They found a maze of train and trolley tracks—some stopped dead in the middle of cobblestone causeways, and others dove into the water. They skidded on the mossy overgrowth on an abandoned pier. They passed through an apple orchard. They waded across murky marshland and through shoulder-high weeds. They hurried past empty warehouses and tried to ignore the hollow strike of phantom footfalls.

It took them two hours to reach Bay Ridge, at Brooklyn's far corner. The waterfront there was tame and vast. A manicured causeway for pedestrians and bicycles ran parallel to an expressway. The girls skipped over the concrete of the Sixty-Ninth Street Pier and headed up the seawall promenade until they came to the Verrazano Bridge.

Wind rushed over the open promenade, inciting the water and twisting the girls' hair into knots. Bicycles and joggers passed them while cars accelerated on the adjacent expressway. The bridge loomed overhead. Its color and ribbed underbelly reminded Val of the giant blue whale that towered over the girls during a class trip to the Museum of Natural History. And standing underneath the bridge, she was filled with the same panic she had felt in the Hall of Ocean Life in the museum—an undeniable awareness of the unknown.

The Bay Ridge waterfront was the farthest either of the girls had ever been from home unaccompanied. Val insisted they keep going. When June wanted to head back, Val leaped over the promenade's fence and scrambled onto the rocks at the water's edge. She tiptoed along the rocks, daring June to follow.

June sat on the railing, watching Val, calling to her that if she didn't turn around in two seconds, she was out of there. And then Val slipped, wedging her foot between two rocks where the suction of mud and water would not let her go.

June picked her way down and calmed her, told her to stop struggling or it would cause her foot to swell and they'd never get her free. She knelt on the slimy rocks and stuck her hands into the crevice without complaining about the filth and mud as she dug to free Val's foot. She'd worked patiently, shredding her fingers. And then when Val's foot was free, she fell backward, landing on her wrist and spraining it.

The doctor charges the paddles once more. The body tenses

and falls limp. He replaces the paddles and walks away. One of the nurses writes something on a clipboard. They discuss where to move the dead girl.

Val approaches the stretcher. The body is turned away from her. All she can see is blood-matted curls.

She places her fingers on the girl's forehead, rotating it toward her. The skin is cool and clammy. The head falls toward Val. She understands that this is not June behind the mask of blood. Val returns to her room.

She sits by the window clutching the figurine of the Virgin. She rocks back and forth in her chair, then leans her head on the glass. The expressway rumbles. Sirens roll in the distance. A woman in an apartment building across from the hospital is sitting on her fire escape. On another fire escape above her two men are lying on a mattress holding hands, watching the sky. On the next roof over three women and a man are sitting in a kiddie pool tossing a beach ball. In the window below them an older man with a telescope is looking at the sky.

On the river two tugs pull a container ship into dock. A bouquet of fireworks explodes from a small fishing boat lit up with red and orange Christmas lights.

Val waits for the moon to slide across the water, showing her where June slipped from her grasp.

The city and river wink and glimmer. Taillights dwindle to beady red points and wide-eyed headlamps draw close then disappear. The water cups the skyline's reflection—a ghost city. Val clutches the plastic figurine until it begins to cut into her skin. She counts backward from ten, and then she begins to pray for the pink raft to appear in the river below.

CHAPTER FIVE

The Seventy-Sixth Precinct smells of burned coffee. The vinyl tile is the color of a murky swimming pool. The windows are double-thick glass and don't look out on much besides the blank stucco of a neighboring town house.

Jonathan sits at a large brown Formica table with a faux wood grain finish. He stares out the window of his interrogation room watching detectives lean into their small desk fans, cooling off the space between their collars and their necks.

When he demanded his one phone call, the cops laughed. He's not under arrest and he can make as many phone calls as he likes. But there's no phone in here and he left his cell in his apartment. The officers assure him that he's in for routine questioning. Missing kids are no joke they say, as if Jonathan might have been under this impression.

Jonathan's hangover has crept past the fog of his Tylenol PM, leaving an infuriating numbness that makes his eyes feel as if they are wearing sweaters. Now he hears his thoughts as he thinks them, a maddening echo of each unpleasant idea.

He fiddles with the table, chipping the Formica, worrying that he has cast doubts on his innocence by asking for a phone call. If the officers return, cuff him, lead him to a cell, he wonders who he can reach.

The only person he's sure to get is Dawn. The girl never sleeps. He can imagine the scene if she waltzed into the station. She'd make him pay for summoning her by wearing an aqua mesh midriff top, hot pants, and platform go-go boots. She swears only "fags" wear heels before dark. *I'm a queen. It's different,* she says.

Jonathan digs his fingers into his temples as if he can squeeze the hangover out. All morning he has been struggling to banish memories of his mother, but when he closes his eyes he sees Eden's body, her seaweed-knotted hair. And now he confuses this picture with the girl under the pier. He mistakes the pale moons of their nails, their shriveled fingers, the mud and gravel on their palms. The last time he'd seen Eden—the last time he'd been out to his parents' summer home—her face was the color of moonstone. It looked as if the bay had sunk into her cheeks and was struggling to push back out.

As the police wrapped her in a blanket, the sun broke over the bluffs on Castle Road on the eastern shore of Fishers Island. A soft orange glow—a warm color that brought no warmth—crept from Eden's chin, to her cheeks, then illuminated eyes that were as still and opaque as marbles. Jonathan watched two men lift his mother into the ambulance. Three days later, when he took the ferry back to the mainland, he knew he wouldn't return.

He stands up and walks to the window so he can watch the detectives who brought him in passing around a photo of a girl in a Catholic school uniform. Jonathan knows this girl as well as the one he found under the pier. He's seen them together waiting for the 61 bus on Van Brunt. He's noticed them in the halls of St. Bernardette's before they faded back into the sea of plaid skirts and white blouses.

The room is soundproof. He watches the police move around as if they are in a silent movie. He watches the pantomime of their lips against the receivers of their beige desk phones. Without noise their business loses its urgency and becomes slapstick—the muted rush of two detectives grabbing their jackets from their chairs and dashing for the door, the comic exaggeration of the station's chief chewing out a uniformed officer.

When two detectives enter his room, they bring with them a tumble of noise—the ringing telephones, radio static, the metallic slam of desk drawers. Then the door closes and it is silent again.

"I know the girl," Jonathan says, before the detectives have a chance to sit down. "Is she okay?"

One of the detectives drops a manila folder onto the table. He's heavyset. He wears a tan suit. There are threads dangling from Detective Coover's green-and-blue-striped tie. His partner, Hughes, is younger and wears a navy suit that's a little too sharp for the station. He leans against the window and crosses his arms as if he has somewhere better to be.

"You teach either of them?" Coover says.

"No. They never signed up for my class."

"You see either girl last night?"

"I was in the bar last night. I made a scene. Ask any of the regulars. Then I went to bed. The bartender will tell you." Jonathan looks at the clock.

"You got into a fight last night?" Hughes says. Jonathan suspects that he's recently been promoted. His inflection rises at the tail of his sentences, leaning greedily toward the next conclusion.

Jonathan shakes his head. "I sang a show tune. Too loud."

Hughes glances at his partner but doesn't catch his eye. "A show tune. Jesus."

"Let's go back to the pier." Coover opens a notepad.

"I was taking a walk. I found the girl, Valerie." Jonathan massages his temple. "She was cold. I don't know how long she'd been there."

"Do you have any idea how she got the cut on the back of her head?" Coover asks.

"No."

"Did you see a weapon?"

"I wasn't looking for one."

"But did you see one?"

"No."

"She'll be fine. But she's got one hell of a cut. Someone or something banged her up." Coover scratches behind his ear. "Any sign of the other girl?"

"No."

"Did you see anyone else down there?"

"No."

"No one on the pier? No kids from the Houses?"

"No one." Jonathan rubs his head. "Yes, maybe someone. I'm not sure from the Houses or not. But he was black, if that's what you're asking."

"That's what he's asking," Hughes says.

"How old?" Coover says.

"I don't know. Eighteen. Twenty-one. I'm not an expert."

"What was he doing?"

"Nothing. Walking. I didn't get a good look."

"Walking. Just walking?"

"Yeah. Walking."

"Can we show you some photos?"

Hughes pokes his head out of the room and signals for an officer, who brings him a binder. The detectives place the book on the table in front of Jonathan. They flip through the laminate pages of mug shots—black kids in their late teens with sullen, wary expressions.

Hughes's breathing is heavy, each breath tense and expectant. He makes a small clicking noise each time Jonathan turns the page without making an ID. The photographs with their numbers and fine print make Jonathan queasy. Hughes's musky cologne just about finishes him off. He looks toward the window, trying to take comfort in the air and light outside.

"Concentrate," Hughes says, tapping the book. Jonathan notices that his nails are manicured.

But Jonathan can only think of Valerie—her chilled, drained body, the band of blood at the base of her skull. He remembers how she hung limp in his arms, the piano beat of her heart, the rasp of her breath. He feels no connection to the other girl, only to the one he found.

Jonathan tries to focus on the book, but he's got nothing for the detectives. If they show him the same mug shots ten minutes from now, he wouldn't be able to say for sure that he'd seen the faces before. Hughes shuts the book and leaves the room.

He's back in a few minutes. "Your bartender friend wasn't too happy we woke her up, but she confirmed your story," Hughes says. "Lucky for you."

After Jonathan signs a statement, he is allowed to leave.

When he gets back to Red Hook, the Dockyard is almost empty. The bartender is the English guy with a manicured Ahab beard and horn-rimmed glasses who spends his shift doing crossword puzzles in all three major papers.

An old-timer sits in the middle of the bar, his hands cupped around his glass. He's short with a concave chest and sparse gray hair that's combed and pomaded into neat rows like crop furrows. Between these rows his pale scalp is visible. His face has broken out in the purplish bloom of determined drinking. He's one of the guys who tells everyone that the Dockyard's bar counter is

made from a single piece of wood salvaged from a tree that fell in
the Visitation of the Blessed Virgin Mary churchyard. He says it's
sacrilegious to use something from a holy place in a bar. *The fuck
you kids think you're doing drinking on sacred property?* This doesn't
keep him from hitting the Dockyard for happy hour. He looks
up from his drink and taps the bar with his fingers, signaling for
Jonathan's attention.

"The other girl turns up hurt or worse, everyone knows where
to find you," he says.

Jonathan drops his gaze to his drink.

There are a few other patrons in the bar—artisans with plaster-
caked fingers who smell of paint thinner and a couple of local
musicians. In the middle of the bar is Dirty Dan, a perennially
out-of-work drywaller who smells of the skunk weed he sells.

Dirty is talking loud. He's yammering with the old-timer, making crude jokes about why lesbians can't be vegetarians. When the
old-timer turns away, Dirty homes in on Jonathan.

"Maestro," he calls, signaling to the bartender. Before Jonathan
can object, a shot of Jameson and a Coke back slide down the bar in
Jonathan's direction. When you drink with Dirty Dan, you drink
what he's drinking.

Dirty's wearing a baseball cap from a long defunct skate-wear
company and a baggy T-shirt with a drunken panda on it. His
cargo pants are ripped and flecked with plaster from whichever
job has recently let him go. Every time Jonathan sees Dirty Dan
he wonders what becomes of people like him in middle age. What
happens when he can no longer make rent by slinging eighths of
weed? How long can he exist on menthol cigarettes, Jameson, and
one meal a day?

"My liquor too good for you? Or are you too good for my
liquor?" Dirty says.

"Neither." Jonathan drains the shot glass and chases it with
Coke.

"So, Maestro, you still tuning up the schoolgirls?" Dirty gives an old man cackle that demands attention.

"Keep your mind off my students."

"I wouldn't screw them with somebody else's dick."

This gets a laugh from the old-timer.

"I wasn't into schoolgirls, even in my day," Dirty says. "Do you slap them with a ruler when they're bad, Maestro?"

The thought of all the afternoons he's spoiled with this creep turns Jonathan's stomach, and the shot of whiskey rises back into his throat. He moves to a stool near the window, out of Dirty Dan's range.

Jonathan nurses his drinks. The bearded bartender cashes out and Lil comes on.

"Maestro," she says, "aren't you going to thank me?"

"For what?"

"That's right, you're this week's hero." No matter what happens around the Dockyard, Lil assumes she runs the show.

"None of yous is heroes," the old-timer says on his way out.

"Maybe one day you'll remember who saved your ass," Lil says, refilling Jonathan's glass.

"What's got you thinking about my ass?"

"It's a slow night."

Lil hovers at Jonathan's end of the bar, outdrinking him. They flip through her vinyl, picking upbeat songs to combat the Sunday evening disappointment.

Around seven Fireman Paulie comes into the Dockyard. Jonathan clocks him and slides down the bar.

Paulie's an ex-Marine and fireman with one of the local engines—a loudmouth who enjoys sounding off on slackers, drugs, and law and order. That doesn't faze Jonathan. What gets him is that Paulie's got a special hard-on for him ever since he barged into the storeroom one night to find Jonathan standing over Lil, who was rolling naked on the floor.

He knew there was no point in explaining that he was just helping Lil out. She and all her night crew had been working their way
through a freezer bag of mushrooms one of the local dealers had
dropped off as a Christmas present. The dealer wished Lil's gang a
Happy New Year, accepted a few drinks, then left them to their hal-
lucinations. Some of the barflies had been tripping on and off for a
week when Lil had her breakdown. Halfway through her shift, her
eyes popped wide and her jaw froze. Her arms began to shake, and
she dropped the bottles of booze she'd brought up from the basement.

Jonathan got his arms around Lil and dragged her to the storeroom. She began ripping off her clothes, tossing them away as if
they were on fire. She lay on the floor, rolling back and forth.
Jonathan was trying to pull her to her feet when the door opened
and Paulie stepped in.

"Fucking junkies," Paulie said. He stood there with his arms
crossed. "You assholes going to get me a drink or am I gonna serve
myself?"

Lil got through the night and Paulie drank for free until he got
drunk enough to tell her she was a slut for giving it away to degen-
erates like Jonathan.

"Fireman," Lil says, pulling him a pint of PBR. "Your daughter
doing okay?"

"Shit," Jonathan says loud enough to get Lil's attention. Both
she and Paulie turn his way. It would be Jonathan's bum luck to
have rescued Fireman Paulie's kid and not even realize it.

"The cops tell me you pulled my girl out of the drink," Paulie
says. He walks over to Jonathan, wedging himself between him
and the bar. "I thought they were pulling my leg."

"Anyone could have looked under the pier."

"No one told me you teach at St. Bernardette's. They run a
background check?"

"Probably," Jonathan says.

"I'm messing with you." Paulie punches Jonathan in the arm,

making him flinch. "You can't take a joke? I thought you were tougher than that. Or are you the type who only talks a big game after you've had a few?"

"I don't talk a big game."

"You do. I've heard it. You're always running your mouth. Right, Lil? He doesn't shut up even when no one's listening." Paulie puts a hand on Jonathan's shoulder and gives him a shake. Lil finds something at the far end of the bar to occupy her. "A music teacher?" Paulie says. "Don't expect Val to take your class."

"Not everyone is into music," Jonathan says.

"You want to tell me what you were doing down by the pier this morning?"

"No. Just be thankful I was."

"I asked you a question."

"I couldn't sleep."

"It's an epidemic around here. You crawl around at all hours like our neighborhood's your living room."

"I live upstairs from the bar. It keeps me up."

"Must be convenient."

"It's inconvenient if you want a good night's sleep."

"Funny," Paulie says, punching Jonathan's arm again. "I guess you don't sleep too much then. I grew up here. All kind of whack jobs hang around the pier, even when the sun's up. Especially when the sun's up. You know what I've seen?"

"I don't," Jonathan says.

"I've seen a couple of your friends from this bar tripping their balls off, lying on the rocks with their toes in the water, like they were at the beach. You know what they had with them? A mounted bass. Who the fuck takes a stuffed fish to the water? You know what I think? I think seeing you drunks hanging out at all hours outside put ideas into the girls' heads. I bet they thought they'd get in on the fun. Some fun. My kid winds up in the hospital. And the other girl, dead or worse."

"What's worse than dead?" Jonathan asks and immediately regrets it.

At the other end of the bar someone is cursing the Mets. Jonathan signals to Lil, but she ignores him.

Paulie slides Jonathan's empty away, signaling that he's been cut off. Lil doesn't offer a refill.

Sunday has drained Red Hook. Not even the warm evening inspires people to come out. Outside the bar Jonathan lights a cigarette and tries to catch Lil's eye through the window.

Lil doesn't look out. He knows she is icing him on purpose—ignoring his heroism because he refused to write her a place in it. Still Jonathan lingers, hoping someone will prevent him from going to his apartment alone. He wants someone to distract him from his day—from the otherworldly cold of Valerie Marino's body as he held her in his arms, from the coarse detectives and their questions. Most of all, he wants someone to distract him from his memory of Eden.

No one appears. He extinguishes his smoke. In his apartment, he opens the windows wide, for once welcoming in the neighborhood noise that will be his only company.

CHAPTER SIX

Cree dreams of the raft—of the girls bobbing from wave to wave, of them caught in the spotlight moon. Their voices carry, distorted by the rush of the water, until the only sound is their rippling laughter that hits the shore in waves. They are calling to him, their voices drawing him in. He jumps.

Cree's bedroom is hot. The dying fan on his bedside table does nothing to relieve the heat. He opens his eyes to the water map on the ceiling, the brown and yellow bubbles tracing the pathways of his upstairs neighbor's leaky plumbing. The dream tingles his nerves—he feels the free fall, then the plunge, followed by the whiplash force of the current as it tackled him.

Cree knew the girls were foolish to take on the river in their flimsy piece of rubber, but he admired the bold way they rounded the piers, treating the raft as if it were as sturdy as a tugboat. He followed them after they bobbed out of sight. He scrambled over the rocks, trying to keep pace with the current and arrived within sight of Valentino Pier just in time to see them burst back into view, the raft ready to sail across a spill of moonlight.

He was standing at the spot where the grass gave way to the jagged rocks and gritty beach. The night was full and humid. The air, too dense to be troubled with a breeze, was burdened with heavy summer stillness. Then the raft hit the moon's reflection and the girls were lit up in front of the heartbeat monitor skyline. Their voices joined the slap of waves on the rocks and the clang of a piece of metal tangling with the pylons below. Cree dashed to the pier to get a better view.

Out on the pier he felt a chill ripple across his skin as if an errant wave had broken at his back. He turned. And when he did, the shadow, the ghost, whatever it was, disappeared and the humidity resettled. Cree took a step and stumbled, expecting to find some form of resistance and finding none. He groped in all directions, grabbing nothing. Then he called his father's name, heard it bounce back off the brick warehouses and tumble into the bay. But his father's ghost, if he had been there, was gone. When he next glanced back at the water, the girls were out of sight. At first he thought he'd lost them. But soon they reappeared, sliding into the moon's reflection.

When Cree walks along the piers at night, he hopes to stumble on some new dimension, something to alleviate the frustration, the sense of being trapped by the only place he'd ever lived. But watching those girls, he understood that it had been a mistake to look for this at the edge of the water. Out on that raft he knew he could feel free of Red Hook yet stay close to it. It seemed that the girls had the entire city, the whole waterfront, even the distant ports of New Jersey at their disposal. They had made the city theirs. Cree couldn't let them keep the night's adventure to themselves.

He's a natural at jumping the pier, accustomed to the currents and the ways of avoiding them. Marcus had taught Cree to swim young, before he let his son come out on the fishing boat. But that night when Cree hit the water, he felt an unfamiliar resistance, a forceful tidal pull. The water at the surface tugged one way and the water around his feet tugged another. His strokes were jagged and choppy as he hammered through the waves, trying to reach the raft.

He was swamped by small waves. He lost sight of his destination. He tried to bob out of the water high enough to see the girls on their raft—but it had sailed out of the moonlight. As the water grew rougher, getting to the raft became a matter of urgency. His strokes turned desperate. He could not reach the girls. Exhausted, he let the current carry him back to shore, wash him on the slimy rocks. Back on land, he'd combed the water with his eyes, searching for Val and June. But they were gone. They had taken their adventure elsewhere, leaving him landlocked.

Cree gets out of bed and opens his curtains. He tries to force the window wider. It's stuck, making him get on his knees and stick his head out to inhale the fresh air. He's slept late. The courtyards are already packed. Barefoot kids are running through the fountain near Lorraine Street—the slap of their feet in the puddled water echoing off the surrounding buildings.

Beneath the window is the bench where Cree's father, Marcus, was shot six years back. At one end is a tattered memorial of sun-bleached photographs and dead flowers. During the drug years, people from the Houses got accustomed to random violence in the courtyards. But Marcus, a corrections officer, had died several years after Red Hook started settling down, setting off a community-wide mourning by people who were worried the neighborhood was backsliding. Cree's lost track of all the folks who still add to his father's memorial.

Cree expects to see his mother out on the bench, eyes closed, mouth shut, communicating with his dad. *We talk without say-*

ing, Gloria told Cree of the hour-long sessions she spends on that bench every day. But this morning, she's absent, which is a relief. Recently, she's been spending too much time down there, ignoring the tangible world in favor of the ghostly.

Ever since Cree finished high school in June, time seems to be moving at a halfhearted pace. Most days he drifts from the benches to the park to the pool. He circles between the pizza joint and the bulletproof Chinese. He plays pickup basketball with a dishtowel tied around his head, waiting for evening, waiting for something to happen.

Cree plans on applying to a community college in Brooklyn with a maritime technology program. The glossy brochure sits next to his bed. But he's delaying, hoping something will come along and take him out of the borough.

When he saw those girls on the water, he understood they'd had the guts to make something out of another do-nothing Red Hook night, transform their neighborhood with a simple raft and look at it from the outside. He wished he'd thought of that.

Cree pulls on a pair of boxer shorts and heads into the living room. He stops when he sees his mother sitting at the small kitchen table across from an elderly woman who lives in the opposite tower. Gloria's eyes are closed. She holds the woman's hands in hers.

The women on his mother's side have always made extra cash communicating with the dead. There's a sign outside his apartment, PSYCHIC CONNECTIONS $10. Someone is always knocking.

Gloria's voice is calm, matter-of-fact. There are no candles or Tarot cards or speaking in tongues. No incense or crystals. There is only the ordinariness of the kitchen with its wire fruit basket, plastic floral tablecloth, and paper napkins flopping over their spindled holder.

As Cree watches, Gloria makes a small, satisfied noise, like a car sliding into gear. Then she opens her eyes and begins to speak.

Cree goes back to his bedroom and lies on top of the covers and struggles to summon the sense of freedom and energy captured by those girls on the water. Instead, he feels the Houses pressing in from all sides.

Marcus's pension and Gloria's nursing salary are enough to allow Cree and his mother to move out of the projects to a better neighborhood and a nicer apartment. But Gloria won't leave the spot where Marcus was shot. She doesn't want to abandon his ghost. *Ghosts don't know to pack up, move out,* she says.

Gloria has given away the last of her husband's possessions. *The spirit is more powerful than this junk. And it takes up less space.*

Cree visited thrift stores, trying to salvage some of his father's belongings—his fishing paraphernalia, his shellacked driftwood clocks and seashell ashtrays, his Tiki god tumblers. He found a couple of dress shirts with Marcus's initials stamped inside the collars in blue ink. He found an old watch with a busted crystal and a scallop shell ashtray, which he can't actually prove belonged to his father. He retrieved his dad's tackle box. He keeps it all in his closet. The best thing that Cree discovered was the old fishing boat that turned up in a weedy lot at the edge of the projects, dragged there by some of Marcus's fishing buddies, then forgotten.

Marcus had promised Cree that when he finished high school, they'd take the small fishing boat down to Florida. They'd drop anchor and sleep in the cabin. They'd fish and cook their dinner over a small camp stove. But when graduation rolled around two months ago Cree and Gloria celebrated alone in a large Italian restaurant near Brooklyn's Borough Hall.

It's Sunday, which means in an hour his cousin Monique will be singing in the Red Hook Gospel Tabernacle choir. A couple of months ago Cree started going to the small storefront church hoping that something there would bring him closer to Marcus. He watched as members of the congregation were swept up, lifted from their seats. He watched them sway, raise their hands, throw back their heads. He hoped they would take him along. But as the faithful lost themselves, Cree only felt more earthbound.

Cree decides to go find Valerie instead. He'll ask her what she felt out on the water. Then he'll take her to the fishing boat and tell her about how he wants to take his mother down to Florida, relocate to a place of sea and sun. He hopes that saying these words out loud will give his plan weight and shape.

Cree lies in bed until he hears Gloria's client leave. He waits until his mother heads off to work. Not long after she goes, someone pounds on the door. Cree pulls on a T-shirt and, carrying his shorts, shuffles through the kitchen to the hall, not all that eager to see who's knocking. He only gets the door open a crack, when plainclothes officers jerk him into the hall. One turns him around, presses his chest against the wall, and pats him down. The officer flips Cree back so they are face-to-face.

The detective is middle aged, with the suggestion of a gut underneath his thin dress shirt. His face is flushed. Blue veins blossom at the edges of his ruddy nose. His partner is young—pink faced and raw, not much older than Cree. He throws nervous glances up and down the poorly lit hall as if he expects to be jumped.

"Cree James?" the younger officer asks.

"Too fucking dark in here," the older officer says. "Take him down."

They frog-march Cree into the stairwell.

Cree hears doors opening as his neighbors get in on the action. He knows what they're thinking. He knows what they're going to be spreading around the Houses later: *Goody two-shoes finally cracked. Got shook down before lunch.*

They hustle Cree down five flights and push him through the busted doorway and out into the courtyard where they back him up against the wall of his building. He covers the fly of his thin boxers with the shorts he's holding.

"Cree James," the older officer says, as if this might have changed on the way down.

"Yes, sir." Marcus taught Cree what he needed to know about

being polite to an officer. Cree checks his badge, another of Marcus's lessons. "Yes, Detective Coover."

"You know a couple of girls? Val Marino and June Giatto."

"Yes, sir," Cree says.

For years it was the older Marino girl, Rita, who made trouble for Cree. Her dad, Paulie, was always cracking down on him for Rita's wildness, blaming the most visible—the most dark-skinned—companion for his twelve-year-old's cigarettes and wine coolers. Never mind that Cree didn't care about that stuff. He couldn't explain to Paulie that he hung with Rita because of some promise he thought she held—a life on the waterside, not the Houses.

Even when they were twelve, Cree knew that Rita was on a fast track that didn't interest him—a path not so different from the project girls who clustered on the outskirts of certain apartments, waiting for admission to the circle of a lawless crew. Cree suspected that Rita let him hang around because of that association with crime and drugs that tainted all the project kids.

It wasn't Rita who Cree mourned when Paulie Marino dragged him out of their three-story brick on Visitation and gave him a tongue lashing that probably carried over to Coffey Park. As Paulie yelled, Cree looked up at Rita dangling out of her second-story bedroom window, her eyes goofy and glazed from two bottles of Bartles & James, and understood she had no plans to defend him. He walked away without selling her out.

That was the same afternoon that Marcus was shot in the courtyard. And that afternoon was the last time that the police had come calling.

"Val Marino and June Giatto," Detective Coover repeats. "You know these girls?"

"Yes. Sort of." Cree blinks, trying to settle his eyes in the harsh sun.

"Which is it? Yes or sort of?" the detective asks.

"Yes."

"You've seen them recently?"

A group of kids are passing by on their way to the basketball courts. They stop a couple of yards behind the officers and dribble. The measured beat of their ball lets Cree know what's going down with him is better than grabbing the court before another crew does.

"I've seen them," Cree says.

"When?"

"Last night."

"When?"

"I said—" Cree takes a breath. "Sometime before midnight. I saw them out on the river on a raft."

A necklace of sweat blooms underneath the officer's collar. A woman pushing a shopping cart slows to a halt. Her gaze lands on Cree. Her tongue clicks, as she dispatches him with the rest of the hoods who've brought her neighborhood down.

"You hang out by the water a lot?" the younger detective wants to know.

"I guess," Cree says. "I fish and so." He turns to the side, as if in profile he might become invisible.

"Fish?" the younger officer says. "You fucking fish?"

"Did you see what happened to those girls on the raft?" Coover asks, grabbing Cree's wrist and pulling his hands away from his crotch.

"No, sir," Cree says.

"Would it surprise you to learn one of them turned up under the pier unconscious while the other's missing?" The cop loosens his grip.

"I had no idea." Cree remembers the water's tug, the way it gripped and released him. He wonders if Val and June had been pulled under too, fighting the tornado of currents as he struggled to reach them. He's embarrassed he couldn't reach them and embarrassed he tried to grab a piece of their night for himself.

"Maybe you know what happened to June, the missing girl?"

"Last I saw," Cree says, "they were out on the water, bobbing and floating, cool as anything."

Detective Coover sticks his hand into his holster strap. "Maybe you swam out there. Maybe you wanted to be part of the fun."

"No, man. No, sir," Cree says. The lie comes easy. The pier had been abandoned. No one had seen him jump into the water, not even Val and June. And no one had seen him return to the rocky beach.

"Let's get this straight," Coover says. "You saw them by the water or earlier?"

Cree glances up into the towers. He can make out shadows and silhouettes watching him through dirty windows. "Both. I saw them on their way down and then I saw them floating."

"So you followed them?"

Cree takes a breath, holds it. "No. I was walking the waterfront is all."

"See anyone else when you were *walking the waterfront?*" the younger detective asks.

"Nope."

"Anyone see you?"

"Probably not."

"You've had trouble with the Marinos before?" Coover says.

"I haven't talked to anyone in that family in six years," Cree says.

"But you've had trouble with them?"

"You'll have to ask them, sir."

"We did," the younger detective says. He clears his throat and looks over his shoulder, making sure he has the crowd's attention. "You like white girls?"

"No," Cree says.

"So you don't like white girls?" The younger officer rubs his hands together.

"That's not what I meant."

"Let me put it another way. You like young girls?"

Cree bites his lips and exhales heavily through his nose.

"I asked you a question," the younger officer says.

"All right," Coover says, taking out a notepad. "The girl, Valerie, said she saw you last night."

"So?" Cree says.

"So you're the last person Valerie talked to before she was knocked unconscious."

"Maybe they had an accident. Maybe the raft just flipped," Cree says.

"Maybe," the younger officer says. "Or maybe she came to shore safely and then she was attacked. Maybe someone carried the other girl off."

Cree looks at his feet.

Detective Coover prods him until he looks up. "One girl is knocked unconscious. The other is missing," he says. "This is foul play until otherwise proven. You get it?"

"But I had nothing to do with it," Cree says.

"Let us be the judge of that." The older officer backs off and nods to his partner. "We're not through with you," he says.

The younger detective shoulder checks Cree, knocking him into the wall. "Don't think of running. And don't even think of hiding out." He pins him back and raises his voice. "Until the other girl turns up, our eyes are on you." He jabs his elbow deeper and holds Cree's gaze, challenging him to look away first.

The cops leave Cree flattened against the wall. The boys with the basketball stare and snicker, then walk off. The woman with the shopping cart mutters. Cree feels the shadows pull back from their windows.

The cops had told him not to hide, but that's exactly what Cree plans to do. Not permanently, just until the shock wears off. He needs to figure out what he has to do to distance himself from this problem. He knows kids from the Houses who've been jailed for offenses less serious than proximity to a crime scene. He knows that once you're on the 76's radar, it's hard to get off—that you become part of every neighborhood shakedown.

As Cree walks through the courtyards, he learns that although the police have declared June missing, the noise on the street is that she's dead. People grumble that whenever someone from the Houses is dropped by drug violence, the neighborhood doesn't pause. But a white girl gets herself drowned or killed, it's news. *It'll be a good thing,* people say, *when the police discover that some white guy killed her. Get them off our back.*

"She's not dead," Cree tells a group of kids sitting by the fountain.

"Hell do you know?" they say. "You swim out there like they said? Get yourself a piece?"

Cree is wise enough not to ask too many questions and turn the spotlight back on himself. He's noticed the appraising looks he's caught just walking through the courtyard. He knows he needs to lie low for the rest of the day.

Cree's an expert in the neighborhood's contours. Ever since he was old enough to be allowed out alone at night, he's been roaming the streets, mapping out Red Hook's best hideouts—a secret lair in an abandoned longshoremen's bar, a sliver of garden wedged between two tenements, a bird's-eye lookout over the water from a towering warehouse. In these corners he indulges his fantasies of life outside of the Hook, transforms his hideaways into the places he would have visited with his father.

He cleared the trash from the empty bar, sanded the splintering wooden mermaid figurehead, and pretended he was visiting Bermuda. He found a busted plastic lounge chair and placed it in the hidden garden. Lying on the chair, squinting so he could see the sliver of the bay beyond the chicken wire fence, he almost believed he was fishing off the coast of Florida. He bought a telescope with a cracked lens from a junk shop and attached it to a tripod fashioned out of a ladder and installed it on the top floor of the abandoned warehouse overlooking the bay, turning the building into a tall ship, from which he could survey the surrounding seas.

Since it's daylight now, Cree knows that only one of his hide-outs will provide adequate cover—the warehouse on Imlay Street at the edge of the water where no one from Red Hook can see in. He hurries through the waterside, skirting the Marinos' house on Visitation. He keeps to the shadows as he darts down smaller, cobbled side streets. He slips through a gap in the cyclone fence that blocks entrance to the warehouse.

The building is cavernous. It takes up the entire block with various wings and sections, all of them empty. The warehouse is seven stories high, each floor with thirty-foot ceilings. Cree's foot-steps echo as he climbs the sturdy steps to his lookout where he's installed his telescope in front of one of the giant, glassless win-dows. In front of the telescope is a battered, leather armchair with a split cushion and a small table, both of which Cree found on the street.

He falls into the chair and stares out over the water at the spot where he saw the girls floating on their raft. The water is calm. He trains his telescope on the bay, then sweeps it west along the waterfront, searching for a flash of pink or a suggestion of flesh. He scans the water up and over toward Governors Island, then north toward the Brooklyn Bridge. He sees nothing out of the ordinary.

Cree takes his eye from the telescope. Something is different about the warehouse. He peers under his chair. Three cigarette butts are crushed into the concrete floor. He picks them up, turn-ing them over in his hands for a clue as to who left them.

All summer, Cree's been under the impression that the shape of Red Hook is changing. Something about the corners, fences, alleys, and streetlamps that he'd memorized in his childhood has grown unfamiliar. The places he used to hide no longer seem comforting or secluded. Even in the darkest nook in the neighborhood, Cree feels exposed. And he can't shake the feeling that he's being followed, marked. A few times he's found evidence of someone else's presence in one of his hideouts, an empty beer can, a couple of junk food wrappers, the telescope pointing in a different direction. And now, these three butts.

He stands up and turns away from the window and staggers back a step, startled by a barrage of color on the opposite wall. He's facing an enormous, newly painted graffiti burner, a massive mural he hadn't noticed on his way in. The piece, framed by palm trees on both sides, is tropically colored—greens and blues, bright oranges and yellows. In the background the jagged Manhattan skyline looms. The letters that make up the body of the piece spell "RunDown" in dense, intricate script.

Cree isn't foolish enough to imagine that no one else ever enters his secret places, but there's other graffiti in his hideouts this summer—hints and signals that make him feel marked or watched. He noticed it first in the abandoned bar, the initials "RD" in jagged, lightning-bolt-style script above the bathroom sink where the mirror should have been. A few days later, one of the walls in the garden was hit with an "RD" in the same style. He found another "RD" next to the window where his telescope stood.

Cree checked the neighborhood for other "RD" tags. He asked his friends and his cousin Monique, who tended to know everyone's business, if they'd heard of a tagger using "RD." No one had.

After a few weeks, the tags grew into bolder and bigger works. In the garden, "RD" was elongated into "RunDown," two words elided in a large piece in steel-gray and yellow bubble letters. The writing was complex but the words were clear.

After RunDown took over the large section of the narrow garden's south-facing wall, he hit the exposed brick of the bar's back room with a piece that featured his name in an oriental style along with the mermaid figurehead. Now he's bombed in the warehouse, enforcing this tropical landscape on Cree's hideout.

Staring at the piece confirms Cree's suspicion that nowhere will ever belong to him. At home he will be harassed by the police until the missing girl is found. And now his secret places are being invaded.

Cree returns to the window and looks back at the bay. If he had reached those girls, he might have been able to save them from whatever was about to happen. Instead of feeling life closing in on him, something might have opened up.

Cree doesn't like to encourage his mother to use her gifts but he wants to know what happened to June, whether she's dead or simply missing, whether he'll have to keep looking over his shoulder for the police or whether this will blow over by nightfall.

Cree leaves the warehouse and takes the subway into the heart of Brooklyn's Caribbean neighborhood where his grandmother lives. He gets out near the museum and threads his way through a line of children wearing name cards around their necks. He passes the Botanic Garden. Its late-summer lawns are dried and brown. He hits Eastern Parkway and spies a couple of Hasidic kids sneaking cigarettes and whistling at girls. They scowl as he passes. He turns down a wide avenue dotted with real estate agents and soul food joints. He keeps walking until he hits a Jamaican bakery.

Lucy Wallace is sitting at a low pastry table folding bright orange crusts over mincemeat. Her fingertips are stained with the dye that comes off the pastry. Her wrists are ringed with flour. Lucy's roots are from the South not Jamaica, but the neighborhood says she folds the best beef patties.

The shop is small. A glass display case of various patties and pastries takes up the entire counter. Two Crock-Pots, one with goat curry and one with lamb, sit on a table behind the register. The owner, an elderly Jamaican man with vertical wrinkles that look like pleats and watery brown eyes is on his cell phone, talking in such a thick accent Cree can barely make out a word.

"Acretius." Cree's grandmother looks up from her workstation. He bends down and gives her a kiss. She smells of biscuit dough and curry spice.

Grandma Lucy is a small woman, much frailer than her daughters. Her gray hair is braided and pulled into a generous bun at the top of her head. Her skin is barely lined. She claims the grease from the dough keeps her smooth.

"Get yourself a patty," Lucy tells Cree, dusting off her hands. She disappears into the back room and returns drying her hands on a dishtowel. "I'm on a break," she says to her boss.

Cree follows Lucy into the doorway next to the shop and up a dilapidated set of stairs to her one-room apartment. He sits on the narrow bed. Lucy takes the rust-colored velour lounger.

The apartment is dim but tidy. All the woodwork and moldings are painted blue green and the walls are baked potato brown. A blue tribal cloth hangs over half the window. The mantel is covered with religious candles to the deities of African American folk magic—High John the Conqueror, Chango Macho, Elegua. A small shrine to the deceased in Lucy's family covers the windowsill.

Lucy kicks up the footrest on her chair and folds her hands. "Something told me you were coming," she says. "I'm guessing this isn't just to see your grandma."

"No, ma'am," Cree says.

"Turn the water on first," Lucy says.

Cree goes over to the small cooker on a stand beside the door and turns on the flame underneath the kettle.

Lucy rubs and flexes one of her hands, massaging the spaces between her fingers. Then she takes off her necklace, a long chain with a brass ball at the bottom. She loops the chain around her fingers and soon the ball starts to rotate in close circles like a pendulum. She squints at the ball and clicks her tongue. "Hmm. So it is," she says.

"What's it say?" Cree asks.

"It's telling me my business. And now you can tell me yours."

Cree is used to his grandma's cryptic divinations, her infuriating need to have all her questions answered by her pendulum. Not that she ever shares these questions or answers with anyone else.

They wait for the water to boil. Then Cree fills a mug for Lucy and brings it to her. She reaches into a string pouch attached to her skirt and pulls out a few sachets from which she sprinkles something that looks like burned confetti into the water. A smell like damp wood swirls up from the mug.

Lucy takes a sip. "Now tell me what's so important that you had to take time to visit me. You haven't applied to that college yet, have you?"

Cree's eyes shift around the room. Grandma Lucy has none of the gentle patience of his mother and aunt. "You've been watching the news?"

Lucy takes a short breath, exhales through her nose, and tightens her mouth into a pucker. "You know I haven't."

"But you heard about that girl who disappeared in Red Hook?"

"I heard."

"I saw her last night."

"You came all the way out here to tell me that?"

Cree picks at the bedspread until Lucy shoos him off. "You think she's dead?"

"It's none of my business," Lucy says.

"But maybe you have a hunch?" Cree looks at Lucy's hand, but the pendulum is clenched in her palm out of sight.

"I might, but this whole thing is none of your business neither."

"Is it my business if I could have helped her?"

"No," Lucy says. "Let the white folks worry about the white

folks. There's plenty else you need to be doing besides bothering with someone else's missing girl." Lucy lowers her lips to her mug and blows, spreading the steam upward. "Acretius, is your mother still wasting her days on that bench?"

Grandma Lucy doesn't approve of her daughters, Gloria and Celia, continuing to live in the projects when they could have lives elsewhere. She never tires of telling them that the whole reason she moved to the Houses in the first place was so that she could save up enough to live somewhere better. But her girls have attached themselves to the place in ways she can't or won't understand.

"Sometimes," Cree says.

"She's down there too much. Be thankful that your daddy's ghost has sense enough to leave you alone. There's a blessing in that."

Cree takes his time getting home. By the time he reaches Red Hook, the light is draining from the sky. Coffey Park is full. Cree passes a crew who've taken over the benches near the basketball courts, perching on the backrests like birds on a wire. He catches sight of Monique surrounded by a bunch of older boys in oversized basketball jerseys. She holds Cree's eye as he passes. He hurries off before she can call him out for being on his lonely.

He heads for the boat. A wind is coming off the water, lifting the litter and tangling it with the dried grass in the lot. Cree ducks and squeezes through a gap in the chicken wire fence. When he looks up, he sees someone sitting on the boat, legs dangling over the prow like a sloppy figurehead. Even though it's a warm night, the intruder is wearing a sweatshirt with a hood that hides his face.

Cree pauses at the fence, preparing to turn around.

"You leaving because of me?" the guy on the boat says.

"Nope."

"Good. That's what I was hoping for." The kid smiles and rubs his hands together, as if he'd been sitting on that damn prow just waiting for Cree to turn up.

"I just didn't expect anyone."

"Oh, so you think you have this place to yourself? You the proprietor?"

"Like I said, nobody comes around much," Cree says, crossing to the middle of the lot.

"Maybe I do now." The stranger pulls off his hood. His face is long and narrow, with drooping eyelids and a down-turned mouth. His hair sticks out in tufts and bunches. His skin is ashen black. Cree guesses the kid is a couple of years older than he is, maybe twenty or twenty-two. "Maybe I'm acclimating to the place."

"You new in Red Hook?" Cree says.

"Been here since before you."

"You live in the Houses?" Cree asks.

"I'm done with the Houses. I've got no more business there." The kid spits to one side. He holds a lighter in one hand, scraping his thumb over the circular flint, letting the flame spark briefly.

Cree gives the kid a look, trying to figure out whether he's messing with him. "So where you living?"

"Bones Manor mainly. Means I live nowhere."

In all his years of wandering through Red Hook, Cree has rarely ventured into Bones Manor. The large lot, a former truck loading zone, is hidden behind a patchwork of corrugated iron fence that runs the length of the entire block. It's a no-man's-land for junkies, hookers, and other Red Hook irregulars. The concrete walls on the lot's waterside are famed for their graffiti—the dopest pieces in the neighborhood it's rumored. Sometimes the lot is empty. Sometimes it feels as if a whole damn city is thriving back there, but no matter how crowded the Manor seems, it has always felt to Cree like the loneliest place on earth.

Nature is out to reclaim Bones Manor and turn it into some sort of inner-city wetlands. A large pond of water, which the residents of the Manor call the Lake, rises and falls with the tides from Erie Basin. People in the Manor make their homes in abandoned shipping containers or the shells of old cars pushed up against the sides of the lot, all sorts of jerry-rigged shelters into which they can disappear in a flash. There's a ghostliness to the way the wind whips from the water and gets trapped inside the place, rattling the corrugated walls, agitating the reeds, and rippling the surface of the Lake.

The kid on the boat lights a cigarette. In the lighter's glow, Cree sees the hollows of the boy's cheeks. "What?" the kid says. "You scared of the place? You intimidated?"

"Nothing around here scares me."

"Not even the police? Those boys can put the fear into anyone."

"I got nothing to fear."

"Is that so?" The kid exhales smoke and looks Cree up and down.

Cree makes a fist and rubs it over his lips. "Truth be told, I got shook down for the first time ever today. Some nonsense I got nothing to do with. Couple of girls took a raft out in the bay. One disappeared."

"Somebody made you a scapegoat."

Cree shrugs, as if a small gesture could brush the whole thing off. "It's messed up."

"What's your business with this boat?" the kid asks. "Seems like at the moment you should be keeping away from all thing aquatic. Don't want to attract improper notice."

"The boat's mine, is all," Cree says.

The guy lowers himself to the ground. "Doesn't look like it belongs to you. This is one dissipated ship."

"The boat's mine," Cree says.

"So how come you just let it sit here? What's the use of a boat without water?"

"I'm fixing it up."

"I could help you with that."

"No need."

"Well, if you change your mind, find me at the Manor. Ask for Ren."

"We'll see," Cree says.

"In the meantime, she could use a little freshening up." Ren scrapes his nails along the hull. "Sorry ass paint flaking like snow." He pulls something out of his pocket. Cree hears the metallic rattle of a spray paint can being shaken.

Cree dashes to the boat and grabs Ren's arm. He tries to jerk the can out of Ren's hand. But Ren's got him by the wrist, turning Cree's arm, burning the skin.

"You should be thanking me for taking the time to ornament her."

"Fuck no," Cree says.

"I'll just come back another time. Make my mark."

"No, you won't," Cree says. "This boat belonged to my pops and he's dead. Everyone knows that a captain comes back to haunt his ship. So I'm hoping you won't dare tagging here."

Ren lets go and steps back. "Your daddy's boat?" he says.

"It's mine now," Cree says. "I explained that."

"Sure," Ren says. "Sure. It's cool."

Cree hops on the boat and looks down at Ren. "You been following me of late?"

"Why would I do something like that?" Ren says. Then he climbs through the fence and exits the lot. Cree glances over to the alley, trying to follow Ren's path down the street. But the kid vanishes, like he'd never been there at all.

CHAPTER SEVEN

This is how you get ready for the vigil. These are the socks you choose—good luck green, the ones you wore when you were chosen for the lead in the school play in eighth grade. Then you remember the last time you wore them you had a fight with June. You wear red socks. This is the necklace you choose, the St. Christopher medallion instead of the gold cross from your confirmation because St. Christopher is the patron saint of travelers and will bring June home.

The toilet paper tears jaggedly, so you tear it again until you are left with a straight line. You make sure the hand towels are hung symmetrically on the rack—something you've never done before. You've never even thought about the hand towels in the bathroom.

The bathmat is flush to the tub. You place an even number of guest soaps in the soap dish. You turn them right side up.

You watch yourself getting ready, calculating the orchestra of small events that will set in motion the larger event. Everything is loaded with significance—the first song on the radio in the morning, June's celebrity crush on the cover of a weekly magazine, the music blaring from a passing car. You are conscious of each of your actions, how you place books on your desk, the way you close the curtains, the arrangement of pillows on your bed, how your shoes line up in your closet. Nothing is left to chance. Details are magic.

Suddenly you do everything in order—size order, numerical order, alphabetical order. You dress from left to right, left shoe first, watch before rings, left arm in left sleeve. If you make a mistake you do it again. All your actions have a consequence, an equal and opposite reaction. If you exercise control, if you organize the world, things will fall into place, June will return.

Choose magic symbols that you write in the steam in mirrors, on the tile in the shower, on the varnish on the kitchen table. Choose sacred objects—ones that meant something to both you and June—that you carry everywhere, that you place next to your bed at night, even under the pillow. Pick secret words you chant under your breath, that you incant until you fall asleep.

Val checks her appearance in the mirror, then leans forward and kisses the glass, leaving a ChapStick smudge. This is June's good luck gesture, her ritual before leaving any room on the way to an important event.

The city has shaken off the heat wave by the time the vigil for June takes place at the Visitation of the Blessed Virgin Mary a week after Val's rescue. It's a Sunday and the congregation has decided to devote their traditional service to June. Across the street from the park, the people from the Houses are holding their summer reunion—a daylong festival of music and barbecue.

Coffey Park is buzzing—every square of grass claimed by a different family. Old-school hip-hop is being pumped from two stacks of speakers. Girls in short denim shorts with rhinestone accents and bright tank tops travel as a team, dancing in time to the music as they check out the offerings on the various grills. Before Val can absorb any of the excitement, her mother ushers her into the church. The heavy door slams behind her and the party is shut out.

The interior of the church is dim. Its walls are the color of putty and the gaudy stained-glass windows forbid daylight. It smells of old clothes and bedding from the basement rummage sales.

The church is too large for the parish. In winter it's drafty and in summer, dank and airless. Today, even at a fraction of its capacity, the building feels stuffy. There are too many pews for the small congregation, and the empty spaces are filled with shadows that stretch from the dusty niches and dark rafters. Near the entrance, Val's mother pauses to light a devotional candle in a red glass holder.

Paulie Marino walks down the aisle first, clearing a path for his wife and daughter. He checks both sides of the aisle, silencing gossip and whispers with his stare. Jo drapes an arm around Val's shoulder. A few of Jo's friends stand up and take Val from her mother, pressing her into their bosoms, filling her nose with their sweet, floral perfumes. June's grandmother sits by herself in the front row, a small woman in a simple dark dress with her dyed black hair wound into a wispy bun.

Jo rubs a hand on Val's shoulders, soothing her. She wipes Val's dry cheeks. Val has yet to cry over June. If she cries, it will mean June isn't coming home. The tears hide behind her eyes, sharp, stinging nettles she blinks away.

Girls from Val's class at St. Bernardette's are sobbing, their faces puffy and blotched. The upperclassmen dab their eyes with handkerchiefs, expertly wiping away streaks of mascara. These girls have rolled the waistbands of their skirts to lift their hemlines. In the back row are the boys who struggle to keep their eyes downcast, longing to stare at the girls in the front rows, hoping that they can get them alone later. Val suspects her schoolmates' grief is all show—especially that of the older girls.

Val's presence in the church is a reminder to everyone of June's absence. She has no friend to beckon her over, no one to hold her hand, fill the space at her side. She knows that when the congregation looks at her, they are thinking of June, that she will always remind them of her missing friend. If June does not return, her absence will deform Val, make it impossible for others to see what is there, not what is gone.

An easel with a large photo of June mounted on poster board stands next to the pulpit. It's a bad picture—the same one that has been circulating since she disappeared. For her school photo June popped several buttons on her blouse so her cleavage is suggested by deep shadow. She wears too much makeup, and her face shines unnaturally.

Expecting a bigger crowd, the priest has brought a microphone to the altar. His voice booms through the church urging the group to pray. His "amen" is drowned in feedback. Val resists the urge to cover her ears. The congregation struggles through a couple of hymns that are supposed to be uplifting but sound like dirges.

Val keeps her eyes on the ceiling. If she ignores the proceedings in the pulpit, if she tunes out the words of the priest, the sniffles of the congregation, if she can will her mind to stay blank until the hymns are over, June will come home. If she can predict the precise moment, by counting to ten, when the priest will close his hymnal, June will walk into the church and all this will be over. While the congregation is singing, Val organizes all the hymnals in her row, making sure they are right side up and evenly spaced. If the hymnals are evenly spaced, June will come home.

A group of Val's classmates approach the microphone. They hold hands and warble the ballad from *Titanic*. The singers trill nervously and breathe heavily, their voices tangling with the scratchy

PA system. One of them puts a hand over her heart, steps forward, and tries a vibrato solo.

No one bothered to consult Val. No one asked her what June would have liked. By surviving she has forfeited any claim to June's friendship. She grips the pew until her hands cramp.

This is your fault. June's voice rises above the roar of blood in Val's head. Val cries out. She opens her eyes. The girls from the next pew are looking at her.

This is your fault, June says again.

Val clenches her jaw. She squeezes her eyes shut. She will not cry. She cannot cry or June won't come home.

This is your fault.

"No," Val blurts. The word is thrown back at her from the arched ceiling. The girls up front stop singing.

Jo widens her eyes at Val. She puts a finger over her lips. The congregation shifts in their seats, resettling after Val's outburst. Whispers whip from row to row. Val swipes the back of her neck, brushing away the stares that are boring into her nape.

This is your fault, June says.

Val is on her feet. Her leather-soled loafers hammer the aisles as she runs for the exit and bursts into the daylight. If she keeps moving, she won't be able to hear June. If she keeps moving, she won't have time to cry.

The crowd in the park has thickened. The air is rich with the sweet smell of caramelizing meat. The music from the sound system is louder, drowning out June's reprimand.

Val dashes toward the park, hoping to escape from anyone who might pursue her, hoping to hide in the crowd where June's absence will be less obvious.

There's a man standing directly in front of her calling her name. It takes her a moment to recognize Mr. Sprouse, the music teacher who found her under the pier. She slows to a halt a few feet in front of him. Their eyes meet.

"Valerie," Mr. Sprouse says.

He will take her back inside. He will remind everyone that she is safe while June is gone.

Val turns and rushes into the crowd. A group of girls are doing a dance routine in front of a small stage where a DJ is spinning. Old men whistle and clap from a nearby bench. Boys Val's age move in a pack, assessing groups of girls in skimpy summer clothes. The girls tease them in a rich singsong chorus.

It's strange to Val to see so many kids her age in the park at the end of her street yet know so few of them. Her parents have their church, their VFW clubhouse, their own block parties. They act as if the Houses are in a different neighborhood with a different set of problems. Even when she and June attended the local elementary, she barely saw her classmates from the projects outside of school. It was known from as early as kindergarten that the white girls were just marking time until fourth grade when they'd head to Catholic schools on the other side of the expressway. Only headstrong Rita had crossed the divide between front and back, bringing Cree to the Marinos' house. His cousin Monique tagged along as an afterthought.

Among these kids Val feels anonymous, which is what she wants. In the projects, no one will look for her. She passes the small playground, skirts the basketball courts, avoids the kids who are skipping through a fountain, sending prisms of water toward the sky. Then she's out of the park and into the first courtyard in the Red Hook Houses.

"Valerie!" Her name ricochets off the projects' walls. She refuses to look back.

The courtyards are filled with people on their way to the park carrying coolers and bags of buns.

She emerges onto a small side street. The doors of the Red Hook Gospel Tabernacle are wide open. Val has never been inside before. The interior is bright. The linoleum floor shines. The walls are hung with airbrushed paintings of Jesus and Mary in ornate plastic frames. The church smells of sweat and fresh air.

Val stays next to the open door. The congregation is seated. The women wear sateen dresses in pastel shades. Some wear hats with netting and fake flowers. The elderly men stick to drab jackets and blazers, while the younger ones wear suits in bright colors—green or deep purple, even bright orange. Several have matched their ties and vest to their suits.

A large man in a white robe is bellowing into a microphone. His bible is balanced on a wobbly stand. Perspiration wreathes his forehead. Next to him, Monique sits on a folding chair. Her arms are crossed over her chest, and her head is turned away. She casts a lazy glance over the congregation, then fixes her eyes on Val. The folding chairs scrape as the congregation rises. Monique takes the microphone. Her white dress is wet at the bodice and under the arms.

She sings with her eyes closed. Her voice is confident, full of knowledge and secrets. She sings over the congregation and they lift their voices to meet hers. As they do, she sings louder, dominating the small room with her song, remaining just beyond the congregation's reach. It seems to Val that Monique is taunting them, making them eager to follow her and cling to her words. The congregation sways. They strain toward Monique, rising and falling— clapping and stomping.

If Monique sings for June, June will come back.

Her song ends. Her eyes remain closed as her breathing slows. The congregation exhales and sits. Monique opens her eyes and steps away from the microphone. Ignoring the women who shake their heads in awe and pleasure and try to squeeze her arm, she walks up an aisle between the chairs and catches sight of Val.

"Got tired of your own church?" she whispers as she passes.

Val looks at the congregation. Four young men in suits the color of Orange Crush are getting ready to sing.

"Came all this way and nothing to say?" Monique says. She pushes past Val onto the street.

Monique looks older than fifteen. She has golden-flecked hair and amber eyes that startle from her dark skin like bright pennies. She's Val's height but with a softer shape—round, polished cheekbones and generous adult curves.

Val follows Monique out of the tabernacle.

"They had a vigil for June," Val says.

"Yeah?"

Monique's dress makes her look as if she's playing some sort of perverse dress-up—squeezing a childish dress over a woman's body.

"June would have liked it if you'd sung something."

"No one asked."

"Remember when you'd sing in my basement when we were little?"

"Not really." Monique fidgets with the lace bodice of her dress.

"One time we sold tickets to people passing by?"

"That sounds whack."

Monique hadn't thought so at the time. She had let Val and June dress her up in Rita's clothes—a black crushed velvet dress and patent leather pumps. At ten, Monique already came close to filling out Rita's party clothes.

The girls turned the Marinos' vestibule into a stage and hung a red blanket over the front door. Val and June hit the pavement, drumming up customers for the "Best Voice in Brooklyn." Four people, one of them June's grandmother, paid fifty cents each to hear Monique. When the audience was assembled, Val whipped back the curtain and Monique sang "Somewhere Over the Rainbow." As she sang, more people gathered. When the song was over, Val demanded that the new arrivals pay up. She handed Monique the kitty.

It was a few weeks later that Paulie dragged Cree onto the street and shamed him in front of the block for being a bad influence on Rita. After that neither he nor Monique returned to the Marinos.

"Maybe you could sing something for June sometime?" Val says.

"Talking to the dead is Cree's mom's business, not mine."

"Who says she's dead?"

Monique tugs at the neck of her dress, letting some air onto her skin. "I'm done with singing today," she says, walking off. "I'm gonna get my groove on elsewhere."

Val half listens to the men's quartet, trying to make up her mind where to go. Her head is beginning to hurt, an ache that rises from the spot at the back of her skull where a large Band-Aid hides a row of stitches.

She's about to head off when she feels someone take her arm. She turns and sees Cree James. He's wearing a brown sateen suit with sleeves that ride down to his palms. He looks good, sharp. His shaved head shines with some tropically scented oil. Cree's not much taller than Val, with a round face and a wide smile that comes easily.

"Sorry about Monique," he says. "Some days she's too big for herself."

"Whatever," Val says. It was always June who was more hurt by Monique's indifference.

Cree steps away and takes off his jacket, revealing a cream-colored silk shirt stuck with sweat to his skinny frame. Val's aware of the looks she's getting from people coming in and out of the church. They take in her uniform and her lanky frame—her pale skin and unremarkable hair. A drab piece of flotsam lost in the sea of Sunday color.

Cree unbuttons his collar and shakes his shirt free of his skin. "It's true you don't remember what happened?"

"Nope," Val says. She turns and shows him the bandage at the base of her skull.

"That's a trip," Cree says. "What's it feel like not remembering?"

"I don't know. Nothing."

"You remember seeing me on the boat?" Cree asks.

"Of course."

"You told the police?"

"Why shouldn't I?"

Cree wipes his smooth head. "I'm just asking. What else did you tell them?"

"Nothing," Val says. On top of everything else, she doesn't need his accusations. But when she starts to walk away, Cree keeps pace. "You're not afraid my dad will see you?"

"That was a lifetime ago," Cree says. "I've got better things to do than be afraid of your dad."

"Why are you following me?"

"To make sure you don't do anything foolish."

Val stops walking. "Maybe I want to do something foolish."

"Well, do you?"

"You coming?"

Val walks quickly in the direction of the water, Cree at her side. It feels good not to be alone. Just having Cree close is enough to distract people from June's absence and from her part in it, Val thinks. All she needs is one friend, one person to stick by her. One person to make her feel less alone and less at fault.

She skirts the Visitation of the Blessed Virgin Mary and the VFW. Noise from Coffey Park wafts through the neighborhood—a sustained echo of the ongoing party. She takes side streets to avoid anyone she might know. The afternoon is emptying out. Red Hook's few shops are shuttered. People are returning home for Sunday afternoon cookouts or heading to the bar to keep the weekend going.

Except for a couple of dog walkers, Valentino Pier is empty. June's shrine is already weathered. The pastel flowers have turned brown. The teddy bears are matted with grime. Val walks to the end of the pier. She grasps the railing and stares at the last spot she saw June. There's a dark spill on the water, a shadow rising from below.

The railing is hot. Behind her Red Hook is unnaturally still. Val flings off her school blazer. She kicks off her penny loafers. She imagines that by now the vigil has let out and the VFW is beginning to fill for the reception. They will be unwrapping foil trays of lasagna and manicotti. The place will be sweltering. The men will drink more than usual. They will talk sports and pensions. They'll go on about the neighborhood's newcomers.

The high school girls will sneak plastic cups of Chianti and cigarettes in the small concrete yard. The boys will congregate on the far end, near the wall. Soon these two groups will meld. Parents will ignore their children who are pairing off and slipping away. And June will be out there somewhere, maybe not far from where Val is standing now.

It's your fault.

"Shut up," Val says.

"I didn't say anything," Cree says.

Val starts unbuttoning her blouse, popping off two of the buttons in her haste. Cree put a hand on her arm to stop her, but she brushes him off. He looks away as if her childish bra embarrasses him. "What are you doing?"

She continues to undress.

Cree holds up his suit jacket, shielding Val even though there's no one around. His silk shirt is untucked. His sweat has brought out the paisley pattern hidden in the fabric.

Val lowers the zipper on her skirt. She knows she looks like a little kid in her cotton underwear. The late-afternoon sun hits her belly and the tops of her thighs. She hoists herself over the railing and stands on the lip of the pier.

The water is the color of slate.

"Don't act crazy," Cree says.

Val doesn't look back. She feels Red Hook fall away behind her as she disappears into the water.

The water smells like Brooklyn. She dives deep and swims away from the pier, combing away the light debris that clouds the bay. She plunges until her lungs feel pummeled and the water turns cold.

Then she feels arms around her waist and she is dragged to the surface.

"Jesus. Were you planning to come up?" Beads of water, like translucent ladybugs, are suspended on Cree's shaved scalp.

Val slips from his grasp and continues swimming, pulling toward Jersey. But Cree catches up and restrains her. "Hey, hey, you know the rules. Watch out for the Governors Island current. Don't get tangled in the pylons. Then you can swim in the bay."

If Cree kisses her, June will be found.

They tread water side by side. The Staten Island ferry crawls into view, inching across the bay. A tugboat chugs out of Erie Basin and begins to cross toward the East River—a small boat, green paint, the letter B on its stack. Its wake knocks Val and Cree together. Her head rolls back onto his shoulder. Cree wraps his arms around her for support. His fingers slip across her skin like a school of fish. She feels him loosen his grip and before he does, she pulls him closer. Then she turns and kisses him.

They plunge beneath the surface, their arms and hands sliding over each other, moving freely, frictionless. Val wraps her legs around his waist, feeling his stomach muscles tighten as he works hard not to sink.

June used to tease Val by telling her that if she didn't practice, when the time came she would embarrass herself. But kissing Cree comes easily. It's as natural as holding your breath underwater.

Through the green-brown water she cannot see how her body is and how she wishes it were. Cree doesn't seem to care either way. Val swims a few strokes, but he's right back behind her, holding on.

She bobs and submerges and rises again. She turns back toward Red Hook and shakes the water from her eyes. The world takes shape, revealing the hard contours of the rocks and pylons.

They are no longer alone. There is a man on the pier—the music teacher. He's waving his arms and shouting Val's name. For an instant, Val thinks of swimming farther out, until she is out of sight of the pier. She doesn't want to hear her name.

If she swims to shore, June will come home.

CHAPTER EIGHT

Since the morning Jonathan carried Val into his store, Fadi hasn't let him pay for a cup of coffee. He usually throws something else in for free—a pastry, a couple of newspapers, a sandwich, even Jonathan's brand of cigarettes. He's clipped several stories about Valerie's rescue and June's disappearance and taped them around the counter. He's highlighted Jonathan's name in yellow marker.

These gestures make Jonathan uncomfortable. He doesn't want to be associated with the missing girl.

"You going to the vigil for June Giatto?" Fadi says, sliding Jonathan's dollar back to him with his coffee. "You're the hero. The neighborhood wants you there."

"I don't think anyone will notice if I'm absent," Jonathan says.

"I will." Fadi glances over Jonathan's shoulder to the street. He hands Jonathan a copy of his local newsletter in which he's listed the time and place of the vigil. "If I had help, I'd go. Take these donuts to Mrs. Giatto for me." He pulls a box of Entenmann's from under the counter.

"Sure," Jonathan says. He doesn't have the heart to disappoint Fadi.

Music from Coffey Park is rolling down Visitation Street, signaling the kickoff of Old Timers Day on the backside of the neighborhood. Overnight, families from the projects have staked out plots of the park, jockeying to get prime real estate for their barbecues. All weekend people who grew up in the Red Hook Houses have been flooding into the neighborhood, taking buses across the country and up from Florida for the yearly reunion—a bittersweet summer rite.

Instead of heading toward the church, Jonathan enters the park. The air smells of sweet char. The police on the perimeter turn a blind eye to the coolers of beer and cups of high-proof punch. It's not even noon, but many of voices already seem liquor loose.

A stage has been set up. A DJ who came up with Grandmaster Flash in the '70s is spinning. Early hip-hop and disco rebounds off the luggage factory lofts and the Visitation of the Blessed Virgin Mary. Jonathan's is the only white face, but no one makes him feel unwelcome.

The party is just getting going, but the park is already packed. Men carrying foil trays of macaroni salad and slaw search out their families' tables. Kids chase one another between the grills. Grandmothers parade their visiting grandchildren, introducing them from group to group. Elder statesmen, newly returned, walk through the park's pathways like homecoming kings, eyeing the women they remember and the ones who are new. Jonathan listens to the baritone greeting of two middle-aged men, the shrill soprano shouts of a couple of grade-school girlfriends now in their thirties, the chatter of a grandmother seeing her nephew for the first time in years. He feels the thunderous claps on the back, the breath-denying hugs, the reverb of kisses as visitors are brought back into the fold.

He drums his fingers on the donut box with the four-on-the-floor disco beat and taps his foot with the syncopated electric bass line. Toward its center, the park is even more crowded. The ice in coolers is refreshed. The DJ turns up the volume and announces a dance contest. A middle-aged woman in a long, floral sundress and bright bangle bracelets passes Jonathan a large plastic cup. She pats his cheek. "Welcome to our party, baby. Have a little sweet tea from me." Jonathan lifts the cup. "Don't worry," she says, "it's plenty boozy."

Jonathan sips the tea. It's as sweet as it is strong and makes his eyes water. He wanders toward the side of the park closer to the waterside of Red Hook where two girls are doing double Dutch, their braids and beads beating time on their shoulders. Behind them is the Visitation of the Blessed Virgin Mary—its stony, grim façade a rebuke to the colorful party. Fadi is mistaken, Jonathan thinks; the soul of the neighborhood is out here, not in there.

As he's looking at the church, the doors burst open and a girl in a school uniform appears on the threshold. She shades her eyes from the sun. The doors close behind her. She begins to run straight for Jonathan.

As she draws near, Jonathan recognizes her.

"Valerie," Jonathan calls.

Val slows to a stop a few feet in front of him. Their eyes meet, then she turns and rushes off. It is as if she is asking him to follow her, to save her from whatever she intends to do next. He drops the donuts and his drink and follows.

Val runs through the party, dodging dancers, sidewalk games, and makeshift dance floors. The crowd parts for her but is less tolerant of Jonathan, muttering and cursing as he bumps into their trays of coleslaw and coolers of beer. He tries calling out but he cannot be heard above the music and the chatter.

He loses Val in a large group gathered around a grill made from an oil drum. Jonathan pushes through this crowd and arrives at the far side of the park. In front of him Val is disappearing into the first of the courtyards.

His lungs feel tight. His breath pinches in his chest and throat. Val picks up her pace. She skirts curbs and tree guards.

Although the girl running from him is strong and agile, Jonathan still feels her limp, clammy body. He remembers the gravel in her hair, the foam that streamed from her mouth. He imagines that it was the proximity of his own body that revived her, made it possible for her to run away from him now.

His legs are heavy. His thighs burn. Valerie darts deeper into the projects and is thrown into shadow. In the first courtyard, Jonathan doubles over and places his hands on his knees. His heart thuds like a bass drum.

"Valerie!"

Two men are sitting on a bench. One of them has a withered face the color of coal dust. He coughs with a tin can rattle. "Whitey lost his baby girl."

His friend, whose face is covered in scrub-brush stubble, takes a pull from a brown-bagged bottle. "Yes sir, indeed."

"No use chasing that little girl now," the first man says. "When a girl wants to be gone, she is gone."

Jonathan stands up and breathes deeply. The whine in his ears is now in sync with the wheeze in his chest. His whole body sounds like a kids' recorder concert.

"Now, what'd you do to make a girl run from you like that?" the man with the bottle says.

When Jonathan catches his breath, he heads out of the projects, taking his time getting back to the waterside.

The sun has passed over Van Brunt and is heading for the river.

"Missing" posters for June still flutter from lampposts and mailboxes. The bench outside the Dockyard is packed with Lil's most devoted drinkers.

"Hey, Maestro, where you been hiding?" Biker Mike calls. "You got a song for us?"

Lil steps outside. She leans up against the door. She's already wearing her shot glass and has been putting it to good use. "How about a drink on the house for my best customer?"

"Since when am I your best customer?"

"Since when weren't you? So how about it, Maestro?" Lil lifts her shot glass to her lips, draining a droplet of whiskey. She brushes against Jonathan's hips. "Keep me company. All I've got is a bunch of dorks inside doing a book club."

"If you're buying."

"For you?" Lil slaps Jonathan on the ass. After her initial shit, she's been extra sweet on him lately. It's as if his association with danger made him worthier.

Before he and Lil head inside, he looks south and catches Val crossing Van Brunt and heading toward the water. The allure of free whiskey fades.

Jonathan's only gone a few steps when Lil calls, "You're not turning down a free drink are you, Maestro? You owe me some company after I saved your ass. If you leave me, I'll drink myself under the table by closing."

A few more drinks and Jonathan's not sure Lil will even make it to the end of her shift. "I'm not leaving you," Jonathan says, turning away.

"Hey," Lil says. "When I'm sober, I'm going to fuck you."

Jonathan can hear Biker Mike and New Steve laugh. Lil turns and gives them the finger.

Jonathan hurries off before he has to hear any more.

He arrives at square of grass that leads to the rocky beach and pier where he found Val. The Staten Island ferry slides across the water.

A tug rounds into view, its engine humming like a muffled snare drum. As he looks down toward the pier, he sees Val strip off her clothes and climb over the railing. Jonathan's breath catches as he watches her jump. Her legs and arms are bent like cricket wings. She sails, her legs pedaling the air, pushing her far from the pier. Then she dips from sight. An image of her holding her breath, weighing herself down, forbidding herself to rise fills Jonathan's mind.

Jonathan begins to rush to the pier. As he approaches, he sees a young black man strip to his boxers and jump in after Val. Jonathan hurries, unsure whether the second jumper intends to harm or help.

When he reaches the tip, he sees Val and the black kid treading water about fifty feet out. He watches them sink below the water—an agonizing disappearance that makes him feel as if he's drowning. They surface, their lips locked. Then they plunge again.

Jonathan calls Val's name, turning his voice into a buoy or a beacon, summoning her home. He wants to dive into the water, haul her to safety, be the person who brings her ashore. She swims farther out.

On the pier, he finds Val's skirt and blouse. He waves them to get her attention. He shouts her name, making a melody of the syllables. He worries that each of his cries is sending her farther out into the currents of the Upper Bay.

Close to Jonathan, two fishermen have cast their lines into the water. Their bucket holds the slick bodies of several glassy-eyed fish.

"Let the kids go," one of the men says. "Your yelling'll only make them drown faster. You can't help them from here. Either get in the water or wait for them to come back."

He watches Val's small, dark head bob as the wake from the tug crests over her. Light waves hit the rocks with a castanet clatter. A seagull chatters to itself. Then Val sees Jonathan. She stares at him, her gaze rising and falling with the waves. She begins to swim for land, cutting through the gray water with uneven strokes.

Valerie hauls herself out of the bay and onto the rocky beach.

She appears at the far end of the pier. Her cotton underwear droops. She wraps her arms around herself as she makes her way to Jonathan. Her stomach is flat and white. Below her small breasts, hidden by a flimsy child's bra, Jonathan can see the outlines of her ribs. He wants to look away.

They meet in the middle of the pier.

"Mr. Sprouse?"

Val drops her hands to her sides. Her hair hangs limp. Her pale skin is almost blue. Goose bumps have blossomed on her arms. Jonathan holds out her blouse. Val reaches for the shirt, then takes one step farther and steps into Jonathan's chest. She is as cool and clammy as when he found her under the pier. Her limbs seem as fragile as dried leaves. He worries that if he wraps his arms around her, he will bruise her skin.

Val bows her head, pressing it into his shoulder. She begins to shake and soon Jonathan feels tears wetting his collarbone. He hesitates, then embraces her, wrapping his arms around the points of her shoulder blades.

The fishermen reel in their lines to watch. Jonathan loosens his grip, but Val only sinks in deeper. Her sobs are audible now. "You found the wrong person," she says. "You should have left me there."

One of the fishermen scrapes back his camp stool. "What do you think you're doing letting that girl stand around in her underpants? You some kind of pervert?"

"You didn't even look for June. Why didn't you find her instead?" Val says. Jonathan feels her mouth move against his shirt.

"You were the only girl under the pier."

Jonathan looks over Val's head and down the pier. Her swimming companion is standing halfway down dressed only in his boxers. "Who the hell are you?" the kid calls.

Val jerks away from Jonathan.

"Get her dressed," the fisherman says, "else I'm going to call someone."

Val grabs her blouse and clutches it to her chest.

"What's going on?" the black kid demands, looking at Jonathan. "What d'ya do to her?"

"I'm fine," Val says. She stoops to collect her shoes, skirt, and blazer, then hurries away from the pier, not stopping for her friend who stands shirtless in the swollen afternoon sun.

Lil is nodding off on the bench outside the bar. Jonathan walks by without disturbing her. He goes to the liquor store and buys a fifth of whiskey which he brown-bags on the way home. He's fumbling with his keys when Lil comes to life.

"Maestro—wanna share that with me?"

"Looks like you've had plenty."

Jonathan gets his door open.

"What?" Lil says, standing up and steadying herself on the bar's window. "You too good for me now you're a hero? I make your life possible," she says. "Don't forget."

He has a half a mind to give Lil his bottle. Instead he slams the door, climbs his stairs, keeps working on the booze, skipping the formality of a glass.

He has no idea how long his phone has been ringing. He's lying on the couch, one foot on the floor. The apartment is dark. His head feels bruised. He's killed the whiskey. The empty lies on its side on his coffee table.

"You bitch," Dawn says when he answers. "I'm up here singing a cappella to a room full of bridge and tunnel ketamine-clobbered beefcake. You *abandoned* me."

Jonathan looks at the time. He's missed his first set at Cock 'n Bulls.

"You're ruining my life," Dawn howls. "You're *ruining* me. I'm having twenty heart attacks up here alone. I can't find my range. I'm sharp. I'm flat. I'm *dying*."

"I'm sure you're doing fine," Jonathan says.

"You don't *do* this to a girl. You don't stand a girl up. I'm working like Martha Stewart on Christmas. And no one's tipping. I need backup."

"Why don't you lip-sync?" Jonathan asks.

"You think I'm just another low-rent tranny with a boom box?"

Jonathan rubs his temples. "If you're not here in half an hour, I'm gonna cut your balls off," Dawn says before hanging up.

The Cock 'n Bulls bar is in full feather when Jonathan arrives. A few drag queens are standing along the far wall. They catch sight of him and snap their fingers, purse their lips, and bob their heads from side to side.

"Girl," one of them says as Jonathan passes on his way to the stage, "Ms. Dawn is ready to kill."

He catches sight of Dawn Perignon in a floor-length pink sequined gown that slithers over her boyish hips, and elbow-length evening gloves. Her curly brown wig ends just below the ear. Her eyebrows are drawn on with thin pencil semicircles. Her eyelashes are so long they cast shadows on her cheeks.

Jonathan waits for her to finish "Age of Aquarius" to take his place at the piano.

"You look like Edith Piaf," he says. "On a bad day."

Dawn covers the microphone. "Fuck you."

"That isn't very ladylike."

"You smell like a sports bar."

He bangs out the opening bars of "Sunset Boulevard" before she can get in another word.

Dawn turns back to her audience and holds out one hand toward

Jonathan, flashing cocktail rings with gems the size of jawbreakers. "A good man *is* hard to find. Am I right, boys?"

As she sings, Dawn lounges on top of the piano, crossing her legs and showing off her six-inch white patent leather platforms.

They run through their repertoire—songs from *Evita* and *South Pacific,* a bunch of Judy Garland numbers, and much of *Cabaret.* Dawn won't look Jonathan's way, but she knows that she's at her best when they sing duets. His voice is the anchor and hers the comedy. They ham up "Me and My Girl" and "The Lady Is a Tramp," which are both good for laughs at Jonathan's expense.

Before their last set they step into the alley behind the bar for a smoke. She makes him hold her cigarette for her. She snaps her gloved fingers when she wants it put to her lips.

Jonathan tries to get ash on her dress.

"Why are you so quiet?" she asks. "I hope you're not about to give me that *I used to be a real musician* crap."

"I didn't say anything."

"You don't *have* to say anything. I can *see* it." She signals for the cigarette. "A girl has to work her ass off to keep a steady booking at a place like this. I don't need you standing me up. You know how many queens are out there selling a show-tune revue? Millions."

"None of them have an accompanist who was once on Broadway."

"Don't you have anything nice to say about me?"

"None of those queens can hold a candle to you. You're a real star, sweetheart. I just bang the keys."

"That's better. Now how do I really look?"

"Like you belong on Park Avenue." Jonathan places the cigarette into Dawn's mouth.

"I read about you in the paper." She inhales without pressing her lips to the filter. "Don't act all surprised that a girl like me reads the paper."

"I bet you even check the box scores."

"It must have been horrible. Do you feel like a hero?"

"I feel like shit."

She pinches Jonathan's cheeks, pulling his lips into a pucker, then she kisses the air in front of his mouth. Her face is so close Jonathan can see the cracks in her foundation. "Well, baby, you should have called. That's what girlfriends are for."

Dawn and two other queens close the bar. They chase tequila shots with Coke. Jonathan sticks to whiskey.

"I'm not letting you head home all on your lonely," Dawn says as they step onto the street at four A.M. The city is still flying. Cabs are streaming up Sixth Avenue and the all-night restaurants are packed.

One of the queens pinches Jonathan's ass. "Why don't you grab us a cab?"

"Get one of those big ones," Dawn says. "A minivan."

Eventually, Jonathan hails a minivan cab. The queens beg the driver to put on KTU, the dance station from Long Island, for the short ride to Dawn's place on Avenue A.

Dawn's apartment has one bedroom that she's divided into three windowless rooms. For someone who wears six-inch heels and can apply mascara on a moving subway, she's handy with power tools. The makeshift bedrooms are occupied by a revolving cast whose stage names blend into one long pun.

The girls kick off their heels, put their eyelashes on the coffee table, take off their wigs, but leave their stocking caps on. They fall back on the leopard covered futon. Maybe it's the heat or maybe it's because the drugs are wearing off, but the energy is low.

Jonathan wakes up feeling the stubble of Dawn's cheeks against his lips. Her breath is hot and sour; her body has a manly odor. He tries to push her off. She presses his shoulders back and covers his mouth with hers. Her tongue is massive.

Jonathan rolls out from under her. "What the fuck?"

"Baby, it's not *good* to be lonely all the time."

"I'm not that lonely."

Dawn raises the smudged remains of her painted eyebrows. "Girl—" she begins.

"Forget it, Don."

Out on the street, joggers, dog walkers, and commuters have replaced the late-night stragglers. People are lined up behind their laptops in coffee shop windows. Jonathan decides to walk to Brooklyn, because he has no real desire to get there.

CHAPTER NINE

The newspaper coverage of the June Giatto story has been disappointing. Except for the free local paper, the *Eagle*, the story never made the front page.

There were a few local color stories in the major papers—a brief mention of Jonathan. No criminal and no body make for no news. Even Fadi recognizes that.

Because of the papers' lack of coverage, Fadi's newsletter has gained traction in a community that craves any news of June— whether rumor, gossip, or fact. Not satisfied by the police's response to their tips, people started dropping slips of paper in Fadi's submission box. He edits and reprints them.

How come the 76 is only shaking down the PJs?

The Po-Po better keep out of the Houses. We got nothing to do with this white girl business.

The Dockyard stays open way past the city-mandated closing time. The police should interview everyone who drinks there. It's inconceivable that none of their customers were out and about when those girls vanished.

Was that June Giatto I saw over in Sunset Park last Friday night?

Fadi knows that he's simply providing a forum for residents of Red Hook to vent their frustrations. At least he's opening a neighborhood dialogue.

In the last couple of days, though, tips that have nothing to do with June have appeared in Fadi's box.

I've recently noticed a group of Latinos engaged in some late-night activity near Beard Street Pier. I'm wondering if anyone can tell me what they are up to?

Yo! Someone stole my bike from 127 Dikeman. You better not be playing with me. Return that shit, you hear? No questions.

Yet again, the Dockyard stayed open past regulation on both Friday and Saturday nights. Plus, I've noticed people smoking inside the bar. This is a clear violation of public ordinance. People, please!

The cast-iron carousel horses on Van Brunt are not toys. They are art.

A van parked on Lorraine was tagged with the letters "RFC." This is the eighth instance of our neighborhood being vandalized with these same letters. Graffiti is a crime.

When I go to the bar to drink, I don't want to deal with underage girls picking out the worst songs on a great jukebox. Take your jailbait somewhere else.

To the fool who calls himself RunDown who tagged over my piece, you better be running scared. Don't mess with Craze.

A lone black male was seen trespassing in the abandoned warehouse at the end of Imlay Street overlooking the water. Please advise.

Fadi knows it's his duty to be objective so he prints everything he receives even if he doesn't like it. Twice a week he assembles his newsletter. The back page is always the same—June's photo accompanied by the police tip line and Fadi's number, as well as the stated $15,000 reward Mrs. Giatto has offered from her son's military death benefit.

To his dismay, people seem more interested in submitting their own complaints than paying attention to what others have to say. Fadi often finds his newsletters in the garbage can by the bus stop.

"You advertise your store by printing trash about the neighborhood," the Greek said when he saw Fadi peeking into the garbage. "Why don't you write something nice? Make us feel good about this dump?"

Fadi keeps his ears open for any leads in the June case. He leaves a notebook on the counter where he jots down the careless comments of his customers who don't imagine that he's listening. From this information, he crafts a biweekly column in which presents his findings and observations in an impartial manner. Rather than making assertions, he poses questions, hoping the community will draw their own conclusions and see the necessity of joining together in an effort to find June.

He knows interviewing Valerie would be a scoop—something the major dailies didn't even manage. He wants to know what questions the police asked her and whether they've been following up. But each time she comes into his store, Fadi cannot bring himself to ask her about June. He notices the way she ignores her friend's photo on the bulletin board and never takes a copy of his newsletter. Her nervous eyes, which look at everything but June's face, forbid inquiry.

Despite the continued good weather, Fadi is aware of the arrival of fall. There's a sharpness to the edge of things, lines coming back into focus, leaves beginning to curl before they crisp, shadows arriving early and sticking around.

When Fadi arrives in Red Hook just after 5:30 A.M., he passes the Greek's where the wino is sleeping in the doorway underneath a pile of discarded clothes. Some time during the night he painted a square of pavement Creamsicle orange and blocked it off with two lopsided sawhorses. The wino is going to catch hell from the Greek and Fadi's sure he's going to be listening to them all day.

Fadi brings in the bundled dailies and frees the *Post* first. It's not the main headline but a teaser on the skyline above the banner that catches his eye. "Get Fresh Brooklyn: City's Largest Local Harvest Megamarket Headed to Red Hook."

Fadi flips through the *Post* and finds the story. The store is going to be housed in a Civil War–era warehouse at the far end of Van Brunt from Fadi's—a dramatic setting at the edge of the waterfront. He skims the piece: water taxi accessible, organic beef cheeks, fresh shrimp, low-cost household items, citrus, gourmet chips, microbrews, microgreens, an outdoor café. A promise to hire staff from the projects and give them a discount. Local Harvest will bring healthy and exotic choices at affordable prices.

Fadi shuts the paper. This supermarket will lure new shoppers to Red Hook—people from Brooklyn Heights and beyond who never set foot in the neighborhood before. But it may also kill his business. He tears the story from the paper so he can tape it to the plexiglass display case to the left of the register.

Just after seven the wino appears. He's the color of a roasted nut with a small, shriveled face and blackberry lips. His hair is the hue and texture of refined oil. He's a tiny man, the size of an adolescent.

Fadi used to shoo the wino away, but the wino persisted, show-ing up to harangue Fadi in his tangled dialect—a harsh medley of Spanish and English diluted by booze. He paced the aisle in front of the coolers, stumbling and leaving handprints on the glass fronts. It often took him twenty minutes to select a drink, but since he always had the money, Fadi eventually let him be.

Ever since June's disappearance the wino has been spending more time in the store. At first he would gesture at the "missing" sign. "Seen the girl. Seen the *muchacha*," he'd say. "She sleeps down at the water. Down by the *fantasmas*." Then he would jab his finger at the reward.

"Tell it to the *policia*," Fadi told him.

"No *policia*," the wino said.

Soon the wino began turning up with strange objects he'd place on the counter—a child's pink sock, a broken barrette, a purse without a strap. "The *muchacha*," he said, stabbing at the objects with a small, gritty finger. "These—the *muchacha*."

It took Fadi a while to understand that the wino claimed to be bringing him objects that had belonged to June. He seemed to have an inexhaustible supply—bracelets without clasps, single earrings, grimy undershirts, a jelly sandal. He presented each object with ceremony, cupping it in his rough palms, then lowering it onto the counter. After he let it go, he would step back and cross his arms over his chest and say, "*Recompensa?*"

"Come back with June, not an earring."

"But the *muchacha* by the water," the wino insisted, pointing at the "missing" poster. "The *muchacha* no come back."

"I know," Fadi said. "That's what the *recompensa* is for."

Fadi usually ended up handing over a beer, a few cigarettes, or a bag of chips.

Today the wino skips the cooler and the "missing" poster and heads for the cleaning products. He brings eight bottles of cut-rate dish soap to the counter. While Fadi's ringing up his purchase, he says, "I see the *muchacha*."

"You want to show me?"

The wino shakes his head, his eyes wide, his mouth shaped into an O. He crosses himself with a shaky hand.

"No *muchacha*, no *recompensa*." Fadi follows him outside and watches him cross back to the Greek's.

The wino rearranges his sawhorses, shooing away a few people waiting for the bus who have come too close to the square of painted pavement. He dumps the dish soap and a bucket of water onto the orange square, then starts scrubbing it with a broom whose bristles are covered in orange paint. In an instant the Greek is outside. He grabs the wino by the collar, lifting him off the ground, yelling in Greek and Spanish.

A crowd gathers, shouting at the Greek, telling him to clean up his soapy orange mess. The paint is poisoning the trees and staining their shoes. It looks damn ugly, someone says. *The hell you go and paint the street for?*

The wino dances around the crowd, trying to slip between them.

By evening the Greek will have forgiven the wino and they will share a meal together. Fadi knows that the Greek believes his evening ritual is a secret. It starts the same way every night, with the Greek passing a tinfoil dish to the wino through the side door after closing. The wino lifts the lid of the dish and smells the food. Then the Greek props the side door open and eventually the wino slips inside. Fadi watches them through the small window to the kitchen, eating across from each other at a table near the stove— the Greek's large bald head and wide shoulders towering over the wino's slumped, child-sized frame.

At lunchtime Fadi orders a deluxe special from the bulletproof Chinese. Their fried rice is school bus yellow and their boneless ribs leave an oily, red dye on the Styrofoam container. As he eats he watches a black kid circle the store, looping around the two aisles, pausing in front of the cleaning products and the cat food. The kid is wearing a black hoodie over a baseball cap—on a hot day, a sure sign of shoplifting. The kid looks over his shoulder now and then, checking Fadi then checking his reflection in the circular mirror angled near the ceiling of the back corner.

Fadi tracks the kid, wondering what he's going to try to nab. The pricey items are either impossible to lift without attracting notice—

diapers and big boxes of detergent—or stowed behind the counter.

The kid's got the low-slung gangster slouch and the oversized duds. But his jeans, which on first glance seemed conventionally baggy, are just too big. They're faded, a little dirty, and of no make that Fadi's heard of. His white sneakers are chunky, more suitable for geriatric ambling than shooting hoops.

The kid's on his fourth circle now, staring down the deodorant and detergent, then he heads for the door. Fadi clears his throat, ready for the confrontation. "You want to show me your hands?"

The kid turns and lifts his shoulders. He walks to the counter with sullen obedience. He withdraws his hands from his pocket and drops a crumpled Wise potato chip bag on the counter.

The kid pokes the turquoise bag with his finger, making it wobble. "Wise's is all."

"Mine?"

"Was."

"Got thirty-five cents?"

"Used to be a quarter."

"Got a quarter then?" Fadi puts down his fork and pushes his half-eaten lunch special to the side.

"Twenty-five cents a bag? Shit. It don't last more than a minute." The kid removes his hood. His eyes are sunken, the whites a little yellowed. "Bet you didn't even clock me eating them."

"You got the change or not?"

"Take it easy, *ese*."

"*Ese?* The Puerto Ricans are across the street. Me, I'm Lebanese. I'm not *ese*. And this is not some dirty bodega where you can lift your Wise."

"That's your problem, boy. Too much fancy shit." The kid riffles the rack of potato chips with one hand, making the bags clipped to the wire display dance. "What's this—Asia-go popcorn? What the fuck is Asia-go? Bet you don't even know." The kid pushes his hand into the rack, sifting through the bags. "Baked rice chips, herb flavored, low-salt kettle crisps. Fuck is all this shit? How come you don't have fried plantains? Potato sticks? Ten cents a pop."

"Are you giving me the thirty-five cents or not?"

"Man, you know what you need?" The kid pulls the Asiago popcorn from the rack and turns the bag over in his hands. "Some straight-up, motherfucking, comprehensible snacks. The kind of shit you don't need a dictionary to consume. Ghetto up, man. Organic blue corn tortilla chips, my ass."

Fadi knows that his new-breed potato chips are outsold by Wise and Doritos. Even he prefers his Hostess and Entenmann's to the stuff with the aging actor on the package. Sorbets languish in the back of the ice cream freezers, while Choco-Tacos and neon Freeze-Pops move. Still, Fadi hopes to lift his store above the other bodegas in Red Hook and bring in the newcomers.

"You buying that, too?" Fadi says, pointing at the popcorn.

"No, I'm cool," the kid says. He lifts his hat, revealing a head of hair twisted into stalagmite tufts. He takes a napkin from the counter and wipes his brow. There's a lean, wolfish look to him. He steps away from the register and clasps his hands behind his back, scanning Fadi's news clippings. "Man, you turn your back on a neighborhood for a second and it's getting ahead of itself. Trying to elevate. Aggrandize."

"You've been away for a while?" Fadi asks. "You don't talk like the kids around here."

The boy pulls up his hood, shielding his face. "Had to get out to educate myself. Just me and my *Merriam-Webster's*." He bends forward, squinting at the newsprint. "I lived here for fourteen years and nothing changed. Disappear for six, and the shit's pretending to be reborn. Cruise ships? Is this shit for real?"

"It's in the paper," Fadi says.

"And the papers are all about the truth?" He looks at Fadi. "Guess you're the wrong dude to ask." The kid plucks at a piece of Scotch tape that's holding one of the clippings to the display case.

"Back when, the Hook only made the news for criminality and such. And mostly, not even that. Shit flew under the radar. Crime was quotidian."

"It's changing," Fadi says.

"I'm reading it, but I ain't seeing it. Looks like the same old decrepitness to me. Poor's still poor."

Fadi comes around from behind the counter with the Local Harvest article. The kid hovers at his shoulder. "That's from today?"

"On the cover," Fadi says, pointing to a stack of *Posts*.

"A supermarket isn't news." The kid glances at Fadi's lunch. "You done with that?" Fadi circles back around the counter and slides the Styrofoam container toward the kid. "I didn't think you Muslims ate pork."

"You want it or not?" Fadi says.

"I'm not complaining. Just observing." He shovels a forkful of bright yellow rice into his mouth. Still eating, he wanders over to the bulletin board near the door. He zeros in on the photo of June. "Missing, bullshit. This girl's dead."

"How do you know?"

"They'll frame some black kid for it. Just wait. I could fish that girl's body out of the water at the end of a line and they'd tell me I killed her. Come on, man, you know the score." He scans Fadi's clippings again, squinting at the newsprint. "You live at the crossroads. This is ground zero, where the front meets the back. But don't waste your time trying to negotiate a truce."

The kid's right. Fadi's bodega is one of the only places patronized by both sides of Red Hook—people from the Houses on their way to and from the bus stop and folks from the waterside looking for early-morning or late-night essentials.

"Do you want my advice? Focus on your own shit. You got a bodega. That's your thing. Your avocation. Leave the dead white girls to the white guys." He saunters out the door, still working on the remains of Fadi's lunch.

Fadi follows the kid outside. He looks up and down the street. The strand of Christmas lights sway in the breeze. Two guys with shaggy haircuts and paint-splattered jeans walk past. They don't return Fadi's nod. A few of Paulie Marino's friends are coming down Visitation. Across the street the door of Dockyard is propped open. Every once in a while the bristles of a broom pop out, sending dust and dirt into the street.

In the last week, Fadi has helped two people from the bar find apartments and helped a kid from the projects get a dog-walking job. From where he stands he can see the water, the polite three-story houses on Visitation, the projects beyond them. He can see the bar and those who hang out there. So it's not too far-fetched to imagine that what happened to June is discoverable right here, under his nose.

Van Brunt smells of turpentine. For the last couple of hours the wino has been on his hands and knees rubbing the painted square of sidewalk with rags soaked in paint thinner. Oily orange liquid is running into the sewer. When Fadi looks over at the Greek's, the wino springs from the sidewalk and rushes across the street. He wraps a hand around Fadi's wrist. His palm is tough, not calloused, but hardened like bark.

"You give him the *recompensa*? The *pandillero,* the homeboy, he come for the *recompensa*?" The corners of the wino's mouth are purple, and his breath smells of Night Train.

"No."

"He tell you about the *muchacha*?"

"No." The wino's digging his thick nails into Fadi's skin.

The Greek pokes his head out from the door of his restaurant to yell at the wino. The wino lets go of Fadi. "The *recompensa es mio!*" he shouts, running back across the street to his scrubbing.

Throughout the afternoon, Fadi listens to the wino shouting about the reward from outside the Greek's. Finally, he closes the door. The usual rush of kids buying afternoon snacks ebbs and flows.

The first wave of twentysomethings stocking up on beer and supplies for the night starts trickling in. Across the street, the wino and the Greek are sitting down to dinner. The orange paint has been stripped from the sidewalk. The sawhorses have been put away. The bus pulls up and drives off. The neon signs in the Dockyard's window flicker. The wino's jagged laugh tangles with the Greek's. Fadi returns to his post behind the counter and waits until closing.

In the last few days, Fadi's store has become the target of small acts of vandalism and petty crime. Twice he's arrived at work to find that all his newspapers have been stolen.

If the newspapers continue to be stolen from the Hafiz Superette, the police will be involved. This is an important intersection of our neighborhood and news must be available to all.

The other night a messy tag—more handwriting than graffiti— appeared on one of Fadi's roll gates.

Vandalism to the Hafiz Superette will not be tolerated. The Hafiz Superette will not serve the needs of the community if it continues to be a target of such attacks.

He wonders if the criminals read his edition.

In his latest newsletter, Fadi included an editorial urging the neighborhood to band together to welcome the cruise ships. "For the first time since the golden age of shipping, Red Hook is going to be a gateway to our city," he wrote. "We have no more time for petty crime and vandalism. We have no room for neighborly discord. We need to show the world the beauty of our colorful community."

But because he wanted to be fair to his contributors, Fadi was forced to print contrary complaints in the same newsletter.

Screw the cruise ships, the mayor, and the antienvironmentalist councilmen who are going to allow these polluting hunks of junk to befoul our waters with their idling engines and pompous smoke.

Keep Red Hook beautiful for the shuffleboarders and smorgasborders who will soon walk among us.

How come the cruise terminal isn't interested in hiring anyone who comes from the Houses? Only the white boys good enough for the waterfront?

Vandalism and thievery are not the only changes that Fadi has noticed. Since June disappeared Paulie Marino and his buddies have made it a point to buy their beer and cigarettes from his Puerto Rican rivals.

It's not even five A.M. when Fadi steps off the subway on the elevated platform of Smith and Ninth Street. The stop is a twenty-minute walk from his store. But since Red Hook doesn't merit its own subway, Smith and Ninth is as close as Fadi can get.

The sun hasn't begun its daily battle with the Houses—its struggle to overcome the bleak fortress of rooftops. The day will be warm, but the dark morning is chilly. Fadi shivers in his T-shirt as he walks down the abandoned platform to the long escalator that leads to the street.

He lets the train roar down into the tunnel before making his own descent. Soon the station is silent. He looks across the platform toward Red Hook barricaded behind the expressway. Like Smith and Ninth, the expressway is crumbling. It's cobbled and patched from parts that rumble and shake when cars hit the fault lines. Between the subway and the expressway is a large sign advertising Kentile tiling, through which the sun, when it rises, will cast a spiderweb of light onto the cars below.

Fadi knows better than to expect the 75—the bus that services the projects—to come. It's simpler to walk through the barren lots, underneath the exhaust-blackened highway, and approach Red Hook through the Houses.

Two weary hookers are strolling on Hamilton Avenue, pausing in the glow of the Pathmark sign to repaint their faces. They call out to Fadi halfheartedly, then heckle him as he crosses beneath the expressway.

He follows the bus route along a desolate stretch of Smith Street on which the only occupied building is a confectionery manufacturer that Fadi's never seen open. Eight columns jut from the building's façade. At the far end of the block a single streetlamp is struggling to stay alight. The street is silent. Then Fadi hears a rattle and hiss. A young man is standing in front of one of the columns, hitting it with a blast of spray paint. His arm arcs, making the spray rise and fall. There's another rattle, and he switches to another can of paint.

Fadi crosses the street, giving the artist wide berth. The streetlight buzzes out. When the streetlight comes back on, he is standing under its yellow spill. The painter is directly across from him, shaking his can, ready to hit the column again.

Even in the dismal glow of the streetlamp, Fadi recognizes the kid who stole the Wise from his store the other day. The kid sees him too. He lowers his can. "Hey, my man."

They stare at each other across the street. Fadi looks at the wall behind the kid. All eight columns are covered in abstract white and black designs.

"Guess I'm caught. First shoplifting and now tagging." The kid smiles—*what can you do?*—and rattles his can. "You going to rat me out?"

"It's none of my business what you do on an abandoned street."

"Abandoned street? This is an important thoroughfare." The kid shakes his head. "The bus route man. The only way people from Smith and Ninth get into the hood. It's not abandoned. It's essential."

"If you're trying to get somewhere else."

"So what happens between point A and point B doesn't matter? I thought you were into this hood."

"I am," Fadi says. "Just not this part."

"Hold up," the kid says. "Haven't you ever heard of neighborhood beautification?" He rattles his can, adds a splash of paint, then drops the paint. "I bet you didn't even notice me working here until this morning." The kid raises the hood of his sweatshirt, hiding the tufts of his hair. "My man, you are just in time. Step back with me."

There's excitement in the kid's gaunt face. His thin, dry lips are quivering. Even the yellowed whites of his eyes gleam. Fadi doesn't want to disappoint, so he follows the kid back down the block. The kid pushes open the door to an abandoned building. Fadi hesitates.

The kid pulls out a flashlight. "It's copacetic. I've checked it out. You coming?" They climb to the second floor and enter a small railroad apartment. Fadi follows the kid to the window, which is nothing more than an empty frame. "Check it," the kid says pointing across the street.

Fadi looks out. The façade of the confectionery factory is dark, the kid's artwork barely visible. "What?"

"You don't see anything, right?"

"No." Fadi turns to leave but the kid grabs his arm. "I've got to get to work."

"What's the rush? Your corner doesn't get going before six. You're getting a jump start on nothing." He looks down the block in the direction of the expressway. "Hold up, here we go." He pushes Fadi back toward the window. The bus has rounded the corner and is coming down the street. "Watch."

Fadi leans out the window, careful not to touch the nails protruding from its frame. As the bus draws closer, its headlights hit the first of the columns and the wall comes to life. A silhouette of a boy leaping into the air—one leg kicking out front, the other bent back behind—each column showing his progression as he flies farther. It's a flipbook, a perfect moving image, taking the jumper higher off the ground. At the end of the building the bus halts before rounding the corner. Its headlights linger on a large tag: RunDown.

Fadi peers toward the expressway, hoping for another bus so he can see the jumper again. "RunDown," he says. "What's RunDown?"

"RunDown is me, Renton Davis. RunDown is also this place, this hood. It's run-down. It's run me down."

Fadi's staring out the window, trying to bring the wall back to life.

"Pretty good, right?" The kid narrows his eyes, trying to read Fadi's expression. "That's what I thought."

Fadi reaches for the flashlight and runs it over the wall. The painting on the columns looks fragmented. He looks down the block again.

"Man, you know the bus isn't coming for another half hour at least."

Fadi looks at his watch. In half an hour it will still be dark enough that he'll be able to see the jumper on the wall. "I'll buy you breakfast."

"You got yourself a deal," Renton says.

They walk to the twenty-four-hour fast-food joints below the expressway and pick up breakfast sandwiches. Ren devours his on the way out the door, so Fadi grabs him two more, which he finishes on the way back to Smith Street.

They wait in the railroad apartment, drinking burnt coffee. Soon they can hear the bus's arthritic groan as it approaches. The headlights swing into view, bumping over the buildings at the far end of the block. Fadi leans out the window. The jumper begins his leap, kicking out and up, away from the ground, transforming the street with a flash of momentary energy, exhilarating the desolation.

As the bus vanishes, leaving the street dark, Fadi half expects to hear the jumper crash to the ground. The sky is softening. He checks his watch. He's late. He'll walk home along this route tonight, watch Renton's drawing leap clear of the neighborhood.

Fadi rushes through the projects. The first lights are coming on in the towers. A few elderly women are pushing shopping carts out of the courtyards and over to Lorraine Street where they will sit in front of the Laundromat until it opens.

On Van Brunt the Puerto Ricans are already open. Fadi lifts his gate, replaying the image of the jumper over in his head, remembering the boy's fluid ascent, the magic of his movement as the bus brought him to life. It's only when he's stationed behind his counter that he realizes his newspapers have been stolen.

CHAPTER TEN

Where is Cree? Since he had jumped the pier after her Val has been looking for him. She needs him to fill the hole left by June, to be the person who completes her sentences, answers her pointless messages, agrees with her silly observations—makes her feel as if she is not cut loose, unmoored, dangling. Because when she opens her mouth, picks up her phone, signs into her e-mail to report a million little things to June, it takes her a moment to remember no one will respond.

When she jumped into the water, Val imagined that if she held her breath and stayed down long enough, she might black out and wake up back on the raft with June at her side. But Cree had pulled her to the surface, kissing her, distracting her from her missing friend, hinting that maybe he'd take her place. Then the music teacher arrived, summoning Val to shore, reminding her, just by appearing on the pier, that she had survived and June was gone. And June was right, Val realized; Val *is* a baby, crying there in the arms of Mr. Sprouse for everyone to see.

But now she must find Cree. So she invents reasons to spend time in Coffey Park, in the gloomy shadow of the Red Hook Houses. She sits on a bench, reading or trying to read—but not reading at all. She ignores the hollers of the boys smoking blunts. She ignores the sideways glance Monique throws her way when she passes with her colorful crew of girls. Instead, she concentrates on summoning Cree. If Cree shows up, seeks her out—if she is no longer alone—people will forgive her for what happened to June. *If Cree likes her—deems her worthy of affection—she will be more than the girl whose friend is missing, more than the girl who lost that friend during a childish adventure.*

She thinks she sees Cree everywhere—at the bodega, at the bus stop, on the pier. She lingers on her stoop before going inside, tricking herself into believing that he is going to be the next person to walk down her street. At night, she stays up late, sitting on her windowsill, her legs dangling, her heels tapping a rhythm she hopes will call Cree to Visitation Street.

On the Sunday following the vigil, Val waits outside the tabernacle. As she listens to Monique sing, she watches the rows of worshippers in shiny suits sway and clap—an undulation of colors like the evening sun spilling across the river. But when the crowd flows back onto the street, Cree is not with them.

Val watches Monique come down the aisle. How far-fetched is it to imagine that they might be friends again, gossiping late at night in Coffey Park, teasing the boys and letting themselves be teased in return?

"You still waiting around for me to sing something for June?" Monique says as she passes Val. "I told you Cree's mom's the one to bother with that nonsense."

"I'm looking for Cree, not his mom," Val says.

"Your daddy knows that?"

"No."

"Thought you always followed daddy's orders."

"Maybe I don't."

"What's your business with Cree?"

"Nothing. I just want to talk to him," Val says.

"You guys a couple or something?"

"No."

"Building closest to Lorraine. Sixth floor. Door's busted." Monique fans herself with her hand. "You're not scared of the Houses? Bet you've never been inside before."

Val won't admit it, but Monique's right. Paulie forbade both her and Rita from playing in the courtyards, let alone entering one of the project buildings. He'd grown up on the waterside and watched the drug slingers from the Houses invade his community, force his friends and family to move away. *People over there got nothing to do with us,* Paulie warned Val whenever she mentioned the Houses.

The projects are a maze. Val tries to appear nonchalant as she looks for the building with the busted door. A couple of young punks whose waistbands ride below their hips circle her. "I got what you're looking for?" one of them asks, reaching down between his knees to grab the sagging crotch of his pants. "You come this way for a little action?"

From a bench in the middle of the courtyard, two old men tsk and tut, their displeasure souring the boys' thrill. The boys run off. Val glances around, willing Cree to appear from every doorway, saving her the trouble of seeking him out.

She finds the building. Like Monique promised, the door is ajar. From outside, Val can smell the pungent stench of summer garbage stewing in the hall. Her palms are clammy. Sweat trickles down her neck. She looks across the courtyard. The boys who taunted her are watching with their arms crossed, checking if she dares to enter.

The stairwell is dark. The floors are unnumbered. Val flattens against a wall, making room for a woman with a baby carriage who scowls as she passes. The baby cries each time the carriage bangs against the stairs, staccato hiccups that bounce off the concrete.

Val pushes through a fire door onto the sixth-floor hallway. The fluorescent lights buzz and flicker as if they're catching flies. A man stumbles out of an apartment, cursing as the door slams behind him.

Halfway down the hall is a door with the name JAMES below the bell and a sign advertising PSYCHIC CONNECTIONS $10. Val's hand cannot find its way to the doorbell. She leans against the opposite wall. She wipes her palms.

The door opens and a large woman in a long purple skirt pokes her head into the hallway.

"What're you doing standing there?" she says, reaching out a hand to Val. "Come inside. I've got the fan running."

Val follows her. She has the same round face as Cree, the same wide, soft features. The apartment is bright and clean. It smells like lavender. Framed prints of flowers hang on the walls in the tidy kitchen. A yellow plastic tablecloth is spread over the small table.

"I'm Gloria," she says. She still holds Val's hand. There is a soft electricity in her fingertips as they press into Val's palm, scanning her life lines and love lines, as if reading Braille.

"I'm—"

"I know who you are. The last time I saw you, you were nine years old." Gloria turns over Val's palm inside her hand. Her hand is soft with deep creases.

If she lets go, Cree will be home. Gloria does not let go. Her grip is strong.

"Is that sister of yours still running wild?"

"I guess," Val says. "I'm looking for—"

"You don't need to tell me who you're looking for," Gloria says, patting Val's cheek with her free hand. She leads Val to the kitchen table. "Sit down, baby. There's no need to be nervous. I don't bite."

Despite the fan, the kitchen is hot. The backs of Val's thighs adhere to the chair's vinyl cushion.

"I could air-condition the place, but it disturbs my flow," Gloria says.

Val cranes her neck, checking to see if Cree is in the living room.

"Water. Lemonade?"

"Water's fine." Val removes the paper napkins from their spindled holder and squares their edges before replacing them.

Gloria fills two glasses with water and places them on the table. She returns to the sink and washes her hands. Then she takes the chair opposite Val. "Are you ready?" she asks. "Give me your hands." Gloria holds out her hands and closes her eyes.

Val hesitates. "Is Cree here?"

Gloria's eyes open. "Cree? No, baby, he's not going to interrupt. Now give me your hands and we'll see if I can talk to your friend."

"My friend?"

"Don't tell me her name." Gloria takes a deep breath and looks up at the ceiling. "I remember now. June. We'll try and talk to June." She flutters her fingers.

If you want to talk to the dead, talk to Cree's mom.

Before Val can object, Gloria grasps her hands and squeezes. A low-watt current passes between them. Val doesn't close her eyes. Instead she takes in the grocery list held to the fridge by an orange magnet, the wire fruit basket hanging over the sink, a coffee cup with a lipstick mark waiting to be washed. She clings to everything mundane to fight back the extraordinary.

Gloria's grip tightens. The light hasn't changed, but shadows have crept over her face, making caverns of her eyes. Although

Gloria is only a few feet away, Val knows she'd have trouble reaching her.

Despite all the rituals she's invented to summon June home, Val doesn't want June to appear here. She does not want to hear her voice come out from Cree's mother's mouth. Until this moment, Val always thought of June's return in the abstract, a miraculous homecoming, a joyful celebration. But in reality, what would June say? What accusations would she make?

It's your fault.

Gloria's face contracts and resettles. Her lips part. Val's breath catches. She doesn't want to hear what Gloria is about to say. She snatches her hands out of Gloria's grasp and covers her ears.

"No!" Val's cry raises a metallic echo among the flatware and pots drying on the counter.

Gloria's eyes snap open. The shadows blow back from her face. "I'm sorry," she says. "I can't find her."

"Okay," Val says. "That's okay." She cups her hand over her mouth and exhales into it, trying to catch her jagged breath.

Gloria leans over the table. "You don't believe she's dead. For this to work, you have to believe she's dead. Do you believe it? Or are you still hoping?"

"Is she dead?"

"That's not for me to say. If you think she's dead, I can try and reach her. But only if that's what you believe. It has to start with you. Sometimes we hold on too long. Sometimes with good reason. Do you know your reason?"

"I just want to know where she is," Val says. "I want her to come back."

"You'll find her, either with my help or with someone else's. You just have to decide how and where to look." Gloria switches to a chair closer to Val and takes her hand. There is nothing probing or searching in her touch this time. "Baby, there's hundreds of people around us we don't see. It's up to you to open your eyes.

You have to choose that this is where you want to find June." Gloria gives her hand a squeeze.

"So it's up to me to decide if she is dead?"

"There's a difference between dead and forgotten."

Val stands up. She rummages in her pocket for money but Gloria waves her off.

They walk to the door. Gloria keeps an arm draped around Val's shoulder. At the threshold she pulls Val into a warm, soft hug. Val closes her eyes. With her face buried in Gloria's shoulder, she sees the raft and the river, the pink rubber buoyed by the water's pulse. She does not see June.

"I'll tell Cree you were here," Gloria says, closing the door behind Val.

This is how you walk home. This is how you look for June—you follow the precise route that led you to the water that night. You see yourself from above—a player moving through a video-game maze. At Coffey Park you turn left. You walk along Lorraine Street, over to the abandoned lot with the boat. You look for Cree among the weeds. You continue down to the Beard Street Pier. You dip your toes into the water at the exact place where you and June launched the raft. You get on your knees, soaking your shorts. You tip your head, lowering your ear into the water. If you can hear the water speak, it will tell you where to find June. You listen for June. The water has no voice. Its heartbeat, the one audible that night from the raft, is silent.

You walk home along the rocks, keeping your eyes on the water, tracing the precise path of the raft, looking below the surface. You pick up trash as you go. *If you pick up trash, if you clean the rocks, June will come home.*

Val follows these commands that pop into her head, letting them guide her out onto a jetty, as close as she can get to the place where she last saw June. The sulfuric mud between the rocks is charcoal gray, iridescent with an oily film.

Val slides her bag from her shoulder. She dumps the contents onto the rocks—a set of barrettes the girls shared in middle school, her half of a friendship necklace, a potholder from a fourth-grade craft project, and a handful of other sacred objects that she's transformed into talismans of June's return. One by one she hurls them into the water. She watches as some sink while others are carried away, bobbing and pinwheeling on the surface. If these things mean anything to June, she'll come back.

She sits on the rocks and drops her chin to her chest. She clasps her hands and places them in her lap. Then she prays to God or the river to shake June free, cough her up, spit her out, send her home.

Starting tenth grade is like being the new girl again, except this time June isn't there to help. Here is what Val overhears during her first week at school. She was raped by a stranger from the Houses and left for dead under the pier. She and June had been high on E when June fell into the water and drowned. They had been turning tricks down by the water when June was abducted.

She does not contradict these wild stories, but allows her classmates to spin their tales, hoping that soon they will forget the story of June's disappearance and notice her presence. Because Val cannot imagine going through high school without a friend to whisper to in the hall, pass notes with in class. So instead of calling her schoolmates out for their lies and speculation, she lets them slide.

In class, she allows her mind to wander from June to Cree, hoping that he will validate her, that his friendship will pardon her. *If he likes her—if one person likes her—she can begin to forgive herself for June.*

During the second week of school, in the middle of geometry she sees him—a hooded figure pacing beneath the scaffolding underneath the abandoned public school that is being converted into apartments. His face is obscured by his hood. But she recognizes Cree's slouch, his noncommittal gangster walk. She glances at the clock. There are twenty minutes left.

The teacher is drawing a line down the middle of the rhombus. He begins to write a formula on the board. Val watches Cree pace to the corner and return. Then she watches him pace to the corner and disappear. Her heart feels as if it's beating against stone. It's a minute before he returns, loping into view like he's walking in jelly. He pauses, then turns toward the corner.

Val grabs her backpack. Her feet echo in the hall. Her bag thwacks a bank of lockers as she cuts a corner too close. She skips the bottom four steps and hits the lobby. Her knees buckle under the weight of her jump. The impact lurches into her chest. Then she's through the doors.

She sees him rounding the corner, heading back in her direction.

"Cree," Val says.

He drops the hood of his sweatshirt. It takes Val a moment to realize that it's not Cree, but a ghost-gray boy in a baseball cap.

"Wrong man." He takes off his cap, revealing twisted cones of black hair. His lips are cracked. The cheekbones are hollow. Val can envision the shape of his skull.

"I thought you were . . . never mind." Val glances over her shoulder to see if anyone is watching her from the classroom window. "I should go."

"Got to get back to class?"

She can sense the tempered noise in the classrooms stacked up inside like shipping containers. After geometry is history. "I don't have to."

"It's good to get an education."

"You never skipped school?" The air feels crisp and illicitly fresh. The street is quiet, as if in deference to the classes in session across the street.

"I'm a different story."

"Why's that?"

"I skipped school until I couldn't." The kid puts his cap back on. "You stare out the window too much. Teacher's at the front of the room."

"You've been watching me?"

"You've been watching me. What's the difference?"

"Only because I thought you were somebody else."

"I know precisely who you are." He pulls a beat-up cigarette from a crumpled soft pack in the pocket of his sweatshirt. "The girl who took the raft out in the water. Big adventure for a young kid."

"I'm almost sixteen."

"Nevertheless. You shouldn't go around blaming others for your own foolishness."

"Who am I blaming? Everyone's blaming me."

"You snitch out the only black kid you know?" The kid flicks his cigarette away. "Careful what you tell the cops. Especially if it's not true."

"I don't know what you're talking about."

The kid rubs his lips and chin. "You caused Cree enough trouble. No need to be checking for him out the classroom window all afternoon."

"You know Cree?"

"I do. And I know you've been looking for him. But I'm watching out for my boy. A considerate kid like that doesn't need people like you spoiling his chances and ruining his outlook." He smiles, spreading the cracks in his lips until Val worries they are going to bleed.

"I didn't do anything. Cree and I . . . we. Never mind."

"That's right. Never mind. Never you mind about Cree." He turns and heads away from Bernardette's in the direction of Red Hook. "Now get back to class."

Val glances at her watch. There are a few minutes left to fifth period. She needs to make it back inside before the bell rings and a teacher catches her reentering the building before dismissal. She is about to head up the school's steps when the doors open and Mr. Sprouse appears. Val freezes, one foot on the bottom step, the other on the sidewalk.

The music teacher is dressed in black and carries a battered leather shoulder bag. June would probably have accused him of trying too hard to be cool instead of just being cool. If it weren't for the shadows beneath his eyes, he would seem boyish. But his distracted, troubled expression ages him, undermines his sharp cheekbones and full lips.

Val lowers her face. It seems impossible to her that she cried in his arms in her underwear and let him hug her nearly naked body.

But now she wants to hide. She feels exposed, caught outside of school during class. She wonders if Mr. Sprouse saw the boy she'd been talking to and made the same mistake she had, taking him for the person he'd seen her making out with in the bay. He probably thinks she dipped out for a quick kiss or worse.

"I'm sorry," she says. "It was an emergency."

Val is already planning what to say to the headmistress when she's hauled into her office. She wonders how long June's disappearance will excuse her behavior.

Mr. Sprouse looks both amused and startled. He smiles and shakes his head. Then he waves her on, away from the school. He puts a finger over his lips. "Go," he says. "Go."

Val hesitates, unsure whether or not to follow his instructions.

"Go," Mr. Sprouse says, waving in the direction of Red Hook.

Halfway down the block, Val looks over her shoulder to see whether anyone from Bernardette's is following, but she is alone.

Val has become a curiosity in school—someone to have around but to keep at arm's distance. She sits silently, hoping the other girls will forget why she is with them and only accept that she is there. She tries to trick herself into forgetting why she is eating at a table of relative strangers instead of with June. She goes out of her way to avoid mentioning her best friend, distancing herself from her disappearance, avoiding memories of her part in it. The problem is, among her more worldly classmates, Val needs June more than ever. Without June, she fears she'll do the wrong thing, expose her inexperience, and be exiled permanently.

Two upperclassmen invite Val to a house party one of the seniors is throwing, the kind of party June would have killed to attend, a party Val is only invited to because June is gone. She can imagine June nagging her all week, planning her outfits, dreaming about the boys who might be there. *If she goes to the party, does exactly what June would have wanted her to do, June will come back.*

Val kisses the mirror, squares the hand towels in the bathroom, doubles back to rearrange the guest soaps. She kisses the mirror again. *If she kisses the mirror, if she goes to the party, if the girls at her school will like her. If the girls at school like her, June will come home.*

Her parents seem relieved that she is going out. Jo compliments Val's outfit and sprays her with perfume on her way out the door. Paulie hands her a ten for a cab ride home. "Midnight," he says, kissing the top of her head. "Midnight and no messing around."

The party is in Brooklyn Heights on the best block where the houses back onto the promenade overlooking the water across to Manhattan. The six-story house with bay windows, the glittering river and city just behind its back garden, belongs to the parents of Anna DeSimone, who went to prep school in the Heights until she started hanging out in bars with her teachers and her parents sent her to Bernardette's. Anna takes a car service to school—a black Lincoln town car with tinted windows.

The front door is propped open by a brick. Val stands in a vestibule wider than her parents' bathroom, listening to the party behind the second set of doors. Through their frosted, etched, and beveled glass she can see distorted figures streaming along the hallway and up and down the stairs.

One group is clustered in the kitchen sitting on the marble counters, pressing their heels into the butcher-block island. The counters are littered with red and blue Solo cups half filled with brown and pink drinks and the pummeled skins of lemons and limes.

Two girls are sitting on the railing of the back deck, smoking and flinging their butts into a barrel planted with herbs. A boy rushes up to one of them and wraps his arms around her waist. He lowers her over the railing, her long hair dangling toward the garden twenty feet below. He bends her farther and her bottom slides from the railing until he is only holding her legs. The girl screams and the boy reels her in.

This is how people die, Val thinks. And tomorrow no one will blame these kids for tiptoeing toward disaster.

Val tours the parlor floor. There are two rooms that open onto each other and neither looks lived in. The walls are creamy yellow and hung with paintings, each lit by its own light.

Most of the faces are unfamiliar. The girls wear discreetly expensive outfits—high-waisted floral skirts, gold gladiator sandals, long cashmere sweaters. Others are dressed like designer versions of the women who loiter outside the Dockyard in cowboy boots and baggy cotton T-shirts. The boys wear khakis and frayed flannel. They help themselves to booze from a dark wooden bar.

The girls from Bernardette's are in the front parlor. They place their drinks on needlepoint coasters. In jeans, tank tops, and jewel-toned cardigans they look like Catholic school kids. Val perches on the arm of the sofa. *If the girls from her school talk to her first, June will come back.*

Anna DeSimone in a short gold dress and no shoes is circulating. Her skin is smeared with sweat and makeup. She is drinking from a martini glass the size of a small vase and holding a fistful of bills, mostly twenties, in her other hand.

"I'm taking a collection." She holds out the hand with the money to Val. "Don't tell me you don't smoke?"

If you act like you belong. If you make them like you. Val teases a five from her back pocket.

"I guess you don't smoke much," Anna says. "Bless you anyway." She tries to make the sign of the cross with her glass.

When the doorbell rings, Anna slips on the parquet and two boys help her up. There's an argument in the hallway.

The group from the hall appears in the living room. Anna is clutching the money and listing to one side. Two boys are trying to take the cash from her to count it. Behind them is a lanky guy in midcalf red basketball shorts and a matching oversized jersey and cap. Val recognizes him and leans back against the wall to disappear.

Irish Mikey is the waterside's petty dealer, a small-time trafficker in dime bags and seeds, nothing anyone gets too worked up about. He's the son of a former detective, which keeps him out of trouble. He used to hang with Rita back in middle school, but when he started spending more time over in the Houses, the Marinos put an end to that.

"Take yo time," Mikey says.

Mikey has the same patchy fuzz he called a beard back when he and Rita were tight. It masks the sprinkling of pimples he hasn't outgrown. He stands with his head cocked to one side, his cap off center, his shoulders slumped. Someone switches the music to hip-hop. The boys take the money from Anna and turn their backs on Mikey while they count it. They keep their shoulders hunched.

"Take yo time," Mikey says again.

Val knows he's laying on the accent, pretending he's dangerous, like he doesn't still live with his parents on one of Red Hook's better streets.

"Three hundred," one of the boys says handing it over.

"Now it's my time to count," Mikey says, taking the cash, counting it quickly with swift flicks of his thumb. He tucks it away, then fumbles in his pocket, pulling out three long Ziplocs of weed wrapped tight like cigars.

One of the boys slides the weed in his pocket, then glances over his shoulder as if he is standing in the middle of the street not on a Persian carpet runner. Mikey laughs and shakes his head. He catches Val's eye and she watches him dial her in.

The boy with the weed glances from Mikey to the floor and shifts from foot to foot. He jams his hands in his pockets. "Man, can you get us anything harder?"

Val is embarrassed for this kid twitching in his baggy khakis and two-hundred-dollar Nikes fronting like he has game. She knows that Mikey hates hard drugs, wouldn't mess with them.

Mikey raises his eyebrows and smiles at Val before giving the boys the once-over. Finally he purses his lips and looks to the side. "Yeah, I could get you some phials."

The boy stares at him, half understanding.

"Crack, man. That what you want?" Mikey tries hard not to laugh. Then he looks at Val. "Valerie, your boy here thinks I make my bank selling crack." He exhales, fluttering his lips. "Like I'm gonna sell crack to any of you kiddies. Like I'm gonna sell that shit period. You set these boys straight for me, Val." Mikey turns back to the boys. "Anything else I can do for you gentlemen?"

The boy with the weed dances in place, then backtracks so quickly he nearly falls over his friend. "No. No thanks."

Anna turns toward Val. "You know the dealer?"

"He was friends with my sister."

"You know the dealer," Anna says, turning away.

Two of the girls from St. Bernardette's slide toward the far edge of the couch so they can get a better look at Val.

The boy with the weed approaches their group. "Your friend is a creep," he says to Val.

"He's not my friend."

"Where do you live anyway?" the boy says.

The party moves upstairs. Some of the kids camp out in the bedrooms or in the walk-through closets that connect the rooms.

Some chill on the third-story deck. A few disappear into the large bathrooms and lock the doors.

Val wanders to the third floor, joining a group of kids in the master bedroom who are sitting in the windows, dangling their legs over the garden and the river. They are smoking a joint that Val accepts.

For a while everything is cool and Val is able to drift in and out of the conversation. One of the girls makes room for her on the ledge. The air is fresh and reminds her of apples. She reaches her hand toward the dancing skyline, fluttering her fingers, blocking out the lights of one skyscraper at a time.

A boy comes into the room and hovers at Val's back. The girls are sitting too close. They are nearly on top of her. She wants them to move away, to be quiet. She wants everyone to be quiet.

Val slides off the ledge and moves back into the room. She lies on the plush carpet. Each fiber is as thick as a caterpillar. She spreads her arms out like a snow angel digging her fingers deep into the carpet, holding on tight, anchoring herself.

She closes her eyes. The interior of each eyelid is a movie screen. The movie is rushing, fast-forwarding, the images blurring. She opens her eyes, but the movie retreats to her peripheral vision, rushing past just within sight. She shuts her eyes again, letting go of the carpet, pressing the heels of her palms over her lids. But the movie only runs quicker, draws closer. And Val feels that she's falling through the carpet. She reaches for the floor, gripping the pile.

The group from the window is standing over her in a semicircle. They are funhouse tall. Their faces are receding. Although they look far away, their voices boom in Val's head.

"Quiet," she says, unable to hear her own voice over the others.

"Why is she yelling?"

"Man, she's messed up."

The heads gathered above Val shift like beads in a kaleidoscope. She raises an arm to shield her eyes. "Stop moving," she says. "Please."

"I didn't move. Did any of you move?" a girl says. Then the whole crowd changes places, rotating like they're playing musical chairs.

"Stop," Val says.

"Someone make her stop shouting."

Val wants people nearby, but nobody close. She wants someone to tell her she's going to be all right, but she doesn't want to hear anyone's voice.

She gets to her feet. She remains bent at the waist as she lurches toward the bathroom. She steadies herself on the bed, then on the dresser, then opens the door and slides onto the cool tile.

"I'm not cleaning up after her," someone says as she closes the door.

The bathroom is a relief. She presses her cheek into the floor, closes her eyes, and tries to make her mind still. But now someone's rattling the doorknob, pulling, shaking the door.

"Take your fucking time," a voice says.

Val lifts herself from the floor. She sits on the edge of the marble tub, cradling her head in her palms. A fist, an open palm, a shoulder slam the door.

"Come on!"

Val stands. She steadies herself, her arms on the sink. The room is spinning. The floor is out of sight. She turns on the water and wets her face, drenching her hair. Someone is pounding on the door.

The only light in the bathroom is the orange glow of a small nightlight plugged into a socket next to the sink.

Val looks up from the sink and into the mirror. Her reflection is a dark shadow in the dark glass. She leans forward, then lolls back, trying to find a distance that won't nauseate her.

You fucked up, June says.

It's June in the mirror, dripping wet, river soaked. Her eyes sunken, her hair plastered down. Her face is the color of dirty marble.

You're a fuckup, June says. And then she slips away and Val is staring at her own face.

"Come back!" Val says. "Come back," Val says again, lifting her hand, slamming it into the glass, watching her own reflection fragment and distort.

There is blood running down her arm. She lies down on the tile. Someone has opened the door. "Just leave her."

Val has no idea how much time passes before the door opens again and a tall man lifts her to her feet, cradling her in his arms. Out in the master bedroom she realizes it's Irish Mikey. He parts the cluster of teenagers, silencing them with some sort of gangster grimace, and shields Val's face from the party as he leads her down the stairs.

CHAPTER ELEVEN

Cree wakes up, his headphones around his neck and his music down low. He lifts the frayed blue curtain that covers the window next to his bed. The grit caked onto the outside of his window makes even bright summer days look overcast.

His mother is already on her bench in the courtyard. Gloria's posture is erect, shoulders straight, knees pressed together. She wears her tight, white nurse's uniform with her solid walking shoes. A bright yellow sweater is draped over her shoulders. She holds a cup of coffee, which she blows on, spreading the steam. She didn't waste time this morning. She headed down to that bench the moment she was showered and dressed, taking her coffee with her. Cree puts his headphones back on, turns up his music, and cancels the sounds of the projects coming to life.

An hour later Gloria is still on her bench. The coffee cup is on the ground. She is sitting sideways, one arm thrown over the backrest, addressing someone who should be in sitting in a position exactly mirroring hers.

A couple of kids in no hurry to get to first period at the junior high pass the bench. They point at Gloria, snapping their fingers to punctuate their laughter. They double over, exaggerate the joke, then point and snap again. Cree knows what these boys are saying. *Crazy lady talking all kinds of shit. Don't care who sees her being all fucked up out in the wide open. Poke her with a stick, crazy lady ain't gonna move—like she's in a motherfuckin' trance.*

They are too young to remember what went down on that bench, how a couple of kids about their age shot Cree's father in broad daylight for no damn reason—an aftershock of the dwindling drug violence. These boys are too young to remember the time before Marcus fell when you had to duck behind your couch as shots rang out, dodging stray bullets that lodged in the lower floors of the projects. They missed out on when their hood was the crack capital of America.

These boys have it easy. They don't have to worry about gangs, crews, or getting jumped in. They don't have to keep track of who owns what bench, what corner. Plenty of drugs are still sold in the Houses and on the streets, but the lifestyle doesn't dominate Red Hook anymore.

So the neighborhood's old ghosts don't mean a thing to them. Cree doesn't blame the boys for calling his mother out. Gloria is down on that bench too often. But he guesses their mothers are among the women who climb the five flights of stairs and ask Gloria to reach out to their own dead.

Cree takes off his headphones and steps into the kitchen. An open suitcase is on the threshold of the kitchen and the living room. A pile of sequin tank tops, tight jeans, gold strappy sandals, pink pajamas, bright brassieres, and fussy thongs is strewn between the two rooms. Dance music is pumping out of the small radio. Cree can hear the shower running in the bathroom. He lowers the music. The bathroom door opens.

"Turn that damn station up," his aunt Celia says. "Turn it up. Don't make me come out there all naked and make you do it."

Cree raises the volume. In a few minutes his aunt appears in the kitchen wearing a towel around her body and another around her hair. She is rubbing pink lotion into her elbows. The scent reminds Cree of air freshener.

"You and Ray have a fight?" Cree says.

"You think this is a decent time to get up?" Celia sits on one of the vinyl kitchen chairs. She wipes beads of water from her forehead.

Unlike her sister, Gloria, who has widened over the years, Celia's slender with just the right amount of curve. Cree has to admit that she's a sexier version of her daughter, Monique. She has high, polished cheekbones and wide-set eyes flecked with gold. Her lips are an exotic pink-brown color that reminds Cree of chocolate-covered cherries.

"I've been up. Just not standing. I remember a time when you didn't get up till noon."

"You were a baby then."

Cree steps over the pile of clothes. "Is this an extended visit?"

Celia gives him a look, like *you don't know what you're talking about,* drawing her chin into her neck, squinting, pursing her lips. "I don't need to tell you how it's gonna be if Ray comes near me again."

"I give it a week," Cree says.

"Whatchu know about it?" Celia gets up from the table, digs through her suitcase, and ducks into Gloria's room to change.

Celia and Ray have a relationship that fluctuates between a simmer and a rolling boil. They've been busting up for years—mad, passionate fights that last for days before resolving themselves with bouts of lust known throughout the Houses. Ray and Celia got together too young, and Monique was born before they figured that out.

Even after Monique, Celia remained the Houses' queen bee, the girl on everybody's mind. Shirts cut down to there, jeans that looked like they took a lot of getting into, earrings that could knock you flat. She traveled farther from the neighborhood than anyone Cree knew. Fast cars were always waiting to take her to clubs in Brighton Beach or Queens. Celia used to walk Cree and Monique home from school through a chorus of whistles and catcalls.

She wasn't more than twenty when Monique was born. And it looked like she was going to stay wild long after that. But after her brother-in-law was killed, she got it in her head to become a corrections officer just like Marcus. The job suits Celia, giving her a useful outlet for her don't-mess-with-me attitude that Cree figures comes from a lifetime of unwelcome attention on the streets.

"Monique know you're here?" Cree asks.

"It was her choice to stay behind. She's a daddy's girl these days."

"And you've talked to Ma?"

"Saw her on my way in. She still out there?"

Cree looks out the window.

"Maybe you should just dig that bench up and take it out of the Houses," Celia says. "Maybe Marcus needs a change of scene."

"Mom's not moving."

"We all like to reach back into the past. No use in getting stuck."

"That's what Grandma says."

"You've been visiting with Lucy?" Celia dumps a pouch of makeup on the table.

"Maybe."

"On what account?"

"There's something I wanted to know about."

"Something or someone?" Celia presses powder onto her cheeks, sending puffs of sparkly beige dust into the air.

"Someone," Cree says.

"Dead or alive?"

Cree watches his aunt line her eyes, drawing their edges outward into the shape of almonds. "That was my question."

"Lucy doesn't give straight answers. But that doesn't mean she doesn't know them. In fact, the less answer you get, the more she knows." Celia puts down her eyeliner and looks at Cree. "Anything you want to ask me, baby boy?"

"Nah, Cee. I'm cool."

Cree knows that Celia's no longer down with talking to the spirits. She's been putting her gift to rest of late, apparently because she doesn't want Monique burdened with a whole bunch of dead people. This is part of the reason she sends Monique to the tabernacle on Sunday—to weed out the family history of ghosts and spirits, crystals and divination.

Cree suspects that Gloria is the real reason Celia's abandoning her gift. She's watched her sister withdraw, choose the dead over the living. She's seen her sit out on that bench too early and too late, unwilling to put Marcus's pension to good use in order to live somewhere better.

Cree heads for the shower. The water is tepid and the pressure's down. It's been nearly three weeks since he jumped into the bay after Val. His thoughts keep returning to her, trying to square her vulnerability with her daring, her sadness with her spirit.

He's been keeping an eye out for her, looping around her block, watching the light in her bedroom window go on and off. He's thought of ringing the bell, but he knows the Marinos won't welcome him.

Red Hook usually seems too small, bringing you face-to-face with people you want to avoid. But now that Cree's looking for Val, the place seems to have expanded. The gap between the front and the back of the neighborhood has widened. For the first time, Cree feels conspicuous on the waterside's streets. He feels as if people know who he's looking for and why. And maybe they also know that he was down by the pier the night June disappeared. So he walks quickly, hoping that his gait will let everyone know he has his own plans, somewhere he needs to be.

Cree and Celia head out of the Houses together. Not much has changed about walking down the street with Celia, except teenagers are now too intimidated to hoot or call. They just whistle behind her back and shake their heads in appreciation. It's the middle-aged men, the ones who don't care that the lady's a law officer, who still call out as she passes. Never mind she's been living with Ray for years.

Midday and Coffey Park is quiet. Two kids about Cree's age are shooting hoops. On the far side of the park a handful of hipsters are sprawled on the grass, letting their dogs mingle as they catch the late September sun through the webbed branches.

Celia's swinging her hips. She's talking something about a nightclub she might go to later. Talking about seeing what's up with her old girlfriends. It's going to be the perfect night for a little bit of crazy she tells her nephew.

Early arrivals for the methadone clinic have claimed the benches along the path through the park nearest the basketball courts. Cree's almost through this gauntlet when he hears his name: "Acretius."

He'd spotted his uncle when he'd entered the park but hoped the man was too strung out to notice him.

"Acretius." Desmond's voice sounds as if it's been trapped inside rusty pipes—a grating, desperate sound. "Acretius, boy."

"Leave him," Celia says.

Celia and Gloria have no time for Marcus's brother—an addict with a bad habit of making his problems everyone else's. Des makes a little bank collecting the neighborhood's empties. He can tell you which houses put out the most bottles, who drinks the good stuff and who sticks to swill.

Cree can smell his uncle behind him, a scent of sour sheets and Night Train. He turns. Junk has melted all family resemblance from Des's face, leaving only the essentials—skin, bone, and raw need. "You got a dollar?"

"No, man."

"Not even a dollar?"

"I said no."

Cree searches his uncle's face for anything left of his father.

A dog that looks like the business end of a feather duster scurries over and starts licking Cree's shoe.

"Leave the boy alone, Des," Celia says. "Else I'll have you written up for panhandling and loitering."

"A dollar. It's not like I'm asking him to win me the lottery," Des says.

"I'll write you up," Celia says. "Don't think I won't."

Cree can't take his eyes off Des's face. His skin is ashy black. There are pockmarks on his cheeks, hollow pockets that look like wormholes. His lips have thinned, vanishing into the pleats of his skin. Every time Cree sees Des he imagines that the world is out to erase every trace of Marcus.

"Traitor. Law man," Des says, looking at Celia.

"I'm a C.O. just like your brother. You'd call him a traitor?"

"Marcus'd be good for the cash."

A guy from the opposite side of the park with shaggy blond hair and wearing tight black jeans rushes over to collect his dog. Before he reaches Cree, Des coughs and spits, splattering the dog.

The rocker picks up the dog. "Fuck you, man," he says to Des.

Des reaches out for Celia's arm with one hand and points toward the rocker with the other. "You gonna write him up too, write him up for talking to me like he own the park?"

"You keep away from us, Des," Celia says.

Cree and Celia leave the park. They head down Visitation. Even though it's a schoolday, Cree keeps a lookout for Val. The parlor floor windows of the Marinos' house are open. Paulie and Jo are settled on the couch.

"Hold up, Cree," Celia says. "Something I got to do."

Celia is standing in front of the stoop next to the Marinos'. She's got her hands on her hips and is staring up at a second-floor window of the neighbor's house. She tosses her head back, opens her mouth. It's a moment before the word emerges. "Bitch."

Cree rushes to his aunt and grabs her arm. She shakes him off.

"Bitch," she calls, "I know you're in there."

"Celia!"

She steps away from Cree, closer to the building. Cree senses people coming to their windows.

"You think I don't know what you're up to? You think I don't know you're getting it on with my man?" Celia stamps her foot.

Cree looks up and sees a shadow back away from the curtain. Invisible hands slam the window.

"You think you can hide over here? You can't come to my house and make time with my man. You hear?" Celia tosses her hair, preparing for more. "Don't make me tell this street about your freaky shit. About how nasty you get." A passing car rolls to a halt behind Celia. She turns. "Whatyoulookingat?"

"Celia, come on."

She's looking up at the window again. "You probably think since I live in the projects you can take what you want."

Now Cree grabs Celia's arm.

"What?" she says, stumbling after her nephew. "You're telling me, I don't have the right to my freedom of speech?"

"Come on," Cree says, speaking softly, hoping Celia will calm down.

"I know you, Cree. You like the white girls. Always did. Just too chicken to admit it. Just you wait till they screw you over. Come to our neighborhood, thinking they can steal what they want."

"It's all one neighborhood," Cree says.

Both Paulie and Jo have come to the window.

"The hell it is," Celia replies.

By the time they reach the corner of Van Brunt, Celia has settled into her good humor. "Bitch never saw me coming. Now that I've ruined her day, I'm ready to start mine. Gonna enjoy every second."

"Later, Cee. Be good."

Celia kisses Cree on the cheek. "No, baby, you be good."

Cree hasn't been down to the fishing boat since he'd found Ren there. Something about that kid creeped him out. In fact, Cree was staying away from all his secret places, worried that Ren will be there or have just left. He doesn't want to find the inconsiderate, intimate touches Ren leaves behind—the cigarette butts, food containers, and graffiti. He doesn't want to know if the kid's been fiddling with Cree's setups, adjusting his telescope, rearranging whatever remains in the abandoned bar, covering the walls with more throw-ups and tags. Why Ren can't find his own places, Cree can't figure.

From a block away, Cree can tell that something is up with the boat. Usually, the hull, mottled with green moss, mud, and brown weather stains, is camouflaged by the weeds that cover the lot. It's only the small deckhouse, whose blue paint has chipped and faded that signals the boat's presence.

Today Cree can see the hull from the end of the street, scrubbed and shellacked, as bright as his father kept it. The wheelhouse has been painted too, not its original navy but a brighter shade of blue.

When Cree reaches the boat, he sees that it's not just the paint on the boat that's been refreshed. The deck and the instrument panels on the cabin have been polished. The torn captain's chair has been patched with vinyl and duct tape. On the stern of the boat is a looped, cursive tag: Cap'n Marcus.

He sits in the chair. It pivots without squeaking. He spins the wheel. It rotates freely. He looks out the window at the wall of the warehouse that backs onto the lot. He closes his eyes, trying to summon the sensation of being out in the bay. But even in his imagination, the boat remains run aground. He leaves the wheel-house and returns to the deck, sitting with his feet dangling over the port side, staring back in the direction of the projects.

He hears Ren before he sees him, whistling as he approaches from the water. The sound is exaggerated, amplified and thrown back by the surrounding buildings. Ren lopes into sight. His black hoodie covers his face. There's blue paint on the front and sleeves. His faded jeans, shapeless and styleless, are dirty and stretched at the knees.

"Fuck you do to my boat?"

Ren removes his hood. His hair is matted and clumped. He slips through the gap in the fence and takes his time making his way toward Cree.

"I said—fuck you do to my boat?" Cree says.

Ren shakes his head. "Any fool can tell I fixed it up for you."

"Who said it needed fixing?"

Ren's eyes are sunken. His cheekbones stick out like tiny fists. He pulls a crumpled cigarette from his pocket. Cree notices his nails are rimmed with dirt. "You gonna thank me?" Ren says.

"You want thanks for messing with my stuff?"

"You think it's nice or what?"

Cree hesitates. He looks over the polished deck and the fresh paint on the wheelhouse. "Yeah, it's nice. But don't you have your own shit to take care of?"

"I do what I want to do," Ren says, blowing smoke through cracked lips.

"Where'd you learn how to do this shit?"

"Let's just say, I took years of shop. Years and motherfucking years."

"You looking for work in one of the shops around here?"

Ren drops the cigarette and exhales loudly as he stamps it out. "I work for nobody but me."

"Don't you have to eat?"

"Don't you? I don't see you with a job. I don't see you thinking all careerlike."

"Truth is," Cree says, "I don't want a job in Red Hook because I don't plan to stick around here."

"Is that so? You making plans?"

Cree nods.

"You still chasing after that white girl? You gonna leave her behind when you go?"

"Man, you are too far up in my business."

"It's not your business when you carry it on in public, jumping into the bay after her. I thought the cops were on you for messing with her. Dumb move to be chasing her in public. How come you don't know that?"

"How come you're so interested in my shit? How come you got nothing better to do?" Cree says.

Ren loops around the boat and examines the starboard side. "I'm just observing is all. Observing and reporting back to you things that will help you out. For instance, that white girl—that's a no-good situation. I'm not saying the girl's a problem, but she's gonna be your problem. You think when the two of you start running around together people ain't gonna put two and two together?"

Cree looks over his shoulder. "Two and two about what?"

" 'Bout you being down by the pier that night before those girls got knocked off their raft."

Cree stands up. "Fuck you know about that?"

"Fuck I don't know," Ren says.

Cree is certain Ren will take him down, but he is ready to jump off the deck, rush around the other side of the boat, teach Ren a lesson about messing with his stuff.

"You better watch yourself," Cree says.

As he's about to run to the starboard side, three kids come down the cobbled street and pause in front of the lot.

"Look at him, talking to himself just like his crazy mama," one of them says.

"She got her bench, he got his dumb-ass boat."

Cree recognizes the boys who were harassing Gloria earlier in the morning. They are dressed in drop-down jeans and oversized polo shirts. Two of them have a dusting of facial hair over their lips while the third is baby faced and baby skinned.

"Get moving, boys," Cree says.

"Maybe we are where we wanna be," baby-face says.

"This lot's off-limits," Cree says.

"Don't look like it."

The three boys climb through the fence. One of them pulls out a joint.

Ren steps out from the back of the boat. "I'd listen to the man if I were you. This lot don't belong to you."

"Don't belong to him, neither."

"Who says?" Ren says.

"Me," baby-face says.

"Maybe I say different," Ren says.

"Fuck you wearing, boy?" the baby-faced kid says. "Your grandpa's hand-me-downs?" He looks at Ren's pants and then his eyes drop to his shoes. "Motherfucking orthopedic shoes and all. You got a walking problem? You lame? Or you just broke?"

"Told him," one of the boys says, clapping baby-face on the back.

"Get a move on," Cree says. "Get to school."

"School fool," baby-face says. "I don't need the son of no crazy lady telling me to get educated."

"What'd you say?" Ren says.

"You seen his mama on that bench in the PJs talking to herself?"

Ren shakes his head.

"You should check her out sometime," baby-face says. "Lady puts on a show."

"Is that so?" Ren says.

The kid nods.

Ren takes a step closer to the group of boys. "You saying that his mama's crazy?"

"Fucked up. Everybody knows it."

"For real?" Ren says.

"Damn straight," the kid says. "Like I said, you got to check it out."

Before he's done talking, Ren's got him by the collar. He lifts the kid half a foot off the ground, then punches him in the face. He lets go and the kid drops. Ren's on his knees, landing blows on the kid's ribs and stomach. The other boys back away.

The baby-faced boy howls as the blows land.

Ren throws short, tight punches. He barely pulls his fist away before he lands another. The kid tries to roll to one side, but Ren's got him pinned.

Cree rushes over. He grabs Ren underneath the arm and lifts him off the boy. "Enough, man. You're through."

Ren's trying to scramble out of Cree's grasp, his arms punching the air, his legs pedaling. Cree drags Ren toward the boat and leaves him there, panting. Then he returns and lifts the kid off the ground. "Go," he says. The kid's friends loop their arms around his waist and shoulders and help him toward the Houses. Cree squats at Ren's side. "You messed him up bad."

"Kids like that made the hood hell in my day. Shit ain't going to happen this time round." He wipes his brow with the dirty cuff of his sweatshirt. His breath is short. There's sweat on his lip.

"Let me buy you a slice or something," Cree says.

"No, man. You don't need to buy me nothing." Ren pulls up his hood and, once again, leaves Cree alone with his boat.

CHAPTER TWELVE

No one lets Monique forget that she had seen those two girls the night one of them disappeared. They had been her playmates until Celia explained that Monique and Cree were no longer welcome in the Marino house. Monique ran into them from time to time on the street and, as she got older, she learned how to cut them dead. She didn't have time for those babies and their make-believe.

Val and June had stopped by the park carrying a big pink raft. Monique was holding court with a crew of older boys. She didn't bother to break away. That raft looked fun, Monique thought—different than riding the park benches every night. Monique wished the girls would ask her to come with. But June only seemed interested in getting an invite to hop the fence.

Monique had been harsh. But when they walked off, she watched the raft bumping between them and tried to imagine where they were headed.

When the news trickled into the projects that June was missing, Monique felt chilled. She didn't have to consult Gloria to know that nothing good would come from blowing off a doomed girl. She should have invited June over the fence. It would have been simple.

People kept asking her about June. Some remembered they'd been friends. Even the boys in the park seemed to take note. *That was some icy treatment, Mo. Maybe you should have let her kick it with you.*

Sometimes the boys asked her questions. *Where your friend hiding out, Mo?* The whole neighborhood seemed out to bug Monique about some girl she barely knew.

Talking to the dead was her aunt Gloria's business, but after a week of getting nagged about June's disappearance, like she had something to do with it, Monique asked aloud, *Girl, where you hiding?*

She didn't expect a response.

The first time it happened, she was listening to her music, headphones on, volume up. At first she thought someone had messed with her playlist, downloaded a bootleg recording—some sped-up amateur street rap. It was a girl mc, that's about all Monique could tell. Her words were indistinguishable, a mad flow of jibber jabber. Monique took off her headphones. The music continued.

She was at home, lying in bed, trying to make something interesting of the ceiling, waiting for the day to prove itself. She figured one of the local girls was trying to rhyme below her window.

When she looked down into the courtyard, it was filled with old men, none of them dropping beats. She opened the window. The volume of the girl's voice didn't change—it just kept on spewing her messy scribble-scrabble style. There was nothing smooth in her rap, nothing complex. She just went on and on, rambling and saying nothing.

Monique put her headphones back on and pumped up the

volume. But the girl's voice conquered all attempts to subdue it. Monique heard her in the shower, in the stairwell, damn, she even heard her when she was talking on the phone.

That afternoon she headed over to the park, hoping for a large crowd to block out the yammering in her ears. She joined a group of girls watching two boys trade crass rhymes.

Pool. Short shorts. Flip-flops. Bikini. Towels.

Monique stood up. These were the first distinct words she'd been able to make out from the flow running through her head. "Cut your nonsense," she said.

The boys broke off their contest and turned her way. The girls stared at her. She recognized the looks on their faces.

"Fuck you staring at?" she said.

She didn't wait for an answer. She knew the looks were the same ones dropped on Gloria whenever she sat talking to herself on her bench.

Sneakers. Sandals. Slingback heels.

Ziti. Cutlet. Stromboli. Cannoli.

Once she was able to make out the words, there was no mistaking June's voice. Monique clapped her hands over her ears. She bit her lip. She fought the urge to talk back. Talk back to the girl, Monique worried, and she would become like her aunt, another crazy yakking with the dead.

When she could dial in June's voice on a distinct frequency, Monique realized that she was talking in lists—birthday gifts, family meals, favorite shoes, what she carried in her purse. She was cataloging days in her life, breaking them into the objects they contained. Monique recognized some of these objects from the afternoons she herself had spent with Val and June. *Popsicle, curtains, high heels, ladder, fence, hose, swing*—an elaborate game of make-believe on Val's backyard swing set on a brutal summer day. Sometimes she figured out what place June was running on about—*subway, roller coaster, boardwalk, sand, water, wave, pizza.* June was looking for bread crumbs to

find her way home. The only problem was that Monique didn't want
to hear it but she couldn't figure out how to make her stop.

The first time after June starting blabbering to her that Monique
tried to sing at the tabernacle, she couldn't silence the girl's voice
and find her way through the hymn. She sang slowly, struggling to
work through a song that was as familiar as breathing. She worried
the congregation knew what was happening to her, that she was
being reached by something beyond. *Window, school bus, boy, yard,
night. Taxi, spaghetti, theater. Ferry, candy apple, concert, tall ship, pier.*
In the middle of the hymn she wanted to scream. She kept her
eyes on the ceiling, ignoring the expectant faces staring at her—the
people who believed that it was God guiding her voice.

When she was done, Monique rushed up the aisle. Val had been
there. She'd stopped Monique and asked her to sing something for
June, as if June would come back if Monique sang a damn song.

Monique brushed her off like she had June. It wasn't until she
was halfway home that she took the time to consider how that had
worked out. Brush a girl off and it comes back to haunt you. Literally.

She dreads returning to the tabernacle. Sunday morning, before the
worship, she heads out of the apartment before Ray gets up. Celia's
been staying over at Gloria's and most nights, Ray doesn't even bother
to come home. Rumor has it he's creeping around the waterside with
a white divorcée he met at his AA meeting. He's been spotted down
at Valentino Pier tossing a tennis ball to the lady's scrappy dogs.

Monique's not much of a smoker, but if it takes getting high
before tabernacle to silence June, so be it. She knows what doors to
knock on in the Houses to score a dime bag, but she doesn't want
word getting out that she's looking. She hustles to the park hoping
to catch the crew of boys up early and up to no good, but the only
people out are a couple of joggers from across the expressway and a
few shaggy-headed white guys walking their mutts.

Monique crosses Van Brunt and heads down Coffey Street. This is the nicest street in all of Red Hook. Single-family brownstones with front yards and backyards and wide stoops flank both sides of the block. A few of them seem abandoned; others overstuffed with too much living—yards filled with stoves and baby carriages. Irish Mikey is riding his stoop as Monique hoped he would be. What Monique has always wanted is a stoop of her own, an open space in the world to sit and relax and not be bothered.

The few times Monique's been on the waterside of late she's noticed Mikey sitting out, sometimes alone, sometimes with a couple of the Puerto Rican dealers. She knows he sells dime bags and quarters—nothing that would attract too much notice from the heavyweight dealers in the projects.

Dressed in a blue basketball jersey and matching shorts, he's presiding over Coffey Street, legs spread, elbows on his knees. Behind him, the parlor floor window's open, and Frank Sinatra's pouring into the street.

"Remember me?" Monique says.

"No doubt."

"You got anything?"

"Such as?"

Monique glances into the open window. A woman in a pink housedress is brushing the leaves of a houseplant with a feather duster.

"You know," Monique says.

Mikey cracks a half smile and rubs the peach fuzz above his lips. "Maybe I don't know."

"Man," Monique says. "Why you gotta make this difficult. Weed. Not a lot, just a dime or a joint."

Mikey makes a clicking sound with his tongue. "I read you," he says. "Must be a million boys over the Houses who could have helped you out."

"Didn't want to ask."

"Yeah, yeah," Mikey says. "Trouble is, I'm not going be called out for stealing their business. So I'm not going to be able to help you. Let's just say my hands are tied." He holds out his palms to Monique like a supplicant.

"Man, a joint," Monique says. "It's not like I'm asking you to cut me in on some business."

"No can do," Mikey says. "But I gotta ask, what's a girl like you doing getting high before church?"

"None of your damn business," Monique says. "Thanks for nothing."

"Call it a favor. I'm keeping you clean. Doing my part for the community."

Monique turns and heads off. She doesn't look around when Mikey whistles long and low at her back.

Sometimes the tougher hoods, who don't cluster in the park for fear of being seen by the 76's squad cars, who keep out of the courtyards until dark, hang near the abandoned lot called Bones Manor. Girls don't go near the Manor unless they're turning tricks, that much Monique knows. But she's latched on to the idea of a joint, just one quick hit, something to silence June.

It's quiet over by the Manor. The corrugated iron fence is a patchwork of overlapping tags and pieces. There's something grim in the graffiti—drab colors and stiff letters. Part of the iron fence is bent back. Monique peeks in as she passes, catching sight of a giant puddle of water, the size of a small pond. Shipping containers and piles of cinder blocks surround it.

Partway up the street, she checks a group of guys, huddled with their backs to her. She knows the leader, Raneem Bennett. He's a little older than Cree. His crew isn't much of a gang, more like a posse of freelance criminals, every man for himself. Raneem tried to summon some notoriety for them by recruiting a few young hoods from Monique's school, handing them each a can of spray paint, and telling them to hit Red Hook with the tag "RFC," which he claimed stood for a new gang he'd formed called "Running From the Cops." A few weeks later the little hoodlums found out they'd been played and had thrown up dozens of "Raneem Fan Club" tags over Red Hook.

Monique crosses the street, passing the crew at a distance. At the corner, she crosses back, turns, and comes at them on their side.

"S'up girl?" Raneem says, as she passes.

"Hey yourself," Monique says.

"Looking for something?" Raneem says.

"Maybe," Monique says.

"Bet I got what you need," one of Raneem's friends says, grabbing the sagging crotch of his baggy shorts.

"I don't need that," Monique says.

"How you know if you haven't tried?"

"So what you looking for?" Raneem says.

"Got a little smoke?"

"Got a little smoke?" Raneem says, making his voice girly high.

"I don't talk like that," Monique says.

"I don't talk like that," Raneem mimics.

"Fuck you."

"Fuck you." It's a cheap tease, but it makes his boys double over.

"Never mind," Monique says, turning away.

"Not so fast," one of Raneem's boys says, grabbing her arm. "Where you running off to?"

"Church."

He jerks Monique's arm and yanks her so she hits the iron fence.

"You been a bad girl? You got something to confess?" He squeezes Monique tight. In his free hand is a soda bottle. He begins to trace the bottle along her collarbone, down between her breasts, over her stomach, and onto the waistband of her shorts.

She wriggles in his grasp. "Let me go."

"Let me go," Raneem mimics.

She tenses her body. Her limbs tingle and go numb. She fights the urge to shut her eyes, as if that could prevent what's coming. There's a screaming in her ears. June's yelling at her from the inside. Her voice is panicked, frantic. Her listing is manic, places and objects tumbling one on top of the other.

Raneem's friend taps her elastic waistband three times with the bottle. Then he digs the cap in hard.

"Stop," Monique says.

The boy with the bottle smiles. "I'm just playing." He thrusts the bottle into her crotch and grunts. He places his crotch against the bottom of the bottle and thrusts toward Monique, driving the cap in hard. Now that he's anchoring the bottle with his body, his hands are free. He reaches down the back of Monique's shorts, underneath her underwear. He grabs her butt with sticky hands and pulls her toward him, grinding her into the bottle. The boy is breathing heavily, grunting and panting. His breath seems viscous. Monique feels it settle onto her collar and chin like film.

She doubles over, folding into herself to keep him at bay. She wants to cover her ears, make June's screaming stop. It's all she can do to stop from shouting to cover the noise in her head. Suddenly, the boy lets go. "You see. No harm, no foul."

Monique rushes up the street. She's surprised that her legs work. Her breath feels trapped. Finally it emerges in tight bursts. At the corner, she huddles in a doorway and lets herself cry.

Ray's out when Monique gets home. She can smell Raneem's friend on her skin—a sour, meaty scent of stale sex and malt liquor. She takes a long shower. Her pelvic bone is sore. She can barely pass a washcloth over it.

She wraps herself in a towel and sits on her bed. Through the window she can see into other apartments where people are gathering for Sunday meals. She knows the courtyards are filled and the park benches are getting going.

June's calmed down. *Movie. Bus. Hot chocolate. Snow.*

Monique knows June would listen if she dared to talk. But she keeps quiet.

CHAPTER THIRTEEN

For the first time in years, the shrine has been tidied. The flowers in the vases are changed every couple of days. A new photo of Marcus sits in a durable plastic frame. The bench has been painted with a coat of forest green. Small plants are arranged in the patch of soil between the bench and the concrete path. One of them has managed a small purple flower. At first Cree thought this was his mom's doing, though he's never known her to care about the shrine before.

Cree puts down his community college application when he hears his mother leave the house for her afternoon shift. He goes to the window in time to see Gloria cross the courtyard and settle on the bench. She doesn't seem surprised by the fresh bouquet of pink and blue carnations in the vase.

School has let out. The courtyards are filled with kids slow-ing time until they are called in for dinner. As Cree watches, the baby-faced kid Ren pounded a few weeks back emerges from the opposite tower with one of his sidekicks. They look at their feet as they walk. The baby-faced kid is carrying a shopping bag and a two-liter bottle of Sprite. Cree tenses as they approach his mother's bench. He tugs on the window, wrestling it up. He leans his head out and is about to call down.

Then the baby-faced boy places the shopping bag on the ground. He hands the bottle of Sprite to his friend who uncaps it. Gloria slides down the bench a few inches. The boy with the bottle kneels and waters the plants. When he is finished, he empties the contents of the bottle into the flower vase and shuffles the flowers, with-drawing a limp carnation and placing it in the brown bag.

While his friend is watering, the baby-faced kid takes a cloth out of the bag and wipes grit from the picture frame. He tips out the dirt that has collected in the prayer candles before lighting them. The boys pick up the paper bag and empty bottle and stand in front of Gloria. Cree can't hear what they say to her, but she smiles and they shuffle off.

When they are gone, Cree rushes to the bench.

"What business do you have with those boys?" Cree asks.

"What boys?"

"The boys who were just messing with you."

"Who's messing?"

"They're messing with me by bugging you."

"Baby, nobody's messing with you. How come you're staring at the courtyard when you should be finishing your application?"

"I'm working on it."

Cree sits on the bench. He looks around to see if those boys are lingering. "Marcus thinks that this maritime program is going to be the best thing for you, baby. You're going to make him so proud," Gloria says. She reaches into her handbag and pulls out a packet of stamps. "Mail it today. I'm going to miss you when you're sailing up that river."

"Maybe I'll get a job out of state. Maybe I'll take you to live somewhere else."

"You know Marcus wants me to stay right here."

"You're hearing him wrong. When I was little, he always told me that we'd go live in Florida. Take his boat down there and everything. How come he changed his mind?"

"Your father isn't going down to Florida. Neither am I."

Cree leaves Gloria on her bench. In the apartment, Celia's suitcase is still open on the living room floor. A hot pink nightgown is draped over the arm of the couch. The cordless phone is missing from the base—probably hurled somewhere after her late-night blowup with Ray.

Cree's tired of this place. It's not just the apartment that's bugging him; it's the entire neighborhood. It's the cops who've kept their eye on him ever since June Giatto went missing. It's the white girls who cross the street as if he might make them vanish too. It's the hoods who cut him dead because he isn't affiliated even though those days are over. It's the rumors that Monique is too messed up to sing at the tabernacle. It's the boys screwing with his mom on her bench and screwing with him at the same time.

Cree gathers the materials for his application and seals them in an envelope. Although Kingsborough Community College is still in Brooklyn, it feels like it's in a different world—east of the Coney Island boardwalk, surrounded by the water. But Cree worries that it's not far enough away, that it will take him years of study to actually make it up the Hudson or out toward where the water gives way to horizon.

He runs down the stairs and dashes through the courtyards. This envelope is too important to trust to the mailboxes near the Houses where kids drop half-empty soda cans, cigarettes, and sandwich wrappers.

He crosses to the waterside, rushes down Visitation, forgetting to look in Val's window. At the corner of Van Brunt, he drops the envelope into the mailbox that is in full view of the bus stop, the bar, the Greek café, and two bodegas—a mailbox he imagines no one would dare to screw with. He lets the blue metal door slam back into place. He wipes the sweat from his forehead and heads into the bodega.

Normally, Cree doesn't think to buy beer. It's always been easy enough to snag a bottle from someone else's six-pack. But now he's got something to celebrate. Cree knows the bodega owner by sight, not by name. He used to keep the *Daily News* article about the small memorial held on the fifth anniversary of Marcus's death taped to the plexiglass case filled with bread rolls. This story has now been replaced with other news.

Cree goes to the refrigerators and stares at the beer. Because malt liquor is the last thing Cree would normally drink, he reaches for a bottle of Olde English. He takes it to the register. The man behind the counter gives Cree the once-over.

"You of age?"

Cree shuffles his feet.

"You don't want a better beer?"

"I don't really drink beer," Cree says. "It's a special occasion. Finished my application to college."

The bodega guy slides the bottle toward Cree. "Problem is I can't sell this to you. Let's just say you took it without my knowledge."

Cree swipes the bottle and tucks it under his arm.

"Hold up," the bodega guy says. He pulls a brown paper bag from beneath the counter and hands it to Cree. "Guess you don't know the drill."

Cree puts the bottle in the bag. "Forgot."

He stands on the corner of Van Brunt and Visitation trying to decide where to take his bottle—which of his hideouts is best for an evening with a forty. At first he thinks he'll climb the abandoned warehouse where he's stashed his telescope. He'll swig the forty and train his lens on the cranes over in New Jersey. But the empty longshoreman's bar is a better place. He can choose a booth and keep company with the old-timers' ghosts and the mermaid figurehead.

When he gets to the bar, the door is open and there's music inside—grinding, whiny rock. The busted furniture is cleared away. The floor is swept clean. A woman with jagged black hair is standing on one of the banquettes. She's using a long pole with a brush on the end to whitewash Ren's Japanese-style "RunDown" piece. A man in a paint-splattered plaid shirt is crouching on the floor with a sander.

They've done a lot of work. The long mirror behind the bar reflects something besides the dust. The wooden shelves shine, as does the long brass rail that runs along the lip of the bar.

He wonders if this couple knows how the late-afternoon light plummets in narrow columns through two holes in the roof of the porch out back, how the wooden figurehead casts a scary shadow if you sneak up on her the wrong way, that the empty liquor bottles with flaking and faded labels sometimes roll off the shelves.

He uncaps the forty. The liquor is sweet and thick, almost syrupy. He winces as he swallows. He closes his eyes and chugs quickly so he doesn't have to taste. His eyes water, and some of the liquor rises back up his throat. He breathes deep, urging the booze to stay down. He pounds half the bottle. The street sways and bucks. His limbs feel as if they are rising through water. Then everything settles.

As he walks down Otsego Street, a cobbled alley with vacant lofts and abandoned lots, he feels the looseness of the evening. The hours that stretch before him feel pliant, as if they are waiting for him to shape them.

He understands what keeps Gloria in Red Hook. It's not what is here now, but what was here back when—the history being buffed and polished away in the longshoreman's bar. As he crosses from this abandoned corner of the waterside back over to the Houses he becomes aware of the layers that form the Hook—the projects built over the frame houses, the pavement laid over the cobblestones, the lofts overtaking the factories, the grocery stores overlapping the warehouses. The new bars cannibalizing the old ones. The skeletons of forgotten buildings—the sugar refinery and the dry dock—surviving among the new concrete bunkers being passed off as luxury living. The living walking on top of the dead—the waterfront dead, the old mob dead, the drug war dead—everyone still there. A neighborhood of ghosts. It's not such a bad place, Cree thinks, if you look under the surface, which is where Gloria lives.

The courtyards and the park are only half full. Cree doesn't recognize the kids on the benches, but he nods as he passes. They clock his bottle and nod back. He sits on a nearby bench and raises the forty in an informal salute. He drinks and listens to the conversation that never opens up to him. No one notices when he walks off.

Cree falls asleep with the TV on and wakes up to the sound of someone knocking. The clock tells him it's two A.M., just about the time Gloria returns from her shift. It's too soon for his buzz to have hardened into a hangover. His brain feels melted and loose. By the blue glow of an infomercial, he stumbles toward the door expecting to find that Gloria has locked herself out.

The baby-faced hood is standing in the hall. He jumps back when Cree opens the door.

"Fuck do you want, little man?"

"Ernesto," the kid says. "My name is Ernesto."

"You know what time it is, *Ernesto*?"

"Don't take me for a fool." The kid crosses his arms, cocks his head to one side.

Cree rubs his head as if he can erase the muddy feeling in his brain.

"It's your ma," Ernesto says. "She went down. Over on Van Brunt."

"Went down?"

"I saw it myself. Me and my boy were tagging the mailbox by the bus stop. She came down the steps of the bus, then she froze like she'd been electrocuted or something. Next thing, she's on the ground. Some of them white kids from that bar called an ambulance."

Although his heart is clenching and his breath comes short and tight, Cree doesn't really trust this kid, this late-night messenger who's been messing with his mother lately. Then his phone starts to buzz, the number of the hospital flashing on the screen.

"She's alive?"

"Yeah," Ernesto says.

As he runs down the hall, Cree listens to the nurse explain that his mom is in the ICU.

"Yo!" Ernesto calls after him. "Tell your boy, I did good by you."

"My boy?"

"Ren. Tell Ren that I did you a solid."

He runs the two miles to the hospital, which takes less time than waiting for the bus. He's out of breath when he places both palms on the admitting desk in the emergency room. When he asks for Gloria, the receptionist takes her time tapping the name into her computer. While the computer pulls up the record, she sorts through files lying on her desk

"Gloria James," Cree says. "Gloria James."

Just as she locates his mother's file, Carmen, one of Gloria's coworkers from pediatrics, appears in the emergency room and takes Cree by the arm, leading him toward the ward.

"I was just clocking out when they brought her in," Carmen says. "We made sure she got a room." Carmen has a deep West Indian accent that can be harsh when she's being authoritative or soothing when she's patient. "It seems she's had a stroke."

"Bad?"

"Bad."

"And—"

"They don't know anything yet. It's too soon. For now they have her hooked up." Carmen pats Cree's hand. "She can't talk, baby. You should know."

His mother lies in a hospital bed. She's hooked up to oxygen. An IV is plugged into her hand. Her face is twisted, and her mouth is partially open like a photo taken at the punch line of a joke. A team of nurses swarms past him and wheels Gloria out. One pushes the rattling gurney; two others keep pace with the IVs and oxygen.

Cree stands alone in the room, listening to the whir of the instruments, the static of the intercom. He's been around the hospital enough to know not to follow when they take Gloria for tests.

Gloria's room has a view of the river, the tip of Manhattan and Jersey. Cree can see the rectangular silhouettes of the Houses—a few windows lit with weak light. The nurses bring Gloria back, hooked up to more tubes and more machines. Her breathing and heartbeat are underscored by short beeps and the rhythmic compression of air.

The doctor, a middle-aged Indian with dead eyes, tells Cree that Gloria is stable. It could be months before they know how much damage has been done. So maybe Cree would like to wait somewhere else, at home, perhaps, where he can sleep.

Cree says nothing and Carmen explains that he will be waiting right here. She's brought him blankets and pillows and converted three chairs into a makeshift bed.

When Cree and Gloria are alone, he takes her hand. Her face is twisted into its painful smile. He squeezes her fingers, careful not to jostle her IV. He wipes the tear that slides down her cheek.

The lights of Manhattan drop their reflections into the river. The taillights of cars on the expressway flow west. Cree watches the boats cut wakes on the dark water. He sees two tugs disappear upriver.

He knows he won't sleep. He goes down to the lobby for a soda. He takes his drink outside, inhaling the Brooklyn scent and expelling the antiseptic hospital air. He steps to the side of the revolving door, making way for patients who stagger in and out.

"Yo. Yo, my man."

Cree turns but can't tell who's calling to him.

"Yo, Cree. Cree James."

Cree glances across the street where a tiered parking garage casts checkered light onto the street. Standing in one illuminated square is Ren. Cree crosses to him.

"You still following me?"

"I heard about your moms. I brought you something," Ren says.

"I don't need it."

Ren hands over a long package wrapped in newspaper. "Your telescope. I thought you might want it to keep tabs. You know, from her window and all." He jams his hands in his pockets and turns. He pulls the hood of his sweatshirt over his tufts of hair. "Be well."

Cree watches him walk down the street, then bolts back into the building, and runs up the eight flights of stairs and rushes to Gloria's window. He trains the telescope on the street, trying to locate Ren. But the boy is ghost.

CHAPTER FOURTEEN

Val feels Mr. Sprouse watching her in the cafeteria. He's standing by the door near the lunch line, a small Styrofoam coffee cup in his hand. Recently, she's noticed the music teacher's eyes on her in the hallway or on the steps of the school—a gaze that lingers long after she expected him to look away.

Ever since Anna's party, Val has eaten lunch alone. The girls at the surrounding tables don't bother to keep their gossip to a whisper. They talk about her breaking the mirror. They exaggerate the story, confident she won't come over and correct them. Irish Mikey becomes her boyfriend, her pimp, a hard-core slinger of crack, a gun-carrying lowlife. She doesn't have the courage to remind her classmates that Anna was the one who summoned Mikey, hoping for something stronger than the dimes of schwag he sells. But even worse, they talk about June.

Val looks up from her lunch and sees Mr. Sprouse walking toward her table.

"Mind if I join you?"

The girls at the neighboring table slow their chatter to watch the music teacher and Val—a girl so lame only a teacher is willing to eat with her. *It could be worse,* she thinks. The teacher standing in front of her table waiting for her reply could have been Mr. Landers, the geometry teacher who scatters seed to pigeons on his way from the subway, or it could have been Mrs. Bloodworth who everyone is sure likes her students more than she should. At least Mr. Sprouse is good-looking. Even the bitchiest of her classmates would agree.

"Go ahead," Val says. "They'll run their mouths anyway."

Her classmates' rumors keep June alive. Somebody's heard that June was spotted near the seedy strip clubs underneath the express-way in Sunset Park. Someone said she ran away with her older boyfriend. Someone is sure she's living in a halfway house upstate.

"Now that June's missing, everybody knows everything about her. They make her up as they go along."

"Ignore it," Mr. Sprouse says.

"Easy for you to say. It's not like I have a million other friends to distract me."

"People prefer a good story to a real tragedy," Mr. Sprouse says. "Don't listen to them." He splays his hands on the table, transforming the scarred Formica into piano keys. His eyelids drop as he bangs out a song audible only in his head.

"What are you doing?" Val asks.

"Tuning them out." He plays another string of invisible notes. "It's Bach. Can't you hear?"

"No."

"Listen." He inclines his head toward the table. Val does the same. She hears the pads of his fingers drumming the plastic, then a four-bar melody whistled into her ear that matches the notes. His lips brush her earlobe, electrifying the fine hairs. Mr. Sprouse pulls his hands back and drops them into his lap.

"You cheated. You whistled," Val says.

"It worked. Ignoring people is an art. I do it all the time. On the other hand, I'm often ignored. You'll get the hang of it."

Erin Medina, a bottle blonde in the class above Val's, starts talking loudly, raising her voice so it carries through the crowded lunchroom. "So last weekend, you know, I had to go to New Jersey because of my little brother and whatever. He wanted to go to this lame theme park."

Val turns.

"Ignore," Mr. Sprouse says.

"The park was supersad, but you'll never guess who I saw." Erin pauses and sips her can of iced tea. "June."

Val stiffens. "Ignore her," the music teacher repeats. Val looks at him, wondering if he'll play his invisible piano for her, lower his lips to her ear once more.

"She was kinda beat-up looking, street kid style."

"You're sure it was her?" one of Erin's classmates asks.

"What kind of question is that? I'm not blind. Of course it was her. She'd dyed her hair black. So I went up to her and I was, like, 'Hey, I like your hair.' And she goes, 'Yeah, whatever. Thanks.'"

"You didn't ask her anything else?" the same classmate says.

"Like what? No, she was with this creepy older guy," Erin says.

Val stands up. She ignores Mr. Sprouse who's trying to draw her back into her seat. She marches over to Erin's table. The girls look up from their lunches. Val grips Erin by the shoulder, tugging so Erin must wheel round to face her.

"You're a liar," Val says. "You're a liar and you know it."

"You're crazy," Erin says, "and *everyone* knows it." She looks to her companions for backup.

Val's face feels hot. Her nose stings with the threat of tears. "You're liars," she says. She's shouting now, at this table of girls and the surrounding ones.

"You're lying about June. You didn't even know her. She'd never do any of the things you say."

Erin and her friends inch back in their seats, as if they are worried Val's going to strike or spit.

There's no way to hold back her tears. June isn't running around with a dangerous, older boyfriend. She isn't waiting on line for a roller coaster. She hasn't started wearing Goth makeup. She hasn't cut or dyed her hair.

"June's dead," Val shouts. "She's dead." The cafeteria falls silent. Several teachers stand up and start making their way toward Val.

June is dead. That's that. The moment Val says this, she knows it's true. It doesn't matter how many vigils are held, how many special assemblies. It doesn't matter how many of her classmates write themselves into June's life, how many of them try to reinvent June for their own pleasure. There are no songs, rituals, shrines, or prayers that will change this. June is dead. She's swollen, bloated, rigid, decaying. She exactly as she appeared to Val in the mirror, except real. And it's Val's fault.

"And none of your stupid lies are going to change that," Val screams, swiping Erin's lunch tray to the floor. She rushes toward the door of the cafeteria. No one stops her. No one prevents her from leaving the school. At the end of the street she turns back to see if Mr. Sprouse is following her, but the street is empty. Then she rounds the corner and heads toward Red Hook.

Val doesn't bother to keep an eye out for Cree. He's kept away from her long enough for her not to get her hopes up. She winds up in the park near Valentino Pier. She stops in front of the shrine to June at the foot of the pier. June's school photo is streaked and pale. The glass jars holding the seven-day candles are filled with rain. How stupid was she to have imagined her babyish rituals would

bring June back, that her dumb games, her ordering and organiz-
ing, had any significance over an event that happened months ago?

Val picks up a photo of June. She wipes the dirt from the cracked
glass. She punches the frame, splintering the glass, reopening the
wounds on her knuckles.

She runs to the end of the pier. She holds the frame like a Fris-
bee and hurls it into the water in the direction of Governors Island.
It wobbles, before stabilizing, cresting through the air in a neat arc,
then crashing into the water.

On the way back home, she passes by the Dockyard. The windows are fogged and when the door swings open, it reveals a dan-
gerously dark interior that smells of rotting wood and stale beer.
She knows Mr. Sprouse hangs out in there. She's seen him outside
smoking and talking to a couple of the disheveled artist types who
drive Paulie nuts. Her father would kill her if she ever went in
there—not that she'd have the courage to push open the door anyway. But she wants Mr. Sprouse to whisper to her again, so that she
cannot just ignore her classmates, but push thoughts of June below
the surface and figure out a way to move on without her.

At home Val cleans her bloody knuckles. Then she grabs Rita's nail
scissors and begins to cut her hair. She watches the strands hit the
sink. She cuts what she imagines will be choppy bangs. Then she
goes to work on the back, removing chunks and dropping them
in the toilet. Her arms ache. Her thumb and middle finger chafe
against the scissors's small loops.

Since Anna DeSimone's party, Val has avoided the mirror. She
washes her face and brushes her teeth keeping her eyes on the sink.
She does not want to see June staring back at her. Val drops the
scissors and rubs her hands through the jagged remains of her hair.
She is startled by her reflection, how the choppy strands make her
neck look long, her ears jump out, her forehead widen.

Her parents are sitting in the living room watching a police procedural.

"Jesus, fuck!" Paulie says when he sees Val standing in the doorway to the living room.

She scuttles into the kitchen, but he catches her. He wheels her around so they are face-to-face. "You look like you escaped the nuthouse."

Val shakes off her father's grip. He smells like aftershave.

"How come you want everyone thinking you're a little bit crazy?" Paulie runs a hand over Val's hair. "Fuck I'm gonna do with this?"

"You don't have to do anything with it."

"I'm gonna have a daughter running around looking like a schizo? You think I want people in this neighborhood thinking Paulie Marino's got a girl looks like a junkie?"

"I don't look like a junkie."

"You do. Like one of those crazy girls who stays up all night in the bar. You want that to be your life? I'm not having a low-life barfly for a kid. You're a beautiful girl. My beautiful girl." He tugs her hair again. "But I'm fixing this mess."

Paulie is famous at his firehouse for giving good haircuts. The boys used to call him Vidal Sassoon until he told them exactly who they could call Vidal Sassoon and it wasn't him. But he kept cutting hair, giving the regulation crops a little something extra that the boys could be proud of.

Val waits until Paulie returns with his clippers, scissors, a towel, and a bowl of water. He opens the door to the stoop and pushes Val out.

"You're going to cut my hair here?" She looks up and down the street.

Maureen, the art therapist who inherited the house next door from her grandmother, is watering her plants. She's got two yappy dogs that look like grimy lambs. Paulie keeps her at a distance. It doesn't matter that her father was a longshoreman and VFW member. It doesn't matter than her grandmother organized the rummage sales at the Visitation of the Blessed Virgin Mary. Maureen's been keeping company with a flashy customer from the Houses, a sleek, black man who's been visiting her late and staying until morning. *It's about boundaries,* Paulie explains. *There's the projects and there's the neighborhood.*

Paulie ignores Maureen as he makes Val sit on the bottom step. He takes a seat a couple of steps up, puts a hand on her head, cupping it in his rough palm, bowing it to her chest. He turns on the clippers and runs them along the base of Val's scalp. Her ears vibrate and the shaved skin prickles.

Val likes the feel of her father's fingers on her head, the pleasurable pain when they tug the longer strands of her hair. She likes how his large hands probe her scalp, searching for symmetry in the mess she's made. Finally he stands up and walks in front of her to even her tiny bangs.

"You look a little like a boy but you don't look nuts."

Maureen has finished watering her plants. "Nice haircut," she says.

Val stares at her, trying to figure out if this woman with her messy salt-and-pepper curls and long batik skirt is fooling with her.

"I said, *nice haircut,*" Maureen says. "Not a lot of girls can pull off short hair. You're lucky."

Lucky? Maureen is crazier than Val thought.

After dark it begins to rain. Val lies on her bed, tugging at the remains of her hair, listening to the wind whipped up by the water. The windowpane rattles. Val pulls back the curtain to watch the storm.

There is someone is standing in front of the converted church across the street. Val can feel the person staring into her window.

At first she thinks she has summoned June home—that by giving up on her she had brought her back. She pulls back the curtain wider. There's an adjustment in the vines as the watcher pulls back out of sight.

Val drops the curtain and turns off her bedroom light, then she peeks through the small gap where the curtain doesn't reach the sill. The watcher steps forward. Val cannot make out a face. Then in the quick, tapered flame of a lighter, she sees Mr. Sprouse. The light goes out, replaced by the ember of a cigarette. Val crouches on the ground, not daring to disturb the curtain as she watches her watcher, thrilled that he will stand guard even in the rain.

CHAPTER FIFTEEN

In the mornings, Fadi no longer walks from the subway, but takes the bus, riding close to the window on the right-hand side, hoping the driver maintains the speed necessary to bring Renton's work to life.

When his cousin Heba helps him out in the store, Fadi hurries through the Houses to Smith Street. He stands across from the painted columns and squints, jerking his head from right to left, trying to make Ren's jumper leap across the wall. He tries jogging down the block. At the corner, he has to sit down to recover his breath. Eventually a woman pokes her head out from the candy factory and glares at Fadi. In the daylight Renton's painting is nothing more than a jigsaw of black on a white background.

Fadi searches for a way to capture the mural for his newsletter but his digital camera only reveals the building's dormant façade. So he writes a small item, telling the neighborhood about the mural, urging them to look for art among their buildings. "Run-Down," he writes, "captures the beauty of Red Hook."

Ever since the morning they ran into each other on Smith Street, Renton's been hanging around the store. Fadi can't ignore the kid's hunger—the way he looks at Fadi's lunches, never asking, vanishing until Fadi has worked his way through fried rice and boneless ribs or a medium pepperoni pie, before reappearing in time to catch the leftovers.

Fadi throws odd jobs Ren's way. He offers him thirty bucks to mop up the back room—a job that allows Ren to make use of the sink to clean himself up. He gives him another twenty to restack the beer in the coolers, imports to the left, domestic to the right, pricey microbrews at eye level, cheap swill down low. Ren always refuses Fadi's offer to let him work the register. "I keep my business behind the scenes," Ren told him.

Ren usually performs his tasks when the store is empty. If customers come in, he often finds something in the back room that needs doing. During an afternoon lull, Ren finds some Windex and begins cleaning the glass fronts of the coolers. When he's finished, he climbs up on a stepladder, takes down all the toilet paper and paper towels so he can dust the tops of the refrigerators. When he's done, he meticulously restacks the paper goods.

"No one looks up there," Fadi says.

"The ship's coming in, boss," Ren says. "You can't be too careful." He's a stickler for order, for making sure Fadi's products are evenly spaced and neatly displayed. He's even more fastidious than Fadi, double-checking the white squares of tile to make sure no dirt shows. The shop is cleaner than ever, the shelves more organized.

Ren finishes reorganizing the toilet paper and paper towels and starts aligning the beer in the coolers. He makes sure not to get prints on the newly polished glass. He's nearly done when the wino enters. When he sees Ren, he freezes. "*Cerveza,*" he says, pointing first to Fadi, then to the back of the store. "*Quiero mi cerveza. Es tiempo.*" He touches his wrist.

"English," Fadi says.

"*Cerveza.* Beer."

"It's always *tiempo* for *cerveza.* Go." Fadi waves toward the back.

"No." The wino hops from foot to foot.

"No?"

"*Tú.*" He points at Fadi.

"Me what? Just get your *cerveza.*"

"*Traeme mi cerveza.*"

"What?" Fadi says.

"He wants you to get him his beer," Ren says. He's come partway down the aisle.

The wino stops dancing. He recoils a few steps as if he's been stung.

"Please just take your beer," Fadi says. He's been considering banning the wino for good. He wants to get rid of him before the cruise ship docks.

The wino tiptoes backward until he is standing outside the store. He curls his fingers and puts them in his mouth. He blocks the entrance. He points a finger at Fadi. "*La recompensa es mia.*" He dances from foot to foot as if he's walking on hot coals. "*La recompensa es mia.*" His voice is getting louder, a sharp, birdlike shriek. Fadi's having enough trouble keeping his own customers and attracting new ones without the wino adding to the problem.

"You want your *cerveza* or not?"

"*Sí.*"

"Go get your beer or get out."

The wino looks at Ren and shakes his head. "*La recompensa es mia,*" he says. Fadi watches two young women cross the street and enter the Puerto Ricans' store.

"Renton, choose him a beer," Fadi says.

"No, no!" He points at Fadi. "*Tu.*"

Fadi goes to the cooler and fetches a forty of Bud. When he returns with the beer, the wino is still cowering in the door, glancing at Ren, then stutter-stepping backward when Ren returns his stare. Fadi hands him the beer. The wino snatches it, stuffs a couple of crumpled bills into Fadi's hand, and scurries away. On his way out the door, he rips down the poster of June, crumples it, and shoves it in the pocket of his trench coat.

Fadi lunges after him.

"Slow down, boss," Ren says. "The girl's gone. Only greedy folk care about rewards."

"You wouldn't care about the money if you found her?"

"There's no way the police would hand over that cash to me even if I led them to her body. They'd cuff me the second I stepped into the station."

"So you wouldn't risk it for the fifteen grand?" Fadi asks.

"No." Ren puts his hands in the pouch of his sweatshirt.

Ren crosses to the plexiglass cabinet on the counter on which Fadi tapes his local news clippings. He points to a picture of the *Queen Mary* docked in the Red Hook cruise terminal. "Forget the girl, boss. You see that? That's where the money is. You've got to be ready. Shipshape."

While Ren takes inventory of the soda, Fadi opens the suggestion box and combs through this week's complaints. Among the twenty slips of paper only one pertains to June.

Tomorrow will mark the two-month anniversary of the disappearance of June Giatto. Please light a candle for her.

Fadi gets out his old laptop and begins to type up the grievances from all over Red Hook—the people from the Houses who want their streetlights fixed, the green thumbs who want people to stop sneaking into the community vegetable garden after dark, the person who wants the Dockyard shut down.

Two of the submissions make him laugh.

Yo, RunDown, you mess with one of my pieces again, I'm going to come after you.

"Creative" as it may be, graffiti is a crime and RunDown is a vandal. Stop defacing our buildings.

Ren finishes with the sodas and sits on a camp chair with the newspapers. The rhythmic rustle as he turns each page creates a comfortable rhythm for Fadi's work. He is almost done cataloging this week's complaints when he pulls a suggestion out of the box that makes him curse aloud.

"You cool, boss?"

Fadi nods and Ren returns to the paper.

Dear Citizens of Red Hook—do you know that our self-appointed community leader employs a dangerous criminal in his store?

Fadi stares at the slip of paper. He turns it over. It's written on a torn sheet of loose-leaf paper. The handwriting tells him nothing. He crumples the paper and drops it in the garbage. This is the first time he's rejected one of his submissions. But calling a graffiti artist a dangerous criminal seems ridiculous even by the standards of his newsletter.

Fadi phones the BBQ place across the expressway. He orders one chicken and rib dinner and one BBQ sampler. He gets a side of everything. He wants Ren to have more than his fill, have extra for the next day and the one after that. He sets up the folding chairs under the awning and puts a couple of beers in brown bags. He wants Christos and the wino to watch him sharing his dinner. He wants the neighborhood to know that he's not alone. He's not a stranger. He has an ally.

The last wave of morning commuters has disappeared up Van Brunt and the bus service has slowed to its midday schedule when Fadi hears someone calling him. He puts down *El Diario* and goes to his door. The Greek is standing in front of his restaurant, waving Fadi over.

"Come," he calls, waving both hands.

Fadi points back toward his counter, suggesting to the Greek that he's got merchandise in there, easy to steal. The Greek should come to him. Then he points at the crosswalk on Visitation. The Greek shrugs. Fadi goes back inside and pours two cups of coffee.

They meet in the middle of the street. Christos's apron is speckled with oil and streaks of red sauce. He smells of fried onions. Fadi offers him the coffee, but he waves it away, leaving Fadi holding a cup in each hand.

"You are too good for my information?" Christos says. "You do not care to print in your paper?"

"I print everything," Fadi says.

"Everything but what has to do with your own business."

"You wrote the thing about Renton? Painting a mural doesn't make him a criminal."

"Mural? What do I know about a mural?" The Greek wipes his hands on his apron. "I only know what Estaban tells me."

"Who's Estaban?"

The Greek jerks his head back toward the Cruise Café where the little wino is peering out the front door. "He says your worker is a criminal. A dangerous man."

"And what has he done?"

"Murder."

Fadi dumps the extra coffee out onto the street.

"I think the neighborhood has the right to know," Christos says.

"Who has he murdered?"

"You want I should tell my customers that you only print the news you like?"

"If you can prove it, I'll put it in the newsletter."

"Sure. Sure," Christos says. "You are killing your business. You don't even wonder why?"

"Because of the newsletter? The newsletter is for the community. It's for my customers." A car is trying to turn from Visitation onto Van Brunt. The driver honks, then leans out the window, cursing. They cross to the Greek's side of the street.

"You even check with your customers before you write? You make other people's business your business. You tell them what to do. Where to go. The vigil for the missing girl? You announce it to the entire world."

"It was a public service."

"For their public." He jerks his head down Visitation toward the Marino house. "You think they like you to advertise their event at the church? That you print your theories about their tragedy. Just sell your coffee and your papers. Better for you."

Fadi takes a sip of his coffee. "Thanks for the tip," he says, crossing back to his store.

"My information, you print it," the Greek calls. "You print it or I tell people myself."

He can't imagine how the Greek is so easily convinced by the wino.

Two kids taking a holiday from school are hovering over the candy bars. They hustle out the door when Fadi returns. He sits on his wobbly stool and picks up his latest newsletter. Submissions for his complaint box are up, but his customers are dwindling. He turns the paper over and stares at the picture of June. She's out of reach. The news and the neighborhood have moved on.

When Ren comes in, Fadi doesn't mention his conversation with the Greek. From time to time the wino appears on the doorstep of the Greek's, dancing in place, biting his fingers and pointing at Fadi's.

"Little man's bugging today," Ren says.

For dinner Fadi orders pizza. It's too cold to eat outside, so he and Ren sit behind the counter. They are nearly done when something crashes through the window. The glass cracks. Fadi rushes outside. The sidewalk in front is empty. From the street he watches the glass slide from the window and splinter on the street and inside his store.

A jagged hunk of metal lies on the floor of the bodega. Shards of glass are strewn over the pastry display, the Coca-Cola cooler, and the floor in front of the counter.

Street sounds flood the store. The night air blows in, rustling the newspapers and making the items on the bulletin board flutter. Fadi looks over at the Greek's. The Cruise Café is shuttered. People in front of the bar cross into the middle of the street to get a better look. When they realize that no one is hurt, they retreat to their post. The Puerto Ricans stay out of sight.

The window, nearly ten feet long and four feet high, will be expensive to replace. It will take a week to get someone out here to do it. Fadi grinds the heels of his hands into his eyes.

He and Ren survey the damage. They take a broom handle and clear the remaining glass from the window frame.

"Boss, I got your back," Ren says.

Fadi will have to survive a week with his roll gate down. Between the ads taped to the glass and the fridges backed against it, the shattered window didn't admit much light, yet with the gate down it will appear that the store is closed.

Ren clears out the last of the large pieces of glass. He brings up the industrial vacuum from the basement and gets to work on the bits underneath the refrigerators. "You trust me, boss?"

"Sure," Fadi says.

"Give me a C-note and I'll get to work. We need supplies."

Fadi gives the kid a hundred and a couple of twenties from the register, hoping that he'll keep the change from whatever he plans to do and buy himself some new T-shirts.

"I'll be back before you open."

Fadi mans the counter until eleven. His only customer is Jonathan.

There's a cot in the basement for emergencies. Fadi's only been asleep a couple of hours when he hears footsteps above his head. He rushes up the rickety basement steps, nearly wrenching the handrail from the wall. Ren is standing in front of the broken window. In either hand he holds a bag from Nuthouse 24-Hour Hardware.

"Easy boss," he says. "I didn't mean to disturb."

Fadi rubs his eyes. "What are you doing?"

"I thought I'd dress up your gate, seeing as how it's going to be down for a while, if that's copacetic. Just a little touch-up. You know, attract business instead of dispersing it." He places his bags on the floor. He selects six cans of spray paint and heads for the door.

"What's the name of this place anyway?" Ren says.

"Hafiz Superette," Fadi says.

"What the hell is a Hafiz?"

"Hafiz is my father."

"Anyone around here know that?"

"Probably not."

"So what'cha want to call it?"

"You want me to rename it right now?"

"Preferably," Ren says.

Fadi stares at the new awning Christos ordered when he renamed his restaurant the Cruise Café. The name seemed desperate, overly aspirational—snubbing Red Hook in favor of the tourists.

"Come on, boss," Ren says.

"The Daily Visitation." Ren nods in approval and rattles the can. Fadi tenses, holding his breath as the first spray hits the gate. It's off to the left—a long black arc, like the opening of a parenthesis. "What's that?"

Ren doesn't turn around.

"What is that?" Fadi says as Ren paints a stripe to the left of the arc.

Ren lowers the can. "You're making me sweat. You trust me or not?"

"I trust you."

"You're acting like the police. Don't you have winks to catch?"

Fadi leaves Ren and walks through the dark interior of his store. With the gates down the place feels like a cave. He sleeps fitfully. At five thirty, he rises. He takes toothpaste and a toothbrush from his shelves and washes up in the industrial sink. Upstairs, Fadi brews coffee, and assembles a tray of pastries. He takes a folding chair from the storage room and carries it out to the street. He places the tray of pastries and a large Styrofoam cup of coffee next to Ren. Ren doesn't look up from his work.

Ren has painted the back half of a cruise ship. The ship takes up the entire length of the roll gate. She's setting sail, heading away from the neighborhood, down Visitation in the direction of the cruise terminal. Half of the upper deck and two of the smokestacks are visible. Lifeboats hang over one side. On the stern is the ship's name: *The Daily Visitation.*

Fadi steps back so he can take it in. The ship's stark colors are offset by the electric blue green water and aqua sky.

"Walk," Ren says, pointing up the street.

Fadi obeys. As he does so, the ridges in the roll gate bring the ship to life, making her bob and sway—sailing in place on Visitation. The water at the base of the ship ripples as Fadi passes.

Ren doesn't wait for Fadi's approval. "It's the bomb," he says. "Now you're prepared. No one from the boat is going to skip over your place."

Fadi paces back and forth, examining the ship from different angles, checking that it animates when approached from either direction. Two tollbooth workers cross from the Greek's to get a better look. When they are done, they buy two large coffees, the papers, and buttered rolls. After they leave the store, Fadi calls out to Ren, "Breakfast?"

Ren wipes his hands on his sweatshirt, adding to the streaks and splashes of paint. He shoves a donut into his mouth and palms two more. "I got to sleep. I need to regenerate." He lopes down Van Brunt toward the water. Fadi watches him go. "I think we're ready for the boat now, boss," Ren calls. "You and me are going to give that mother a New York welcome."

When Ren is out of sight, Fadi stalks the pavement in front of his gate watching the ship ripple and sway. People stop to stare at Ren's work. Someone nearly misses the bus. Christos comes to the door of his restaurant and curses at Fadi in Greek.

CHAPTER SIXTEEN

A few minutes after the bell rings, there is a knock at the door to Jonathan's classroom. Val is standing outside, a slip of paper in her hand.

"I transferred into your class, Mr. Sprouse. I hope that's okay."

Jonathan can hear the arrhythmic thunk and metallic reverb of a basketball being dribbled in the gym downstairs. He hesitates, taking in Val's choppy haircut that makes her look like a 1960s film star, then steps aside so she can enter. The rest of the girls bow their heads together, only separating so she pick a path through their chairs. Val finds a seat at the back of the room by the window.

Jonathan presses play on the stereo and soon his mother's voice fills the room. He knows he should retire his mother's second-run Broadway recordings and introduce something like *Le Nozze di Figaro, The Magic Flute,* or *The Goldberg Variations*—music that's worth teaching. But ever since he found Val under the pier, he feels drawn to his mother's music, as if by playing her recordings he might rescue her as well.

Val rocks back in her chair.

"Hey, Val, don't break that window like you broke Anna's mirror."

Jonathan glances up and catches two juniors, Stacy and Meredith, looking at Val.

Jonathan puts a finger to his lips. His students barely tolerate his class, so why should he care if they know adagio from allegro, recitative from aria? They use his class to sleep or catch up on text messages. When their whispers rise to conversation level, he turns up the volume on the stereo so they'd have to scream to hear one another.

The girls lean closer together. "I still can't believe how fucked up she was at that party."

"We never should have invited her." They glance back at Val.

For a couple of weeks the girls in Jonathan's class have been whispering about a student who got high and put her fist into a bathroom mirror at a party. He's heard of worse transgressions, but the school seems fixated on this story.

Jonathan approaches Stacy and Meredith. "If you two are going to continue to talk, I think it would be better if you did it in Sister Margaret's office."

"Sorry," Stacy says.

"Yeah, sorry," Meredith says. They pull their chairs apart.

"It's too late for sorry," Jonathan says. "Get out."

The whole class stares at him. His heart is beating fast, and his fingers tingle as he points to the door.

"What?" Stacy says.

"I said, get out. Or have you never been sent out of a room before?"

"Not in high school."

"Now."

The girls hesitate. Jonathan walks behind their chairs and grabs hold of the plastic backrests. He tips the chairs forward. The girls scramble to their feet, grabbing their book bags as they head for the door.

Jonathan sits down on the piano bench and clasps his hands to hide their trembling. "Does anyone else have something to say? Maybe I'm missing something? Is it too much for you to sit and listen to music quietly? Or perhaps this *is* too difficult. Perhaps it *is* too much to ask. Maybe one of you has a story about last weekend's party you want to tell. Or maybe now is the time to share some critical information on the behavior of one of your classmates. Maybe because this is not math or history and because we don't have any homework, now is the perfect time for you to discuss your hangovers and how cool you all are for being able to handle more Jell-O shots or Slippery Nipples than your friends."

The girls shift in their seats. Some look at the ground. They're either ashamed or smiling. Jonathan doesn't care which. "So now I suggest you shut the hell up and listen to *Cabaret*." Jonathan slides down on the piano bench. One of the girls will probably report him to the headmistress for telling the class to shut up but there's nothing he can do about it now. He turns the volume up as loud as it will go so he doesn't have to hear himself think.

When the bell rings, Val approaches the piano. "Mr. Sprouse?" She draws a hand along the piano's black lacquer finish. "Never mind."

Before she can whisk it away, Jonathan reaches out and takes her hand. He squeezes, feeling her long, delicate fingers and smooth palm, trying to erase her classmates' words. Val stares at their hands, then pulls hers back.

"I have to go, Mr. Sprouse."

The door slams. Jonathan listens to the noises of the school emptying, the voices carrying down the stairs and out onto the street.

.   .   .

Even though he's sure he'll be caught in the impending downpour, after school Jonathan walks back to Red Hook.

It's Friday and the rain brings an end-of-week melancholy. Soon he will be in the bar, wasting time until he goes into the city to accompany Dawn and stay up late and sleep it off tomorrow. But for now, on these blocks between Carroll Gardens and Red Hook, he can cling to the quiet and the calm, the gradual Friday emptying, the slow release before the gearing up. For a few blocks he can pretend that he's just another commuter walking home at the end of the workweek, ready to settle rather than hurtle into the weekend.

The charmless pedestrian bridge over six lanes of snaking traffic is empty. Before long the expressway will slow to a standstill—traffic chained together like a borough long subway, the whir and splash of motion replaced by a solid, plaintive honk.

At the end of the walkway, Jonathan catches sight of Val. She's halfway up the street, her kilt plastered to her legs by the wind. At first he considers turning back and taking a different route. He remembers her delicate hand briefly inside his—an innocent gesture so easily transformed.

She's looking back and slowing her pace so they are now side by side. Jonathan switches his umbrella from one hand to the other, gathering Val under its canopy. She pulls in closer to Jonathan. He looks over his shoulder to see if anyone else is on the block. Their footsteps fall into sync.

"Weren't you the one who told me to ignore other people?" Val says.

"They weren't disrupting the class."

"You know, Mr. Sprouse, now that June's gone, you probably know me better than anyone."

"You don't have to call me Mr. Sprouse outside of school."

"Okay. But you do know more about me than anyone else does."

"I'm sure that's not true," Jonathan says.

He wonders if Val has spotted him outside her window, watching her from behind the vine-covered gate of the abandoned church, making sure she doesn't run down to the water or other places he might not be able to reach her.

"You even know about my first kiss," Val says. "You were there. You saw. Down by the pier. You're the only person who knows."

They cross from Carroll Gardens into Red Hook where the wind is making the telephone wires whine. The rain falls fiercely. It's not even four o'clock, but the sky is the color of carbon steel. The tops of the Red Hook Houses are invisible in the storm. Val draws in closer, huddling under the umbrella.

"June used to tell me everything," Val says. "Now that I finally have a secret to tell her she isn't here. It's not fair."

"So you want to hear one of my secrets instead?"

"Yes," Val says. "Tell me something good."

Jonathan pats his pocket for a cigarette, then thinks better of it. He could tell her about Dawn, the drag queen who he guesses is his best friend. But the girl is an open book and will share the nitty-gritty of her life with the person next to her on the subway. He could tell Val about his father, whom he hasn't spoken to since his mother's death, who turned a blind eye to Eden's flirtations. But these secrets are not his own. In fact, since he has so few friends, secrets are hard to come by. "There's this bartender that I sleep with once a month."

"Yeah?"

"That's it. Not satisfied?" Jonathan says.

"No," Val says.

"Okay, okay. I never enjoy it."

"Really?" Val stops walking.

"You sound happy."

"No. It's just that's a good secret."

Jonathan's arm aches from holding the umbrella. His hips and stomach muscles feel tired from the effort of keeping some distance between him and Val. He worries that if he relaxes too much, the accidental collision of their hips will become comfortable.

From down the block, he can make out the neon glow from the Dockyard's window reflected in the wet sidewalk. The bench outside the bar is empty. They stop outside his door. Val waits before stepping out from under the umbrella. After she goes home, Jonathan knows he will be obliged to check on her. He will stand beneath her window, keeping her safe, until he has to join Dawn.

"If you have homework or anything to do, you can do it here," Jonathan says, indicating the door to his building.

"Cool . . . Jonathan." Val lets his name hang between them, before following him into the entryway.

At the threshold, Jonathan realizes what his apartment must look like to someone unaccustomed to the sight of all-week insomnia— the sticky-bottomed whiskey glasses, the stack of empty jewel cases, the crumpled bedding, the greasy pillow on the couch.

"Nice place," Val says.

"It's a hole." Jonathan collects a few glasses from the coffee table and walks them to the sink.

Val throws the pillow back onto the bed and sits on the couch. "So," she says. She puts her feet up on the coffee table.

Jonathan walks to the far end of the studio and opens a window onto the fire escape. He lights a cigarette. He takes three deep drags, then flings it to the concrete garden below.

"Don't worry," Val says, "my mother smokes."

"So did mine."

"She quit?"

"No, she drowned."

Val drops her feet to the floor and sits up straight. Her mouth opens and shuts. "Jesus. Really?"

"She was drunk. She was always an imperious drunk, which

made it hard to argue with her. She took out our speedboat and flipped it."

"You saw?"

Jonathan picks up an empty bottle of Jameson and tips it to see if the green glass is hiding anything. "She'd been drinking from long before her five o'clock cocktail hour until after dinner. As usual she was paranoid about being a washed-up singer—which she was. No shame in that. She'd had a long run. But you couldn't talk sense into her. *Patti LuPone this, Bernadette Peters that*—she was always running her mouth about stars with staying power. She blamed anyone in spitting distance for the end of her career—my father, the housekeeper, our cook." Jonathan busies himself with his drink so he can ignore Val's reaction to his admission of wealth. "Most of all she blamed me. You know, *If I didn't have you to look after I wouldn't have missed out on this and that role*. Which was bullshit, because by the time I was born her career was coming to an end. Anyway, that night she outdid herself. I wouldn't take the bait when she needled me, which infuriated her. Eventually she told me I was boring her and she was going to take the speedboat out. *Good*, I thought. *That'll get rid of her for a little while at least*. I was basically pushing her out the door, daring her to get in that damn boat. Anything to shut her up."

Eden had laughed as she climbed on board the boat, the keys on their orange key float in one hand, a highball in the other. Whiskey sloshed over the dash of the Chris-Craft. It took her a few minutes to get the key in the ignition. Jonathan came outside to watch her struggle. He enjoyed it, seeing her fumble with the key, get her scarf tangled in the steering wheel. She hadn't even untied the ropes, so he figured Eden would just run in place, give up, and pass out on board. But she took off and took part of the dock with her.

About a quarter mile out into the sound the boat banked hard. It flipped, then barrel-rolled, and flipped again. Eden crested into the air, her long scarf fluttering like a useless wing. Then she disappeared into the inky sound.

"Did you swim out?"

"No."

Eden wasn't found until the next morning washed ashore on a rocky stretch of beach. As Jonathan watched the paramedics lift her lifeless, frigid body into the ambulance, he knew he wouldn't come back to Fishers Island. He should have stopped Eden, but he'd wanted her to suffer, if only for a moment. She hadn't bothered to come into the city to see his jazz quartet. She'd even laughed when he told her they'd been written up in the *New Yorker*. "Don't get your hopes up, Jonny," she'd said. "You don't have the stomach for the business."

One look at Eden's rigid, pale form told Jonathan that the brittle noise of the dock shearing off and the whoosh and crash of the splintering boat deep in the sound would replace all the tranquil music summoned by Fishers—the low rush of the grass, the cresting wail of a soaring seabird, the call-and-response of two buoys. He knew he could never cross the sound from the mainland without seeing Eden flying into the water and that the memory of him standing on the dock and letting his mother drown would haunt him if he ever set foot in their seaside home again.

Val picks up a CD from the coffee table and scrapes a nail across the scratched jewel case.

"That's one of hers." He points at the recording of *Mame* in Val's hand. "My mother, Eden Farrow, the drowned smoker."

"You've been making us listen to your mother in class?"

Val teases out the liner notes from the case and looks at the photo of Eden in a long red coat with mink collar. She bites her lip, worrying it with her teeth until the flesh turns white. "Can I ask you something, Mr. Sprouse?"

"Sure."

Val takes a deep breath and flops back on the couch, pulling into herself. She turns and looks out the window across Van Brunt. For a moment, Jonathan thinks she's given up on her question. Then in a distant voice she says, "Are you still mad at her or are you only mad at yourself?"

"What a question."

"Sorry." Val tosses the CD back onto the table. "If you have stuff to do, I can do my homework."

"I have a few things to do," Jonathan says, looking around.

Propped against the wall are the storyboards for a jingle for a chain of women's gyms in the tristate area. The drawings show women in a step aerobics class, women on StairMasters, women sipping smoothies at a juice bar. Jonathan's mind is blank. The images conjure no music. He props them on the windowsill. For two weeks he's been deleting voice mails from the advertising agency. In a few days they'll take him off the job.

After a while, he realizes he's not looking at the storyboards. He's watching Val's reflection in the window. She has curled up on the couch, a textbook cradled in her arm. She lifts her head, and their eyes meet in the reflection.

"I'm working," Jonathan says.

"You're writing music? Can I hear?"

Jonathan puts down his pen.

"A song? Jazz? Classical?"

It's been ages since Jonathan wrote anything other than these ridiculous jingles. "A ditty," he says. "Not worth your time."

Val sticks the top of her pencil in her mouth and chews the metal below the eraser, then begins writing in her notebook. Jonathan tries to focus on the exercising women, but all he can hear is the scrape of Val's pencil across paper.

Val drops her pencil and slams her book. "Can I order a pizza? Is that weird?"

Jonathan reaches into his pocket for his wallet.

"No," Val says. "Let me pay. I *owe* you."

"Do you?"

"I owe you my life."

"I'm flattered," Jonathan says. He's surprised by his own sincerity.

He can tell that Val's not really paying attention to her book while they wait for the deliveryman. Her eyes keep lifting from her work, searching out his in the window.

When the doorbell rings, she leaps from the couch. "Don't you feel bad for delivery boys in the rain? They have to work so hard so we can stay dry." Jonathan looks at Val, half expecting a cloud of sarcasm to have swept across her face. But her eyes are wide open, and a considered smile plays on her lips.

Jonathan listens to her rush down the stairs. He hears the sound of the front door opening, then the amplification of the street noises. Soon she is running back. She puts the pizza on the coffee table and lifts the lid. Steam rises toward her face.

Jonathan walks to the foot of his bed and looks out the window onto Van Brunt. The rain has brought the night down with it. The street is dark. The streetlights come up, unsteady behind the downpour.

"Want some?" Val asks.

He sits down next to her. She frees a slice for him, but he lets it sit on the cardboard. While Val eats, he flips through her textbook. Her notes on World War I slide to the floor.

Thunder roars. He is holding Val's textbook, tapping a lively beat onto the cardboard cover. A lively energetic beat of young legs running to stay young, legs trying never to grow old. He's thinking of Val running down the stairs to get a pizza, running through the Houses, running down to the pier. A rhythm, a beat, a repetition, a jingle. Now he has something.

Thunder again and the sound of rain beating against his window.

"You're not going to eat?" Val asks. "Are you one of those people who prefers cold pizza? Or maybe you don't eat at all."

The start of the jingle—the first few notes, the pattern that will become the rhythm—is trapped between his mind and his fingers. It's not quite there. But almost. He turns and watches Val. She's finishing her slice, smiling as she wipes her mouth.

"Whatcha looking at, Jonathan?" she asks.

"I'm not sure," he says.

Then her lips are on his, not moving, not opening or closing, neither making room for his tongue nor offering hers. Just still. Waiting. Jonathan lets his lips linger a moment too long and Val draws closer.

"No," he says, pushing her back. The gesture is too forceful.

For a moment she stares at him, her mouth still shaped around their kiss. Then she leaps to her feet and dashes out the door.

Jonathan is chasing her, trying to catch his breath, trying not to slip on the sidewalk in the rain or get hit by a bus, or splashed by a car. At the end of Visitation, he sees the door to the Marinos' house open and close.

A trio of smokers from the bar watch him as he walks back, including Dirty Dan who's wearing Lil's shot glass around his neck. They see him skulk across the street, shoulders pulled up to his ears.

"Everything cool, Maestro?"

He hears Dirty Dan's old man cackle. "Looks like she got away."

Back upstairs, he puts Val's books in her backpack and walks down Visitation. He rings her bell. He knows from the angle of her curtains that she's in her room looking down.

Val does not answer his call. She does not come to the door. Jonathan is soaked. His T-shirt is plastered to his chest. Rain drips into the waistband of his jeans. He leaves Val's backpack in the shelter of her doorway.

Twice on his way down Visitation he checks behind him to see if she's come to the window.

He knows that tonight he will drink but be unable to wash away the feeling of Val's lips on his. He will play loud, hammering out "Me and My Girl," and drain whatever free swill the bartender at Cock 'n Bulls slides his way. He will let Dawn flirt with him, even kiss him onstage. He might kiss her back. He will try to shift his focus to the boys in the bar, but he will see Val instead.

CHAPTER SEVENTEEN

Cree's acceptance letter comes with a glossy guide to the Kingsborough Community College campus and a course catalog for maritime technology. He tucks these under his mattress. He doesn't return phone calls from the departmental secretary asking him if he plans to enroll. He hopes they will forget about him.

Using the telescope Ren brought him, he watches the tugs on the river from Gloria's hospital window. He focuses on the deckhands—their confident gestures, the way they coil rope or check the towlines. He follows the boats' muscular bodies leading compact wakes and tries to forget his ambition to become part of a crew.

His mother speaks with difficulty. She prefers to squeeze his hand and to point at the water following her son's gaze. But Cree knows that leaving Red Hook is impossible. He will put off school until Gloria is well enough to take care of herself.

The doctors warn Cree that his mother will have some lingering paralysis as well as mood swings. She will cry unexpectedly. He shouldn't worry if she becomes angry for no reason. The doctors have told her she's lucky, that she got to the hospital in time. Still, there will be months of rehabilitation, hours of relearning basic mechanics and simple words.

Gloria submits to the therapists' prodding and stretching. She allows Cree to manipulate her arm and fingers, activating the nerves and muscles. She seems untroubled by her disobedient body.

When she does speak, her voice sounds unfamiliar, stilted. She loses track of her words on their way out and has to pause and retrace her steps. Her sentences have a childlike simplicity.

"My ears," she tells the doctor. "I can't hear."

They order tests and a new CAT scan but find nothing wrong with her ears.

"I can't hear," Gloria insists, her jaw trembling with each word. She curls her hands around the edge of her blanket in frustration. "Can't," she says. A tear slides down her cheek. The doctor refuses to do more tests.

Two days before Gloria is released, Grandma Lucy visits for the second time. On her first visit, Lucy had taken her daughter's hand in her small smooth palm and whispered something Cree couldn't hear.

Before she left, Lucy clasped her pendulum in her fist and let it drop toward the floor. It dangled from its thin gold chain, then swung back and forth once before she gathered it up. She told Cree she would come back when Gloria could talk.

On her second visit, Lucy wears a purple scarf that smells like moss. A large amber amulet hangs between her breasts. She carries a brown paper bag of Jamaican beef patties. The grease from the dough has soaked through the wax wrappers and blossomed onto the paper. She puts the patties on the tray table.

"Eat," she says to Gloria.

Gloria shakes her head. Her eyes are dull. Her lips and cheeks are drawn.

"You're not happy you're going home?" Lucy asks.

"She says her hearing's not right," Cree says.

Lucy takes Gloria's chin in her hand and looks into her daughter's eyes. Standing by the side of the bed, she's barely eye level with Gloria who is propped up on the pillows. Lucy looks whittled down. The only thing she has a lot of is hair—her large gray braids coiled into two ropes then wound into a bun at the nape of her neck.

"Nothing wrong with her hearing," Lucy says.

"Ma," Gloria says. Her mouth and jaw work, trying to shape her thoughts into sound. "It's not good. Not right."

Lucy lets go of Gloria's chin and moves to the foot of the bed. She crosses her thin arms over her chest. "The only problem with your ears is you can't hear Marcus inside that head of yours anymore," Lucy says. She holds her daughter's gaze until Gloria looks away.

"Why don't you go ahead and tell these doctors that's what the trouble is. You're wasting their time with all those tests. There's no medical cure for what ails you, baby." Lucy sits in a chair the color of milk chocolate. "You should enjoy the silence. Maybe you'll listen to the rest of us for a change."

Gloria comes home from the hospital on a thin, gray morning. She leans on Cree as they walk through the courtyard. The memorial to Marcus is being maintained by Ren's crew of hoods. Cree's noticed them picking up litter, chasing off smaller kids who come too close with fat tagging markers.

Gloria passes her bench without a glance. Her right leg drags. She keeps her eyes ahead, her shoulders as stiff as she can manage. Her hand, inside Cree's for support, clenches and relaxes in an unbidden rhythm. Cree helps her up the stairs to the apartment where she collapses on the couch.

She looks at the pile of sparkly tops and tight jeans stacked next to the couch. "Celia?"

"Celia," Cree says. "She wants to stick around until you don't need her."

"I don't," Gloria says.

Cree helps his mother into her room. Later he helps her into the bathroom where he runs water for her bath. He heats up a tray of macaroni one of the neighbors dropped off. He pulls a small table up to the couch. He stacks pillows so Gloria can eat comfortably. He turns on the TV.

"Baby," she says covering her ears, "too loud."

They watch TV on mute.

After Gloria is in bed, he goes to his room and shuts the door. He puts on the radio, listening to the late-night call-in show on HOT 97. It's not long before Gloria asks him to listen to the radio through his headphones.

They live in silence. Even the ambient noise of the Houses is too much for her. She squints and strains when the pipes bang or the kids in the courtyards shout. When it gets noisy, she tenses, cocks her head to one side, leaning toward some inaudible sound. She waves her good hand at Cree, ordering him to stop whatever he's doing so she can focus—tune in something beyond the everyday noises of their apartment and the courtyard. She closes her eyes and holds her hands in front of her, as if her crooked fingers might draw Marcus's voice back.

Gloria often looks as if she's forgotten something—as if a piece of music is trapped in her head and she can't remember its name. Sometimes she will stop whatever she is doing, pausing with a hand on the kitchen counter before looking up as if it's come back to her. But then she will shake her head, dismissing whatever's she's hit on as wrong.

Celia can't stand the quiet. She goes dancing after work, shaking off a day spent at the jail. *You should come, baby,* she tells Cree. Word around the Houses is that she's found a new man to show Ray that two can play his game.

Twice a week Ernesto turns up at the door with a bag of groceries. "From my man," is all he says when Cree tries to hand him cash.

At night when they watch TV with the sound off, Cree notices tears slip down Gloria's cheeks.

"Want me to put on some music, Ma? The soul review?"

"Quiet." She fumbles for his hand. "Please."

The secretary from Kingsborough Community College calls again. Gloria is at the kitchen table. Cree pulls the cord as far as it will stretch, nearly dislodging the phone from the wall.

"Maybe next fall," he whispers.

The secretary tells him that he needs to speak up.

Gloria is watching him from the table.

"Take me off this list," Cree says.

One of Gloria's clients knocks on the door. At the kitchen table, Gloria takes the woman's hands in her good one. She closes her eyes. But when she opens them, instead of the clarity Cree and her client expect, her lashes are damp.

"Same thing happened to my mother," the client says to Cree as he shows her out. "After her stroke, she'd cry at nothing."

Cree does not explain that his mother is finally mourning Marcus.

"I'll come back in few weeks. We can try again," the woman says. But the look on her face tells Cree she won't return. She'll seek her solace elsewhere. That afternoon, Gloria removes the PSY-CHIC CONNECTIONS sign from the door, her unsteady hands tearing the paper as she rips it down.

After Gloria goes to bed, Cree goes to his closet and retrieves the box filled with Marcus's trinkets that he salvaged from the thrift stores where Gloria had donated them. He takes the box to the living room.

Celia is sleeping on the foldout. Her uniform hangs from a hanger on the curtain rod. Her after-work clothes—orange patent heels, shiny jeans, and a top that looks like a handkerchief—are in a pile on a chair.

Careful not to wake his aunt, Cree distributes the few possessions of Marcus's that he's been able to recover—a couple of scallop shell ashtrays, a framed photograph of a fishing boat against a sherbet sunset, a single glass from a set of Tiki tumblers. He hopes his mother will make do with these reminders of Marcus.

In the morning, Cree butters bread for his mother. Celia spoons sugar into her coffee. Gloria keeps her back to the living room while she eats. She doesn't acknowledge Marcus's stuff.

Someone knocks on the door.

Cree answers it expecting Ernesto but it's Monique. She's done something to her hair—tinted it iridescent maroon and shaped it into coils like Christmas ribbon.

"Is my ma here?"

"Hello to you too, Mo," Cree says. "Where've you been hiding out?"

"You gonna let me in?"

"I'm just saying I haven't seen you around lately."

"I've been around."

"Not at the tabernacle."

Monique stands on her tiptoes to see over Cree's shoulder. "Shut your mouth, Cree. It's not even your church to begin with. Is my mother here or not?"

"She's here. Where else?"

"I know where else she goes. I know what she gets up to when she's not here."

Cree wouldn't swear to it but his cousin looks a little stoned. Her eyes are rimmed with red, and her gaze sharpens and fades as they talk.

"Are you high, Mo?"

"Are you?"

Cree steps aside, letting Monique pass.

Celia drops her fork. "Baby," she says, "how come you're not in school?"

"Jewish holiday." Monique pulls out a chair but sits at a distance from the others. "Hey, Aunt Gloria. You doing better?"

Gloria's eyes are fixed on Monique's face. Her head is cocked to one side. "Aunt Gloria?" Monique says.

Gloria's mouth opens but she says nothing.

Monique turns to Celia. "You ever coming home?"

"I'm helping out my sister, baby. You know that," Celia says.

"Guess it's easier to step out on Ray if you don't come home. Not like Ray's there either. Not like he notices where you are and what you do." Monique takes a bite of toast. "I need money for food, Ma. I ran through all the frozen dinners."

"Why don't you eat here with us?" Celia says.

"Nah," Monique says, taking a piece of toast from Cree's plate. The way his cousin is going at the toast Cree's starting to think that he was right about her being high.

Monique avoids Cree's glance.

"Come on, baby," Celia says. "I'm sure your aunt would love your company."

Cree looks over at Gloria. Her head is still tilted, her eyes fixed on Monique.

"Wouldn't you, Gloria? Wouldn't it be nice if Monique came over for dinner?"

They all wait for Gloria to break from her trance. Her jaw starts to work. Her lips tremble. She points a shaking finger at Monique. "You hear them," she says. She takes a breath, her mouth clenching and releasing. "You hear them."

Monique shakes her head and looks away. "You're talking crazy, Aunt Gloria. I don't hear anything or anyone." She turns to Celia. "So, Ma, you got cash or not?"

Celia reaches for her purse. "I'm cooking tonight, Mo. Eat with us."

"I don't know. Maybe I'll eat with Ray."

"The hell you will," Celia says. "The hell you'll eat with Ray and his white piece."

Gloria is still pointing at Monique, her rigid finger quivering. "You can't hide it from me."

"I don't know what you're talking about." Monique holds out her palm until Celia drops two twenties.

"You spending that on food?" Cree asks.

"Shut up, Cree," Monique says.

"Don't ignore me," Gloria says. "You can hear them."

Celia looks from her sister to her daughter.

"I don't hear anything," Monique says. She won't meet Gloria's eyes. "All I know is that I need some cash to get some dinner so I don't have to eat at this table with a bunch of people who talk crazy." She stands up. "I don't know how you stand it, Cree. This whole place smells like ghost." The door slams behind her.

"Why'd you drive her off, Gloria?" Celia says. "You scared the hell out of my baby."

Celia and Cree wait as Gloria shapes her words. "She can hear Marcus. She lied to her aunt."

"Don't drag her into your nonsense. Dead is dead," Celia says.

Cree dashes into the hall. He takes the stairs two at a time and grabs Monique as she's leaving building.

"You need to get out of there too?" Monique says.

Cree takes a few breaths. "What my ma said, is it true?"

"I don't know what you're talking about. I don't know what any of you are talking about."

"That you've got her . . . gift."

"The gift of crazy? No. I don't have that. I can't hear jack shit. So don't ask me again." She turns and walks away. Cree watches her go, avoiding a group of her friends. They call her name, but Monique doesn't turn. Just before she disappears, she covers her ears, then shakes her head, as if she's trying to banish an unwelcome sound.

The next morning all Marcus's trinkets are missing. Gloria's bedroom door is ajar. Cree calls her name. There is no answer.

Cree calls her name again as he heads for the stairs.

Shut the hell up, is the only response.

He loses his footing on the stairs. He tumbles into a wall on one of the landings, scattering the litter that's accumulated in the corner. He hurries down to the exit.

Gloria is halfway between the bench and the door. She's frozen, the right side of her body lagging behind her left. From the outskirts of the courtyard people are watching her. But they keep busy with their own conversations, their own ball games. They don't break from their midmorning rhythms to give Gloria a hand.

Cree is at his mother's side. He takes her arm and wraps it around his waist.

"I gave it back to him," Gloria says. "I gave it back." With her good hand, she points toward the bench. All of Marcus's knick-knacks are scattered underneath the slats. "If your daddy's going to leave me, he might as well take his junk." Gloria turns, tugging on Cree's arm, pulling him toward their building.

Cree's feet don't move. He knows the moment he closes their apartment door, he'll lose everything that's left of his father once and for all. There will be no way for him to retrieve these few mementos once they are scavenged by strangers.

He drops Gloria's arm. She wobbles, then regains her balance.

"Cree," she says. "Leave it."

Before he reaches the bench, there is a disturbance in the courtyard. Conversations cease and then resume at a lower level. Three coded whistles zip from the windows. Movement at the outskirts stops. Cree knows this adjustment, the drawing back, the retreating before the arrival of the police.

He's caught between Gloria and the bench when two detectives reach him. The air around him is still, as if everyone has drawn a breath and held it in.

"Cree James?"

Cree nods and reaches out a hand to steady his mother.

The older detective, Coover, takes the lead. "Would you mind coming with us? We've got an eyewitness who puts you at the scene the night June Giatto disappeared. Saw you carrying a girl from the pier."

"The person saw me or someone like me?" Cree says.

"Don't be a smart-ass," Hughes says. He tugs his shirt cuffs and straightens his jacket.

"I got to take my mom inside," Cree says. "Then I'll come."

He keeps his head down as he takes Gloria to the door. "It's nothing, Ma," he says.

The detectives follow him as he helps his mother up the stairs. They wait in the hallway as Cree settles Gloria on the couch, then they lead him to an unmarked car parked on Lorraine Street. Cree feels the courtyards shift as he passes.

They drive to the 76. The radio is tuned to WFAN. Two radio jocks are tearing apart the Mets for their postseason collapse. When the call-in show reaches a frenzy, Hughes punches the radio and they continue in silence.

They take Cree in through a side entrance and leave him in a windowless room with four other black teenagers. Cree wonders if the others know that they're only here so someone can identify him.

One of the boys is working a toothpick back and forth in his mouth. "What are we supposed to have done?" he asks.

"Kidnapping. Murder too," a smaller boy replies. "They pay you to come in today?"

"They don't pay me shit." The kid spits his toothpick to the floor. Cree sweats hot then cold. He keeps his back to the room.

The door opens and a uniformed cop enters. "Line up," he says.

Cree takes the fourth position. He stares at his toes as he files past the one-way glass in the adjacent room.

Over an intercom someone tells the lineup to stare straight ahead. Cree catches his reflection in the two-way mirror. He's not all that different from the kids to his left and right—boys culled from juvee or jail or rounded up from a pool of known trouble-makers. He tries to stand straighter, look brighter, confident but not arrogant. But the eyes staring back at him show a panicked and uncertain teenager.

The fluorescent lights hum. Cree can hear static from the intercom. One by one the boys are asked to step forward. They are instructed to turn and stand in profile. Cree thinks about contorting his face, stiffening his jaw, altering his appearance. But when it is his turn, he is too nervous to do anything but follow orders.

The second kid in the lineup is asked to step forward again. Cree watches him turn and show his profile to the mirror. There's a slight smile on his face—a smirk that suggests they've got the wrong guy.

The uniformed officer opens the door and the boys file out.

"They pick right?" boy number two asks. "Or are you all wasting everyone's time again?"

"You can leave through the front door," the officer says.

Celia is sitting on a bench outside the holding room. She's wearing her CO uniform, which hugs her a little tighter than regulation.

"Cree, baby," Celia says, standing up and taking his arm. "Gloria called and told me they scooped you up."

"It's nothing, Cee."

"Yeah? What nothing are they trying to pin on you?" Celia asks. Before Cree can answer, Celia whips her head around and narrows in on the officer who's just escorted the boys from the lineup. His eyes are dropped, fixed on her rear. "What the hell are you looking at? You've never seen a uniform before?"

"C'mon, Cee, let's get going."

"Not before you tell me why they brought you here in the first place. If you're in trouble, you let me know about it."

"It's nothing. Something to do with that girl who disappeared near the pier. I don't know what," Cree says.

"How come you're mixed up in that?" Celia says.

"I'm not."

The door to the observation room opens and the two detectives who brought Cree in emerge. Between them is the wino who's often passed out on Van Brunt. He's a buddy of Cree's uncle Des—the two of them haunting the methadone clinic until it opens, then flopping on the park benches, riding out their synthetic high.

Celia slides between Cree and Detective Hughes.

"You taking IDs from crackheads now?" Celia says.

"The witness says he saw a person the same age and build as this young man carrying a girl out of the water that night."

"You mean the same color," Celia says.

"That too," Hughes says.

"So you're gonna pin it on my nephew. You know how many boys his age live in Red Hook?"

"He was seen near the water that night," Coover says.

"Near the water, not in it," Celia says.

Cree peers over Hughes's shoulder, trying to catch sight of the wino. He wants to see if he can read in his shriveled face whether the little man really saw him jump into the water that night or if he's just making shit up to claim the reward. If the wino saw him swim after the girls, Cree wouldn't put it past him to invent the rest of the story, tell the cops what they wanted to hear to close their case.

The wino steps out from behind the detective and takes Cree's hand and shakes it. It's his customary greeting, which precedes begging for a dollar. Cree usually crosses the street to avoid it.

"You two know each other?" Hughes says.

"He's a drug buddy of my uncle's," Cree says.

"*No fue el,*" the wino says pointing at Cree. "*Fue el tio con el barco.* The boat."

"You got a boat?" Coover asks Cree. "The girls saw you on a boat."

"The hell my nephew would do with a boat," Celia says.

"*No fue el. El otro. El otro.*"

The two detectives exchange a look and take the wino by the collar and hustle him toward the door.

Celia and Cree give them a head start. They exit the station onto Union Street. There is no relief in the fresh air.

Cree watches *Monday Night Football* on mute. Without sound, there is a comical quality to the game and its presentation, as if all the players fell through the looking glass and decided to run and stop at random.

"Yo?"

Someone's in the hall, calling out instead of knocking.

"Yo?"

The voice is low. Secretive.

Cree stands up and goes to the door.

Ernesto is standing outside.

"A little late for delivery," Cree says.

"I got nothing for you. My man, he wants to see you."

"Your man?"

"Ren."

"How come he doesn't come himself?"

" 'Cause he sent me. You coming or not?"

"Maybe I'm busy," Cree says.

"Ren says you aren't. Says you barely leave the apartment. Says you need to get some fresh air."

Cree follows Ernesto down Lorraine Street and over to Otsego. The kid stops on the corner and points down to where the cobblestone street dissolves into darkness. "He's over there."

"You're not coming?"

"Not needed." He pulls his hood over his head and dashes back toward the Houses.

Ren is standing next to a mid-1990s Honda Civic hatchback with the engine running. He's still wearing the same sweatshirt and dirty jeans. His face looks fuller.

"You couldn't make the walk over to get me yourself?" Cree says.

"Heard you got picked up by the police today," Ren says. "I like to keep clear of authority. What'd they haul you in for?"

"Nothing. That missing girl nonsense I had nothing to do with."

"That doesn't matter," Ren says "They'll haul you in until you do. But I got it covered. It's copacetic."

"You have it covered?"

"I'm taking care of the situation," Ren says. "First off, I made sure the other white girl, Valerie, didn't hang around you anymore."

"You what?"

"Don't you understand how the game is played? The more you hang around that white girl with the missing friend, the more guilty you make yourself look. It's bad enough you jumped in the water with her, got all hot and heavy for the whole neighborhood to see. That's crazy time. One girl goes missing and you get with the other even though you know the cops are trying to finger you for it. That's why you need me. I watch out so as you don't get yourself in trouble for some shit you didn't do. Your only crime is being in the wrong place at the wrong time. You ready for an expedition?" Ren nods toward the car.

"This is yours?"

"Call it a loan." Ren opens the passenger door and hops in. "You drive?"

Cree peeks into the car. The wires under the steering wheel are loose. "You can hot-wire but you can't drive?"

"I was indisposed during my formative years. You getting in?" Ren reclines the seat and puts on his seat belt.

"Indisposed how?"

"It's no big thing. I was in the wrong place at the wrong time with the wrong people. I did the wrong thing."

"You were in jail."

Ren nods. "You driving? Or you expect this thing to drive itself."

Cree gets behind the wheel. Gloria paid for driving lessons for his seventeenth birthday. But since he passed his test, Cree hasn't had many chances to test out his skills. He jerks the car over the cobblestones until they hit Van Brunt.

"Left? Right? Where are we going?" he asks.

"Staten Island," Ren says. "You know how to get there?"

Uncertain of the expressway, Cree takes the city streets. He heads over toward Park Slope, then turns up Fourth Avenue in the direction of the Verrazano Bridge, figuring if he keeps his eye on that, he'll eventually get to the other side.

The avenue ends in Bay Ridge. They are under the bridge. After a few wrong turns, Cree gets the car onto the ramp. Then they are hurtling across the water, leaving Brooklyn behind, sliding through the tollbooth into the smallest borough.

"Where to?" Cree asks.

"Keep to the water," Ren says.

Cree finds a road that runs parallel to the bay. One side is derelict houses, the other a wasteland strewn with garbage and scrap. Ren rolls down the window. The air smells like landfill and saltwater.

He peers out his window. "Go slow," he says.

The wasteland gives way to an assortment of mismatched businesses. Between an animal feed depot and a car wash, Ren tells Cree to stop. Cree puts the car in park. Ren reaches over and fiddles with the wires, killing the engine. He hands Cree a flashlight.

Ren leads the way, stopping at a battered Do Not Enter sign.

"Where are we?" Cree asks.

"Graveyard," Ren says.

"We have graveyards in Brooklyn."

"Not for ships."

They pick their way around a twisted fence and a maze of old shipping containers. Soon the ground grows soft, then muddy. Then they are wet to their ankles.

Cree casts his flashlight in front of him. Its beam finds the giant husks of ferries and tugs—boats reduced to skeleton shapes, rust in place of paint. There are container ships and freighters, all sculptures of decayed iron. Smokestacks poke out of the water at odd angles that fill Cree with the same uneasiness as the sight of a broken limb. Blind portholes swallow his light. Near the shore four large fishing boats are lined up, their prows pushing in toward land, nosing the rushes. Their paint is stripped away, revealing salt-dried wood.

"This way," Ren says, heading along the shore toward the fishing boats. He stops in front of the boats, bouncing his flashlight off each of them in turn.

"What are you looking for?" Cree asks.

"Parts. For our boat. I'm getting her shipshape, ready to sail."

"You're taking my boat?" Cree asks.

"Me? Us," Ren says. "We're going together." He chooses one of the four fishing boats and begins to climb aboard.

"I'm not going anywhere," Cree says. "My ma—"

"You're going to spend your life in the Houses?" Ren asks.

The deck is splintered. Through missing boards they can see

into the cavernous hull. Cree's flashlight finds a dead fish. He closes his eyes, trying to find the boat's sway.

Out on the boat in the dark with the water at his back, it's easy to imagine he's adrift with Marcus. The summer before Marcus died, he had taken Cree to Jersey City on the fishing boat. When they began the return trip, the sky had filled with heavy clouds and was nearly as black as the water. Marcus thought he could beat the storm, but the first thunder erupted five minutes from shore. The little boat pitched. Water swamped the deck. The lights of Red Hook bobbed in and out of view as the boat was rocked between the waves.

Cree hadn't been scared. He'd stood by his dad at the wheel, confident that Marcus would get them home. Marcus steered with one hand on Cree's shoulder, catching him each time the boat plunged. The water was too rough for them to tie up on their illegal mooring just off the sugar refinery, so they'd dropped anchor and huddled in the tiny deckhouse, watching the blurry lights of the distant city dip and sway as the storm tossed their boat. When the weather settled, Marcus brought them into shore.

"Fenwick Island," Cree says.

"What?" Ren is silhouetted behind him, his flashlight dancing in the remains of the cabin.

"It's in Delaware. That's where my dad said we'd spent our first night on our way to Florida. He died before we made the trip."

"So that's where we'll go. First stop."

"What makes you so sure we're going anywhere?"

Ren shrugs. His flashlight rises and falls. "You got a boat. You got a first mate. Why would we stay put."

"You think I can just up and leave?"

"I'm not saying relocate. I'm saying adventure."

Cree looks over the side of the boat, deeper into the dark water. Two months had passed since he'd seen those girls on their raft and believed adventure had been within reach.

Ren follows Cree's gaze. "Proactive man. That's what we're after."

Ren has Marcus's talent for making everything sound easy—as if shipping out is no big deal. The wind gusts. The abandoned boats sway.

"Fenwick Island," Cree says. "And then the Keys. We were always planning to head down to the Keys. My moms would fly and meet us there for a family vacation. But the real vacation would have been the trip down."

They begin to move the scrap and parts. By the end of the night, both boys have an animal scent—a barnyard musk of mud and sweat as well as the murky stale odor of stagnant water. It takes them three round trips to the car to load all the materials Ren's salvaged.

They drive back to Brooklyn, their haul bumping and clattering in the trunk. Cree parks in front of the lot where his father's boat is moored.

"That was a trip," Cree says. He and Ren bump fists. "Want to come back to mine, get cleaned up?"

"Go on," Ren says. "I got work to do." He looks at the scrap at his feet. "Give me a couple of days. Then we'll take her out for a ride. See if we can get to Jersey and back."

Cree wants to take Ren to a place where they can drink beer and talk girls. He wants to walk side by side into the courtyards or the park, claim one of the benches, laugh louder than necessary, prove that he's not alone.

He wants to hang in the pizza parlor, grab takeout from the bulletproof Chinese. He wants Ren to come with him to one of those house parties he no longer braves alone.

But Ren seems to dodge the Houses in favor of the empty backstreets. Maybe out on the water he will shed his secrets, let them go as they pass beneath the Verrazano and head toward the Atlantic.

CHAPTER EIGHTEEN

It sounds to Monique as if June is giving up. Her voice has lost some of its confidence and grown flat and robotic. Sometimes she confuses words, mispronouncing simple things, adding syllables or tripping over vowels. *Kitchen. Breakfast. Pancake. Frying-panhandle.* Her memory is fading, taking with it her certainty of how and who she was.

Hammer. Workshop. Homeworked. Noterbook.

Even at this uncertain register, June's voice rings in Monique's ears. It wakes her from her dreams. It nags her during school. She skips tabernacle, worried that the congregation will suspect that she's possessed.

The reverend shows up at Monique and Celia's apartment. Monique watches him through the peephole. She holds her breath. She can feel her heartbeat against the metal. The reverend's head balloons over his foreshortened body. The distorting glass makes his eyes bulge. He leans into the door, pressing his eye to the wrong side of the peephole as if he can see in, the dark of his iris inches from Monique's own.

He calls her name. He bangs on the door—deep blows that vibrate in Monique's chest. Somewhere down the hall a door opens and a voice calls out to quit his racket. He straightens his jacket and walks down the dim hall to the stairs.

In the projects she is besieged by voices of those who died in the towers and in the courtyards. She hears the cries of old ladies who died all alone as well as the gangbangers and drug slingers caught in their own cross fire. She cups her hands over her ears, but it only makes the noise louder. She drops her hands and catches sight of a couple of kids watching her. *Monique's buggin'*, one of them says. *Yo, Monique, how come you're buggin'? You smoke the bad shit?*

Her gang is in their usual place in Coffey Park clustered around two benches, making pointless trouble for anyone who passes. Shawna, Monique's shadow, has risen in the ranks, and now sits in Monique's place.

Yo, girl, where you been?

You missing out, Mo. How come you weren't at Dee's crib last night? That shit was phat. We took it late. Till dawn.

Shawna got down.

Shawna's doing a poor job of seeming uninterested in the boys' attention. She lets them tease her too long. She takes too many gibes and punches. She acts hungry for notice, especially at Monique's expense.

Didn't know we interested you anymore, Shawna says. *Thought you were hunting the rough stuff with Raneem's boys.*

Only three weeks ago, Shawna couldn't get her hair done without calling Monique for advice. Now she's ribbing her. But that's what happens—the boys tease the girls, then the girls trash the girls. It's a drop-down system, and Monique's fallen to the bottom.

Monique knows how to put Shawna in her place. It would be simple to remind the crew that Shawna had accidentally gotten with a twelve-year-old at the beginning of the summer, mistaking the kid for his older brother.

What's the matter with her?

She's tripping.

She's high.

She's high on Raneem's shit.

Their words hardly register.

Monique heads toward the waterside. It's quieter on the cobbled streets. Next door to Val's house a woman in a long purple skirt is sweeping her stoop. She looks up as Monique passes. Monique is almost at Van Brunt when she stops and backtracks to the bottom step. "Is my father shacked up here?"

The woman leans on her broom.

"Ray, my dad. His boys tell me he's shacked up in this house."

The woman pushes up the sleeves of her white blouse, revealing slashes of black paint or pen on her forearms. Her hair—light brown turning gray—is frizzy, framing her head in a wedge. She doesn't wear any makeup. Two small dogs are yapping in the doorway behind her, springing up and banging against the glass.

Monique can't believe that Ray prefers this woman to Celia. It makes her wonder what they're preaching in his recovery meeting.

This woman reminds Monique of the volunteers who sometimes visit her high school to teach creative writing, women who seem to pity the students for the first half of class and then spend the second half glancing at the clock.

"Monique? I'm Maureen," the woman says. "I was wondering when we'd meet." She comes down the steps, places a hand on Monique's shoulder, and draws her inside.

The interior of the small row house is dark and smells like turpentine. Large pieces of paper with smudged charcoal drawings of women's bodies are taped to the walls in the hallway. Women's arms, legs, thighs, butts. Women's breasts spilling over their prostrate figures.

Maureen leads Monique into the living room. The walls are
covered with more sketches. Women with their legs gaping open.
Women crawling into bathtubs. Women considering themselves in
the mirror. Women with their fingers creeping down to their privates. In the middle of the room is a large easel with a half-finished
drawing of three female figures—two bursting from the body of
the first.

"You do all these?" Monique asks. She averts her eyes from the
vaginas that stare at her from all sides. "You're working on that
now?" She points at the easel.

"Those are my selves," Maureen says.

"Your what?"

"The three aspects of my nature. They're born from me."

The couch is covered with magazines and sketchbooks. Two
hanging plants are dying in their planters, their brown tendrils
curling and withering.

"Ray's at work," Maureen says. "He'll be back around five."

"I know what time my dad gets off work."

"Of course you do." Maureen slides art books and sketchbooks
from the couch onto the floor. "Sit."

Monique perches on the edge of the couch with her knees
together and her hands clasped. She can feel the springs poking
into the backs of her thighs. She can't imagine Ray in this place.
She can't see him without his booming TV and his animated fights
with Celia.

"So my father's living here now? Like permanent?"

"He and I are learning about new parts of our selves," Maureen
says.

"So there's more than one of him now too?"

"This must be difficult for you," Maureen says.

"My father running out? It happens all the time." Monique

stands up. The voices, which had subsided when she entered the house, are starting again. She walks around the room, lifting drawings, poking through coffee cans crammed with charcoal pencils and china markers. She enters the small kitchen. Maureen's shelves are filled with grains and beans stored in glass jars.

From the kitchen window, Monique looks into the garden, then over the wall that divides the Marinos' backyard from Maureen's. She can see the top of the white-and-blue swing set Val and June would make-believe into outer space and fantastical lands Monique didn't quite grasp. The other girls always took the lead on these imaginary adventures, bringing to life stories from books Monique hadn't read and movies she hadn't seen. She'd tagged along, drugged by the exotic-sounding names, the complicated rules and customs of these imaginary places.

Rust has crept onto the swing set. The crossbar sags in the middle.

"I don't know anyone who has a garden," Monique says. "It must be a trip."

"I don't spend that much time out there," Maureen says.

"You don't have kids?"

Maureen shakes her head.

"This big house and no kids? How come you don't have kids?"

"I never wanted them."

"Cramps your style, I guess," Monique says. "So is my dad coming home or what?"

"You should talk to him about that."

"I'm talking about it with you."

"Let's have this discussion when Ray's here," Maureen says.

Monique looks around the kitchen. She doesn't want to hang around until Ray comes back. The Ray who stays in this house is not her father—at least not in any way recognizable to Monique. Without making excuses, she heads for the hall.

On her way out she passes Val, who's got a funky new haircut.

"Hey, Monique."

Monique tries to speak, but June's voice is pounding in her ears, saying Val's name.

"You hanging out with Maureen?"

Monique opens and shuts her mouth like a nutcracker.

"Monique? Is everything cool?"

Monique wants to follow Val inside her house, go down to the basement, and pull out the old costumes and scarves. She wants Val to invent one of her complicated adventures set in a kingdom far away. She wonders if Val still remembers these places, if perhaps that's what she was looking for that night on the raft, a world that hovers just out of reach.

"Um, okay. Whatever," Val says.

Monique struggles to sort out her own thoughts from June's chattering. "Val!" she says. Her voice is not her own.

"What?" Val says.

Monique clamps her hand over her mouth, then lets it go. "Shut up." She twitches, trying to break free of June.

"Are you talking to me?" Val looks more confused than angry.

Monique shakes her head. She looks past Val into the homey interior of the Marinos' house. No amount of make-believe will get June to let her be.

She rushes away.

"Monique, wait!"

She heads for the desolate streets on the tip of Red Hook. June's voice is still a rhythmic chant but she's no longer just saying Val's name. She's incanting a whole host of names, some Monique recognizes, some she doesn't, and others she's sure are nonsense.

Halfway up the block the corrugated siding that hides Bones Manor from the street begins. As she passes, a slight wind lifts from the water, rattling the fence. She slips through a gap and enters the Manor's barren empire.

She's standing at the edge of a large pond filled with rushes that bow and sway. The top of the water ripples, distorting her reflection. All around her are makeshift shelters, concrete foundations with tarps as roofs, shipping containers with laundry lines strung across their short ends, and shopping carts for storage. Battered chairs sit in a semicircle under a sheet hung between four stripped saplings. Trash rolls like tumbleweed.

The highest point of the Manor is a blue building that looks like two stacked trailers. They are balanced on a staggered cinderblock platform. The top trailer has smudged windows, one of them partially blocked by a ragged curtain. As Monique looks up the curtain is pulled back.

A chorus of new voices joins June's. They are rough and eroded. They sound like the ache of the wind in a charred forest, the rattle of a can rolling down an empty street, the whisper of dust in a gutted building—hollow noises unaccustomed to an audience. They suggest a loneliness worse than pain.

This is what people become, Monique thinks, voices crying out in an abandoned lot, groping the forgotten air of an old boneyard, hoping for someone to hear them and reaching a person who won't listen. So what does it matter if Ray runs off with Maureen, and Shawna becomes queen of the benches? Everyone's heading in the same direction.

Still, there is charm in the desolation of the Manor, invention in the ruin. It's as close to make-believe as Red Hook gets, a world created out of scrap—containers transformed into mansions, a muddy puddle into a lake. Monique imagines she'd like a shipping container of her own, a shelter from the madness of the Houses where people will let her be.

"Boo!"

A hand claps over her eyes. She jumps.

"I said, boo. Did I scare you? Or were you waiting for me?" The hand lifts. Monique turns to face Raneem. His boys are behind him. "Did you come looking for me?"

"No," Monique says.

Raneem stands back. His jeans are slung low, revealing three inches of his boxers. He's capped two of his front teeth in gold.

"You know, not many girls like you come to this place. Not unless they want something."

"What I want," Monique says, "is to be left alone. You can do that for me, can't you?"

"Why don't you sing something for us," Raneem says. "Word is you've got a fine voice in there." He taps Monique's chest. She flinches and he presses harder. "Sing," Raneem says.

Monique opens her mouth but nothing comes out.

"You won't sing for me?" Raneem puts his hand over her throat. "How about now?" He takes his hand away. "I'm just fucking with you. Tough girl like you can't take a joke? I hear you're a girl who likes to run with the big boys. So what? You got bored of those kids, wanted to find some real adventure?"

Perhaps she has come here looking for Raneem.

"Tell you what. How about we all relax and enjoy ourselves?" He pulls something from his pocket and holds it in front of Monique's face. "I seem to remember this is what you came looking for last time. A little smoke. Get a high with the crew."

It's a pristine blunt, plump and golden brown.

"No thanks," Monique says.

"You're scared of the good shit? You prefer smoking that project schwag?"

"I'm not in the mood."

"Silly rabbit," one of Raneem's crew says, "this is what gets you in the mood. Spark it, boy." He jerks his chin to Raneem.

Monique shakes her head. "I'm cool," she says.

But Raneem is already forcing the blunt into her mouth. She takes a deep breath, inhaling and holding it so Raneem doesn't have to hold her lips shut. She exhales and the world flip-flops. She wobbles and knocks against Raneem. "You see, I knew you'd come round." His capped teeth glint. He brushes his tongue over them. "This shit is catnip for the ladies," Raneem says, putting an arm around Monique. She doesn't remove it. If she does, she worries she'll rock back and hit the ground.

Monique closes her eyes. Raneem's breath is hot on her face. He's exhaling warm, soured smoke into her lips. She knows she'd only make it a few steps before they get her down. So what's the point of trying to run?

"You see," Raneem says, unbuttoning the top button of her jeans, "like taking candy from a baby."

Monique closes her eyes. She hears Raneem fumbling with his belt buckle. She braces herself. Then he lets her go. She staggers back, hits the ground, and opens her eyes.

At first Monique thinks that the voices in her head have come to life, materializing from the bunkers and containers—sallow faced and ashen eyed. But these are no ghosts. Silent and grim, the Manor folk circle Raneem and his boys. Their clothes are dirty and torn—scrap layered over scrap. Belts of twine and wire. Ponchos made from curtains and sheets. Plastic bags for shoes.

"What?" Raneem says. "What you all looking at?"

They keep coming. Monique gets to her feet and brushes herself off. June is talking louder now. Her voice is fevered and panicked. *Water, watered, wave, unwavering. Rock, rocker, rocking, rocked.*

Raneem grabs for a piece of scrap metal near his feet. But before he can lift it, one of the Manor dwellers breaks rank, stepping forward and landing a punch to Raneem's jaw. In an instant, this scrawny kid in a black sweatshirt is all over Raneem, pouncing and pinning him, driving him hard into the gravel and concrete.

"You leave her," the kid says. "You leave her alone."

Raneem's bigger, but the kid has the jump on him. He fights quick and hard, landing fast punches that give Raneem and his boys no time to react. After barely a minute, the kid lifts Raneem to his feet and shoves him back into the arms of his friends.

"Don't come back to the Manor anymore," he says.

His hood falls back, revealing a head covered in matted tufts of hair and a long, drawn face with sleepy eyes.

"Yo!" one of Raneem's crew says. "Don't I know you?"

"You don't know shit," the kid says pulling up his hood. "Go."

The Manor folk watch Raneem and his boys hurrying toward the lake and out of the Manor, before retreating into their own shadows.

Monique remains where she was standing. She wraps her arms around herself. She hadn't noticed growing cold, but her entire body is shivering and shaking.

"Come on," the boy in the sweatshirt says, extending a hand to her. "Let's get you warm."

He leads her to a pair of large shipping containers set side by side spray-painted blue and green. The door to one of them is open.

Monique hesitates.

"It's cool," he says.

The interior of the container is tricked out. The light from the door shines on walls covered in elaborate graffiti. The pieces are tropical—surf and sand with stands of loopy palm trees. One wall shows the sun rising in a burst of orange and yellow. On the opposite wall the sun sets in a melting firestorm of reds and pinks.

"RunDown," Monique says, reading the tag at the base of one of the pieces. "Is that you? You're called RunDown?"

"Used to be. Call me Ren. It's easier."

"Okay, Ren." She wraps her arms around herself, trying to fight off the chill.

"You're Cree James's cousin."

"How come you know Cree?"

"He's my boy. He and I are about to travel together."

"Cree? He only travels in his mind."

Everything in Ren's crib is neatly stacked and folded. There's a bed made out of forklift palettes with a twin mattress. The blanket is tucked with hospital corners. Shelves made out of boards and cinder blocks run along one wall. These are stocked with cans of soup, soda, and vegetables, as well as cleaning supplies and toiletries. A few books are stacked next to the bed. At the far end of the container is a beat-up recliner and a clip-on lamp that runs off a battery. Ren switches on the lamp, and the colors on the walls come to life.

"This all your work," Monique says.

"My oeuvre."

"It's tight."

Ren hands her a different black sweatshirt, which she pulls over her head.

"How come you saved me?" Monique says.

"'Cause it looked like you needed saving."

It's quiet in the storage container. The air is still but fresh. The weed is making Monique's head spin. "Do you mind if I lie down for a moment?"

"It's all yours," Ren says. "I'll wait outside."

"No," she says. "You can stay."

The boy sits in the recliner. He switches off the light.

"Leave it on," Monique says. "I want to see the colors."

She lies down on the bed. The pillow and sheets smell of soap. She falls asleep to the gentle creaking of springs and pleather as Ren rocks back and forth, watching over her.

When Monique wakes up, the sky has faded from blue to slate. Ren is still in his chair, rattling a spray can in time to his rocking.

"You up for walking home? This is no place to be after dark. I'll walk you partway."

Monique's back and neck are sore from where she hit the ground. Ren takes her toward the hole in the fence. Shadowy figures pull back as they pass. Her heart beats hard at every dark alley, every abandoned lot.

"I got you," Ren says. "It's cool. With me you're unassailable."

They pass the automotive chop shops closing for the day. The local kids volunteering at the community vegetable garden are padlocking their gate. Monique and Ren pause on Otsego Street and look back toward the water. At the far end of the street, a pewter sliver of the bay is visible through the arched windows of an empty warehouse. As they watch, the sun drops, electrifying the water with the same neon palette Ren had painted on the wall of his container. Monique slips her hand into his. They stand, silently watching the sun burn up the water until it falls behind the Jersey waterfront, leaving the neighborhood in darkness.

They emerge onto Lorraine Street. Ren walks slower now, slinking almost. He pulls the drawstrings of his hood, tightening it over his face. Soon they are at the entrance to one of the courtyards.

"This is as far as I go," Ren says. Monique starts to take off his sweatshirt, but he stops her. "Keep it. I'll get it from you sometime."

"Sure thing," she says.

"And tell your cousin to come find me. We've got places to go."

"Not without me, I hope."

He takes Monique's hands and looks her up and down. "Yeah, I think you can ride with us."

Monique doesn't notice Celia until she's on top of them. She and Ren spring apart.

"Later," Monique says.

Ren's about to turn away when Celia catches his arm. She pulls his hood back. Her mouth opens and a slow scream begins to emerge, gaining power, like a train whipping through a station.

Ren shakes free of Celia's grasp. He breaks into an all-out run. Monique takes her mother by the shoulders. "Stop screaming at him, Ma. Stop," Monique says. "Stop! He's good!"

But Celia's scream continues to pierce the newly fallen night.

CHAPTER NINETEEN

Val hadn't planned to kiss Jonathan. In the moment that he allowed his mouth to linger on hers she felt his lips relax. If Jonathan had simply pulled away and apologized for giving her the wrong impression, that would be one thing, but the near violence of his reaction, the way he pushed her back, told Val that he was stopping *himself* from kissing *her* as much as preventing her from kissing him. His reaction was passionate. She was sure of this.

It was like something out of a movie the way he chased her down the street, shouted her name into the rain. She'd run quickly, sure he'd follow. And he had for half a block. But when Val ducked into her parents' house, Jonathan was nowhere in sight. She kept a lookout from her window, checking to see if he was at his post behind the iron fence across the street. When Jonathan turned up on her step, she'd remained hidden behind her curtain, unsure of what would follow if she opened the door.

Now she regrets her hesitation. With Jonathan she was able to forget June's hand sliding from hers, the black curtain of water pulling them away from each other. Jonathan would forgive Val for June.

She stares into the window of his apartment on her way to St. Bernardette's. She lingers on Van Brunt, at the bus stop, on the school steps, hoping they'll bump into each other. She takes her time in the lobby, on the stairs, in the cafeteria, in front of the teacher's lounge. She counts the minutes until Music Appreciation.

In class, Jonathan tells them they're going to be watching a movie, a modern production of *Le Nozze di Figaro* set in an Upper East Side apartment. This is the only introduction he gives before inserting the DVD, dimming the lights, and pressing play. He takes his seat behind the piano and doesn't say a word until the bell rings. He fidgets with his sheet music and the stack of CDs beneath the piano bench, but Val can feel it when his eyes dart to her face. When she dawdles in front of the piano for a moment after class, Jonathan doesn't look up from the sheet music he's arranging.

Val turns sixteen on an unremarkable and overcast Wednesday. There won't be much fanfare—probably just a white cake with a seam of raspberry filling from one of the Italian bakeries on Court Street and a couple of small gifts from her parents and Rita.

The bus lets Val off on Van Brunt. The Dockyard's windows are fogged over. The door to the bar opens, revealing a dark interior lit up by green Christmas lights. She glances inside, hoping to see Jonathan, hoping he'll come out. But the room is too dark for her to distinguish the faces of the drinkers.

She heads to the bodega to buy a pack of gum. Ever since June disappeared the bodega owner has been a little sweet on her, slip-

ping her candy bars and single cigarettes. He even offers her a
breakfast sandwich some mornings.

She slides a pack of spearmint across the counter. She hates herself for forgetting his name.

"Gum? That's it? How about a soda?"

"No, thank you." Val glances at the flyer with June's photo on
it still taped next to the counter. "Did you ever get your T-shirt
back? The one you lent me that morning?"

"Don't worry about that."

Val pops a piece of gum in her mouth. "It's my birthday."

"Happy birthday. Are you doing anything special?"

"No," Val says.

He slides off his stool. "I have something for you." He squats
down, showing Val his broad back, then pulls out a white pastry
box with a torn top. He puts it on the counter between them. He
opens the top. Inside are assorted golden pastries, some shaped like
egg rolls, others like bird's nests. "They're Lebanese," he said. "Let
me get some tape."

He disappears into a back room.

"Fadi!" a voice behind Val says. *Fadi,* that's his name.

Val turns and sees Jonathan entering the store. When their eyes
meet, Val cannot remember any of the dozens of things she planned
to say to him, things that would prove she wasn't a little kid, things
that would make him like her back, invite her over.

"Fancy meeting you here," Jonathan says. He digs in his pocket
and teases out some crumpled bills.

"I liked that opera you played today," Val says. "It was cool."

"The usual?" Fadi says, emerging from the back and toward the
cigarette display.

"Pack of Spirits," Jonathan says.

Fadi finishes taping the box. He pulls a plastic bag from a
hook and edges the pastries inside. He adds a stack of napkins. Val
glances from Fadi to Jonathan, trying to recall the only other time

the three of them were alone together here. But she remembers nothing until she woke up in the hospital, nothing of the man who pulled her from underneath the pier, carried her seven blocks to the store, and nothing of the man who called 911.

"Did you wish Valerie a happy birthday?" Fadi says.

"I didn't know," Jonathan says.

"She's sixteen," Fadi says.

"Wow." Jonathan unwraps his cigarettes. "Sixteen, that's something." He stares at her while Fadi hands her the box, then shakes his head. "Well, happy birthday." Jonathan pats Val on the shoulder before heading for the door.

Val grabs the pastries and rushes out of the store. She catches Jonathan at the corner in front of the Greek's. "Hey, can I have one of those?" She points at his cigarettes. "Since it's my birthday."

Jonathan looks at his cigarettes, flips the pack over, and is about to tuck it away.

"It's not like I'm hooked or anything. I'm not going to turn into my mother. She thinks she's healthy because she smokes 120s. They taste like caramel."

Jonathan takes a cigarette from his pack. "Don't get your hopes up. These don't taste like caramel. Just don't smoke it where your dad will see you."

"Like you need to tell me that." Val takes the cigarette from Jonathan's hand.

"Hey, Maestro!" Jonathan and Val look across the street. The redheaded bartender, whom Paulie complains about although he usually drinks during her shift, is leaning against the doorway. "Kind of young for you, isn't she?" The bartender shades her eyes. "What is it, sweetheart, you hot for your teacher? Come across the street, Maestro, let a grown-up buy you a drink."

"Gimme a second here," Jonathan says.

"Offer's not going to stand." Lil puts her hands on her hips. "Enjoy your homework, kiddo."

"Happy birthday." Jonathan pats Val's shoulder once more before crossing to the bar.

Did he let his hand linger a little longer this time? Was it her imagination, or did it seem that Jonathan would have preferred their conversation over talking to Lil?

On her way home, Val goes over all the details of Jonathan's apartment, the smell of old smoke and stale laundry, the sound of honky-tonk trickling in from the bar. She focuses on the battered couch, the piles of jewel cases, the scraps of paper. She replays their kiss, trying to recall the precise texture of Jonathan's lips. She closes her eyes as she stumbles blindly up her stoop, holding on to the memory, thinking of Jonathan to banish thoughts of June.

In bed, she continues to replay the entire afternoon at the music teacher's apartment, examining it until the sheen comes off, until she can no longer conjure the thrill of her lips on his. Until her obsession with the details makes the details lose their meaning.

In her dream she is drowning. She is fighting to keep her head above water. The raft has popped out from under her. It's being carried away. Val splashes, trying to grasp the corner of pink rubber. She slides under the water and cannot breathe. She thrashes and pounds on the walls, trying to break out, escape the water that is swallowing her.

The covers are in a pile on the floor. She goes to the bathroom and splashes water on her face. But she's still thinking of the raft. She remembers the water, murky and turbulent below the surface with tangled, labyrinthine currents.

Val lies down at the far edge of the bed, one leg dangling to the floor. She closes her eyes. But her heart is still racing. She can't get the raft out of her head. She feels herself slipping into the water where she is tackled by a wave and pushed under. She'd opened her eyes, but June was already too far away.

The clock says 2:30 A.M. Val tiptoes as she goes into the hallway and down the stairs. In the vestibule she pulls on a sweatshirt and a pair of sneakers.

Van Brunt is quiet. Val passes a few stragglers from the bar. She hasn't quite shaken off her dream. The nerves in her hands tingle, and her breath is quick and irregular. When she reaches the corner of Visitation, she pauses and glances over at the Dockyard. The windows are fogged and the neon signs cast a fuzzy glow onto the street. From where she stands, the place looks like a clubhouse, forbidding and uncertain behind its steamy windows.

The door opens and a figure lurches into the street. He takes several staggered steps, then collapses onto the mailbox at the corner, splaying himself over its rounded hump like a body washed up on the beach. Under the yellow light of the streetlamp, Val can tell she's looking at the crown of Jonathan's head. She watches him for a moment, hoping he'll stand on his own and get himself inside his building. But he doesn't move, not even when two of the bar's patrons slap him on the shoulder on their way home.

"You motherfucker," one of them says. "You sorry motherfucker."

Val hesitates. She doesn't want the redheaded bartender to see her with Jonathan and she doesn't want her father's friends to catch her out so late. Jonathan groans and rights himself. He takes several steps backward, then falls onto the bench outside the bar.

Val rushes across the street. "Mr. Sprouse? Mr. Sprouse?" She shakes his shoulder. "Jonathan?"

He moans.

"Jonathan? Mr. Sprouse. You can't sleep here, Mr. Sprouse."

His head nods. His eyes are two slits, no bigger than coin slots. "Valerie," he says. "Valerie." It sounds as if his mouth is full of pebbles. He reaches out a hand and tries to pat Val's cheek. "You're so beautiful and you have no idea. So beautiful," he says, dropping his hand toward the sidewalk.

"Jonathan, you can't sleep here. You need to go home," Val says.

"Can't go. Lost my keys."

She finds the keys clutched in his palm. "No, Jonathan, they're right there in your hand. Please stand up." She takes the keys and shakes them in front of his face, like she's enticing a dog with a toy.

"My keys. You found my keys. You're an angel."

"Okay, Jonathan," Val says. "I'm going to go open the door to your building. Then you'll follow me, right?"

It takes Val a few minutes to figure out which key fits the lock. In the hallway, she finds a piece of brick, which she uses to prop open the door. She returns to Jonathan's side, crouches down, and tries to coax him off the bench. "Just stand up for me, Jonathan. Please." Val glances into the bar, hoping no one is paying attention to what's happening out on the street.

"For you, Valerie, anything."

Jonathan lumbers to his feet. Val braces herself, catching one of his arms and throwing it around her shoulder. "Okay, just follow me." They lurch toward the street. Val shifts her weight, directing them toward Jonathan's door and up the stairs. She pulls him out of his coat and sweater and yanks back the covers of his bed before he tumbles down. Then she unlaces his shoes, removing them along with his socks. She pulls the covers over him.

"Can I get you anything?"

"Water."

Val finds a glass, rinses it, and fills it with water. When she returns, Jonathan is fumbling with a bottle of Tylenol PM. She taps out two pills and holds up his head so he can drink.

Val sits on the edge of the bed. The clock next to the bed tells her it's just after three. A late-night bus rolls into the stop across the street. The apartment shakes in time with its idling. Voices rise from the bar below. Country music slips in through the floor-boards. Someone breaks a glass. Jonathan shifts position. One of his hands flails, then gropes at the blankets. Val laces her fingers through his and watches the clock work its way toward four.

Val's eyes grow heavy. She reaches over Jonathan and eases the second pillow out from under him. She tosses it to the foot of the bed. Then she climbs to the inside of the bed, stretching her feet toward the headboard. She curls into the crook behind Jonathan's knees and, wedged between his body and the wall, falls asleep.

Val wakes up in the same position. At first, she doesn't want to disturb Jonathan who's snoring lightly at the head of the bed. She closes her eyes, searching for sleep.

She had slept without dreaming and without fear of the nightmare that had driven her from her own bedroom. She'd felt anchored by Jonathan's proximity—the regularity of his breathing and the sonar of his sleep.

After twenty minutes, Val knows that sleep is futile. Her legs feel cramped and her back aches. She worries that when Jonathan discovers her there, he'll be angry, furious at the liberty she's taken. *He let his lips linger,* she tells herself, *He chased me down the street.*

The clock shows that half an hour has passed since she woke up. Van Brunt is still quiet. The sun, just a suggestion. She knows she should go home before her parents wake up, slip into her room, and pretend she was there all along. But Jonathan hasn't stirred except to press closer to Val. Even if he's sleeping, this means something.

Val grows cramped. She stretches out one leg at a time. Then with as little adjustment to the covers as possible, she slides out of bed. The second her feet hit the floor, Jonathan rolls over, grasping for the space she'd just evacuated. His eyes flash open, a startled look on his face. "Where are—?" he says. Then he turns and sees Val. She watches him bring her into focus, his eyes narrowing and widening as he searches for explanation or memory.

He props himself up on one elbow. "Valerie? What are you doing here?"

"You don't remember? You couldn't get home? You were on the bench outside the bar?"

"Jesus. Fuck," he says, falling back against the mattress and pulling a pillow over his head. "Did I . . . Did we . . ."

"No, Mr. Sprouse."

"My God, don't fucking call me Mr. Sprouse." His voice is muffled by the pillow and Val can't tell if he's angry or not.

"I'm sorry, Jonathan."

"I'm not mad at you, Val. I'm just—this is fucked up."

"It's okay, Jonathan. Nothing happened. I just helped you upstairs. That's all."

"And you slept here, in my bed." He tosses the pillow at the window. "I could lose my job. Worse, your dad will kill me."

"No one saw."

"In this neighborhood? Someone saw."

"I'm sorry," Val says. "I should have left. But I was worried. You were kind of messed up. I didn't think I should leave you alone. Should I have left you alone? What if something happened, like you choked or passed out and hurt yourself?"

"God." Jonathan balls his fists and presses them into his eyes. "That would have been better."

Val takes his water glass and goes to the sink to refill it. She finds some antacid in the bathroom. "My sister takes these when she's hungover. She says they're better than aspirin."

Jonathan pulls back the covers and sits at the edge of the bed. He takes the pills, then hangs his head. "Hangover advice from a teenager. I'm a real fucking mess. I'm going to take a shower," he says. "I smell like death. I feel worse."

Val watches the bathroom door close behind him. She pulls on her shoes and finds her coat.

Jonathan hadn't said *stay* but he hadn't said *go,* either, which was encouraging. So maybe the mature thing to do, the thing that would demonstrate her independence, would be to leave on her own terms without being asked.

Val pulls on her sweatshirt and opens the door.

"Valerie? Val?" Jonathan pokes his head out of the bathroom. The shower is still running in the background. "I need to get out of this fucking place."

"Your apartment?"

"Red Hook."

"So why don't you? You're an adult. You can just leave. I'm stuck with my parents."

He wishes he could jump into his mother's battered Mercedes wagon that's parked around the corner on Imlay Street and whisk Val away to Fishers Island where the water isn't hemmed in by the industrial ports in Jersey and the jagged Manhattan skyline. He could collapse in an Adirondack chair and let the sea air wash the hangover from his head. His brain throbs. His stomach clenches, and he sees Eden's blue figure stranded on the rocky beach.

Jonathan ducks back into the shower. "You're not leaving, right? I owe you something. At least a cup of coffee."

Still wearing her sweatshirt, Val waits by the door until Jonathan emerges from the bathroom. He's shirtless and has wrapped a towel around his waist. He's got more muscle on his skinny frame than she imagined. His chest is sprinkled with sparse black hairs. She watches him go to the kitchen and search the cupboards.

"Shit. No coffee. No milk. Nothing."

"It's okay," Val says.

Jonathan rubs his temples. "No. It's not. None of it's okay. You're too young to know people like me. People who can't even keep instant coffee in the house."

"I'm not."

"This is not an ideal example of adult life." He sweeps an arm around the apartment. "Please don't think it is."

Jonathan goes to his dresser. He pulls on a T-shirt, then finds fresh underwear and a pair of pants. "Do you mind?" he asks. Val turns her back and lets him finish dressing. "It's way too early for any of my degenerate friends to be up, so maybe I could buy you a cup of coffee since I can't provide one here. Let's just make sure the coast is clear."

They kneel on the bed and look out the window. Fadi is standing outside his bodega talking to the black kid who warned Val to stay away from Cree. There's no harm in these two, Val thinks. She checks the clock—not even her parents will be up this early.

The interior of the Cruise Café is hidden behind a film of greasy steam. A couple of methadone addicts are pantomiming something in the bus stop.

"Okay?" Val says.

"I think we got it."

Now they are accomplices—the coffee run, an illicit adventure.

They walk down the narrow staircase. As they step outside, the door to the Dockyard opens and a ragtag crew in last night's clothes stumbles out.

"Inside," Jonathan says.

He fumbles with his key and gets the lock open. There is a moment of silence, before Val and Jonathan erupt into laughter. They are inches apart from each other. Val can feel Jonathan's laughter in her own chest. She laughs harder, bending forward. Her head hits his breastbone. She feels Jonathan's lips in her hair. Then his mouth finds his way down to hers.

This kiss develops slowly, taking its time, assuming a depth and a rhythm as their tongues dance and twist. Val is uncertain whether it lasts seconds or minutes.

Then they are standing apart. "Jesus, my head hurts," Jonathan says. He peers through the smudged glass window in his doorway. "Maybe it's better if I go alone," he says.

Alone in the apartment, a wave of giddiness overtakes Val. He hadn't told her to leave. He'd kissed her. He trusted her. He left her alone. He's coming back. Val bows her head to her knees. There is no one to watch her clap her hands and fist-pump the stale air.

CHAPTER TWENTY

Cree hauls the red metal shopping cart piled high with bags of folded laundry up the dark stairwell, the rubber wheels bumping as he climbs. He drags the cart into his hallway, steadying his load with his free arm. At the door to his apartment he searches for the key. Before the bolt slides back he knows something is up.

Gloria, Celia, Grandma Lucy, and Monique are gathered in the living room. The older women are lined up on the couch while Monique sits off to the side in the room's single armchair.

Cree closes the door. The women remind him of the female hosts of one of those midday talk shows—young, fiery, and feisty alongside old, wise, and maternal.

"What?" Cree says.

He knows them well enough to recognize that each of them is sequestered in her own style of anger. Monique is sulky and pissed. Her arms are crossed over her chest, her body angled away from the group. The lower half of her face is clenched, like she's biting down hard on a word she doesn't dare say. Celia is simmering with the animated anger she brings to her arguments with Ray. She is unable to sit still. Gloria's face conveys disappointment and deep sadness. Grandma Lucy is alert and intense, her fury honed to a fine point.

"Darnell Renton Davis," Celia says, standing up. Her hands are on her waist, her amber eyes glitter, and the gold highlights in her hair seem to have caught fire.

"Celia," Gloria says, reaching for her sister's arm with her good hand. "Celia, sit."

Celia allows herself to be pulled down to the couch.

"What about Ren?" Cree says.

"So you know him?" Celia says. "You admit you know him."

"We hang sometimes. Why? Why's it matter?" Cree says.

The women look at one another. Celia raises her eyebrows and nods at Gloria. Gloria opens her mouth. Her lips tremble, but the words don't come out. She shuts her mouth and tries again. "Baby," Gloria says, "Darnell Renton Davis is the boy who shot Marcus."

Cree becomes aware of every detail in the room: the teacups on the coffee table, the remote control forgotten on the windowsill, a towel hanging on the door to his bedroom. "What? No, Renton's cool," Cree says. "We're, you know . . . he's my . . . Friends and whatever."

"Nevertheless," Gloria says, "he's the one who did it."

"He did," Celia says. "He certainly did."

Grandma Lucy dangles her pendulum, watches it spin, and says nothing.

"No," Cree says. "You're wrong. You're all wrong. He's a strange boy. But not that. No."

"He wasn't much older than you were," Lucy says. "A baby himself."

"I've seen him in lockup when I worked the juvee wards. I've seen him. I know," Celia says. "That's the boy. Plain and simple."

The nerves in Cree's hands tingle. His chest tightens and his breath catches. "You never told me his name."

"You were twelve," Gloria says. "His name didn't matter to you."

"How long's this boy been messing with you?" Celia says, looking from Cree to Monique. "With both of you?"

"What's Mo got to do with this?" Cree says.

"Nothing," Monique says, drawing farther away from the circle, so she's looking out the window.

"Boys like that don't change," Celia says. "I see it every day. Turn them loose and they're back where it started. Boost a car, get a gun. Murder's no thing after that."

"What are you going to do?" Grandma Lucy says. She folds her brittle arms over her chest and stares at Cree until he looks away.

"Do?" Celia says, standing up from the couch and spinning around to look at everyone at once. "What he's going to do is to stay the hell away from that boy, and tomorrow I'm going to search out his parole officer and let him know that Renton's been harassing our family." She falls back on the couch and fixes her gaze on Cree.

"No one's harassing no one," Monique says.

Gloria pulls her cardigan tight. "If Marcus only knew," she says, with a look at Monique.

"Well, he doesn't," Monique says. "And he's not going to." She stands up, stomps to the bathroom, and slams the door.

"Don't start with Marcus, Gloria," Lucy says. "This is a question for the living, not the dead. Cree has business with this Renton. He just needs to figure out what it is."

"Cree's got no business with him," Celia says. "None."

"You'd think Marcus would have something to say about this," Gloria says, sinking back on the couch, retreating into herself.

"Well, if he does, he's not saying it to you," Grandma Lucy says. She sits up straighter, her composed posture a rebuke to her daughters.

"This isn't about Marcus," Celia says. "This is about Cree. You need to tell us what you've been doing with this boy. What has he gotten you into?"

"Nothing."

"Does this nothing have anything to do with that lineup I hauled you out of?" Celia asks.

"No."

"He's a gangbanger, baby. Don't you know how your daddy got killed?" Celia says.

"Of course I know." Cree stares at the women, wondering what they want him to say. Should he apologize for his stupidity, plead ignorance, swear vengeance? Should he make a case for Ren?

They are waiting. Cree wants to kick something and kick it hard. He wants to splinter the coffee table, splatter whatever tea Grandma Lucy has brought over on the walls and carpets, stain the room with that brew of sticks and twigs and moss.

He wants to yank down the curtains, break the TV. And he wants to curse his father for dying in the first place and then coming back to steal the only friend he's got.

"Fuck this," Cree says. "Fuck all of this." He dashes into the hall before the women can see him cry.

For once he's thankful for the dim hallway, the dark staircases, the broken streetlights in the courtyard and along Lorraine Street. He's thankful for the projects' residents who turn a blind eye to other people's suffering so they can get on with their own.

Shit. He'd known something was up with Ren all along, but he couldn't figure what it was because, Cree realizes now—too fucking late of course—he doesn't know a thing about the kid. He doesn't know about his parents, his past. He doesn't know where he came from and why. He's never seen where he lives and has no idea how he makes bank. The only fact he had about Ren was that the kid had done a stint in jail. But in Red Hook that doesn't raise too many eyebrows.

He hadn't wondered why the kid turned up one day, why he knew so much about Cree, why he seemed to care so much. Ren had invaded Cree's hideouts, laying his RunDown tag on the small corners of the Hook Cree had carved out for himself. He'd deputized those shitty little hoods to care for Marcus's memorial, but worst of all, he'd reclaimed the boat. He'd polished it and sanitized it, colonizing the place where Cree had felt closest to his father. It wasn't enough for Ren to have fucked up Cree's life in the past, he was fucking with it now. That's what this was—a complete and total mind-fuck. He either pitied Cree or wanted to torment him. And Cree had been too fucking blind—too flattered by the attention   to notice.

Cree's pretty certain he's the only boy in the Houses who never got into a schoolyard fight. After his dad was shot, kids had left him alone. Teachers let him window-gaze in the back of their classrooms. Bullies knew better than to get caught picking on him. For years, it was as if a cloak of invincibility (or was it invisibility?) had been dropped around his shoulders. He could pass through the projects' more disreputable corners and run the gauntlets of gangs, crews, and posses and attract no more attention than a "What up, kid?"

But Cree's ready for it now. He's ready for the fight he wasn't allowed to have. The fury and rage is pressing into his hands, curling them into fists, driving them to pound his thighs.

Marcus's death had become a symbol of the senseless violence of Red Hook. To engage it directly—to talk to Cree, to comfort Gloria, to smile at Celia without leering—was to admit how fucked up the place was, how far they'd all fallen. For years,

Gloria had diverted Cree's grief with her belief in Marcus's ghost, making the boy disappointed rather than angry. But now his anger has a face.

Cree reaches the lot where the boat is moored. He sees Ren crouching near the stern, fiddling with something in the motor. He's focused on his task, tuned into whatever nut or bolt needs attention. Cree approaches as quietly as he can. Then he says Ren's name. Ren stands and Cree lands a square sucker punch on the kid's jaw. One on the jaw, one on the right eye. Ren stumbles back. Cree gets in another punch to the stomach. He grasps Ren by the shoulders and feels him go limp as if he's not going to resist the next hit. And the one after that and the one after that.

Cree lets go. There's no satisfaction in a one-sided fight. Ren struggles to catch his breath.

"I was in juvee for seven years. I can take my hits," he says. "So bring it. I'm not going to fight you."

Cree is panting. His fists are sore. "You killed my dad."

Ren slides to the ground and leans back against the boat. "I killed your dad."

"You've been lying to me this whole time, pretending we were friends or whatever?" Cree says.

"No," Ren says. "I never lied to you. I just didn't tell you the whole story. You think you would have talked to me if I told you the truth?"

"Why do you care if I talk to you in the first place? I should be the last person you'd want to talk to."

Ren dabs blood from his lip with the cuff of his sweatshirt. "No, you're the only person I want to talk to."

"That's fucked up," Cree says. "You're fucked up."

"What do you know?" Ren says. "You don't know a thing about me. You don't know how I tick."

"And I don't care," Cree says. "All I need to know is that you shot my dad." He turns and starts to walk out of the lot.

"What?" Ren says. "That's it? You're leaving? You don't even want to hear my side?"

Cree stops walking and kicks the ground. "Shit."

Ren doesn't wait for Cree to turn around before beginning his story. "It's a fucked-up story," he says. "The first thing I remember after I dropped the gun was watching this little kid walk across the courtyard. A small boy, a couple of years younger than me. I didn't know you or know your dad. But I knew I'd fucked up. You looked lost even before you saw your father'd been dropped."

Cree had been crying when he reached the courtyard. Marcus's death hadn't been the source of that day's grief, but it had immediately taken over, made the other thing seem inconsequential.

It had started when Rita Marino had decided to steal one of her mother's cigarettes. She had already downed two wine coolers and was looking for some new diversion. She'd spent an hour worrying about where she was going to smoke the slim 120. Eventually she decided on the upstairs bathroom in her house. There was a small vent that opened onto the roof where she could exhale smoke. She brought Cree in after her and locked the door.

The smoke made Rita choke. She said it made her head spin. Cree tried to quiet her. But it was too late. Mr. Marino was pounding on the door. The Marinos didn't allow them to play with the door closed and here they were in a locked bathroom that reeked of smoke. Mr. Marino dragged Cree down the stairs. He shoved him out the door, then thought better of it and reached for Cree's collar. He held him tight and berated him until people came to their windows to watch.

"I couldn't shake the memory of your face," Ren says. "I thought I'd do you a solid when I got out. Help you out and such. I wasn't wrong in thinking you needed someone on your side."

"Fuck you," Cree says.

"Here's what's messed up. It could have been anyone who got into the trouble I did. It could have been you."

"No. Not me."

"Why? Because you had a lot of friends growing up? You were the popular kid? I didn't think so," Ren says. "All it takes is for the right guys to pay you mind. Call your name across the courtyards, allow you to hang on their benches, chill in their corner. You never wanted to belong? You never wanted a crew?"

"Not when I was twelve."

"Bullshit. Fuck, man, I didn't even know that I was being sized up until it was too late. The attention was addictive. Suddenly all these older dudes—these cool dudes—wanted me to hang with them. I saw that they were getting into some rough shit. But that was better than sitting at home alone with a busted TV. I became habituated to their lifestyle." Ren finds a crumpled cigarette in the pouch of his sweatshirt. "One day we were chilling in an apartment on the second floor of one of the towers. A guy from my crew had a gun. Someone always had a gun, but this time I was allowed to hold it. I felt like a real sophisticated baller. Apparently there was another crew hanging in an apartment across the courtyard who my boys wanted to put a scare into. The guys told me I'd be the real deal—a hard-core banger—if I sent out a warning to their rivals. I didn't even think about it. I just pointed the gun out the window."

Cree puts a knuckle into his mouth and bites down, hoping the pain will distract him from the threat of tears.

"Remember how often you heard gunfire back then?" Ren says. "It was nothing. I heard it all the time. It was part of the everyday every day. But I never saw anyone brought down. I figured I was just adding to the background noise, the atmospherics. It took us a beat to figure out that the screaming outside the window meant someone'd been hit. My boys told me to wait in the apartment. I was still waiting there when the cops rolled in. I watched the whole thing unfold like it had nothing to do with me. Like I was watching TV. I was lucky to have been tried as a juvenile, otherwise I'd still be inside." Ren tugs some dried grass out of the earth and tosses it away.

"So you're lucky," Cree says. "So what?"

"I'm sorry," Ren says. "I'm real sorry."

"Whatever that means."

"My parents didn't visit me more than a couple times a year. Then they moved upstate to Troy. I didn't even know until one of my letters got sent back. They don't even know I'm out."

"I'm supposed to feel bad *your* family's not together?"

"I'm explaining something to you," Ren says. "I'm a fuckup. I got no one on my side. And that's my fault. But what about you?"

"What about me?" Cree says. "What's your business with me?"

"You've got a whole neighborhood full of people, but you're lonely by choice. That's what I can't figure."

"I don't know what your game is, but it's better you don't think about me at all."

"Too bad," Ren says. "It's a habit. In juvee, I used to think about you a lot. In my eye you were still that little kid crossing the courtyard. When the weather was nice, I'd try to guess what you were up to. Because whatever it was, was better than the nothing I was doing."

"If the weather was nice, I should have been out on this boat with my dad. But thanks to you that never happened," Cree says.

"When I first got out, I just wanted to see what you looked like. That's all. I wanted to check that you were okay, not getting into any sort of trouble. It's fifty-fifty out here that trouble's going to find you. I followed you around, caught wind of all your hiding spots. Then I started thinking, this boy's looking for an escape—a reprieve. He wants an adventure but is too afraid to leave Red Hook. And that's my fault. With your father gone, you're frozen. Stuck in that courtyard because of what I did. You dream of getting out but you're too scared."

"Fuck you," Cree says. "You don't know the first thing about me." But he knows it isn't true.

"I don't? Don't tell me you haven't been wanting to get that boat out on the water, go all those places your father promised to take you," Ren says. "The boat's ready. I had enough years of machine and shop to fix her up."

"So then what? You thought I'd just jump on board with you? That we'd sail into the sunset? That was your plan? When were you going to tell me about what you'd done?"

"When I made it up to you as best I could."

"You must be crazy to even think that's possible," Cree says.

"No," Ren says. "You're the crazy one planning to spend his whole life in this neighborhood. There's no such thing as ghosts. The dead don't come back. You just pretend they do so you don't have to get on with it."

"What do you know about ghosts?" Cree says.

"You want to know what ghosts are like? Try living in a dormitory full of teenage killers. You'll see mad ghosts everywhere you look. On the faces of twelve-year-old boys who can't forget who they killed. Who see their dead everywhere. You'll see them in the fucking mirror when you just want to check if you're still breathing. There wasn't a goddamned night on the inside when I wasn't woken by somebody haunted by the person he dropped. Ghosts aren't the dead. They're those the dead left behind. Stay here long enough, you'll become one of them—another ghost haunting the Hook."

"There's nothing wrong with Red Hook."

"There's something wrong with being too afraid to see any-place else," Ren says. "I saw you watching those girls on the raft. I watched you watch them."

"You what?" Cree says. He was sure he'd been alone on the pier. But there had been the shadow disappearing into the night that had made him turn from the water.

"You followed them along the pier. I was with you every step of the way. I was even close enough to touch you. You were too mesmerized to notice. You were so jealous of their adventure, you wanted to grab a piece for yourself. You followed them into the water," Ren says. "You swam out."

Cree shakes his head. But he remembers the strange chill at his back, the eerie sensation that Marcus had been close by, watching.

"You did," Ren says. "But you couldn't reach them. The current was too strong. You think I'm the only person who saw you swim out? How long do you think you're going to keep this a secret? Red Hook only looks abandoned. But it has eyes."

"Yeah," Cree says. "Yours."

"You should be thankful that I'm keeping watch over you— distracting the cops from the fact that you were in the water the night that girl drowned."

"Drowned? How come you know that?"

"I told you. I was watching. I watched the raft flip while you were swimming out. Then I watched you struggle back onto the shore."

"You saw what happened?" All it would have taken is a word from Ren to clear Cree of suspicion, to get the damn cops off his back. "And you didn't say anything?"

"Like I said, I saw the raft flip," Ren says. "And I saw you in the water with those girls. You know how many innocent kids were in juvee with me? How many of them were guilty of being in the wrong place at the wrong time? You're guilty of nothing but your own foolishness. Swimming out to a couple of white girls couldn't end well. One day your friend Val will remember that you were trying to reach her. Then what are you going to do?"

"I don't know," Cree says.

"You need me," Ren says. "I know you had nothing to do with that raft. But the cops can't wait to slap their cuffs on some black kid for this sort of crime. Even if there was no crime. They still have their eyes on you. You have to think about these things if you're going to survive," Ren says.

"I'm going to survive. I'm surviving."

"You're putting one foot in front of the other. That ain't life."

"What do you know about a life? You spent most of yours locked up."

"Exactly. And so will you, one way or another. I'm not saying in jail. But I'm implying by circumstance." Ren stands up.

"You stay away from my boat," Cree says. "And you stay away from me. I'm not going anywhere with you. Now or ever. Keep away from me. Keep away from my mom. Keep out of anywhere you think I might be. If you see my shadow, I suggest you run." Cree takes a deep breath. His chest feels tight. His eyes and nose sting. "If I see you again, I'm going to tell everyone who you are and what you did. The biggest mistake you made, after killing my dad, was coming back to Red Hook."

Cree rushes away from the lot. The fucked-up thing, the really fucked-up thing, is that in the last weeks with Ren—on the boat or wherever—Cree had felt closer to Marcus. So maybe Ren's right. Maybe the dead do cling to those who brought them down.

Cree circles the neighborhood. There is no comfort in his hideouts. The renovation of the abandoned bar is nearly complete. A sign in the window advertises an opening night party. He retreats toward the Houses. As he crosses Coffey Park, he sees his uncle Des nodding off on one of the benches. Next to him is the wino who fingered Cree for the lineup. He's swigging wine from a bottle in a brown paper bag. Des lifts his head as Cree passes.

"Acretius," he says.

Cree stops. "Des, ask your buddy why he's been selling me out to the police. Greedy little shit."

"Give me a dollar and I'll ask him," Des says. His voice is all rattle and rasp.

"I'll ask him myself then," Cree says. He approaches the bench, towering over the wino who's trying to shrink into his filthy coat. "Yo." He takes the bottle out of the wino's hand and drops it in a garbage can. The shattering glass makes the wino flinch.

"Estaban," Des says. "His name is Estaban."

"I don't care what his name is," Cree says.

"*Perdoname,*" the wino says, clutching Cree's hand. "*Perdoname. No era usted. No era usted.*"

"He says it wasn't you," Des says. "How about a dollar?"

"Fuck your dollar," Cree says.

Cree stares into Des's face, searching, as he always does, for any remnant of Marcus in his uncle's withering skin and cloudy eyes. But there's nothing.

The lights are out in the living room. The apartment is silent. Cree drops his keys on the kitchen table and listens to them skid across the Formica.

"Acretius?"

Cree jumps at the sound of his grandmother's voice.

"Turn on the light, Acretius."

Cree switches on the overhead in the kitchen. Grandma Lucy is sitting at the far end of the couch. Her hands are folded in her lap. A small valise is next to the window. "Where's Celia?" Cree says.

"I sent her home. Everybody in this family is running from something. I'm tired of it. Sit." She pats the spot next to her on the couch.

Cree pulls out a chair. Grandma Lucy fingers her pendulum. "Don't think for one instant I don't know how badly you want to talk to Marcus's spirit. But let me tell you something. A spirit is not something you see or hear. It's something you feel. An idea. And you can't go looking for it. It comes to you."

"But not to me," Cree says.

"Is that so?" Lucy folds her arms across her chest and stares at the silent television. "Is that so?" she says again. "You have less sense than I imagined. You can switch off the light."

Cree stands in the dark for a moment, aware of his grandmother's irritation. He hears the knife edge of her breath. "Good night, Grandma," Cree says, crossing to his bedroom.

"You ever think about why this boy's come for you? You ever think about that?"

"Not until I had to," Cree says.

"Well," Lucy says, "if you thought about things the way I do, you might alight upon the idea that this boy is the means by which Marcus talks to you. But that is a decision you'd have to make for yourself."

Cree hovers at the bedroom door for a moment, but Lucy is done.

In the morning when he gets up, Lucy has run Gloria's bath, fixed coffee and toast. The two women are looking through an incense and oils catalog and don't notice when Cree slides out the front door.

He rushes down the stairs, dashes through the courtyard, and breaks into a run on Lorraine Street. He arrives at the lot. The boat is gone.

CHAPTER TWENTY-ONE

When the taxi is midway across the Brooklyn Bridge, Jonathan squints at the numbers on the meter, trying to distinguish them from the numbers on the radio and the glowing digits on the clock, which are all jumping up and down and melting into one LCD trail. His eyes swivel in their sockets. His optic nerves shake. He tries to focus on one number, but it jitters side to side, then disappears completely.

The radio is turned to KTU. Dance music is flooding the cab. Jonathan's jaw is tense. His head, lolling against the vinyl headrest in the backseat, is velvet and heavy. He closes his eyes and the insides of his eyelids feel like satin. His stomach is melting. The window is open and one of his hands is trailing outside the cab. The air between his fingers seems mentholated.

Dawn is next to him. He rolls his head to one side to get a look at her, but he can't focus well enough to see how disheveled her drag is. He feels her vibrating next to him, her head dropping toward his shoulder as she caresses his knee with her hand. Jonathan worries if she stops rubbing he'll come down.

The drugs had been Dawn's idea—one E each to celebrate a successful night during which they'd brought down the crowd with a showcase of "Patriotic Songs of War." Dawn had worn a floor length red, white, and blue sequined dress, with a sash that read "Miss America." She'd chosen a blond wig that reached for the stars. She topped it off with a tiara.

A week ago a man who claimed to be a talent scout from a cruise line gave them each his card. Dawn nearly shoved her tongue down his throat in appreciation. Tonight the scout was back in the audience. He told Dawn that he loved her act. "We're going international!" she said, squeezing Jonathan's ass.

"Yeah, I can just see myself on the lido deck," he said. "When that ship sails, you'll be cruising alone."

"Don't be a dead fish. Let's celebrate." She pulled a pillbox out from the crevice between her falsies. "One pill doesn't do anything," she said, forcing the capsule between Jonathan's lips before their final set.

Now Jonathan's in the cab with Dawn. He draws a deep breath, which takes forever to fill his lungs. He sits up and wills the clock on top of the Watchtower building to hold-fucking-still for a second so he can find out how late it is or how early. The suspension cables on the bridge collapse and separate.

The driver's yelling at them over the music.

"Fuck you two say you're going?"

Jonathan steadies himself on the divider between the front and back seats. He rests his chin on the hard metal lip. "Take the expressway," he says. "Toward Staten Island."

They overshoot the exit and have to double back below the

expressway's dirty underbelly. They thread their way through the projects and pull onto Van Brunt.

"You sure know how to treat a lady," Dawn says, stepping out of the cab. Jonathan notices that she's wearing jeans, a fur jacket, a girl's T-shirt, and the white platforms. She's brushed out her wig so it falls around her shoulders.

Jonathan overpays the driver and slams the door without offering to direct him back to the city.

Dawn had taken E to celebrate, but Jonathan had other reasons. He knew the drug would lift his spirits. He disregarded the inevitable comedown—the morbid Sunday of self-reproach that awaited him.

When he kissed Val in the dark corridor behind his front door, he knew he'd made a mistake. He was aware of the relief coursing through her body. So he kissed her because he believed that's what she wanted. At least, that's how it started.

It had been nice, Val's mouth on his, the quick excitement of her breath giving way to the easy flow of their tongues as the kiss found its pace and rhythm. There was none of the smoky char of kissing Lil's barrel-aged mouth—the sour aftertaste of whiskey and beer. There was nothing needy or demanding in the simple movements of Val's lips. With Val, Jonathan realized how much he missed being kissed by someone who wanted to kiss him because he was Jonathan and not just because he was the last man standing at the end of another long night.

This was something he'd skipped in high school. He'd preferred to tangle with bad girls, the ones brave enough to talk their way into stale-smelling dive bars on Second Avenue—the ones for whom kissing was a gateway drug quickly abandoned in favor of more serious pleasures.

Jonathan had let the kiss go on too long. He'd pulled Val in tighter, as if he was trying to squeeze everything out of the moment. Because he knew when he let go, that had to be the end of it.

When he returned from the bodega, Val had made herself comfortable on his couch. There was no way for him to avoid the expectant look on her face that told him she wanted more. But he didn't kiss her again.

All day, he consoled himself with the fact that it could have been worse. In his deep, drunken stupor, he could have rolled over and grasped her. He could have mindlessly gone through the motions, only regaining consciousness when it was too late. He couldn't think about that. That's what the E was for.

He and Dawn stand shivering on Van Brunt. Jonathan takes a moment to collect himself. The Dockyard's vibrating neon signs come to a standstill. The street feels solid beneath his feet.

"Jesus," Dawn says. "This fresh air is going to kill my high. Get a girl inside." She heads for the door.

Inside, the night has wound down to its hollow core. No one is tending bar. A few drinkers are huddled at a table near the window, one slumped, his head wedged between a stand of empties, while two others talk at each other over his rounded back. Jonathan is too gone to determine who they are.

"What's a girl have to do to get a drink?" Dawn says.

"The question is not what but who," Jonathan says. Then he sidesteps before Dawn can pinch his ass.

Of course Dirty Dan is there. His hangdog, puppet face is distorted with a sloppy smile, which widens when he sees Dawn, who has taken off her fur bolero, revealing a tiny T-shirt that ends a few inches above her navel. "I didn't know chicks with dicks were your style, Maestro." Dirty Dan lets out his cackle.

Even though Dirty's trying to cling to youth by wearing skater clothes, Jonathan can tell what he will look like when he's old—a spindly, withered drunk with a booze-distended belly.

Fucked up as he is, Jonathan knows the best thing to do is let Dirty ramble until he runs out of fuel. The reason Dirty doesn't get thrown out as often as Jonathan is that he's the only drug dealer who sticks around until late, using more than he sells, then giving it away for free.

Jonathan taps Lil on the shoulder. "Is it open bar tonight?"

Her face has a late-night gloss of sweat and booze. Her eyes are narrowed.

"Nothing wrong with experimenting, Maestro," Lil says. "It's good for you to play with someone strong enough to carry you home." She gives Dawn a half-mast stare. "He was mine first you know."

"I just want a drink," Jonathan says.

"Help yourself," Lil says.

Jonathan slides behind the bar.

"Real chic scene out here," Dawn says. "How come you never invited me over before?"

"I didn't think you'd like my friends," Jonathan says.

"These are your friends?" Dawn arches a penciled eyebrow. Then she pounds her drink like a sailor. "Well, that's the saddest thing I've ever heard." She kisses the top of Jonathan's head. "I'm going to powder my nose."

Jonathan watches her walk to the back of the bar. There seems to be a little more hip and dip to her walk as she transforms the Dockyard into her personal runway. Dirty Dan catcalls as Dawn passes. She stops walking and turns to face him.

"Oh yeah?" she says.

"Yeah," Dirty says. But there's a glitch in his gab. Dirty Dan is tall, but in her heels, Dawn towers over him.

Dawn takes Dirty by the shoulders as if she is about to kiss him. Then she pushes him away. "Not with these lips, honey."

Jonathan's high has lowered his guard. He doesn't notice that Paulie Marino is standing in front of him. Paulie has to bang the table to get Jonathan's attention.

"You little fucking pervert," Paulie says.

Jonathan's eyes widen as he tries to get his vision to stop shaking.

"You little perv."

Jonathan struggles to his feet, but slips and slides back to the bench. The muscles on either side of Paulie's neck are twitching. Lil and Dirty lower their glasses and stare at Jonathan.

"I couldn't find my kid all day, then I learn from your druggie girlfriend that my little girl carried you home last night."

Jonathan's head is spinning so fast he can't figure out how to glower at Lil.

"You don't get it," Jonathan says. He glances over at Lil and her crowd. But no one steps forward.

"What the fuck did you do to my little girl?" Paulie's voice rises above Lil's wheedling country music. "Tell me." He takes a step closer.

The things that get forgiven in the Dockyard—the late-night slipups, the guys Lil's hooked up with after their girlfriends went home, the couples who've been discovered naked in the storage room, the two-day benders that have wrecked marriages, the people who've vomited, who've wet themselves, who've propositioned police officers, the people who've stolen and destroyed—all of them excused when the sun rises. Jonathan's mistake is not one of these.

Lil's crew watches with detached fascination—immobile and riveted, eager to see what unfolds so they will have a story to tell the next night.

"Lil?" Jonathan says, hoping she'll step in, deflect the inevitable, and preserve the night's debauchery. Lil doesn't move.

Jonathan doesn't resist when the first punch lands on his right eye. The second summons a warm gush of blood from his nose. The third splits his lip. His eye is already swelling shut. He struggles to keep the other one open, which is how he sees Dawn stride over and clock Paulie in the jaw.

Paulie staggers back.

"You wouldn't hit a girl, now would you?" Dawn says. She

squats down at Jonathan's side. Her wig is in place. Her makeup is refreshed—her lips relined, her cheeks matte. She wipes blood from his nose. "Oh, baby," she says, "what have you done?"

Jonathan tries to speak, but his bruised and bloody mouth won't let him.

Dawn helps him to his feet. "Excuse us," she says, pushing past Paulie. She turns and waves her glossy red nails at Lil and Dirty Dan. "Now, you all know how to show a girl a real good time."

Jonathan's face throbs. His swollen eye has its own pulse. When he talks, his busted lip feels as if it's going to explode. Dawn stays with him for two days. She borrows his clothes. Except for her carefully shaped eyebrows, in Jonathan's black jeans and T-shirts, she is simply Don from New Jersey a trim, well-muscled man with glowing skin. Don knows how to take care of the wounded with icepacks, hot compresses, tea, and steamed vegetables from the bulletproof Chinese. But these attentions only ease Jonathan's physical discomfort.

Eventually Dawn has to return to the city. She has a meeting with her cruise ship talent scout. She does a pretty good job of hiding her disappointment that Jonathan won't accompany her.

"You'll knock 'em dead on your own," Jonathan says. "How many times have I told you that you don't need me?"

After Dawn leaves, he turns the radio on for company. A jingle he wrote a year ago for a used car dealership plays on a constant loop. Its artificial joy is a rebuke. He wishes he could drink less and sleep more, but he does the opposite.

By Tuesday morning, the area around his eye looks like the inside of a plum—concentric circles of purples, pinks, and yellows. His lip is still busted and cracked. He takes a long shower and shaves carefully. He finds his cleanest clothes. Despite his battered appearance, he's determined to go into work.

Fadi notices Jonathan's bruises but doesn't say anything. He doesn't charge him for his coffee. When Jonathan exits the bodega, Valerie is standing at the bus stop. He raises his hand to cover his swollen eye. She's wearing pink knee socks with her loafers—a direct violation of St. Bernardette's dress code. An open textbook is in her hands. Twice she glances up from the page and into Jonathan's apartment. He resists the urge to call out to her. Valerie looks down the street for the bus. Then she closes her textbook, slides it into her book bag, and begins to walk to school. As much as he'd like to catch up to Val, he can't risk being seen with her in Red Hook.

While Jonathan was watching Val, a black teenager has come down Visitation and stopped in front of the mural of the cruise ship someone painted on one of Fadi's roll gates. He paces in front of the painting. Eventually he catches Jonathan's eye. It takes Jonathan a moment to place him. It's the boy Val jumped into the bay with the day of June's vigil.

"S'up?"

Jonathan nods. If this is the first person Valerie kissed, then Jonathan is the second. Even he has to admit that this is not a step in the right direction.

"You cool?" the boy says.

He remembers how this boy had stood on the pier, watching as Jonathan dressed Val. He feels like an adulterer, a thief. Next to this kid he feels deformed.

The boy shrugs and rubs his bald head. "Okay, man. Enjoy your day."

The 61 rumbles into the stop. Jonathan dashes toward the open door.

Every time the bus hits a bump or pothole, Jonathan's eye throbs. He anchors his chin with his hand, softening the impact. As the bus crosses from Red Hook into Carroll Gardens, Jonathan catches sight of Val. She swings her arms as she walks. Her chin is tilted upward, her eyes trained on something in the sky. It was enough to rescue her that first time. The second time he found her in the water, he should have let her be. She didn't need him. It was the other way around.

He waits for the steps to clear of students before entering St. Bernardette's. He will take the back stairs up to his classroom and hide behind his piano. He will keep the lights off and show the girls another film of an opera. The second bell rings. He can hear the lobby quieting down, the last footfalls of students rushing to class.

He is alone in the lobby when the school secretary pokes her head out from behind the door that leads to the chapel and administrative offices. "Sister Margaret needs to see you, Mr. Sprouse."

Perhaps Valerie was looking into his window this morning to warn him, as if she could spare him his fate. Jonathan enters the administration wing. The swinging door closes behind him, shutting him off from the rest of the school.

Sister Margaret sits behind her desk, watched over by a stained glass window of the Blessed Virgin. She and Jonathan have had little to do with each other since he was hired two years ago. A manila folder is open on her desk. She does not look up when he enters.

"Take a seat, Mr. Sprouse."

Her wimple throws her face into shadow.

"I'm going to ask you a question plain and simple, and I'm going to expect a plain and simple answer."

Jonathan glances around the office. He inhales its scent of musty paperwork, old wood, and pencil shavings. This is the last school where he will work.

"Mr. Sprouse, did you tell two of your students to *shut up*?"

"What?"

"Did you use inappropriate language when addressing your class?"

Jonathan laughs. "I believe, Sister Margaret, what I actually said was *shut the hell up*."

Sister Margaret looks up from her file, noticing Jonathan's face for the first time. "You may teach music, Mr. Sprouse. You may think of yourself as a bohemian, but that doesn't give you the right to speak like a heathen. Even a music teacher must abide by our rules."

"I'm not a music teacher," Jonathan says. "If I am, I'm a terrible one. My students don't pay attention to what I say and I don't care. Appreciate music? My ass. Since the start of the year only one student has contributed to my class in any way you might consider constructive. And do you know what she said? She said the music was *cool*. That's real insight for you."

Sister Margaret closes the folder and clears her throat.

"I pretend my students need to learn, and I pretend I need to teach. It's a farce. I'm wasting their time, and they are wasting mine. I'm even wasting this school's time. This whole thing has been an experiment in complete and utter fucking time wastage." The nun recoils from his profanity as if he's spit on her. "Do you know why I teach music? Because I don't have the energy to play it or write it."

"Are you done?"

"Am I done? I am most certainly done. Permanently done. Have my students sit in silence this afternoon. They'll get more out of it."

Jonathan stands up. Sister Margaret brushes the front of her dress with both hands. She is making small movements with her mouth, trying to find the right words or restrain the wrong ones.

"Don't bother," Jonathan says, waving her back into her seat. "I quit."

The lobby is empty. He hurries toward the door. Anna DeSimone is getting out of a Lincoln town car. A black lace bra is poking out of her blouse.

"Whoa, Mr. Sprouse," she says. "Looks like you had an exciting weekend." She comes up the steps until she is standing a few inches from Jonathan. "Lovers' quarrel or barroom brawl?"

"Anna," Jonathan says. "You're seventeen. Act like it."

That evening Jonathan lies on his couch trying to listen to Eden's recording of *Mame*. The doorbell rings during the overture. At the start of the second number a pebble hits his window. He has no interest in finding out who wants to see him.

Jonathan switches off the stereo and turns off the lights. He lies in the dark, his ears growing used to the neighborhood noise while his eyes adjust to the yellow cast of the streetlamp on his floor.

The screen of his phone is lighting up with Dawn's name.

He answers it but says nothing.

"I know you're there, sweetness," Dawn says. "Aren't you going to say hello?"

"Hi," Jonathan says.

"Congratulate me." Dawn is clearly getting an early start on a late night.

"Congratulations."

"We're going to the Bahamas. We're going to Jamaica."

Jonathan has no energy for Dawn's exuberant hysterics. "Did you win a sweepstakes?"

"*Jo-na-than*." Dawn draws out each syllable as if she is speaking to a small child. "The cruise, sweetness. We booked it. This is my Carmen Miranda moment."

Jonathan's heart falls like a counterweight against Dawn's excitement. "That's great, Dawn." Even the fucking drag queen is moving on to something better.

"You don't sound thrilled," Dawn says.

"You'll be a real rum swizzle."

"And you?"

A groan of rusted iron followed by a crash comes from his fire escape. A shadow slides across the table.

"I have to go." Jonathan hangs up the phone.

He gets to his knees and crawls across the floor toward the door, figuring he can hide in his building's stairwell. Before he opens the door, he looks over at the window and sees a hand pressing against the glass. He leaps to his feet and rushes to the window.

"Val! What are you doing?"

"I tried the doorbell."

The gush of fresh air that follows Val into the apartment makes Jonathan cough. He shuts the window. He can sense Val shivering and resists his urge to touch her.

"Did anyone see you?"

"I knew you were home. How come you're sitting in the dark?" She reaches for the lamp next to the table, but Jonathan swats her hand away. "Jesus," Val says.

"You can't be here."

"We had a sub in Music Appreciation. She made us listen to something called madrigals."

"You're not supposed to be here."

"Says my dad."

"Says me."

She crosses the living room and sits on the couch. "I can't believe he beat you up. He's an asshole."

"I would have done the same thing."

Jonathan checks that the blinds over the window next to his bed are as flush to the glass as possible. Then he turns on a small lamp next to the TV. Val is wearing a pink peacoat. Her skin is rosy with cold. She barely looks sixteen.

"Whoa," Val says. "Your face."

"It's the least of my problems."

"When are you coming back to school, Mr. Sprouse?"

"I'm not."

"Because of my dad?"

"No, because of me."

Val sits on the couch and fiddles with an empty pizza box. "You didn't do anything."

Jonathan sits on the bed. Then he thinks better of it and stands. "Valerie, really."

"I mean, it's not like we slept together or anything. It's not that big a deal."

"It doesn't matter what we didn't do. No one cares about what didn't happen."

"I'll tell them it was my fault. That I was the one who kissed you. I crawled into your bed."

"You can't do that."

"Why not? It's true."

"It doesn't matter what people think of me. You're just starting out."

Val pulls her peacoat tighter and shrinks back into the couch. "Why should I care what people think of me?"

Jonathan feels exhausted. He wants to flop down on his bed and close his eyes. "It's more complicated than that. Let me be the bad guy. Let people think I took advantage of you. They'll pity you for a while, then things will get back to normal."

"Nothing will ever get back to normal."

"You have to go."

"Where? Home? To my dad who beats up my friends?"

"Your dad loves you," Jonathan says.

"How do you know? How do you know what goes on in my life?" The pitch of Val's voice is rising.

"I don't. But you can't stay."

"I know what you're going to say. You're going to say that I'm too young. That this is inappropriate. That I should go sleep with boys my own age. You're going to say that you're a *teacher*. Like that makes you so old and wise." She wipes her eyes with the cuff of her coat. "But you know what? You don't know everything. You were wrong. Everyone was wrong."

"About—"

"It *is* my fault June's missing."

Jonathan shakes his head.

"It's true." Val sounds triumphant. "It is."

"No," Jonathan says.

"You don't believe me?" Val crosses her arms over her chest. "June told me that I still acted like a baby and that the raft was stupid. She told me I'd never have a boyfriend because I was too weird. She wanted to go into shore and hang. But I wouldn't let her. Everyone thinks that what happened was an accident, but it wasn't." She stares at Jonathan, holding his gaze, daring him to look away. "I pushed her."

Suddenly Jonathan is not thinking of Val and June, but of Eden, arcing through the air, flying backward from the boat to the water. He didn't push her, but he let her go. His guilt doesn't make this distinction.

Jonathan rarely thinks of what led up to the moment his mother boarded the boat. He only remembers what came after—the terrible noise of the splintering dock, the barrel roll, then the awful silence as the engine died and the boat began to sink. At night, before the booze lets him sleep, he still tries to imagine what might have happened if he'd plunged into the sound and churned the water with panicked strokes. Could he have reached Eden? Would he be able to forgive himself if he had tried?

"I pushed her and she fell off the raft. I told her to swim home if that's what she wanted. She was my only friend and I pushed her. And for a moment it felt good." Val's shoulders start to shake, and her words are swallowed by a loud sob. "I just watched her tread water. She was always bossing me. She thought I didn't care." She swallows hard. "But I did."

"You almost died yourself. You couldn't have known what

would happen to June." Jonathan steps toward Val, ready to wrap his arms around her, still her sobs. But he stops himself. He stands in the middle of the room, his arms limp at his sides.

"But I pushed her." Val wipes her nose on her sleeve. "June was such a bitch. She didn't like hanging out with me anymore. I embarrassed her. But she didn't have anyone else. And now neither do I."

Jonathan sits on the couch, near enough to try and reassure Val but not close enough to touch.

"I didn't know what would happen when I pushed her off the raft. I tried to grab her, but then the raft flipped. I had no idea how strong the current was. It pulled me under and I couldn't reach June. I tried. I really tried. But I couldn't. I couldn't even see her in the water." Tears stream down Val's cheeks, running over her lips, dripping off her chin. "I miss her every day. Every minute of every day even though it's my fault she's gone. And I can't tell anyone what I did to my best friend, because then they would know that we weren't friends and then I wouldn't be allowed to miss her. Because missing June is all I have left of her."

"I'm sorry," Jonathan says. He wonders if any of Val's classmates have ever commiserated with her for her loss instead of gossiping about it.

"I can never tell anyone what happened. I killed her. Everything's my fault."

"You have to stop saying that or you'll make it true," Jonathan says.

He looks at Val, shrinking into herself on the couch, pulling away from him, retreating into her sorrow. This is how it starts, this guilt that grabs you like a vise, that grips and squeezes tighter every year, that goes from memory, to refrain, to persistent baseline—that embeds itself and echoes throughout the day. The guilt that eats away, leaving half a person behind and makes you search out other broken people for company.

Part of him has never left the dock in Fishers Island and still stands there, drink in hand, watching Eden stumble onto the boat, watching the boat bank hard, and his mother fly away and sink into the inky sound. And part of him still watches himself from a distance, watches him watching Eden, watches him staying on dry land, watches him doing nothing. "You have to forgive yourself," Jonathan says. "It was an accident."

"I killed my best friend," Val says. She doubles over, burying her face in her lap. Jonathan reaches over and strokes her back, then pulls his hand away. "Now you won't even touch me," Val says. "You're as bad as everyone else."

"I'm not the right person. I think you should talk about this with your parents."

"No," Val says. "You can't tell me to go home. You're the only one who understands. There's no one but you. You've been watching me, at the pier, in school, outside my fucking window. You understand me. You have to. Because no one else ever will." Her eyes are wild with tears. "Because you know what I did and you'll forgive me because you did the same thing." Val's words are aspirated by sobs. Her throat sounds raw and scraped. "You and me—we're the same."

"No," Jonathan says. "We're nothing alike." Val stares at him. Her mouth is slightly open. Her bottom lip vibrates. "You don't want to be anything like me."

"I do," Val says. "I am." She puts her head in her hands. "I am."

Jonathan closes his eyes and rubs his eyelids. Now the winnowing begins—possibilities tossed like trash from a car window. This is the moment where Val will step out of her young, fresh shell and accidentally join the ranks of the incomplete or the damaged, people like Lil and him. Once Val mistakes herself for one of them, it will be too late. "What happened to June was not your fault," he says.

Jonathan finds a paper napkin from the bulletproof Chinese and hands it to her. She wads it up and tosses it away. He wants to hold her until she stops shaking. He wants to let her cry herself out. He wants to be the one to restore her. Instead he walks to the window and peeks out a slat in the blinds.

"Don't do that," Val says. "Don't fucking do that. Stop being paranoid that someone's watching us." She rushes to the window and opens the blinds, bending them in her fury. She wrestles with the latch and yanks up the pane. She sticks her head out into the street. "Hey," she shouts down to Van Brunt. "I'm up here with Jonathan Sprouse. All by myself. I'm up here—"

Jonathan pulls Val back from the window. She breaks free from his grip and wheels around to face him. "Get off me," she says. "You're hurting me. Let me go. You don't care about me."

He lets go of her arm and steps back from the window. He doesn't want their argument to carry out into the street. She lunges back toward the window, but Jonathan gets there first, slamming it shut with such force a hairline crack appears in the glass. He looks down. Biker Mike and New Steve are smoking outside the bar, their faces turned upward in the direction of his apartment.

"You're going to get both of us in a lot of trouble if you don't stop," Jonathan says.

"Trouble? What trouble could I possibly get in? I killed someone. My life is over."

"It hasn't even begun." Jonathan's swollen eye has begun to throb. The things he wants to say to Val tangle with the things he shouldn't say, and in the end no more words come out of his mouth.

Val stops crying. She wipes her face on her sleeve. Her eyes are red and swollen, her cheeks mottled, but when she speaks her voice is calm. "Yes, it *has* begun, Jonathan. And you can't tell me what to do, because you don't care."

Her sudden composure startles him. She buttons her coat and heads for the door.

Jonathan goes to the window and watches Val leave his building. The calm in her voice chills him. He wants to follow, but there are too many unwelcome faces outside the bar. He will wait and then he will break his promise to himself and stand guard across from Val's bedroom for one more night.

He finds a bottle with a couple of fingers of whiskey left. He kills the booze, and chain-smokes his last four cigarettes, lighting one off the other.

"Nice face." Lil has emerged from the bar for a smoke. "You're a real piece of work, Maestro. What'd you do to her this time?"

"I don't know what you're talking about."

"Fireman Paulie's kid. She came into the bar looking like hell on wheels. You break her heart?"

"You served her? You served a sixteen-year-old?"

"You want to report me? She got Dirty to buy her a drink. I didn't notice."

"Jesus, Lil. Jesus. Dirty-fucking-Dan?"

"Yeah?" Lil picks a speck of ash off her fingerless gloves. "He actually got pissed off when I threw the kid out."

"Where is he?"

Lil crushes her cigarette under her cowboy boot. "Left."

"When?"

"Right after I eighty-sixed the kid."

"*Together?*"

"Maestro. What happens outside the bar is none of my business."

Jonathan has to resist the urge to slap her. He paces in a circle, looking from Lil to the point where Van Brunt gives way to the water.

"C'mon inside, Maestro. Leave the kid alone. Don't you remember being sixteen?" Lil says. "And we're still standing even after all the shit we did."

All the shit we did. "When I was sixteen, I was at Juilliard."

"Yeah?" Lil says. "Then what happened?"

Then I let go, Jonathan thinks, *in increments.* So slowly that he didn't know it was happening until it was too late.

"I chose wrong," Jonathan says.

"Who doesn't?" Lil says. "Live with it."

"I do. Barely. But she shouldn't. We are not a life anyone should choose."

"Fuck you, Jonathan."

"Does Dirty still crash over on Conover?"

"Maestro, leave it."

"So she can grow up to be us? You're a shining fucking example to us all, Lil." He hurries down Van Brunt.

Dirty Dan lives in a dilapidated one-bedroom ranch house in an incongruous row of shotgun shacks that are hidden on a small, dark street. One side of the street is taken up by a lot that contains a giant satellite. A fifty-foot fence topped with concertina wire surrounds the lot.

At some point, the row of ranch houses might have seemed charming—working-class shanties for seafarers. But now their yards are stuffed with discarded junk—children's playhouses, bicycle skeletons, the rusted shells of car parts. On most of the houses, the clapboard siding is peeling away revealing Tyvek and fiberglass.

Jonathan is ashamed to have been to this house before. Several times, he'd joined a caravan of late-night creatures in Dirty's living room, splaying themselves on his stained and scarred couch, allowing Dirty to chatter in exchange for keeping them supplied with whatever they needed.

From the street, Jonathan can see the blue glare of Dirty's enormous flatscreen. Like most dealers, Dirty lives in squalor but has all the latest toys—televisions, stereos, numerous video game consoles.

Jonathan pounds on the door. It swings opens. He steps into

the narrow living room, which is only illuminated by the channel guide on the television. The sticky smell of weed hangs in the air.

"Dirty?" Jonathan calls. "Dirty."

Smoke curls from underneath a closed door near the back of the room. A toilet flushes and Dirty walks into the living room smoking a menthol cigarette. He's shirtless. His chest is shriveled and distended like a female orangutan's. "Now, now, now," he says. "Guess I should install better security."

"Where is she?" Jonathan says.

"I know not of whom you speak."

"Valerie!" Jonathan calls.

"Why don't we just sit down for a moment," Dirty Dan says, trying to guide Jonathan to the couch.

Jonathan shoves Dirty to the side.

"Slow your roll, Maestro. The kiddo's just taking a nap. Over-indulged in Granddaddy Purple. Speaking of which . . ." He holds up a joint toward Jonathan.

Jonathan opens the door to Dirty's bedroom. Val is sitting up against the headboard. Her knees are drawn to her chest. She's shaking.

"You said she was asleep," Jonathan says.

"I thought she was. I gave her some pills to calm her down. Your little girl here was on a mission. Her wish is my command." Dirty opens his arms like a showman.

"Val," Jonathan says. He sits on the bed.

"I'm going to be sick," she says.

Jonathan pulls back the blanket. Val is stripped down to her underwear. He turns to Dirty. "You sick fuck," he says.

"Jailbait's not my style," Dirty says.

"Bullshit." Jonathan takes Val's chin in his hand. "Did he touch you?"

"Not really," Val says. "A little."

"I guess you just saved the day, Maestro," Dirty says. "Maybe Fireman Paulie will give you another hero's welcome."

Jonathan unclenches Val's fist, takes the two blue pills from her grasp, and flings them at Dirty.

"What's going to happen to me?" Val says.

"You're going to remember who you were when you took that raft out. You're going to start being that person again."

Val puts her arms around Jonathan's neck. She sinks her head onto his collarbone. He lets her rest for a moment.

"Cute," Dirty says, sparking his joint.

Jonathan disengages Val's arms. He finds her pants. Her sneakers are under the bed. Jonathan loosens the laces and slides her feet into them, then he swings her legs down to the floor. He kneels in front of her and ties her shoes. He adjusts her socks so they are not bunched around her ankles. Her peacoat is on a chair. Jonathan threads her arms into the sleeves, then buttons the coat and turns up the collar. He secures Val's arm around his waist and loops his arm around her shoulder. He holds on tight as they head outside.

There's a low sonic disturbance in the air, something that rattles the waterfront, its energy trapped behind the warehouses along the bay. Jonathan steadies Val, guiding her over the cobblestones. A foghorn hollows out Red Hook, rattling the skeletal buildings, bouncing off the solid brick walls. It envelops the neighborhood's strength and frailty—the crumbling waterfront that endures.

They turn onto Visitation and look down toward the water. The lights of several tugs clear-cut the dark. The small boats take shape—four of them spread around a black mass. Jonathan can feel the *Queen Mary* idling as it's pulled in. It's passing right in front of the terminal, the lower levels, hundreds of dots of light, visible above the tugs' wheelhouses. The rest of the ship is lost to the fog and dark.

Val lifts her head from Jonathan's shoulder. "Birnam Wood," she says. She lets her head drop. "We had it in English."

The foghorn bellows again as the cruise ship starts easing into the terminal—the hulking mass stiffly taking its place in the dock.

It towers over the narrow waterside streets, taller than the tallest of the Houses, an unreal skyline that eclipses the skyscrapers beyond. Its engine is cut—leaving the night to its silence. The tugs are untied. They chug away, slipping home underneath the fog, leaving the massive ship behind.

Jonathan and Val keep to the shadows as they approach Van Brunt. Jonathan stops before they reach the Dockyard. "This is my exit," he says.

Val nods.

"You got it from here?"

"Yes." Her voice is small. She looks over his shoulder to the looming ship in the distance. A light goes on and off in one of the portholes. "What do you think he sees?" Val says.

"I don't know." Jonathan kisses the top of her head. "I'll be right behind you. I'll be watching you home."

Val crosses Visitation, then Van Brunt. Jonathan waits for her to pass the Greek's. Then he follows. He stands underneath Fadi's awning, in front of the mural that shows the ship that's just come into port, and watches her stumble up the street. Val's pink coat recedes, fading into the dark of Visitation. Jonathan takes a few more steps down the block, sheltering under the tree canopies. Val climbs her stoop. The front door opens. Then there is the bass drum beat as it slams behind her. Jonathan hesitates for a moment, wondering if she'll peer out at him from behind her curtain. But before she can make it up to her room, he turns away. Tomorrow Val may look for Jonathan. But he will be gone. She will not be able to mistake him for a viable option.

Jonathan walks to Imlay Street where he parks his mother's battered Mercedes wagon. The engine rumbles to life and the car lurches forward, bumping over the cobblestones. He turns up Visitation then onto Van Brunt.

. . .

From the parking lot of a rest stop on 95 he dials the custodian in Fishers Island. For the first time in eight years he lets the phone ring without hanging up. The voice that comes on the line is unfamiliar. Jonathan is tempted to apologize for dialing the wrong number. Then he hears himself say his name, explaining who he is. Only silence meets his words.

"Never mind," Jonathan says.

"Hold on, I'll get your father."

Jonathan watches the red taillights of the northbound traffic streaming away from him.

His father's voice, no longer ironclad and confident, wavers as he tests out Jonathan's name.

"I'm coming out to the island," Jonathan says. "If that's okay."

The only response is the wind rush static of the bad connection.

Jonathan takes a deep breath. He could turn back, join the sparse southbound traffic, head toward the city. But he cannot imagine where he would go, what new descent he would embark upon. "Dad," he says, "I need to come home."

"The boat will meet you," his father says.

Jonathan leaves the car in the parking lot near the dock in New London and waits for his father's custodian to arrive on their newest Chris Craft. As they cross to Fishers Island, Jonathan tries to locate the spot in the water where Eden drowned. Halfway out, he tells the driver to kill the engine. They float in silence.

In the distance, Jonathan can make out the lamp on the edge of the rebuilt dock, holding steady as the boat rocks. Behind it is the large shadow of their massive, shingle-style house. A figure comes down toward the water, silhouetted against the backlit lawn beyond. If Jonathan jumped, it would take him more than ten minutes to swim to shore.

By the time he reached Eden, it would have been too late. He must have known that then. It's only time that made saving her seem possible—clinging on to her convinced himself her death was something he might eventually undo. He closes his eyes, sees her tearing the boat from the dock, ripping across the water, and flipping too far out for him to have saved her.

He tells the driver to start the motor. They glide toward shore and he lets Eden go. Missing her does not mean he cannot forgive himself. He hopes Val can figure this out. But he cannot be the one to show her.

It's nearly three A.M. when Jonathan collapses on an Adirondack chair on the wraparound porch overlooking the sound. He waits for the sun to rise, eager for it to crest behind the house and electrify the bay. The night owls he's left behind will also be up late, but they will pull down the grates over the Dockyard's windows to block out the sun when it arrives.

CHAPTER TWENTY-TWO

The day the *Queen Mary* docks will be the last time that Fadi prints his newsletter. He'd meant his pamphlet to unite the community. But all it has done is fracture his vision of the neighborhood. It's made him aware of the pointless grievances, the petty arguments, the irrational hatreds. Now he cannot help trying to put faces to the complaints he receives, figure out which of his customers resents his neighbor for listening to music with the window open, who wants to prevent Local Harvest from opening, who thinks dogs should be banned from Coffey Park, who is demanding that the Dockyard close. The gripes are unceasing, self-generating—one complaint spawning a host of related complaints and retaliations.

In the last week the tone of the submissions has changed from civic concern to personal vendetta.

Did you hear the one about the drag queen and the fireman? You'll never guess which one of them went down.

What kind of self-respecting black man stoops to walk a white lady's dog? Don't debase yourself.

I didn't know that "Me and My Girl" was about statutory rape!

Fadi's heard the gossip about Jonathan and Valerie, but he dismisses it with the rest of the misinformation that passes through his store every day. He wants to tell his customers that he'd witnessed the stricken look on Jonathan's face when he carried Val into the store, the helpless panic that he'd gotten to her too late. Fadi can't imagine he'd cause her harm. But he keeps his mouth shut. Fadi can't stop himself from thinking that perhaps the Greek was right. He'd intended to give people a place to discuss June's disappearance. But all he's done is open up old wounds and create new ones. Now he wants to quiet the voices of complaint, go back to pretending that, after his customers leave with their six-packs or sandwiches, they are at peace with one another. From his station at the counter, he hopes that he can continue to see Red Hook as a neighborhood on the verge, instead of a community struggling against itself.

The cruise ship will be a new chapter. It will draw the attention of the city. It will allow the locals to show their neighborhood off to the world.

At seven A.M. on the morning of the first docking of the *Queen Mary* in the Red Hook Cruise Terminal, Fadi steps outside his deli and looks up and down Van Brunt. The remnants of a fall fog hover over the neighborhood, muting the slow sounds of a Sunday that's barely started.

He spent the night in the store, getting ready for this arrival— the mad rush of passengers and those who've come to greet them. Around two A.M., he'd walked down Visitation and watched four tugboats guide the massive ship into port. But the night was dense with fog that clung to the outline of the *Queen Mary,* dissolving her edges, transforming the boat into a vapory phantom. The ship devoured the coastline, blocking out New Jersey and the tip of Manhattan. What a shame to sneak into New York at night, Fadi thought, sleep through the magnificent arrival, the ocean giving way to the river, giving way to the glittering city.

Back in the store sleep eluded him. He put on the twenty-four-hour news channel and watched a cheerful reporter interview some of the Dockyard's regulars who had gathered at the terminal. They were glazed with drink. They bellowed nonsense. The reporter tried to make light of their inebriation. But there was tension beneath her smile.

Fadi keeps the news on all morning. By seven, the reports show local catering companies arriving at the terminal, preparing a "Best of Brooklyn" festival—famous cheesecake, famous hot dogs, local beer. The borough president is set to arrive at ten to glad-hand the arriving passengers.

Out on Van Brunt, the only change is the clusters of cops on each corner, arms crossed over their chests, chatting, relaxing as the day starts to show. At the far end of the street, where Red Hook gives way to Carroll Gardens, Fadi can hear a distant bustle of traffic, a new noise of taxis and buses jostling for position as they approach the terminal.

Fadi had hoped that Ren would watch the store while he went down to the terminal. But he hasn't seen the kid in a while. The last time Ren stopped by was when he put the finishing touches on the mural. On that last visit, Ren had filled two large grocery bags with supplies. He'd taken more than usual—more canned goods and pastries. Fadi hadn't said anything. He just let Ren stock his bags and undercharged him.

After he loaded his bags, Fadi walked him out to the street. He watched him head toward the water, not the projects. Halfway down the block Ren looked over his shoulder. "I owe you." He jostled the bags. "You think I don't know?"

It didn't sound like a good-bye.

Each time the door opens, Fadi expects to see Ren. He hides out behind his counter in the evenings, not wanting to see Christos and the wino having dinner together. The wino seems to sense that the coast is clear. Instead of hovering in the door, peeking inside to make sure Ren isn't there, he resumes lingering by the coolers, pawing the forty-ounce bottles until Fadi gives him something for free.

Fadi has attracted a few new customers—both artsy-looking newcomers and younger kids from the Houses who stop in to comment on the ship mural and ask who the artist is. Fadi made up flyers advertising "The Daily Visitation" printed on glossy paper in full color—one side giving his address, the other a photograph of Ren's mural. He plans to hand these out at the terminal, draw customers up the street, and send images of Ren's work out on the ocean.

By eight, the sun has started to burn off the fog, restoring the sharp edges to the neighborhood. A beautiful day to land in Brooklyn, Fadi thinks—crisp and clear, with a sharp hint of fall. Fadi's cousin Heba is sitting behind the counter, shoving coffee cake into his mouth and watching a talk show. Heba shows no interest in the ship.

Fadi pulls out the New York Lotto chalkboard where he sometimes posts the daily jackpot, squats down, writes: "Welcome to Brooklyn. Free Coffee." He hangs a small pouch on the board that he fills with his flyers, then carries the board down Visitation to the terminal and draws an arrow pointing up the street toward his shop. He ties three balloons—red, white, and blue—to the board to match the balloons on his awning.

He returns to the store and dumps a box of donut holes onto a foil tray and pierces them with American flag toothpicks. He places this on the counter next to a stack of small coffee cups. One of the late-night newcomers—rumpled clothes and bleary eyes, out for a walk with his dog—pokes his head into the deli. "Free coffee? Iced?"

Fadi forces a smile. "Only hot. For the ship."

Later, leaving Heba at the register, Fadi heads back out to Visitation, falling in line with a handful of joggers and early-morning locals there for the spectacle, ready to take stock of the ebb and flow of people heading for Van Brunt. As Fadi passes the Dockyard, he hears a mournful song slipping through the splintered doorway behind the half-pulled grate. He checks his watch and hopes it's the cleaning lady who's in there this early.

When Fadi closes in on the *Queen Mary*, perspective is lost. New York and New Jersey are lost. There is only the boat and the sky. The massive hull and looming prow block all the beyond that comes at the end of the street, the light bouncing off the water and the distant promise of the skyscrapers.

Despite the fresh air, the boat brings a sense of claustrophobia to the neighborhood. This was a place of space and water, but with the Houses in the back and now the boat in the front, Fadi feels trapped. He thought the ship would expand his world, blow the place open with activity. But for now it's just sitting there, blocking the view.

In the last hour, the cruise terminal has come to life. A line of limos, taxis, and tour buses stretches from the ship back toward the expressway. The traffic pattern has been designed so cars can slip in and out of the neighborhood without passing through it, sliding in from the expressway on a small street guarded by police, avoiding Van Brunt, avoiding Red Hook.

Fadi watches as the cabs pull close to the ship, whisking passengers out of the neighborhood without a second glance. Busloads of people are taken from the boat, their feet barely touching down in Brooklyn. None of the arriving passengers notices his sign. No one takes a flyer.

Fadi leaves his chalkboard, hoping it will allure the cops if not the passengers. Two kids have been batting his balloons around until one popped and now hangs limp and withered. He heads back to the store to wait for something he's not sure will ever happen—for the first passengers to decide to walk off the ship and avoid the line of taxis and limos.

Business is better than on the average Sunday, with people stopping by on their way down to the boat. By lunchtime things have started to taper off. In the early afternoon, Fadi sends Heba home with a sandwich. He stands in front of his store, looking at the boat at the far end of Visitation, then checking the water end of Van Brunt to see if Ren is approaching. He can't believe the kid would miss the ship.

Christos steps out of his restaurant and looks up at his Cruise Café awning. "We get a supermarket. We get a ship. We get stuck with nothing."

By nightfall the only business on Van Brunt to benefit from the cruise ship's arrival is the bulletproof Chinese two doors down from the Greek's. A line of Filipino and Thai deckhands runs from the greasy, scratched window in the shop's interior down toward the Greek's storefront.

In a month, visitors to Red Hook will dwindle. The joggers and Sunday strollers will choose other battles than the one against the bitter wind whipping from the bay. No one will respond to the For Rent signs on Fadi's bulletin board. In a few weeks, when the clocks fall back, the tone of the neighborhood will change from a place of light and space to a neighborhood where echo meets shadow. And the Christmas lights that never come down will almost be back in season.

The first cycle of nightly news is replaying the footage of the "Best of Brooklyn" festival at the cruise terminal when a black kid in a hoodie comes into the bodega. "Welcome back," Fadi says before realizing his mistake.

The kid lowers his hood, revealing a smooth shaved head and a round, inviting face. "You know me?"

"No," Fadi says, interesting himself in the metro section of the *Times*. "Just trying to be welcoming."

The kid nods. He pauses in front of Fadi's bulletin board, scanning the ads. He tucks his hands into the pouch pocket of his sweatshirt. From time to time he glances at Fadi.

"Are you looking for something?" Fadi says.

"I'm looking for someone. Is this your place?"

"It is."

"I think a friend of mine works here. A kid named Ren. Renton Davis. That's his painting outside. Is he around?"

"I haven't seen him in a few." Fadi closes the paper and pours himself a cup of coffee. "Are you the boy he's looking after?"

"Looking after?"

"With the groceries. He was always putting bags aside for someone."

The boy eyes Fadi. "He sent stuff for my mom when she got sick, if that's what you mean."

"What's your name?"

"Cree. Do you know where he is?"

"I don't. I don't even know where he lives."

"Bones Manor." Cree takes a newsletter from the counter, flips it over, and stares at June's picture. "June Giatto," he says. "That seems like a lifetime ago."

"The guy who rescued her friend Valerie brought her in here. Laid her down right where you're standing. I thought she was dead. She's a good kid."

"I know," Cree says. "She's cool." He shuffles his feet. "I was on the pier that night." He bites his lip and looks away. "It was amazing—those two girls just floated on moonlight. You know what I normally see by the water at night?"

Fadi shakes his head.

"Crazy shit. But those girls were like nothing else. They were *possible*."

"You never told anyone you were there?"

"Only Ren. But he already knew. He was there too." On his way out, Cree takes a newsletter, folds it, and tucks it in his back pocket.

He was there too. These words keep Fadi up all night. They run through his head on the bus from the subway. They distract him from paying attention to the jumper on the façade of the confectionery manufacturer.

Ren had never mentioned that he was near the water the night June disappeared. But he was certain that she wouldn't be found. He'd discouraged Fadi from looking for her. Fadi knows it's a long shot—that Ren is probably miles away from Red Hook—but he wants to know what the kid saw on the water that night. He wants to know why he never bothered to tell Fadi he'd seen the girls.

The neighborhood, just waking up, is bang and clatter. The first iron gates are rolling up. The early delivery vans are trundling over the faulty asphalt. Fadi walks past his store. When he gets to the water where Local Harvest will be, he doubles back. He finds a small cobbled side street with a derelict bus stop. There's a man inside, huddled on the bench, keeping warm in his puffy black coat. He stirs as Fadi passes.

"Excuse me," Fadi says. "Can you tell me where Bones Manor is?"

"A dollar," the man says. His face looks like spent charcoal.

Fadi fishes out a five.

The man shakes his head, then coughs and spits. "Up there, there's a hole in the fence. Between the iron walls. But they don't want you."

Fadi's footfalls echo like gunshots. He walks parallel to the corrugated iron fence, searching for the gap. Soon he sees a corner that is bent back. He leans in close and hears the whisper and rustle coming from inside.

Fadi circles the block. Each time he passes the gap in the fence he rushes by. It is only when the first hint of sun dulls the sky over the Houses that he dares to peek inside.

A stagnant body of water, larger than a puddle and smaller than a lake, stretches out in front of him. Around it is a sparse shantytown of makeshift abodes—containers used as houses, lean-tos made from trees and tarps—a ghost town left to the ghosts.

He picks his way along the edge of the water and up onto a concrete platform that allows him to look over the lot. The water whispers as he passes. The reeds talk behind his back.

On the far side of the Manor, someone is bringing a small fire to life. Two figures huddle over the narrow flame, their thin shadows stretching across the water. The Manor has the same hungry, haunted look Ren first had when he turned up in Fadi's store. Fadi can imagine him here, in this world that seems halfway between the living and the dead.

At the back corner of the lot, Fadi nearly trips over the little wino. He's slumped underneath his coat. Fadi nudges him with his toe. The wino rolls over and curses in Spanish.

"Estaban," Fadi says.

The wino opens his eyes. His shriveled face looks like a peach pit.

"I'm looking for Ren."

The wino shakes his head.

"Ren. Renton. You know who I'm talking about."

"*No se.*"

"Yes," Fadi says. "Yes, you do. He works for me. He lives here."

"*No mas,*" the wino says. He closes his eyes. Fadi nudges him again.

"Where does he live?"

"Gone," the wino says. He flutters his hand in a wavelike motion.

"Where?"

"*No se.*" The wino pulls his coat over his head, blocking Fadi out.

Fadi hovers for a moment, wondering whether it's worth his time to drag the wino from his sleep, to lift him and shake him until he tells Fadi what he wants to know.

Suddenly, the wino bolts upright. "The *recompensa,*" he says. "You come for the *recompensa.*"

"No," Fadi says, "I'm only looking for my friend."

"No friend. *El Diablo.*"

The wino's words barely register. Fadi's eyes are drawn to the mattress on which Estaban had been sleeping—a pink inflatable raft. He takes the wino's arm and yanks him off his bed. Then he holds up the raft.

"Where did you get this?"

The wino shakes his head.

"Where?" Fadi says. His voice echoes off the metal walls. He feels the Manor shift as eyes peer out from behind tattered curtains.

"Ren-ton," the wino says. He waves his hand toward two shipping containers next to each other.

Fadi lets go of the wino's arm. The little man staggers backward.

A pile of rubble—concrete shards and fragments of rebar—blocks Fadi's way toward the containers. He picks his way over this heap and arrives at the place the wino indicated. The door at the short end of one of the containers is open. The other container is shut tight.

Fadi slides through the opening, then pushes the door wider, letting in a dim rectangle of light. The container is clean. A pile of discarded bedding lies crumpled in the corner. Murals in Ren's familiar style cover the walls. There's a low shelf made from cinder blocks and boards along one wall holding several cans of spray paint. Fadi picks one up and shakes it, summoning the familiar rattle. Then he uncaps it, presses the button, and releases a hiss of paint into the air. He's too late. Ren is gone.

Fadi exits the container and closes the door. The little wino is peeking at him from behind the rubble heap. Fadi walks away.

At the entrance to the Manor, Fadi pauses and looks back. The sun has broken through the jagged skyline of the Houses, illuminating the murky pond and the drab concrete landscape. It has pulled the shipping containers from the darkness, highlighting their muted colors—red, blue, or orange metal.

The locked container next to Ren's former hideout does not have these industrial hues. Unlike the others in the lot, this one jumps from the dreary landscape of the Manor with a vibrant swirl of deep blues and swampy greens.

Fadi immediately recognizes the seascape depicted on the ridged metal as the bay beyond Valentino Pier. He sees the distant skyline of Manhattan, the looming hump of Governors Island, the suggestion of Staten Island. As the sun jumps the final hurdle of the projects opposite the Manor, it lands squarely in the middle of the container, illuminating a round spill of moonlight. Centered in this opalescent shimmer is a pink raft with two figures silhouetted against the reflection of the full moon.

Fadi does not have to pry open the door to the sealed container to know that this is where Ren hid June in order to protect Cree from a crime he didn't commit. This is the place that Ren had suggested with his hypotheses and hints. This is the secret grave that no one except the wino ever suspected. This is where the *recompensa* lies.

CHAPTER TWENTY-THREE

A few more days is all he needs. That's all. In lockup there had been nothing but time, identical days endlessly repeated, each one providing a chance to make good on yesterday's mistakes. Improve yourself. Educate yourself. Atone. But out here, time slips through Ren's fingers. He can't slow it down, he can't rewind. He can't undo.

He'd tricked himself into believing that he'd win Cree over, get him to come adventuring without explaining himself. Without coming clean. But the fine CO lady, the one who brightened up the wards just by passing by, had made him. Screamed to high hell as if she'd seen a ghost.

How come these Red Hook girls couldn't stay out of trouble, first those white girls, then Monique? Ren had been tailing Cree the night Val and June hit the water in their raft. His plan had been to sidle up to Cree on the pier, open up a conversation, and figure a way into Cree's life. But then the kid had started following the girls on the raft, tracking them from pier to pier.

Ren had kept close to him, so close in fact they'd nearly collided in the park in front of Valentino Pier. Ren had just enough time to hide behind a low wall before Cree rushed past him, jumped in the water, started swimming for the girls.

Ren ran to the pier. The current was swirling. Cree was thrashing out toward Val and June. Ren could see that the boy would have to turn back before he made it out to the raft. After five minutes, Cree gave up and let the waves bring him in.

Cree was paddling back to shore when the raft flipped. Ren could see one of the girls still clinging to the raft. The other was flailing in the drink. As Cree hauled himself onto the beach, Ren took two steps down the pier, ready to reveal himself to Cree, yank the boy back in the water, and head toward the raft. But the dark water with its hidden currents scared him. If Cree couldn't fight the current, Ren knew he didn't stand a chance. He never learned to swim before getting locked up. He couldn't take more than a few strokes without panicking. Val and June had already been pulled apart by the current. The boys would never reach the raft in time.

Before Cree could catch sight of him, Ren hopped over the side of the pier, crashing onto the jagged rocks and sand below. He scanned the bay. The raft was floating empty in the direction of Governors Island. He began to head along the shoreline, trying to keep pace with the raft, hoping the girls would be swept in the same direction.

Just once he took his eyes from the water, checking over his shoulder to see if Cree had made him. But all he saw was the boy's silhouette heading across the park away from the pier.

Farther up the shore, Ren caught sight of a white shape, fish belly pale in the moonlight. Val was swimming toward a rocky outcrop, paddling with weak strokes. A tugboat was passing too close to the coastline, churning a wake that roiled the water and sent waves crashing into the shore. Before Ren could reach Val, one of these waves lifted her and knocked her into the rocks at the foot of the parking lot. The tide pulled her out and another wave sent her back in. Val sank from view. When she resurfaced, she was no longer paddling, but floating limp, letting the water buffet her.

Ren had no choice but to get in the water now. He was terrified of going in too deep, so he waded chest high, until the bottom gave out. He kicked his legs, fighting to stay afloat. He felt the current grip him. Water flew up his nose and ran down the back of his throat. Then a wave swamped him and washed Val's body on top of his.

He looped an arm around her waist and began to drag her to shore. Blood trickled down her neck from a cut somewhere under her hair. He listened for her breath. Eventually it reached his ear, faint but even. Ren lifted Val and carried her to higher ground. He searched around for somewhere safe to stow her while he looked for her friend. He stumbled over the rocks toward the little beach. He propped her up against a pylon under the pier, praying she'd be all right until he could return.

Once more, he decided to follow the raft. He passed the rocky outcrop, the cruise terminal, and the container terminal. Half a mile up the shore, at the border of Red Hook and Carroll Gardens, he spotted the pink raft, washed up in a stand of rusted and disused pylons. A few feet farther on, he glimpsed the other girl's body, floating facedown. Ren rolled her over, slapped her face a few times, blew into her cold mouth. He knew enough to know she was gone. He freed the raft from the pylons and placed June on top of it. He waded into the water and floated her back to Valentino Pier.

Ren was a nobody, a ghost with no name. He could disappear

from Red Hook and no one would have known he had been back in the first place. He could leave June for someone else to find and be done with it. But Cree was a different story.

The boy thought he was a master sleuth, that he snuck in and out of his hiding places unobserved, that no one saw him tiptoeing around the waterfront. The kid believed he had Red Hook to himself. But Ren knew better. Someone might have seen Cree by the water that night watching the girls on their raft. Someone might have seen him try to swim after them. Ren had heard enough stories in jail to know how these things play out. Chances were Cree would serve time for something he had nothing to do with. Life would slow to a standstill, and if he ever made it out everything would have passed him by, all because he'd foolishly tried to attach himself to a misguided adventure. So Ren hid June in the only place he knew no one would look. No body, no crime. It was as simple as that.

He carried the girl to Bones Manor along side streets he hoped were abandoned. The only person he'd come across was the crackhead wino—but he hoped the little man was too strung out to notice his cargo. After he locked June away in the airtight storage container next to his, securing the door so no one could get in, he doubled back to the water's edge where he sat with Val until the sun began hovering behind the Houses. Soon the dog walkers and joggers would appear near the pier and Val would be safe.

On his way back from the pier he'd nearly collided with a white dude in crumpled black clothes on his way down to the water. The guy was shuffling across the park either up all night or up too early—trailing a scent of smoke and booze. Fog had rolled in, smothering the river, hiding the distant bridges and other boroughs. Even New Jersey was out of sight. The white guy stared at the water as if it might tell him something.

At the edge of the park, Ren ducked behind some raggedy bushes. He watched the white guy on the pier, willing him to look down and see Val. The Staten Island ferry rolled into view. Some sound in the pylons caught the white guy's attention. He looked.

Ren had planned to keep a low profile when he returned to Red Hook, hiding at the edges and never entering the Houses. But he couldn't help himself from walking Monique home. There was something lost but adventurous about her, as if she'd purposefully allowed herself to get off the path in order to find a better route. He wanted to keep her safe, but he also wanted to follow her wherever she was going. After the CO lady started screaming, Ren knew it would only be a couple of hours before Cree came for him. He took his beating, told his story, knowing Cree would walk away.

When Ernesto and his tiny hoods checked in with him later that night, he told them he had one final job. They had to help him haul the boat down to the water. With or without Cree it was time for Ren to go.

Ren had painted the escapes he knew Cree dreamed of—electric pieces he hoped would entice the boy away. He'd wanted to show Cree, Fadi, the rest of them what they had—amp it up, draw attention to the everyday. Too bad folks insisted on dwelling on what they lacked, the adventures that were out of reach, the customers who didn't come, the people who went missing, the people who got dropped. Ren wanted to shake them free. But some fools seemed destined to run in place.

Ren knows he has to get out before the CO lady starts asking questions. Soon someone will come down to his container. It won't be long before they open up the one next to his.

After he let Cree pummel him, Ren sits up all night waiting for the boy to return, make good on the adventure they'd planned. He sits on the deck of the boat, watching the shore, willing Cree to appear. By the next morning, the boy hasn't shown. Ren gets ready to leave. Soon the sky is fading from black to gray. Cree isn't coming. It's time to get going.

The small boat is surprisingly powerful and sways under Ren's inexperienced command. He tips left and right, trying to find balance in the water. He is afraid to pick up speed. He inches out into the Erie Basin.

Cree hadn't needed to tell Ren that a captain returns to haunt his ship. Ren knows Marcus is with him on the boat. Hell, Marcus has been with him ever since he dropped the gun onto the windowsill of that second-story apartment in the Houses. The man had jumped up off the ground and flown into Ren's heart, took up residence in his mind, infected and informed each of Ren's ideas, each of his dreams. He was the ghost in Ren's reflection, the shadow he cast on the sidewalk. As Ren guides the boat away from shore, he hopes he's doing Marcus proud.

At first the chop of the water unsettles him. He clenches the wheel, jerking and bucking with the waves. But soon he relaxes his grip and dares to accelerate. And suddenly he understands that the boat is more powerful than the slight waves and the current.

The sun is rising over Brooklyn, and the bay blazes like a vivid burner—the kind Ren would have like to have painted on a subway or a billboard. But instead of painting it, Ren is part of it, sailing into it—all the colors in his cans come to life. As he passes below the Verrazano, crossing out of the borough, he feels Marcus take the wheel, guiding him into deeper waters where he hopes Cree will have the sense to find him.

June crosses from the Manor to the pier, fluid and slow. She pushes through the world that has grown as heavy as mud. From habit she reaches out to touch people she passes but catches nothing. She absorbs the wind, grass, benches, and flagpoles. Distances that once took her minutes to cover now take hours. She is unaware of the sun's touch and the woodwind sounds of fall. Her world is drained of color and sound.

It wasn't always this way. Initially, she had clung to life. That first month after she'd drowned in the dark, chilly bay, she'd tried to latch onto others, hovering near the action, hoping to be brought back. She had been drawn to the bright world around the Houses—the music from the tabernacle, the parties in Coffey Park. She haunted the cookouts, seeing whether there was a place for her between the clusters of grills that shimmered with heat and smoke. She wondered if she might come back to life as someone was opening a bag of chips or squeezing ketchup. June stood watch, as solid as the smoke that rose from the coals. She tried to lend a hand, but she was as ineffectual as air.

She fell into step with girls who had ignored her when she was alive. She lingered in the pizza parlor, soundlessly flirting and chatting with the fine boys she was too chicken to approach in life. She lay out by the pool, untroubled by the heat of the sun, trying to remember the music that came from the boom boxes. She stared from the pier to Manhattan, still dreaming of checking the place out on her own, imagining that one day she'd float across the water, fly up and down the streets, capable of more in death than in life.

Things began to fade. Music was the first thing to go. Then the sound of voices. Soon talk became pantomime. June's memory lost shape like a stratus cloud. She became an imperfect chronicler of the past, cataloging the days of her life in obsessive detail. Listing birthday gifts, family meals, favorite shoes, what she carried in her purse. Turning her life into a litany of possessions and events, replacing her memories with the objects that comprised them. The day she cut out of school and walked to Bay Ridge—*bridge, wind, rocks, expressway.* Her last birthday—*cannoli, sleepover, dance music.* Soon words lost their significance and she forgot the importance she once attached to "lip gloss" and "perfume."

June knew that Val came with offerings—teenage magazines, pieces of jewelry, ribbons, things she thinks June misses. When Val left, June forced her fingers into the real world, the old place of weight and substance, and pulled these trinkets over to her side, objects she barely recognized and could not remember.

Eventually, June stopped trying to work her way back to the other side. She gave up on Val's offerings. During the day, she folded herself inward, pulling herself away from what had made her old life electric and loud. She stopped wandering Red Hook. She forgot the resonance of things, the allure of pizza, the beat of music, the comfort of sprawling on a towel by the pool. But today something is breaking through the fortress of silence that encloses June. And she feels drawn to the pier.

After school, Val lies on her bed. A week has passed since Jonathan saved her for the second time. Although she knows that he is gone, she stares up at his apartment when she passes on her way home.

That afternoon one of the detectives who visited Val in the hospital pulled her out of history. Val watched him rub his ruddy neck as he told her that June's body had been discovered in a sealed shipping container. The detective's hand kept working his dry skin as he explained to Val that, despite the condition of the body, the medical examiner could see no signs of foul play. June drowned and someone hid her. Crazy people often think they are doing God's work by burying a body, he explained. It's not unusual for folks to cover up crimes they didn't commit.

Val stares at her ceiling, trying not to think of June falling apart in a forgotten corner of the neighborhood. When did she stop being June and become June's body, her remains?

"Valerie. Yo, Valerie!"

Val pulls the curtain back. Monique is standing across the street, not far from the spot where Mr. Sprouse used to stare into her window.

"Yo, Valerie, you wanna come down for a minute?"

"Why don't you come up?"

"I got something to show you. Don't leave me hanging out here."

Val slips on her shoes and meets Monique on the sidewalk.

"You still have all those costumes in your basement?" Monique asks.

"You remember that?"

"I remember stuff," Monique says, heading for Van Brunt. "Like all those games you made up."

"All that make-believe was for babies."

"It was dope," Monique says.

Val checks Monique's face to see if she's messing with her.

"Honest," Monique says. "You made up some crazy fun games."

"Where are we going?" Val says.

"Valentino Pier." Monique takes hold of Val's wrist. "Listen, you asked me to do something once, you remember? You wanted me to sing for June."

"You wouldn't."

"You know, I was jealous of you with your raft. But I just sat there like that damn bench might carry me away." Monique begins to lead them toward the water. "If I tell you something, you promise not to ask any questions? I'm going to sing for June, and she's going to be listening. I know she's going to be listening."

The girls walk to Valentino Pier. Val doesn't look at the tattered memorial to June. She refuses to glance at the rocky beach where Jonathan found her unconscious. She tries to ignore the spot on the pier where she'd let the music teacher hold her while she cried in her underwear. She does not pick out the place in the bay where June's hand last slipped from hers. The water is darker now that the weather is getting colder. Val sits on a bench at the far end. Monique faces the Port of Jersey. She puts her hands on the railing and leans out over the water like a ship's figurehead.

Val recognizes the song from tabernacle. There's no way that Monique could have known that it was one of June's favorites, "Prayer Changes Things." When Monique gets to the line "I've been out on the stormy raging sea," her voice deepens. She repeats the phrase. Her voice rises and falls with the waves. It goes out into the bay, then breaks back onto the shore. "I've been way out on the stormy, Lord, Lord, raging sea."

Val listens to Monique's hymn and tries to believe that June is nearby. When Monique is done, she sits down next to Val and they watch as the massive cruise ship that's been docked all week begins to pull out of the terminal.

"Sing another," Val says.

Monique stands up and goes to the rail.

Val knows that June is listening.

Ever since Fadi found June and received the reward from Mrs. Giatto, his bodega is popular again. He clips the articles about the discovery but only because they have pictures of Ren's murals— the one on the shipping container and the one on his store. He filed these away to show Ren if he ever sees the kid again. But as days pass, he starts losing hope that this will ever happen.

Fadi has stopped dreaming of improvements he wants to make to his store. Ren's mural is enough. One afternoon, he spots the little hoodlum Ren had deputized into his errand boy. The kid gives Fadi the address where he'd been delivering the groceries Ren put aside. Fadi cashes his reward check and tucks a fat envelope into the waistband of his pants.

Cree answers the door. Two women are sitting at the kitchen table. The smaller one, with long gray braids, is rubbing oil into the palms of her companion.

"The bodega guy," Cree says after a second.

"Fadi. My name is Fadi."

The two women look over from the table.

Fadi takes the envelope out of his waistband. He taps it on his opposite hand, before passing it to Cree.

"From Ren," Fadi says.

Cree takes the envelope. "Do you know where he is?" Cree asks.

Fadi shakes his head. "You don't want to open it?"

The woman with the gray braids drops something small and shiny attached to a chain from her palm. It spins once. "He wants you to get moving," she says, then looks up. "He was a good boy."

Cree looks from the old woman to the envelope. He runs his thumb under the seal. His eyes widen as he looks inside. "Whoa." He hands the envelope back to Fadi. "I can't. You're the one who found June, right?"

Fadi shakes his head. "Only officially. Ren was the one who really found her."

"So this money belongs to Ren."

"No," Fadi says. "It belongs to you."

"You going to do something useful with that?" the older woman asks. "Or are you going to sit around all day like your mother holding on to something that just isn't there?"

The other woman wriggles her hands free from the older woman's grasp. "He's going to use it to go to college." Her speech is slow but determined. "It's a gift from Marcus. He just reached back into this world and handed this miracle over to Cree."

"No Marcus. No miracle, Ma," Cree says. "This is Ren's doing."

With difficulty, Cree's mother folds her arms over her chest. "Reward money for that dead girl isn't going to make up for killing your daddy."

"Nobody's trying to make up for nothing," Cree says. "Somebody's just trying to be my friend." He turns to Fadi. "Thank you." Cree offers Fadi his hand. "And thank Ren if you ever see him again."

When Fadi crosses back to the waterside, the foghorn is sounding for the *Queen Mary*'s departure. Even though the ship brought little business and no real change, Fadi wants to see her off. Jonathan got a job on board. "Show tunes and smorgasbords," he said when he'd visited the store one final time to say good-bye. Fadi knows he won't be back.

He heads down to Valentino Pier. It's crowded with people watching the ship. The foghorn bellows three more times, then the *Queen Mary* begins to ease from the dock, four tugboats leading her out.

Fadi walks to the tip of the pier, trying to see if Jonathan is on the top deck as he said he would be. There are two girls at the end of the pier—Valerie and Monique, the girl from the Houses who came into his store to buy gum the same day June drowned. Val is sitting on a bench. Monique is standing at the railing, leaning out over the water. She is singing a gospel hymn. Val listens with her eyes closed.

Fadi sits on a nearby bench and watches the *Queen Mary*. Monique's song drifts over to him—a story of hope and prayer and stormy seas. He imagines her voice carrying over the water to Jonathan, blessing him on his journey.

The *Queen Mary* slides away, revealing the edge of Manhattan it had obscured. Red Hook's shoreline is restored. The last taxis and buses that had deposited passengers pull away.

Instead of returning to his store when he reaches Van Brunt, Fadi crosses to the Dockyard and goes inside.

Happy hour is gearing up. He pulls out a seat at the bar. He keeps his head down so other patrons don't embarrass themselves by saying hello without remembering his name.

The bartender has a beard like Abraham Lincoln. He smokes American Spirits and drinks his coffee black. Twice a week he buys a tin of mints.

"Hero Man," he says, placing a coaster in front of Fadi.

"Excuse me?"

"Hero Man, right? You found that girl's body. First drink's on the house."

A few customers look in their direction. They raise their glasses.

The walls of the Dockyard are covered in memorabilia from a different Red Hook. Photos of sea captains, bustling docks, tall ships pulled up to the old warehouses, long decommissioned tugs and fishing boats. All these are interlaced with the strange junk the newcomers seem to relish—busted taxidermy, Christmas lights, nautical refuse. On these walls the old lives among the new, the true Red Hook with the imagined one.

"Hero Man." Someone slaps Fadi on the back. It's the redheaded bartender, the woman Fadi often sees walking home alone as he's opening up, the sad echo of her footfalls welcoming him to work. "I was beginning to wonder if you'd ever join us," she says, sliding behind the bar.

The redhead pours Fadi another beer. It's the same brew he sells for half the price, but it tastes better here. He looks over his shoulder to the glow of his shop across the street.

Hero Man. Maestro. RunDown. *We let people invent us as they please,* he thinks. *The truth we keep to ourselves.* Fadi sips his beer and thinks of Jonathan on the boat, disappearing underneath the span of the Verrazano. He will no longer have the musician to transform the neighborhood into one of his songs. Fadi will do this himself, listening for the melody of the local noise, the grinding, rattling, slamming, and silence. The music leaking from the bar, from passing cars, from open windows. The sad moan of the telephone wires on Van Brunt. The voices over his shoulder and outside the Dockyard's window coming into concert, finding their own harmony to lift this place up and carry it along.

ACKNOWLEDGMENTS

Gratitude unmeasured to my teachers Doug Bauer, David Gates, Alice Mattison, and Lynne Sharon Schwartz. Thanks to my wonderful agent, Kim Witherspoon at Inkwell Management, as well as to Lyndsey Blessing and the incomparable William Callahan.

I know I'm punching above my weight to have had the amazing fortune to work with an editor such as Lee Boudreaux, likewise Michael McKenzie, Ashley Garland, Karen Maine, and Dan Halpern at Ecco. And Dennis Lehane, my gosh, *thanks*. In the UK, thanks to Peter Straus at Rogers, Coleridge & White and Suzie Dooré and Francine Toon at Sceptre.

To everyone at the James Merrill House—especially Lynn Callahan, Sibby Lynch, and Stuart Vyse—thank you for giving me a magical place to begin this book. Much love to Tiffany Briere,

Sandra Ramirez, Lisa Fetchko, Carlin Wing, and of course, Louisa Hall for their advice and assistance. It goes without saying, but thanks to Justin Nowell, Matt Stewart, Mary Kelley, and Judyth van Amringe for their love and enthusiasm.

Most important, thanks to my parents, Philip and Elizabeth Pochoda, who are the best and most careful readers (in entirely different ways) whom I could have asked for. You might have had reason to worry when I was up all night in Red Hook—but, look, it worked out in the end.